THE LIGHT THAT BINDS

The Sundered World Trilogy
Failed Empire
Shadow of the War
The Light That Binds

By Nathan Garrison

The Sundered World Trilogy
Veiled Empire
Shadow of the Void
The Light That Binds

THE LIGHT THAT BINDS

Book Three of the Sundered World Trilogy

NATHAN GARRISON

HARPER

VOYAGER

IMPULSE

An Imprint of HarperCollins Publishers

This is a work of fiction. Names, characters, places, and incidents are products of the author's imagination or are used fictitiously and are not to be construed as real. Any resemblance to actual events, locales, organizations, or persons, living or dead, is entirely coincidental.

THE LIGHT THAT BINDS. Copyright © 2017 by Nathan Garrison. All rights reserved. Printed in the United States of America. No part of this book may be used or reproduced in any manner whatsoever without written permission except in the case of brief quotations embodied in critical articles and reviews. For information, address HarperCollins Publishers, 195 Broadway, New York, NY 10007.

Digital Edition OCTOBER 2017 ISBN: 978-0-06-245197-2
Print Edition ISBN: 978-0-06-245293-1

Cover art by Cover photograph © Amble Design / Shutterstock

Harper Voyager, the Harper Voyager logo, and Harper Voyager Impulse are trademarks of HarperCollins Publishers.
HarperCollins is a registered trademark of HarperCollins Publishers in the United States of America and other countries.

FIRST EDITION

17 18 19 20 21 HDC 10 9 8 7 6 5 4 3 2 1

To Kathryn

PROLOGUE

A Page from History of the Veiled Empire,
Chapter 10

Uva Thress, Imperial Historian
11,748 A.S.

It should be noted that while the Non-Battle for
Humanity marked the first instance of *open* conflict in the Chaos War, hostilities truly began
almost two years earlier with the assassination of
the Panisian royal family, which was subsequently
blamed on Sceptrine soldiers. Not only did this act
spark a war between Panisahldron and Sceptre, it left
the child Queen Arivana alone amongst the throne's
councilors, who sought to prolong the war for their
own ends. Had not the two great sorceresses of the
age, Jasside and Vashodia, come to the aid of Sceptre,
and forced a once one-sided war to a conclusive, yet
(modestly) peaceful resolution, humankind would

have been significantly less prepared for the invasion that came soon after.

And had not the prodigal warrior Mevon Daere returned home to his father, the emperor (who had thought his son dead at the time), it seems unlikely that the mighty Imperial war machine would have ever stirred from its slumber . . .

PART I

PART I

CHAPTER 1

Vashodia sat atop the bird statue's head, dangling her legs from the tip of its upturned beak. Red-and-orange wings stretched a hundred paces to either side, wind whistling through magically forged feathers in tones doubtless meant to invoke a sense of peace and prosperity. A lithe, glowing body flowed down towards monstrous talons that clutched the tower's edge. A phoenix, the locals called it. A myth from another age, another world, both long dead, supposedly symbolic of hope and rebirth or some such nonsense. It didn't make for the most comfortable seat, but she'd required a clear vantage point, and this, inarguably, was the highest one around.

The staff of the royal tower below were less than thrilled by her choice of perch.

The statue blazed incessantly, as if competing with

the sun, forcing her to maintain a wreath of shadows about her at all times. No doubt her dark stain ruined the thing's intended effect. The Panisians, who swarmed like ants along bricked streets and buzzed like mosquitos in vessels that flew between each of the city's hundred towers, must have cursed the sight of her as they made their way to and from their mostly pointless occupations.

Vashodia couldn't help but giggle at the thought.

She took a break from her vigil to peer down at the shipyards along Panisahldron's western edge. Men and women toiled by the tens of thousands in a frenzy of activity that made the rest of the city seem sluggish in comparison. Two hundred fifty-one skyships, at last count, occupied the space, all of various sizes and shapes and stages of completion. Crafted by mundane means then outfitted with energy-infused constructs to enable flight and control—and, occasionally, weaponry—the vessels stood as testament to this people's renewed unity and their dogged preparation for the trial to come. Expediency demanded they place function over beauty, as witnessed by the plain, blocky hulls; an indication, perhaps, of the nation's changing heart.

The problem, Vashodia knew, was that all of it was a waste.

Some delusions are too strong to dispel with logic, she thought. *And hope is the worst offense of all.*

She sighed, returning to her study of the continent.

She'd spread her little machines across the land's far reaches months ago. They examined every village and town, every city and fortress, every lone farmstead and rarely trod trail, observing and collecting news from the waking world, then transmitting their findings through commune. She parsed the data, sifting through oceans of it, gleaning insights and making connections no one else could have possibly seen.

Far, far to the west rested the Veiled Empire. Though no longer protected by the Shroud, the voltensi—the sensor towers—still stood sentinel, and for the purposes of the coming war, were just as effective. North of that sat the mierothi colony and another voltensus. It held sway over most of Weskara, and the farthest corner of Sceptre. The valynkar reigned in the south, a lodestone of blinding power.

And that was it. There was little else in those three directions that might be considered a tempting target. Not so, the east.

The horseshoe-shaped island nation of Yusan stuck out of the Endless Sea all alone, a sick buffalo culled from the herd. Like the other coastal nations, it sported few casters of any worth. *Unlike* them, however, its people would have a hard time fleeing were they to come under attack.

And they would, Vashodia had warned; it's where *she* would strike first.

Few enough of the petty rulers had listened when she'd made the pronouncement, and fewer still had heeded her recommended course of action. How could she possibly tell, after all, what their enigmatic enemy planned to do?

Not that it mattered. In the end, they'd all be forced into action. If not by her . . . by *them*.

We are the ruvak, the woman had said. The young queen's false handmaiden, Flumere. The assassin and spy, Sem Aira Grusot. One and the same. She'd proven reticent to give up anything else, however. And that was even after Vashodia had . . . played with her. Extensively. Her interrogations, however—normally swift in extracting information from her subjects— only drove the creature to deeper defiance. Vashodia had wrangled nothing more than those four words from the spy before the queen demanded a cessation of the questioning. Not even a curse.

She could almost respect the resolve were it not so infuriating.

Vashodia knew more about them, of course. Ruul's memories, when she'd visited him a few centuries ago, had been delicious to dig through. Still, she possessed little *useful* information. She knew who they were, where they came from, and could surmise what they wanted, but she did not know what drove them, what they valued, how they *thought*—all things that would soon become crucial. The ignorance threatened to drive her mad.

History will remember me, one way or another. Either as the savior they followed, or the mad prophet, the doom-sayer, they ignored. Though I'm partial to the former, either one will do.

If nothing else, her siphoning of the gods' knowledge had proven how intractably history treated its most memorable souls. None were recorded with accuracy; few in a manner they would wish. And the greatest sin of all was how many faded to legend, then obscurity, then were forgotten entirely as a new age surmounted the old, grinding it all to dust and dreams in the ever-persistent march of time.

Such will not happen to me. I will make sure of it.

A chord struck inside her mind, a dark string thrumming, and she quested towards the construct that had sent the signal. Before she'd even isolated the source, half a dozen more notes rang out in the vicinity of the first.

Warning bells, sounding off. Large masses descending out of the chaos of the void.

Over Yusan, of course.

She smiled at her own prescience, proven right once more.

No time like now for the end to begin.

Dark clouds rolled around and behind Jasside, a seething mass crackling with energy, just waiting to release. She tapped a booted toe in a slow cadence on the deck, the sound quickly swallowed by the wind as she strained her senses for any sign of movement below. Storms brewed, inside and out. The rumbling of thunder grew more insistent, quickening both her foot and her heartbeat, as if seeking to merge with the aching ocean of darkness she held at the ready. Eagerness warred with weariness, and she hated them both.

A lot of people were about to die. She just had to make sure as few as possible were human . . . or those once called it.

Footsteps approached, and Jasside ceased her tapping. She clenched her hands, which hung rigid at her sides, trying to release the strain in them while still holding on to the power she'd gathered. Power that partially flowed through the figure now stopping at her side.

"Grandmother," Jasside said, then turned to face the woman. Angla was dressed, as Jasside was, in dark leather, layered and covering every stitch of ebony skin below the neck. Black but greying hair hung free to the shoulder, a style most mierothi women had adopted, as if they couldn't bear, since its miraculous return, to keep it contained. Jasside's own blond hair fell past her waist, bound in a braid.

Angla raised her eyebrows in an unveiled expression of worry. "Are you all right, Jasside?"

"Fine," she snapped, and instantly regretted her tone.

"I can see that," Angla said, crossing her arms. "Clearly."

Jasside sighed. "Sorry."

Angla's stance softened, and the mierothi woman leaned in and squeezed Jasside's hand, wringing out the tension in a manner the younger woman could never do on her own. "Worried about the battle?"

"Worried?" Jasside asked, surprised that it should even be a question. More surprised that the answer was no. Another lingering effect from Vashodia's teaching: irrepressible confidence. "Always. But I just—"

Angla raised an eyebrow as Jasside forced herself to stop. She didn't know how to convey her desire for the abyss-taken thing to *start already*. Not without sounding bloodthirsty. This fervor, this hunger for battle—a clash was inevitable and there were people to protect, a job she trusted to no one more than herself. Even so, it scared her. Most times, when examining herself for negative attributes, Jasside found the fault to lie with her former mistress. On this occasion, however, it didn't seem like something she'd learned from Vashodia.

It felt more like an attitude that Mevon would share.

Just the thought of him drove a spike through her gut. To think he'd been alive all this time. That he'd also thought *her* dead. That Vashodia knew . . . and held it from her. Jasside didn't know whether to feel rage at her mistress's deception, joy that he still lived, or shame that she'd moved on so quickly. So she did what she'd always had and stuffed it *all* away—right alongside her desire to drop everything and fly across the world to find him.

There will be time for . . . personal matters later. We've an enemy to deal with first.

"We can't save them all," Angla said, pulling her back into the present. "But we do the best we can. No need to punish yourself for that."

Jasside nodded, realizing how much she'd let show on her face. She didn't know which was worse, though: that she didn't correct her grandmother's false conclusion, or that the conclusion she'd reached wasn't correct. Jasside knew she needed to focus. Lives would soon be at stake.

"You're right," she said at last. "We do the best we can."

The answer seemed to satisfy Angla, who dipped her head briefly then looked out across the cloud-scape. "Are sure you want me and my sisters linked? The added mobility could be useful."

Jasside smiled, noting the hint of eagerness her grandmother now showed. "Want to test your wings again?"

Brown eyes flipped up and away, and the woman shrugged. Wings sprang from her back, blacker than a starless void, and fluttered a few times. Angla groaned like someone stretching their legs after being cramped in a tight space for too long.

"I don't blame you," Jasside said, once again marveling at the most impressive measure of mierothi transformation. "But your son's report made the situation clear. You're best suited where you are."

"Of course, dear. Of course."

"And besides," Jasside added, reaching out to rub her grandmother's protruding belly. "We wouldn't want to put the little one in harm's way."

Angla, smiling blissfully, laid one hand over Jasside's, while the other gently cradled the round bump.

Draevenus clung to handholds in the rocky hull above him, inhaling lungfuls of something bitter and biting with every steady breath. Eddies of air swirled at his back, threatening to suck him out into open sky. He smiled as he remembered he no longer needed to fear falling.

The mirth died quickly when he returned his mind to what he was about to do.

Hand over hand, foot over foot, he crawled across the vessel's back side, searching for an opening. He'd boarded the thing in haste after its destination became clear, and had no time to study it beforehand. Three crevasses he'd already explored, but they'd turned out nothing more than cracks or folds in the misshapen hull. With his grip starting to fail, and time running short, he hastened his inverted, spiderlike creep.

Around the next chunk of rock he caught sight of another likely opening. He altered his path, angling for it.

This had better be it. I don't think I can hold on much longer.

He'd thought about blessing himself with increased strength before attempting his infiltration, but there was still too much unknown about the enemy, and he couldn't risk them sensing the casting. As always, assassination required a certain balance of risks far different from that of normal combat.

And a certain forceful numbing of the soul that he thought he'd long ago left behind.

Palms aching and slick with sweat, and fingers sharply stung by the porous stone, Draevenus at last pulled himself into the shadowed alcove. He stood upright for what seemed the first time in days as he caught his breath and shook out the fatigue from his limbs.

I guess I'm not quite conditioned for resuming my old line of work.

He shook his head at the incompleteness of the thought.

I guess I wish I didn't have to be.

He strode forward. The space ended just two paces in, and he nearly gave up until he saw a thin crack too straight to be natural. He pressed a finger into it and followed the groove, eventually tracing the outline of a half-oval, flat at the bottom. A doorway of some kind. It had to be.

For several marks he felt around in the rock surrounding the door, searching for a knob or button that would open it, but found nothing. It must have been a rarely used portal, one only for escape or other emergencies. Which meant he'd have to do this the old-fashioned way.

Drawing a dagger, Draevenus wedged its tip into the crack and began working it back and forth, up and down. The wind of the ship's passing tumbled into the alcove in spurts, and his sweat had long since been dried by the time he heard a metallic rasp and the door clicking open.

A second dagger sprang into his other hand as he crouched and stalked forward through the shadows.

Jasside felt it: a change in the wind. A slight push in the air's pressure when a moment ago there had been only pull.

The enemy had arrived.

Again.

Images of their previous incursions scraped across her mind: bodies shorn by ruvaki blades, or shattered by ruvaki sorcery, scattered like obscene driftwood across endless coastlines. Red tides washing up on red shores.

Rather than banish the memories she clung to them, keeping the reminder fresh as fuel for what she now set out to do.

Destroy them. Utterly.

The dark energy she now held drew them, like the ocean drew a river. It was formidable. Menacing. A threat they would strike at, hoping to bring down quickly before moving on to easier targets.

This time, though, she had a surprise in store.

Just a little bit closer.

Inhaling, Jasside energized further, pulling power through her own capacity as well as that of the dozen mierothi women behind her, until she held tenfold the energy of just beats ago. She extended a hand. Darkness swirled at her fingertips into a spinning disc, then shot forward faster than thought. The clouds near the black beam's path were sucked forward, adding to the churning, icy vortex as it raced towards her unseen enemy.

At her command, the spell constricted into a ball . . .

Then expanded.

The fog cleared in an instant, at last revealing the scene. Six ruvaki ships, midsized as far as she could tell, hovered low along the wide beach, slowed down enough to drop rank upon rank of ground assault troops onto the sands. Though no two were exactly alike, these ships were made of dull, pitted stone, shaped like nothing more than enormous oblong boulders. Now unloaded, they surged up in her direction.

Below her marched a throng of refugees, thirty thousand strong, flanked only by a too-thin line of alliance soldiers. Panisians and Sceptrines mostly, with some Phelupari, along with the shattered remnants of the army of Corbrithe, the coastal nation from which they now fled.

"Forward," she commanded.

The pilot heard her clearly, and the back end tilted up before they swept forward out of the clouds like a specter. Wind rushed by as they picked up speed. The enemy ships pointed their noses at her and began glowing with half-lit hues that changed from green to purple to yellow to grey.

This is where it gets tricky.

Their straight line wavered, blinked, and they were suddenly staggered and farther apart. Another blink and they were in a circle. Now back to the straight line. Now in no discernable pattern whatsoever. If she focused her sight on one, it would seem to follow a logical pattern, but doing so made the others fade almost to nothing.

Sem Aira's few words upon the last battlefield between men—revered now like scripture—rang ever true: uncertainty empowered the ruvak, driving their magic and their tactics and probably their thoughts, as well.

Chaos. It was a bitter enemy to have.

Let's add some order to this equation, then, Jasside thought, raising her hands, closing her eyes, and getting to work.

A blanket of darkness fell in a wide swath across their likely path, and she immediately felt them. Six objects swimming through her dark pool, their shields still soft, rebuffing her sorcery but not yet hardened against it.

Before she could pinpoint their locations, however, energy blasted out from six points.

She took a beat to trace their likely trajectories. Two sped towards her. The other four were aimed directly for the heart of the stewing mass of civilians.

She conjured dozens, now hundreds of her nullifying fields, bursting them across the sky between the refugees and the ruvaki ships. Highly modified from their original incarnation to account for the peculiarities of enemy power, they scoured the four lances of chaotic energy from existence, the last spiraling away harmlessly just paces above human heads.

That left the two aimed at her.

"Evade!" she cried.

She summoned a shadow that appeared solid even as the deck beneath her lurched sideways. The shadow became a ship—identical to hers—that stayed in the space they'd just occupied, while the real one vanished from sight.

You aren't the only ones well-versed in deception.

The lances crashed into the shadow ship, exploding. Lurid fire spread like lightning, and the stench of sulfur filled the air. Jasside reduced her power to almost nothing, hoping it might trick the enemy into thinking they'd been consumed in the blast.

Hoping it would at least buy her the few beats she'd need to launch her own offensive.

Jasside counted three slow breaths, building her anger with each one. Then, energizing to the limit of her harmonized capacity, she struck back.

A thousand tendrils of virulent darkness shot forth from her hands. They sought the enemy ships, quickly latching on, forcing their shields to harden in response. Six fish, soon caught in her net.

Unfortunately, that was all she could do.

Because once attuned, a ruvaki ship could defend against anything, no matter how much power—the *same* kind of power, anyway—was poured into the attack.

But Jasside was aware of that, and didn't waste any of her own. With her spare energy, she sent blasts down upon the hillsides, where the enemy troops were now closing with the outnumbered protection force. A volley of wrath-bows arced their missiles out from below just as her own spells crashed from above. The hills turned into a bloody, smoking wasteland in an instant, thinning out the attackers to more manageable numbers.

While all this was happening, however, the half dozen ships had pooled chaos for another attack.

And looking up, she saw another ship approaching, far away but closing fast. It was massive, larger by far than the other six combined. The command vessel, then. For this squad anyway.

"Send the signals," she shouted over her shoulder. "We can't wait any longer."

No one responded, but Jasside felt two small puffs of energy behind her.

One dark. One light.

Draevenus was squatting on the balls of his feet and peering through a crack in the entranceway into the irregular chamber beyond when he felt an urgent brush against his mind from commune. A few beats later, and another brush from the same source.

That's the signal. Time to kill again.

He stood, already pushing through another door, this one deep inside the ship, which he'd spent the last few marks silently working loose. Reaching to the opposite forearms, he clutched eight throwing knives between the fingers of each hand. He energized for the span of an eyeblink. Thrusting forward, blades spun through the air past a pair of guards just three paces away. As they arced across the room, he consumed his gathered energy to give them additional velocity and to direct their path. Four other guards, facing him and some fifteen paces distant, crumpled as the knives sank hilt-deep through each of their eyes.

In silence, except for the clattering of their metallic armor as it struck the floor, they died. Not so different than any other species, really.

The two nearest guards turned, swinging wide, tapered blades towards Draevenus. He was already ducking, though, and while their swords passed over his head, he had pulled his own heavy daggers and lunged forward. Unnaturally honed edges tore through their armor with a grinding squeal.

They both spun away, screeching in pain.

Draevenus stabbed upwards, finding the gap between their back plates and the rear rim of their helmets. Two more bodies slumped dead to the deck.

The other five occupants of the chamber turned wide-eyed gazes toward him, expressions of fear that needed no translation.

Four stood in a roughly circular depression at the center of the room, hands pulling away from control devices of some kind, while the fifth sat on a raised platform overseeing their work. None wore armor. They were instead clothed in tight suits with exposed heads, revealing the intricacies of their strange bodies.

Though subtle differences showed, most notably between the sexes, ruvak tended towards the tall and thin, with pale, waxy skin and joints that bent at angles too severe to seem real. Vertical slits replaced nostrils, and their upper lips protruded like shallow, fleshy beaks. Faint traces of fat fuzz adorned some heads, but not others, perhaps indicating a trend to remain shaven. Curled holes on the sides of their heads stood in place of ears. It was a familiar face, yet so alien.

It was the face of the enemy.

They didn't look like much. Nothing like a match to the terror they induced, or the countless corpses they left behind. It didn't matter. As always, Draevenus would do what was necessary.

Only two beats had passed since he'd finished off the guards. He energized another half, took one step to his right to line up the attack, then shadow-dashed forward.

Draevenus felt only the barest hint of resistance as dagger edges passed through two thin necks. Twin heads rolled, spouting blood more orange than red. He landed, quickly thrusting forward. The hearts of his latest victims pulsed once, sending a faint shiver up the steel that had pierced them.

Four bodies fell at once. Draevenus turned to the last ruvak upon the raised dais.

The man's hands shot up in a universal sign of protest, but Draevenus knew he couldn't afford mercy today. He leapt up and grabbed a bony shoulder. Unable to watch the life leave another set of eyes—no matter how dissimilar from his own—Draevenus turned away as he stabbed one last time, shuddering as the weight fell against him then slid slowly, messily down.

Disentangling himself from the twitching body, Draevenus pivoted to face the chamber's center.

Amidst the four crew members sat a rectangular box, waist high and half again as long as he was tall. He hopped down and stood by it. Tugging off his bloodstained gloves, he shoved dark, bare fingers into the crack just below the rim, then heaved forward. The lid sloughed off with a hiss and release of mist that reeked like bile.

Another ruvak lay in the coffin-like space. Tubes spread like a spider's web from the seemingly unconscious body to the surrounding walls.

Unbidden, memories sprang forth into his mind. Memories he hadn't known he'd possessed. A deep cave. Darkwisps shaped like a face. His back pressed against a box just like this.

His god resting within. Speaking.

Travel across the void requires certain expediencies, Ruul had said, *discomforting as they might be. I've no doubt they will have learned the lesson as I and my counterpart have.*

Draevenus slouched, grabbing on to the coffin's edge to keep from falling as he wrestled to slam shut his mind's eye.

Not again!

His remembrance of entering and leaving that dark god's haunt was clear. The rest was less than fog. Yet, somehow, bits and pieces occasionally floated up out of that murky gap in his memory, always relevant to his current situation, if not always opportune. It felt intentional. Ruul, even as he willingly set in motion his own death, had implanted inside Draevenus's mind what he thought would be necessary for the future.

Then promptly locked it all away, only to be revealed in moments such as this.

Truth was, as annoying as it could be, at least it meant he knew what he needed to do.

Fighting off the light-headedness that accompanied his visions, Draevenus began slicing through each of the tubes.

A glob of sweat trickled down Jasside's back despite the wind's chill. She'd been forced to deflect three more volleys while still maintaining her stranglehold on the enemy ships, and had beaten back the same number of ground assaults as she waited. The strain had started getting to her.

Where are *they?*

Light glimpsed through parting clouds answered her a moment later.

A silverstone mass surged out from behind the thunderheads, like a leviathan of the sky. It soon filled the whole of her vision on the right side, casting a natural shadow that covered the entire battlefield beneath her. Roots dangled below, easily a thousand paces long and dozens across.

Halumyr Domicile, uprooted.

Light burned along its leading edge, an aura surrounding a cluster of white-clad figures that sang of their intentions clearly, even to a caster of darkness such as her.

The ruvak saw their doom and tried to escape, but too late.

Like rays straight from the sun, six beams lashed out. They made contact with the enemy ships and met no resistance.

And that was always the plan. For once attuned to darkness or light, the ruvaki shields had no defense against the other.

The half dozen vessels morphed into molten slags, glowing with the pure red of fire as their masses dripped down upon hillsides, setting grass and trees alike on fire. Also part of the plan: the smoke would cover their retreat should enemy reinforcements arrive.

One threat down. As for the other . . .

Jasside glanced up. As if on cue, the approaching command ship banked sharply down, like a vertically thrown stone surpassing the apex of its flight. From that height, and at its speed, the impact it made with the ground sent a shock wave she could feel a league distant.

She focused her eyes on the crash site, until she finally saw a single dark speck fly free of the wreckage.

At that, Jasside allowed herself a single breath,

then dissolved the link. Angla stepped up to her side once more.

"They'll need help below," Jasside said, sagging. "Looks like your sisters, at least, will get to flex their wings after all."

Her grandmother offered a bittersweet smile before gesturing to the other mierothi. They dove off the ship's ledge, unfurling as they fell. Joined by valynkar from the domicile, the sky below filled with flying figures, each striking at the enemy formations with bursts of both light and dark energy. Rather than flee, however, the remaining ruvaki threw themselves upon the defenders in a frothing rage. She didn't blame them. With their ships gone, there was little possibility for retreat. Still, it was futile and meant more deaths that weren't necessary.

Jasside straightened as a figure thumped down on the deck beside her.

"Well fought," Gilshamed said, golden hair glowing in the sunlight. "Your tactic seems to have worked wonders."

"This time," she replied. "The next—who knows? With a foe that seems capable of bending to any situation, how long will it be until we've run out of ways to counter them?"

Gilshamed only sighed, turning his face away.

Jasside followed his gaze. The battle was all but over. "Best start your landing," she said, ever surprised, given their history, that he never balked at taking orders from her. "Thirty thousand people will be needing a ride."

He nodded. "Today, we managed to save them. I only pray we'll enjoy as much success tomorrow."

Jasside didn't know how to respond as he flew off.

Who does he have to pray to when I've already murdered his god?

CHAPTER 2

Arivana had taken to staring at her councilors as they spoke, blinking as little as was humanly possible. It seemed to unnerve them. Not that she derived any pleasure from that—at least she tried not to—but she'd finally reached the point where they'd listen to her without obvious contempt. She'd cling to anything that kept them from realizing how precarious her newfound authority truly was.

Even now, the Minister of Song, a middle-aged man from House Trelent, babbled on in protest to the reallocation of resources, which he claimed rightfully belonged in the hands of the great families. Every few beats his eyes would dart her way, and each such glance was accompanied by the same series of gestures: licked lips and a short hiss of breath before returning to his prepared speech.

She drummed fingers on the armrest of her throne, her own anger building with each syllable he uttered.

People are dying in numbers unimaginable, and still all they can think about are their abyss-taken profits.

Once, there would have been little she could have done about her anger except bury it beneath the veneer of royal repose, staying obedient to the limits of her station, which had been far more constricted than she'd even realized at the time.

But no more. Being a queen finally *meant* something. Beyond being a pretty face to parade before the crowds, a trained monkey to do and say all the right things at the right times. After five thousand years, House Celandaris again had power and respect.

And the change had nothing to do, she was sure, with the manner in which her new councilors had attained their stations.

Arivana spared a small smile for that. Jasside's handling of her former council, and the two other most senior members of each house, had been the subject of much debate among both the high and the low in Panisahldron. Eighteen very public deaths will have that effect. But her own continued association with the dark sorceress had kept any such talk to the most respectful tones. Fear wouldn't have been her weapon of choice, but it had done enough to tip the scales in her favor.

And besides, it wasn't the only tool she had at her disposal at the moment.

She stood, disregarding the fact that the Minister of Song was still in the middle of his speech. He shut up immediately. All eyes turned to her, staring with the kind of rapt attention she could no longer afford to shy away from. Not that she felt any such need to anymore.

Arivana took a moment as she rose to smooth down her gown, noticing with some pleasure the feel of her newfound hips. Nearly sixteen now, she'd grown fully into womanhood, more alike to the portraits of her mother than to that frightened child who'd become an orphan on the same day she'd had a crown placed upon her head. This, too, was a tool, one she didn't even need to consciously use. Not in any lurid way; though seduction might have its place, she didn't have the skill or desire to use it effectively. Nor the need. Rather, her body proclaimed a simple statement of fact: *Before you stands a* woman. *The child you once knew is dead.*

"Ministers," she said, allowing only the barest hint of disdain to enter her voice. "Need I remind you again that the interests of your individual houses are insignificant at the moment. Too many lives are at stake to waste time squabbling over petty concerns."

For a long moment no one spoke. The other members of the council darted glances at the Minister of Song, the only one of them standing, as if hoping his posture would absolve them from having to respond.

He shrank back under their glares, then licked his lips, seeming to accept the burden none of them were willing to bear.

"'Petty,' Your Majesty?" he said at last, raising an eyebrow as if he himself weren't sure if it was truly a question. "Panisahldron has long stood upon the strength of our exports, and you've stripped the very means of our production. We'll be facing a systemic financial collapse if we keep this up much longer."

"For good cause," Arivana said. "For what is financial collapse measured against the collapse of our people? Of our allies' very nations?" She paused, lifting her chin. "Unless you think otherwise?"

He shook his head. "Most assuredly not. Only a monster would withhold aid from those in such dire need. These . . . unfortunates . . . must of course be taken care of."

"Now it is my turn to question a choice of word. Unfortunate might describe someone who makes risky business decisions that fail to turn out in their favor. But I do not think it applies in this situation. Those we seek to help are not *unfortunates*. They are refugees, fleeing an enemy who've induced more slaughter in a month than we did upon the Sceptrines in a year and a half of war. Their homes are gone, their nations are crumbling, and lucky are those among them who haven't watched loved ones turned to ash or torn to shreds by invaders that know no mercy.

"So no, let us not use *unfortunates*, because that,

minister, is far too mild a term. These people, these innocent, helpless people, are *dispossessed*."

He looked around at his cohorts, probably hoping one of them would add their voice to his. When five beats passed, and no help came, he hissed in a breath once more and said, "But they're just foreigners, Your Majesty. Send aid, by all means, but it's not worth impoverishing ourselves for them."

"And what cause would be worthy, then?" Arivana said, unable to hide the anger any longer. "Must Panisians, too, be slaughtered by the millions before you'll lift your noses out of your ledgers? Must more members of your own houses?"

Looking thoroughly chastised, the Minister of Song tucked his chin to his chest and rigidly took his seat, clearly unwilling to face her wrath alone. No one else in the chamber had the courage to meet her eyes.

Cowards, she thought, then immediately regretted it. She couldn't exactly blame them. They'd all been thrust into their positions unprepared and without warning, expected to fill roles just recently occupied by those far more qualified and experienced.

Promotion through death was no easy thing to bear, a truth she knew far too well.

And yet if they couldn't understand the hardships that war could create, then she couldn't find much cause for true sympathy either. They could help her carry out her plans, or they, too, could be replaced.

No longer would wealth buy anyone freedom from responsibility.

"The shipyard operation will continue, unaltered," she said at last. "And you'll be grateful it doesn't require *all* of your resources. If you're still having trouble managing your coffers, I suggest you start by putting an end to your weekly parties. Some denial of gratification might help you empathize with those millions now marching through the wilderness, wondering when—or even *if*—their next meal will come."

The six ministers lifted their heads just long enough to mumble their assent. Grudgingly, but at least it came.

Arivana sighed. She wished, once again, that she didn't have to shame them into agreement. *Some day you may be the council I need, providing advice and guidance for the betterment of our nation. But times such as these have no patience for potential. Until you're ready, I'll have to take . . . other measures.*

"If there are no further comments," Arivana said, "let us progress to today's last order of business." She peered towards the guards stationed by the entrance. "Bring in the prisoners."

The two men shifted their shock-lances to their outer hands, then pulled open the vaulted double doors, revealing the procession waiting just outside: nine prisoners, bound hand and foot in chains, and flanking them, twice as many of the prison guards.

Two of the guards marched closer to their charges than the others—close enough to touch. Recent acquisitions, the man and woman held no weapons, and wore tunics conspicuously lacking in sleeves.

Bare skin was a necessary part of a void's uniform when escorting criminal casters.

Jasside's stories about her homeland had inspired the hiring of such people. It seemed more humane than keeping sorcerous prisoners drugged at all times. Arivana had known such people existed, of course, but had heard little else about them. She'd been unsurprised to learn of their historical treatment at the hands of the great houses. Voids had been marginalized, buried beneath a veil of superstition and carefully cultivated fear. Tior Pashams himself had kept strict tabs on each one in Panisahldron. Ironic, then, that his own records had been the key to finding such gems, and elevating them from outcasts into positions of respect.

The city clocks stuck fifteen as the wardens marched the prisoners in. Arivana spared a glance between the council chamber's sculpted pillars to the shipyards just visible over the tops of the hundred towers. A flurry of motion, greater than the norm, announced the change in shifts, as day-workers headed home, and night-workers began activating multitudes of lightglobes that would illuminate their nocturnal labors. Too many ships were and would be needed to halt production for any reason.

The sight was nothing new. Arivana knew she'd only looked that way to avoid facing those now arrayed before her. Nine prisoners. Nine casters.

The woman she'd once called aunt among them.

Arivana gestured towards the Faer family pod. The Minister of Forms stood, smoothing out the creases in her ceremonial robe, and cleared her throat. She began by reading off a name, followed by a list of the prisoner's crime or crimes. Most were fairly minor offenses, all things considered. Nothing violent or seditious. The process was repeated until all—but one—of the prisoners had been addressed.

"Now," the minister said, "you will all be given a choice. Workers are needed for the great undertaking at our shipyards. You may not have any skill in construction, but you can still be useful by lending your power to those who are. Take part willingly, and without incident, and for every day you labor, a week will be subtracted from your sentence. That, or you return to your cells.

"We will have your answers now."

One by one, the prisoners muttered their replies. Eight more bodies to add strength to the effort.

"You have chosen well," Arivana said. Then, facing the wardens, she added, "Unbind them. They'll begin immediately."

Eight sets of chain fell clattering to the marbled floor, and an aide from House Faer left the family pod to escort them down to the shipyards. The procession departed in visibly better spirits than when they'd entered.

Leaving but a single soul at the chamber's suddenly stark center.

"Claris Baudone," Arivana said, knowing no amount of self-control could prevent the tremor that now entered her voice. "We will now discuss an alteration of your sentence, which for obvious reasons, will differ significantly from that of the others."

Claris stared back, her face unreadable. Did arrogance and pride rest behind those eyes? Or did humility and regret? Perhaps it was a bit of both.

Or perhaps there was only vengeance.

Arivana didn't know. She hadn't allowed herself to visit the woman, no matter how desperately she'd wanted to, needed to. This had to be done in the open. Playing favorites and making secret deals seemed like the surest way to undermine her position. Whatever was about to happen would be a surprise to them all.

"You stand condemned of treason," Arivana continued, "a crime normally punished by death. Yet, here you are. Granted clemency once already, though your actions were indisputable. Have you anything now to say in your defense?"

Claris slowly lifted her eyes to meet Arivana's gaze. "Eight months," she said.

"What?" Arivana replied, suddenly chilled by what she feared was about to happen.

"Eight months. That's how long it's been since

Tior's death. Since you realized the same thing I did. Since you had him and all his corrupt peers eliminated in a single stroke. Yet that whole time I was kept locked away. And for what? It seems my only crime was failing to finish him off, a task you cannot claim didn't need to be done, seeing as how you did it yourself."

"News reaches even the darkest cells, it seems. But not, apparently, all of it." Arivana sighed. "Tior was killed, along with the other ministers, upon a battlefield, by an enemy who had come to negotiate peace. It was his own fault for being unwilling to talk. His death only came because he chose to break peace and tried to have her killed."

"What difference does it make? The end result was the same."

"You made a unilateral decision that wasn't yours to make!"

"*Someone* had to. Tior was—"

"We're well aware what he was. What they *all* were. It is a mistake that will not be forgotten or repeated. But that doesn't give anyone the right to conspire with foreign entities to elicit violence against our own. Loyal guardsmen died, Claris. One, in my very arms. No matter what ends you sought to achieve, their blood will always be on your hands."

To this, Claris did not respond. Arivana considered it a wise move.

"I will ask again," Arivana said, "have you anything to say in your defense?"

"No," Claris said, a word barely heard above the city's faint hum. "I'm . . . sorry."

With a queen's eyes, a queen's judgment, Arivana examined the woman standing before her. This was a serious matter. An *adult* matter. There was no room for the often blind adoration of a child for their favored aunt.

She was glad then, in her scrutiny, to find nothing but sincerity.

"Very well," Arivana said at last. She lifted her chin slightly, a signal to her council that the words were now for them. "We are living, now, in unprecedented times, in *desperate* times, even if some would refuse to see it. We cannot continue acting according to the measure of relative peace. Concessions must be made. Advantages grasped, in whatever manner they might appear. Our nation needs guidance, direction, leadership, and no one in this room can give it better . . . than Claris Baudone."

Murmurs and nervous shifting accompanied the announcement. The ministers were expecting it, if not exactly pleased. Claris, though, flared wide her eyes and nostrils, poorly hiding her surprise.

Arivana focused once more on her adoptive aunt. "These, then, are the details of your revised sentence—you will become my personal advisor, providing information and advice freely, with no thought for political gain either for yourself or your house. You will command no troops, hold no titles, own nothing but what the crown provides for use during your service. If need be, you will guard the royal person, putting my life above your own.

"You will accept this new sentence, or you can return to your cell until old age claims you. The choice is yours."

Arivana had seen the dungeons. She couldn't imagine anyone would willingly return to them. Still, when Claris gently nodded, she felt relief flood through her, an end to the held-breath tension that had been choking her for four-fifths of a year.

"Let it be," Arivana said. "Guard, remove her chains. The rest of you, please leave us. My new advisor and I have much to discuss."

Arivana waited patiently as the ministers and their aides shuffled out, exchanging honorifics with muted tones and attention. The doors closed behind them, and a woman no longer a prisoner stepped quietly up to her throne, rubbing wrists now unshackled.

Some part of Arivana—a large part, if she were being honest with herself—wanted to vault across the distance between them, to leap into Claris's arms, as she had on so many occasions, and weep her apologies. But she knew she couldn't. And to be fair, she *shouldn't*. For Claris *had* committed treason—she was unshakable in that belief. And as she'd taken it upon herself to make something worthy out of the title of queen—to make something worthy of herself—she refused to give in to the demands of her past self. If she had any lamentations, they would be saved for those who needed them most.

"Thank you," Claris said. "I don't know—"

"I meant everything I said," Arivana interrupted. "I freed you because you are needed, nothing more. Your actions betrayed my trust, regardless of your intentions, but I will not let my personal feelings get in the way of doing what is best for our people."

"I . . . understand."

She didn't, Arivana knew. Not really. For the hurt Claris had dealt her had at least been understood, in time, if not condoned.

Flumere's betrayal had stung far, far worse.

The ripple of equine muscles between his knees and the familiar sway of that rugged, ash-colored mane made Mevon feel that much more at home. Riding Quake again, one of so many things he'd left behind, felt like reinserting a missing piece back into the self he used to be. Comforting, yet, at the same time, strange.

Mevon knew he wasn't the same as when he'd left. Before, when he served Rekaj and the old mierothi regime, things had always been simple: follow orders; deliver justice; kill.

Then, the revolution. And the laying bare of all the lies his life was built upon.

He'd dedicated himself to the cause of freedom as much because of his father as because doing so had not forced him to change his ideals—he'd only changed his targets. Yet even as the conflict drew to a close, he'd begun to war with his place, with his purpose. He still didn't know if disappearing as he had, leaving behind everything he knew, everyone he loved, was the right way to do things, but he was convinced the journey had been crucial to his own understanding. Of the world, and more importantly, of himself.

Too, externally he was not that different, but the peace he now felt made it clear that he would never see things through the lens of the man he used to be. The realization had slowly dawned the more he'd re-acquainted himself with familiar places and people and things. It had been difficult to accept at first, but Mevon no longer minded. He was done doing things the easy way.

He stared at a faded scar along Quake's neck that hadn't been there before and smiled.

I'm not the only one that has changed.

Mevon turned his head to glance at the man riding beside him. Warrior. General. Emperor.

Father.

His hair and beard had faded from grey to nearly white, and the lines around his eyes, once sharp from endless laughter, had withered and sagged. Two years since Mevon had left, but Yandumar looked to have aged two decades. Slick Ren, who had stayed behind in Mecrithos, and who—thank the gods—hadn't tried acting like a mother to him, assured Mevon that his return had worked wonders for Yandumar's well-being. But if that were true, it only demonstrated just how far into despair his father had fallen. For all of it, Mevon couldn't help but feel partially, if not totally, to blame.

Still, when his father caught him staring, he peered back, smiling widely just as Mevon remembered. It was good to see, especially since such expressions now came so rarely.

"Any chance you've relented?" Mevon asked, keeping his tone light in hopes of extending his father's good mood. "Or are you determined to keep our destination an Imperial secret?"

"Can't you just let it be a surprise?" Yandumar said, a thin hoarseness to his voice as new to Mevon as the man's white hair. "Some of the best things in life are the things you don't expect."

"You'll get no argument from me there. But still, a hint or two wouldn't be remiss, now, would it? How can I expect to build anticipation when I don't have the faintest notion what's in store?"

"Come now, son. I know you're smarter than that. Look around and you'll see enough clues to get your mind running in the right direction. Don't expect me to enable your laziness."

"Laziness? I'll admit, this is the first time anyone's accused me of *that*."

Yandumar shrugged. "It's what fathers are for."

"What are emperors for, then?"

"Not much."

Mevon laughed. Then, taking his father's advice, he studied the environment for hints of their destination.

Ochre grasses as high as Quake's chest bracketed the trail, stretching across the plains to the Godsreach Mountains on their right. A deep sniff brought scents of salt and freshly turned soil. Wind blew in conflicting bursts: glacial and sporadic down from the passes, while warm, moist and steady from directly ahead.

"We're headed for the Shelf," Mevon declared, "and its farthest north point in the eastern territory, if I'm not mistaken."

"Right you are," Yandumar admitted. "And what does that tell you?"

Mevon shook his head. "Nothing much."

"Oh?"

"I was stationed out here, if you remember. Back when I worked for Rekaj. I know this area well, and I'm telling you there's nothing out here."

"Is that right?" His tone had just the right touch of infuriating condescension that only a son could hear from a father.

"Yes, Father. Why, that pass right there is where . . ." Mevon trailed off, finger shaking as it pointed up the mountain.

"Where you brought back Jasside after capturing

her for the first time," Yandumar said, completing the sentence.

Mevon smiled, a warmth filling him as he lost himself in memories of her. "I still can't believe she's alive."

"You would have known if—"

"If I'd never left." Mevon gulped harshly. "I know, Father. I know."

Of all the wounds stemming from his disappearance, that one bled the worst. *Jasside lived.* The woman who'd made him believe that he could be more than just a mindless killer. Who'd found a way to love him regardless of what he'd done in the past.

The depth of her forgiveness even now left him breathless. *How great the light in her soul must be. More than enough for us both.*

It had not surprised him when he'd learned what she'd accomplished. First stopping a war between the other great powers of humankind, and now leading the defense against the mysterious invaders from the void.

Mevon could think of no better hands for the world to be in.

And though he didn't dare pronounce any sort of claim on her heart—he'd been dead in her eyes, after all—the fact that she lived meant there was still a chance for something, *anything* to grow between them. Even if not to the extent that he hoped, he'd cherish any time he got with her.

Abyss, I'd be happy just following her orders. Something tells me I'll be doing that soon anyway.

He wondered, briefly, if he would still have faked his own death if he'd known she yet lived. Probably not, he decided. But then again, he doubted he would now be the man that he was, a man possibly worthy of her, if he hadn't. And in turn, she wouldn't have been in position to do as she had, to be exactly where and when the world needed her most.

No regrets, then. No going back. If something comes, it comes of who we are now, not the static image of each other we hold in our minds.

"You still love her, don't you?" Yandumar asked.

"How could I not?"

"A lot of reasons, son. But they'd be the wrong ones."

Mevon grunted.

"If you've a doubt, come out and say it."

"Sorry, Father. It's just . . . this conflict we're headed towards. From the reports you've shared with me, it seems likely to be all-consuming, even more bloody than the one we fought for the empire's freedom. How can anyone find time for love when the very tides run red?"

"Abyss take all that," Yandumar growled. "That's *exactly* when the world needs love. It'll happen if it's meant to."

"You make it sound like I don't have a choice."

"Choice? There's always a choice. Love, guilt,

anger—they're emotions all right, and powerful ones at that. They sometimes make us *think* we have no control, but that's just weakness talking. How you respond when they show up is another matter. *That* is a person's true measure, what choice they make. *That* is what separates us from beasts."

Mevon inhaled deeply, letting the breath out between narrow lips as he absorbed his father's words. There were truths in his statements. Powerful truths. And ones most people—Mevon included—seemed to go their whole lives missing. Mevon had always told himself he was in control of his emotions, when in reality he had merely suppressed them. He'd let his training and instinct guide him, never wanting or wondering if there was another way. A *better* way.

I can claim ignorance no longer. Time to start owning my choices, no matter how hard that might be.

Nudging Quake with his knees, Mevon drifted nearer his father and laid a hand on his shoulder.

"I'm sorry," he said. "I shouldn't have left without saying anything. I shouldn't have made you think I was dead."

Yandumar stiffened. "That's not what I . . . You don't have to . . ." He turned his head away.

Mevon felt the aging muscles beneath his hand begin to shudder.

"It was selfish of me," Mevon said. "And beyond inconsiderate. I don't expect forgiveness—"

"But you have it!" Yandumar croaked. He turned his head, allowing Mevon to see red-rimmed and brimming eyes. "Don't you see? You're my son. No matter what you do, you'll never *not* have my forgiveness. Even for this. *Especially* for this. After what I did . . ."

Mevon lifted an eyebrow. *What did you do?*

Then, he remembered.

After realizing the similarity of their sins, he couldn't help but laugh.

"What is it?" Yandumar asked.

"Nothing. I just guess you can say, we've both had our turn coming back from the dead."

His father's eyes widened, then he too began to laugh.

They were both still in the throes of mirth when Mevon noticed the grasses cut sharply away and a sudden intensity to the wind in their faces.

They'd finally reached the Shelf.

Yandumar pointed down. "This, son, is what I wanted you to see."

Wooden stairs traveled down the cliff upon switchbacks carved out of its side. They hadn't been there before. A league down they traveled, connecting at the distant surface with a maze of wharfs and piers and jetties sticking out into the glittering sea. Between them sailed ships by the hundreds.

"You've built a fleet," Mevon said, unable to withhold the wonder from his voice.

"Not just a fleet," Yandumar said. "An *armada*. Some old friends of ours are going to need all the help they can get. Once more, the Veiled Empire is going to war."

CHAPTER 3

Dread welled within Tassariel as another patient began to stir from their already fitful slumber.

I hate this part.

Padding softly on slippered feet to avoid waking any others, she glided up to his bedside. Cracked lips parted, mumbling. She placed the jug's stem between them and dribbled as much water as she dared. His eyes still fluttering in an effort to let in light, he lifted his nearer arm towards her hands, likely trying to tilt the jug up even farther.

He failed to reach, of course.

Another effort, almost a lunge this time, which elicited a groan too high-pitched to match the bulky frame it came from. Something now clumsily brushed the backs of her fingers, but it wasn't a hand.

Just the tender nub of his arm ending four finger-widths below his elbow.

The man's eyes and lips burst open, the latter sending a fresh runnel of watery-blood down his chin while the former fixed her with a frantic stare. Breaths once steady now became a harsh, rapid wheeze. Shaking, he lifted both arms before his face, examining the horror, the dichotomy that hadn't been there the last time he'd been conscious.

Tassariel took a long step back.

The man clenched his teeth and his one remaining fist. His face turned red.

"Where . . . is . . . my . . . *arm!*"

Not all of them responded with anger, but even when they did, Tasserial didn't mind it so much. She understood that reaction. And unlike most of the other caretakers, she knew how to protect herself against a flailing, raging patient, and could do so without causing them further harm.

She set the jug on the bedside table, then stretched out her fingers in case she had to restrain him.

The preparation proved unnecessary.

Both arms flopped onto his belly, then slid to the sides as his whole body went limp. Blood and tension drained from his face. Leaking out from the corner of each eye, a pair of tears marked trails toward his ears. He sobbed, once.

Why couldn't you have just stayed angry?

"Where is my arm?" he repeated, softer this time.

It took Tassariel a moment to realize he actually expected an answer.

"It was lost on the battlefield," she said.

"But you can heal me, right? I thought . . . I thought magic could cure anything."

She shook her head regretfully. *Most times I wish it could.* "Magic can mend most sorts of broken flesh, but it can't regrow something wholly lost."

"I've heard stories, though. Soldiers losing limbs only to be made whole again. I even talked to a lad once who had it done to him!"

"We can reattach one if it's recovered. But we were retreating when your shield was struck by an enemy chaos bolt. There was . . . no time to go searching for it."

"What about Derolan? Trask? My squadmates. They were right beside me. I'm sure one of them would have picked it up. Did you ask them?"

Tassariel felt her eyes drift to the side, as if against her will. Two beds, empty. A human attendant was replacing the sheets.

She said nothing.

Nothing needed to be said.

"No," the one-armed patient whispered. "No."

He began shuddering, a reaction that bore no relationship to his injuries. Tassariel remained frozen in place. There was nothing to do for him now. Nothing *she* could do, anyway. She'd taken care of his physical needs, but the wounds now assailing him—wounds he would carry the rest of his life—were beyond her power to heal. Beyond, even, her power to soothe, if only temporarily.

All valynkar children learned the basics of healing magic before the age of fifty. Tassariel had taken emergency service among the healers simply because she had nothing else to do. And despite her calling, she didn't think she'd be much use in a fight. Her heart wasn't in it. Or in anything, really.

Experiencing the death of a god—*her* god—from within her very bones had felt as if her own soul were passing through to the light beyond the abyss. Only there had been no light on the other side, and she'd returned to a body left numb. She understood this on some level of her awareness, but had no defense against it, no means to combat it. And no one, not even her aunt, who'd been miraculously released from the prison of her own mind by the final act of Elos, could understand what she was going through. How could they when she didn't even understand it herself?

Tassariel looked down upon the broken, grieving soldier, understanding his need and trying to summon something for him: pity, maybe, or even the smallest measure of comfort.

But for him—for anyone—she had nothing to give.

"I'm sorry," she said at last, knowing he likely didn't hear her. Probably for the best. If he had, he wouldn't have been able to ignore the lack of sincerity in her voice.

She turned and strode down the hallway, through the dining room, and out the front door to the street. The temple of healing was perpetually full, and half the buildings in the domicile had been converted for one use or another during the conflict. Or, more accurately, the evacuation. She wasn't even sure who owned the house she'd just left. Not that it mattered now; her shift was over. She told herself she could ask tomorrow, but knew she wouldn't.

Sighing, Tassariel tucked her ragged, lavender hair behind her ears and began her morning trek towards home.

The sun's red rays made the silverstone buildings around her gleam like so many misshapen garnets. Wind from the domicile's passing fluttered her robe behind her, a thing once white but now stained by more types of fluid than she cared to name. The streets alternated, with little transition, between abandoned and frenetic. The newcomers hailed from warmer climes, and weren't used to the cold at this altitude. They ran everywhere they went to keep their forays outside brief.

How nice to be able to flee such mundane discomfort.

No one spoke to her as the ground beneath her feet changed from paved street to grass-lined path and back again, a small thing for which she was grateful. She'd been too eager to escape and no one she'd left behind would have still called her a friend. Her return hadn't made matters any better. If anything, her isolation from her own people had deepened. They didn't know how to deal with the girl who'd been inhabited by their god.

The girl, some said, who was responsible for his death.

She understood their frustration, even their hatred. If gods could die, after all, then the faith that shaped their lives was without meaning, and all acts that faith inspired had to be called into question.

If gods could die, then faith itself was dead.

Tassariel envied those who could throw themselves into new causes, replacing one kind of devotion for another. But she had been too close to Elos; close enough to burn. The wound stung deeper and sharper for her than it did for any other valynkar, far surpassing any reasonable tolerance for pain.

Numbness is a gift. Though I don't know what I did to earn it.

Lifting her head, Tassariel found herself standing before the door to her residence. Her feet must have brought her there by instinct. She hesitated, swallowing hard, and tried to make something presentable out of the mess that was herself. But she knew there was nothing she could do to really fix what was broken.

She ran a fingernail across the chimes. A moment later, the silverstone door panels ground, rasping, to the sides. A haggard-looking woman, human, stood in the entrance, balancing an infant on her hip.

"Well, don't just stand there, girl," the woman said. "This is more your home than ours, after all."

Tassariel stepped inside without a word. Three other children ran around—doing what, she didn't know—sparing her only the briefest of peripheral glances. The father and two oldest children were absent, likely off to their assigned tasks for the day. She no longer chafed at being called "girl" by a woman who'd seen sixty fewer turns of the world, nor at sharing a dwelling meant for one with eight other people. Few and lucky were those, since the invasion began, who hadn't been forced to make considerable concessions.

She snatched a loaf of bread from a cabinet, tearing off chunks and shoving them into her mouth as she trudged out to the balcony. Eying her hammock, she lifted a leg to climb into it.

Gravity shifted, and she toppled forward, barely able to catch herself on the ledge.

Tassariel cast out her gaze, long past the distant edge of the domicile. Scores of impossibly tall buildings lay beyond, with a cluster at the center taller still.

Panisahldron. They'd reached her at last, already braking to come to a stop over the city. A simple maneuver, really. Just a single controller at the center of the domicile, pulling a few levers. Here, the great would gather and discuss how to stem the tide of blood, but she had no hope they'd find a solution as easy as that.

The world, and her soul, raced further toward the abyss every day, and there was little she could do to slow either of them down.

Jasside waited until both the skimmer from below and the golden-winged figure from above had landed upon the royal tower's ledge before waving over her shoulder to Angla and stepping off the edge of her ship. Expending a tiny pulse of energy, she shadow-dashed across the thousand-pace gap through open air. Upon arrival, she realized that she'd misjudged the distance, coming in a pace too high. Though only a slight error, it was enough to cause her to smack down amidst the others with reverberating force.

King Chase of Sceptre and Queen Arivana of Panisahldron both jumped back in surprise. Gilshamed shook his head and frowned.

"Pleased with yourself, are you?" the valynkar asked.

Jasside wiped away the smile she'd been wearing, meant to convey her apologies. Too much of her exhilaration must have shown through, causing him to have interpreted it differently. "No," she said. "Why should I be?"

"Vashodia always knew how to make an entrance.

Should it be cause for concern to think there might be too much of your mistress in you?"

"Only the harmless parts, I assure you. But if it becomes otherwise, I hope and expect you'll let me know."

"Trust me, I shall."

She smiled at him again, hoping this one conveyed the gratitude that words alone could not. "Besides, Gilshamed, it's a two-way exchange between her and I. Don't the benefits, in our case, outweigh the risks?"

Reluctantly, he nodded. "I see your point."

"If we're going to jabber on, can we at least do it away from the edge?" Chase said, glancing down nervously at the drop. "These gusts of wind are a bit strong for my tastes."

"That's right. You don't have buildings this tall in your country," Arivana said. "I suppose the height takes some getting used to."

"That," Chase said, "is one way to put it."

Jasside watched as the king of Sceptre and the queen of Panisahldron pointedly avoided each other's eyes. Not that she could blame them. It was a miracle that they were talking at all after years of bitter war between their peoples. There was bound to be a little mistrust, a little . . . awkwardness.

Nothing like the threat of mutual extermination to help put the past to rest.

Arivana cleared her throat, then turned to the attendant at her side. "Claris, lead us inside."

"Of course, Your Majesty," the woman said, then lifted an arm. "This way please."

The four of them marched in the direction Claris indicated, Jasside in the rear. As she passed the raven-haired woman, Jasside felt the power within her: dormant, yet substantial. Not quite on the same level as herself, or even Gilshamed, but far more than those not of pure valynkar or mierothi blood.

Just as strong as the former council members. The ones I . . . took care of.

The thought made her perform an even deeper inspection of Claris. The woman may have worn the same shapeless grey accoutrements as the rest of the palace staff, but her eyes saw too much, and her movements were far too graceful for any mere servant.

Gilshamed, she noticed, was also casting glances over his shoulder at the woman, but they seemed more confused than wary. Jasside waited until they'd passed through the hall into a round chamber filled with red velvet seats before leaning in close to the valynkar.

"The attendant, Claris," Jasside whispered. "Do you know her?"

"Yes," Gilshamed replied, "but only by reputation."

"What have you heard?"

"She was the former head of House Baudone and Minister of Dance."

"Dance?"

"A dual meaning, like most of their titles. She was—

and probably still is—the foremost Panisian expert on combat."

"Interesting. And useful. But why the servant's garb, then?"

Gilshamed, now taking his seat, could only shrug.

Jasside sat as well, intrigued, as always, by any sort of puzzle; another trait she'd picked up from Vashodia. As surreptitiously as possible, she studied Claris as the woman went to stand behind Arivana's chair. Everything about her posture spoke of subservience, but there was a fierceness to her as well, a desperate loyalty laid bare every time she glanced toward the queen.

She's trying to prove herself.

As soon as she thought it, Jasside saw it was true. Whatever Claris had done to fall from—then seek to climb back into—the queen's good graces didn't matter. She'd be both ally and asset to Arivana, and thus, to the greater cause.

Jasside eyed the girl with renewed respect. No— not a girl, but a woman come into her own. Jasside had known since they'd first met that Arivana had a good heart, and she'd proven soon thereafter to have the loyalty of her people. That she'd display such wisdom and shrewd judgment for affairs of state was a welcome surprise.

Perhaps this new alliance won't fall apart after all.

A single servant brought in a tray, which Jasside was intrigued to find held only water.

"I apologize for the lack of traditional Panisian hospitality," Arivana said. She wore a maroon silk dress, crossed by dizzying patterns of gems, with feathers fanned out from her neck to frame her head. The ribbons tied into her elaborately styled hair looked made of pure gold. "I've sent all but the most crucial servants onto more important tasks, and as for refreshments . . . well . . . you all know how many extra mouths we have to feed."

"I'm not here to be entertained," Chase said. His plain outfit stood in stark contrast to the queen's: a mud-brown tunic and trousers, lined in grey like quarry stone. He wore a slender sword on one hip, its pommel smooth with use, and a metal scepter on the other, but bore no other ornamentation. "I take no offense at the gesture."

"Neither do I," Gilshamed said, taking a cup from the servant and sipping gratefully. "I propose we begin. There is, after all, much to discuss."

"Indeed," Jasside said. She turned to the queen. "Perhaps you'd like to start, Your Majesty?"

"I'm afraid for my part there isn't much to tell," Arivana said. "I've put every resource at my disposal toward building more skyships, but the number of refugees increases a thousandfold for every seat we create."

"What do you need to increase production?"

"Casters are the limiting factor, but to bring in

more I'd have to pull them from the weapons factories."

"I'd not recommend that," Chase said. "Those magically forged armaments are the only things keeping our ground troops from being outright slaughtered in every engagement. We've barely enough of them as it is. Take those away, and we'll only be useful as human fodder."

"That won't happen," Jasside assured him, then turned to Gilshamed. "Any luck bringing in more valynkar?"

He shook his head. "A week ago, I personally sent word by commune to my kin, nearly a thousand strong, who are spread out alone or in small groups throughout the world. Not long after—" he paused, fists clenching "—their stars began going out."

"What!" Jasside said. "How many?"

"Nearly half so far, but only those closest to the eastern coast."

Jasside closed her eyes, pondering possible explanations and quickly arriving at the most alarming one. "Is it possible that the ruvak can somehow trace us through commune?"

"Light and dark are entirely separate realms, and neither have ever been breached by the other. Believe me, we have tried. What makes you think ruvaki magic can achieve in months what no one else could in thousands of years?"

"Chaos," Jasside said, "does not play by the same rules."

Gilshamed raised both eyebrows. "You are convinced that is what their power stems from, then?"

"Their source could be none other."

"A wonderful observation," Chase said dryly. "But how does that help us fight them? Chaos doesn't sound like something easy to predict."

"Like I said, the rules have changed. That doesn't mean they don't exist. We'll just have to figure out what they are, and how to exploit them to our advantage."

"Yes, well," Arivana said, looking more than a bit lost, "back to the original point. How many of your kin can you send, Gilshamed? And when can we expect them?"

The golden man sighed. "All of the domiciles are roaming up and down the eastern coast, fighting alongside the ships of your great houses. We've . . . had losses. My priority right now is to reinforce them, and make sure no more lone valynkar are hunted down."

"So, that means . . . ?"

"One hundred," Gilshamed said. "I can spare no more than that. They'll be here within the week."

The queen, to her credit, hid her disappointment well. "Every hand will be put to good use. Thank you."

Gilshamed gave her a tight-lipped smile.

Jasside turned to the king of Sceptre. "What about the situation on the ground? Anything more you need to help your forces?"

Chase grunted. "I wouldn't mind another ten thousand of those daeloth. Have you got any hidden away?"

"Unfortunately, no."

"A pity. The only other thing," Chase said, "is communication. I hate putting aside talented casters as little more than glorified messengers. It's a waste. Have we no other resources we might put to use for that? Perhaps the young or the very old? They'd stay back from the front lines of course."

Arivana's eyes flared. "I don't think we're so desperate as to start sending children off to war."

"The war is coming to *us*," Chase said. "And the ruvak don't discriminate. Once the fighting men are taken out, they will rain down mass slaughter with no regard for age or sex or station. Maybe my reports don't do it justice." He shrugged. "I guess only those who've witnessed it with their own eyes can appreciate how desperate we truly are."

The queen lowered her eyes, sadness now mixing with ferocity. But not, Jasside saw, replacing it entirely.

"Sixteen is the minimum age," Arivana said. "And volunteers only. I cannot in good conscience order anyone younger than myself into harm's way. And they *will* be, make no mistake. I expect you will all do everything in your power to keep them safe."

"Before our own safety," Chase said. "Trust me, this will help tremendously, and will be better for them than simply waiting around to die."

"How can you know that?" Arivana said.

"Because I've seen it in action. We start training young in Sceptre, you know. By necessity."

The queen sighed. "Very well. I'll see how many, if any, are willing."

"As will I," Jasside said. "Gilshamed, have you anything to add?"

The valynkar slowly shook his head. "No. You all seem to have everything well in hand."

Jasside nodded. "Well, then, if there's nothing else, I see that we all have quite a bit of work to do."

They stood, but Arivana came up last. "There's just one more thing. A minor matter, really. But one I can't seem to do anything about." She lifted her eyes to the ceiling.

Jasside followed the queen's gaze. She felt the pull of familiar power above them.

"Vashodia," Jasside said. "She's still giving you problems?"

"You . . . might say that."

Jasside ground her teeth. Her mistress hadn't been listening to her of late.

But there is someone *she might listen to.*

"Have no fear," Jasside said, forcing a smile. "I'll take care of it."

Draevenus circled the great bird statue twice, gliding on the warm air that rose from the city. Flapping a few times to surge over the crest of the giant head, he landed on a plumed ridge jutting up from the neck— half in, half out of darkness.

He dismissed his wings, then stepped forward into his sister's cold, comforting sphere.

"Good evening, dear brother," she said, sitting legs crossed and with her back to him, the loose folds of her robe billowing like black ribbons. "How nice of you to join me. I hope you didn't have to go too far out of your way?"

Draevenus braced himself as a gust of wind sang by. "Hello, Vash."

"Not the most convenient place to corner me with your demands, I know. But then, you never did do things the easy way."

"*Your* way, you mean."

"One and the same, of course. At least here you can't argue about the quality of the view!"

She raised her arms as if to embrace the city. Draevenus spared it only a glance. His eyes instead locked on to Vashodia's hands, still covered in scales and tipped by sharp, curled claws. A reminder of what the rest of them had left behind, and of the completion his sister had willfully disdained. He'd stopped feeling pain at the sight of her months ago, and now felt only numbness.

A heart could only break so many times.

"Magnificent, isn't it?" she went on. "A thousand hues of lights glittering across the faces of a hundred unique towers, the least of which rises many times higher than any structure back home. Why is that, you think? Why, in nineteen hundred years, did none of our people try to build something so grandiose as this?"

"We didn't care," Draevenus said, feeling confident in speaking for his entire race on this. "We had dominion of the continent. There was no one to impress."

Vashodia snickered. "On target as usual, dear brother. You might even say you've struck right to the heart of the matter."

"What 'matter' would that be?"

She turned her head, assaulting him with her pale face, and gave him a sharp-toothed smile. "That we cannot win this war fighting as we have. As those . . . children would have us wage it."

"Do you include your apprentice in that category?"

"Her most of all. She should know better. You see, we ruled the Veiled Empire in absolution. The concerns of both the outside world and our own citizens were negligible at best. It simply didn't matter what they thought. We could do whatever we wanted with no regard for our reputations. Have you caught on yet to what I'm getting at?"

Draevenus nodded slowly. "The ruvak are the same as we were."

"Oh, well done! Wits about you at last. I was starting to worry."

"I don't see how that affects the way we fight them."

"And there they go again. Pity. It was fun while they lasted."

"Vash . . ."

"A point. Right. Small minds always need to hear the point of things. Very well." She sighed, turning back to face the city again. "The ruvak hold all the cards. They can do as they please. And every action we take only plays further into their hands . . . as long as we keep doing the expected."

Draevenus swallowed the lump in his throat. "You're talking about the refugees."

"Of course I am. We should have abandoned them to their fate and gone on the offensive right from the start. We might have stood a chance then. As it is, we're only losing slowly, thinking it right to waste the lives of valuable fighters defending those too weak to defend themselves."

"But—"

"No. We must put the survival of our species above all other concerns. Oh yes! We've all grown different coverings, but mierothi and valynkar are all undisputably of human stock. We're not just fighting for the right to hold dominion over this world, dear brother. We're fighting for the very right to exist."

Draevenus hung his head. He could always tell when she'd set her mind and knew there'd be no budging her from this stance. The only consolation was that no one was listening to her. That fact, however, didn't put him at ease. On the contrary, it filled him with dread.

"So go on, then," Vashodia said. "Deliver your messages, the concerns of those who dare to rule in a time such as this. Go on, if you think any of it actually matters."

At the moment, Draevenus wasn't sure if it did, and the messages he'd rehearsed turned to ash on his tongue. So, finally, he decided on something else.

"Our brother was born last night."

Her flinch, so slight only his assassin's sight was able to perceive it, was the most surprising thing he'd ever seen her do.

"Half brother," she said, recovering her composure so quickly he wasn't sure she'd ever lost it. "And we've got countless numbers of those."

"Not like this. No scales for one, and his skin is grey. Perfectly healthy, though. And perfectly natural. He's something we've never seen before, Vash. Something new."

"And you think this is cause for celebration?"

"How could it not be?"

She scoffed. "Of course you think as such. You still view Ruul's final act as a gift."

"It made us whole. Ended our stagnation. Gave

hope to a people that had forgotten the word's very meaning. If that's not a gift, I don't know what is."

"It also promised death."

Draevenus shrugged. "We'll still live as long as the valynkar. But our kin are able to have children now. *Real* children. They'll be able to leave a legacy beyond themselves, their own achievements. And maybe, just maybe, the rift between our sexes will start to heal."

Vashodia said nothing for several beats, then slowly rose to her feet. She turned, stepped forward, lifted eyes that were, except for the ever-present malice, unreadable. She laid a palm against his cheek.

"And what of you, dear brother? Will you not partake of our god's gracious gift?"

He sighed, closing his eyes, and shook his head.

"Why ever not?"

Draevenus glanced down at his arms. "This skin, my wings . . . those are enough for me. My soul is too stained to taste anything else. My heart is a burden. I wouldn't wish it upon my worst enemy. Especially knowing what role I'm to take in this war."

"The remorseful assassin. But you play the part so well!"

"As do we all, we puppets, dancing and jerking every time you twitch a string. Please, tell me that you at least have a plan?"

She hesitated, a slight tightening around the eyes. His stomach twisted at the sight.

My second surprise of the day.

"Find the weakness in our enemy and exploit it," she said, a bit too cheerfully. "It's only a matter of time until it's discovered, a task in which you'll play a most important part."

Draevenus lifted an eyebrow. "What do you mean?"

"Naturally," she said, lowering her hand and stepping away, "we can't waste someone of your talents in open battle. You're to go behind enemy lines—farther than you'd normally dare. If the ruvak have secrets, you can be sure that's where they'll be kept. I expect you'll prove efficacious at prying them out of their cold, waxy fingers."

"It seems it's all I'm good for."

"Nonsense. And besides, I'm sure you'll have such a good time getting to know your new apprentice."

"What the abyss are you talking about?"

"Light and dark together have proved an exceptional combination for combating ruvaki energies. It's dangerous to go alone." She pointed to the valynkar domicile hovering above the city. "I'd suggest you take one of those."

"A valynkar apprentice, huh?" He smiled. "I think I know just the one."

"Wonderful," Vashodia said, clapping her hands. "Now off with you. My little machines are probably growing worried that I've been away from them too long."

Nodding once, he turned, preparing to unfurl his wings. At last, though, he remembered what he'd originally come here to say.

"Vashodia?"

"Yes?"

"Jasside asked me, on behalf of Queen Arivana, to see if you would stop attempting to interrogate Sem Aira Grusot."

"The spy, you mean. The assassin who started a worldwide war." Vashodia giggled. "If the queen wants mercy for that one, I suppose I can relent. I'll soon have others to play with. Perhaps they'll prove more willing to answer my questions."

Draevenus shivered. "And there's . . . one more thing . . ."

She waved an arm. "Out with it."

"People are wondering when you're going to join the fighting. You'd be an unmatchable asset, you know. Beyond your apprentice even. Think how many lives—"

She glared at him.

"How many *soldiers* you could save, then."

Vashodia peered to the northeast, narrowing her eyes, as if she could see something out there that no one else could. "Tell them all not to worry. The option to avoid combat will soon be taken from me, from all of us here. The only choice left will be whether to fight . . . or to die."

CHAPTER 4

Mevon leaned against the rail at the stern of the ship, entranced by the frothing white wake behind them. The gentle rise and fall as the vessel surmounted swells, the lap of waves against the hull, the warm breeze laden with the scent of salt, the sprays that left the deck coated in a slim, slick layer of water—Mevon had never felt more at peace.

The armada sailing behind them, however, reminded him constantly of war.

The nearest less than a hundred paces away, the farthest lost in the dusk's orange haze, the ships seemed countless.

"Quite a sight to behold, eh?" Yandumar said, patting Mevon's shoulder as he joined him on the rail.

"Quite," Mevon said. "How did you manage it?"

"Oh, we started building right after I took the

throne. Lots of people looking for work about then. Came from all over the empire. For them, a newly freed people, the project became a point of pride."

"They're impressive. I've seen river barges and fishing boats, but never anything like this. Where'd you learn how to build them?"

"Archives below the palace. Deep below. Held all sorts of oddly shaped trinkets, each filled with information of some kind. 'Repositories,' Orbrahn calls 'em. Can only be read by a caster, of course. Ship designs were in one, ancient but still serviceable. I added what little bit I'd learned from my time outside the Shroud and, well, you're standing on the results."

Mevon smiled, as much for the explanation as for seeing his father in such good spirits. Such moods no longer seemed quite so fragile.

He looked up along the main mast and pointed to the flag standing stiff in the wind. Three vertical stripes—white, black, and red. "What does that represent?"

Yandumar flicked his eyes up, then closed them. "White, for the light we lost. Black, for the darkness we overcame. And red, for the blood we shed to earn our freedom."

Mevon nodded once. "I approve."

"I thought you might."

Turning back to the railing, Mevon rubbed a hand along the stubble garnishing his jaw. He breathed out heavily through his nose.

"Something troubling you, son?"

Mevon grunted. "They're waiting, right? That's what you came to tell me. I suppose we should get this over with."

"Ha!" Yandumar said, clapping Mevon on the shoulder again. "I'm sure it won't be that bad."

"We'll see."

They departed the railing together, marching past the man at the tiller and down the steep steps to the main deck. Sailors bustled about on tasks Mevon had little notion of, but seemed to involve a lot of ropes. Other than those barefooted, shirtless men, and a few archers and crossbowmen, the deck was mostly empty, making the massive ship seem far too vast for its crew. Most of the troops he'd seen spent the majority of their time in their cabins; even Mevon knew that wearing armor on a swaying deck was the surest way to find yourself in a cold, watery grave.

Yandumar led him near the prow and held open the door to his personal cabin. Mevon stepped inside, squinting as he transitioned from natural if fading light to the bright blue of dark-forged lightglobes; a paradox if ever he heard one.

His eyes adjusted quickly. Three figures stood waiting before him.

"Hello," Mevon said. "I suppose it's been a while."

Idrus and Ilyem greeted him with a respectful nod, the former with curled corners of his lips. Orbrahn, kneeling over some strange box, rolled his eyes and chuckled.

Mevon had anticipated glares or crossed arms or outright sneers. This . . . he didn't know what it was yet, but it wasn't nearly as hostile as he expected.

"I'm sorry about what I did," Mevon continued. "Disappearing like that. Making you all think I was dead. I don't expect you to forgive—"

"Do you honestly think we care?" Orbrahn said.

Mevon stared at the young, dark-haired caster, whose face seemed locked in a perpetual smirk. "I don't understand."

"You think any of *us* wanted to hang around after the fighting was over? Pah! Administrating an empire's boring business. We're not mad at you. Well, maybe a little. But only because we didn't think of it first!"

Mevon shook his head, disbelieving his ears.

"He's right, you know," Ilyem said, blue light reflecting off her close-shaven head. "So much changed in so little time. Everyone had to readjust, even our kind." She gave him a slight, knowing look, not quite a smile. "*Especially* our kind."

"Besides," Idrus said, his uncannily observant eyes giving Mevon a thorough examination, "whatever it was that you set out to do seems to have done you good."

Mevon sighed, standing a little straighter. He hadn't realized how much of a burden he'd placed upon himself trying to justify his actions in their eyes. But they'd proven, once again, far greater friends than he could ever be, their understanding lifting that weight from his shoulders like it was nothing. Nothing at all.

"Well, now that we have that settled," Yandumar said, "let's move on to more pleasant matters."

"You call planning a war *pleasant*, old man?" Orbrahn said, still tinkering with the contraption at his feet. "More like an exercise in tedium."

"Quit your bellyaching, boy. You know as well as the rest of us that this is what we were all bred for. And what can be more satisfying than doing what you *know* you're meant to?"

Mevon smiled. "I couldn't agree more, Father."

"Using your own child to gang up on me now?" Orbrahn said. "Not the most sporting tactic, old man. Fine then. I'll just be over here trying to get this abyss-taken thing to work while you all chat. Come get me when you need something sorcerous solved."

Yandumar sighed as Orbrahn dragged the box-thing into the farthest corner of the cabin and turned his back on them. "Sometimes I wonder why I appointed him to my inner circle."

"You couldn't trust anyone else," Idrus said. "And despite his arrogance, he's always been willing to learn."

Yandumar grunted. "I suppose he has at that."

"What that he's working on?" Mevon asked.

"Either a puff of smoke and a pile of ash . . . or something that might actually prove useful. I'm sure we'll find out which soon enough."

"You don't sound very hopeful."

"Just mindful of history, son. It hasn't always been kind to our young friend."

Mevon smiled.

"Gentlemen," Ilyem said, wearing a look unreadable to most but which Mevon knew for impatience. "May I suggest we begin?"

"Aye," Idrus added. "We'll need to make preparations for every conceivable circumstance with this one. The situation is . . . tricky."

"How so?" Mevon said. "I've only heard the basics."

"For one, the enemy—ruvak, they're called—are mostly airborne."

"Airborne? You can't mean . . . ?"

"They have ships that fly," Yandumar said. "Not too fast, mind you, but still highly mobile. The only upside is that our . . . allies . . . have similar capabilities, if not quite so many."

"But not us," Mevon said.

Idrus flicked his eyes toward Orbrahn. "Not yet."

Mevon crossed his arms, one hand reaching up to rub his chin. "Tricky indeed. I suppose we could use sorcery to bring them down."

"Not on our own," Ilyem said. "Though plentiful, we only have dark casters. From what we've been told, only dark and light *together* can do them harm."

"That's going to be a problem."

"Which is why we're sailing southeast," Yandumar said. "We're to land on the western shores of a land called Panisahldron, then march inland through their jungles to reinforce the main allied force at their capital. Their light casters outnumber the dark more than three to one. What we add should help even those numbers a bit."

"Seems a sound plan. But what about ground combat? I assume these *ruvak* do not stay in the air entirely. What capabilities do they possess on foot?"

"They've at least three troop types that have been identified so far," Idrus said. "Large, heavy infantry, and lightly armoured skirmishers. The latter, apparently, have been seen jumping over the heads of upright men."

"Interesting. And unprecedented. What measures have you taken against them?"

"I've made spears our primary infantry weapon, and had the troops practice against thrown sacks full of sand. Our bowmen have switched to shortbows and drill all day for speed. The worst of them can release nine shafts a mark." Idrus sighed, holding up his hands and shrugging. "Until we meet them in battle, though, this is all just guesswork."

Mevon nodded. He knew that no plan lasted long past first contact, and you couldn't truly know an enemy until you've crossed blades with them. Still, the preparations seemed effective based on what limited, secondhand information they could get.

"You mentioned a third type," Mevon said. "What do you know about them?"

"Little," Ilyem said. "But we've been told they tend to keep their distance in battle, ravaging our allies' lines with strange, chaotic energy."

"Magic?"

"Most think so."

"Do we know if—"

"Our kind can negate it?" Ilyem shook her head. "It has yet to be tested."

Mevon grunted. "We'll find out quick enough once we face them."

He felt energy surge from the corner of the cabin as the air filled with a crackling hum. He glanced over at Orbrahn just as the young man lifted his arms in triumph and shouted, "I got it!"

The box, the contraption he'd been working on, now floated of its own accord.

"If we can get those working on a larger scale," Yandumar said, nodding forlornly towards the flying device, "we'll find out sooner still."

Gilshamed slid a finger along Lashriel's forehead, pushing a strand of long, violet hair out of her face, giving dawn's rays free rein to dance across her cheek, her jaw, her lips, the tip of her perfect nose. Her breaths came steady, each a whispered assurance that all was well. Though her eyes were closed, he knew that when they opened there would be awareness and intelligence behind them. There would be a soul.

If he could choose one moment, one sliver to pull from time's merciless, raging river, it would be this one. Here, lying beside his wife, watching as she slumbered, forgetting the centuries they'd been separated, the torments they'd both endured, was as close to bliss as he would likely see this side of paradise.

And since he was no longer sure that anything waited for him beyond abyss's dark, cold curtain, he would cherish such moments all the more.

He dropped his hand to the bare peak of her shoulder, brushed it down her side to the valley that was her waist, then up her hip's smooth, curved mound. She stirred at his touch, back arching, arms stretching out to encircle his neck. A sound, half moan, half yawn, purred from her throat. Her lashes parted above a growing smile.

Joy, thought Gilshamed. *So this is what it feels like.*

"Good morning, my love," she said.

"It is indeed," he said, drinking in the sight of her lively, violet eyes. "The best that ever was."

She snuggled closer. Breath pulsed from her open, anxious mouth, so sweet it seemed holy. Their lips touched with a spark. His hand fell to the small of her back and pulled her closer, tighter and tighter, until he could no longer tell where he ended and she began. As it was meant to be. As they had been, once, so very long ago.

With a sigh and a laugh that threatened to sink Gilshamed into ancient memories, Lashriel pulled away. He regretfully allowed the space between them to widen, at least enough to where they could look once more into each other's eyes.

"Trying to make up for lost time?" she asked.

Though her tone was obviously playful, Gilshamed still felt a hollow ache in his chest. For her sake, though, he responded with what he hoped was a convincing smile. "There are many things I feel I *need* to make up for, but this is the only one I *wish* to."

"As do I." She kissed him again, lightly, bringing a hand down to rub his chest. "But another day awaits, my love, and you have a world to go save."

"Do I?"

She frowned. He'd meant to phrase it as a jest, but in her arms he was laid open, vulnerable, his soul's truth too raw to conceal. Hiding anything from her would require a great deal of effort, a task made more difficult by the fact that he did not want to. He wanted only to be honest with her, in every way.

I just wish I could spare you from worry.

Her furrowed brow let him know that he was failing.

"Don't say that, Gil. People need you. *Nations* need you."

"But I only need you, my love. The abyss can have the rest."

"It will unless someone stands against it, spitting defiance in its face. No one does that better than you."

"I used to think that, as well." Gilshamed sighed, rolling onto his back to stare at the vaulted white ceiling of their bedchamber. "But I'm afraid that's no longer the case."

"How could that be?"

"The world moved on, Lash. You were lost, and I spent every waking moment searching for a way to bring you back. I spurned all responsibilities, all relationships, all cares, became single-minded in my quest. Destructive. I went . . . a little mad. More than a little.

"The world moved on, and now others have taken upon their shoulders the mantle of its protection. People more skilled, more motivated, more selfless than I have the heart to now be. People better than I ever was.

"The world moved on . . . and they do not need me anymore."

Lashriel buried her face between his shoulder and neck, and for the longest time said nothing. He stroked her hair gently, content to let be the silence and stillness. So long as he was with her, he could endure anything.

It wasn't until he felt a smear of wetness across his upper chest that he realized she was crying.

His hand froze, still entwined in her curls, and his mouth went dry. He did not know what to say, what to do. His instinct for such things had died alongside so many other parts of him along the way. The ability to give comfort seemed as alien as the ruvak.

"What's wrong?" he said at last.

"Nothing," she said, wiping her cheeks.

"No, what is it? You can tell me."

Lashriel breathed deeply, shaking and clutching him tight. "We've lost so much of ourselves, Gil. We aren't what we used to be. I look at you and it's like peering through clouded glass at my own memories. I look in the mirror and I see a stranger."

She lifted her head, now pinning him with wide, glistening eyes. "We found each other, though, after everything we've been through. And despite the brutal odds, we managed to reclaim *us* again.

"We won't ever be the same as the selves from before. I know that. But if there's a chance, any chance at all, to hold on to the old parts of us, the best parts, then we shouldn't give up on them without a fight."

"What are you saying?"

"You loved who you were, Gil. Leading people. Fighting with all your strength to save the weak. Standing up to those who would use their power to dominate those without it. It was your entire identity . . . and you loved it. You were whole."

"Maybe," Gilshamed said, touched by her words, her insight into the one soul he never dared delve too deeply. "But that part of me only brought us both to ruin."

"That was *not* your fault. You have to know that!"

"I do not. Had I only paid you the kind of attention you deserved, you never would have—"

"Hush now, my love. I never blamed you for trying to keep me safe from the ravages of war. I still don't. But the young and able-bodied are not meant to sit idle while others die on their behalf. The urge to action itched strong in us all. And Voren? Voren was . . . inspirational."

"He was," Gilshamed admitted. "He was indeed."

"So," she said as she rose, hair tumbling like a silken waterfall over her shoulders. "You get up, my love. You walk out that door. You attend to your duties. You go and save the world. After all, it's what you were born to do."

Seeing her standing there, with hands now planted on her hips, wearing nothing but an all-too-serious gaze, Gilshamed couldn't help but laugh. He rose from the bed, grasped her hands and pulled them to his face, planting kisses across the backs of her fingers. Spinning away, he strode to the wardrobe and began to dress, filled, for the first time in centuries, with a small but welcome measure of peace.

Tassariel stepped lightly down the corridor of an unfamiliar level of the tower. The stone walls bled cold, consuming all sound, while the lightglobes did little more than stab needles of illumination into the shadows. No other soul had yet crossed her path. She had been hesitant to follow the directions she'd been given; during her stay—however brief it was—she'd never known this place to be used.

She glanced down at her dirty caretaker's robe, unsure if it was fitting attire. Having just come off her shift, she probably should have gone home to change first, but exhaustion pulled at her limbs, and she knew that her hammock would have been too tempting a sight to resist. Besides, her home was only really good for sleep, nowadays. Sleep, but no rest. She had no desire to see any more of it than was necessary.

Eventually, the corridor ended, splitting to either side in a broad arc that wrapped around to meet itself somewhere nearer the tower's core. This was the fifth such round chamber she'd arrived at. Oval glass the size of her torso, spaced evenly along the inner circle, slanted inward to grant viewing of the sunken space beyond. The windows of the other chambers had been dark. These, however, glowed with faint but steady light.

Looks like I've finally found the right one.

Tassariel turned right at random, and was rewarded by her choice of direction less than a quarter of the way around the circle. Arivana glanced towards her as she approached.

"Tassariel!" the queen said, lips curling in obvious delight. "I didn't expect to see you here."

The valynkar stopped three paces away and bowed. "Your Majesty."

"Oh, abyss take your formality," Arivana said, and before another heartbeat passed, spread her arms and lunged forward.

Cringing, Tassariel absorbed the impact, then tried to push the young woman away. "Please, I'm filthy! I couldn't bear getting a stain on your dress. You don't even want to know what I'm covered in!"

"What's a little mess going to hurt anything? I won't let it get in the way. I need a good friend too much right now to care."

Tassariel felt the tension inside her release at the words. "Me too, I think," she said, hugging the queen back with the same ferocity. "Me too."

They shared a sigh, then stepped apart, though Arivana grabbed hold of one hand. "I meant to visit you at some point, once I'd heard your domicile had come to roost. How have you been? I haven't seen you since . . ."

"Fasheshe," Tassariel finished, having sensed a slice of hesitation in the queen's eyes. *Since before the god inside me turned everything upside down.* "I've been . . . fine. I suppose. Busy. They needed help uprooting the domiciles, a task almost as difficult as convincing our high council it needed to be done. Then once the fighting started . . ." She shrugged, gesturing at her caretaker's outfit.

"Noble pursuits. It's good to stay occupied, I know. Helps take your mind off things you can't afford to linger on. Like having Elos inside you, only to witness his death firsthand." The queen gave her hand a squeeze. "I can't imagine what that must have felt like."

Tassariel squeezed back. "Probably like watching your closest confidant revealed as a betrayer."

Arivana flinched, glancing over through the nearest window.

Tassariel followed her gaze.

At the center of the round chamber—called a "theatre" by the servants she'd talked to—rested nothing but a thin pallet, upon which sat a single figure, hazy in the half-light. Wearing what looked like a grain sack, the woman bore features that, while too close for comfort, weren't close enough to identify as human.

Sem Aira Grusot. The one once known as Flumere.

Arivana lifted a hand to the glass, resting it there as if she could reach through and touch what lay beyond. As if that might make a difference, somehow.

"Elos," Arivana said. "He knew right away, didn't he? From the very first time he saw her."

"Yes," Tassariel replied.

A sad smile tugged at the corner of the queen's lips, vanishing quickly. "That explains why you acted so strangely. Did he ever say why he waited so long to reveal her?"

"Never explicitly. But he was always harping about the need to keep his intentions—his knowledge, even—as close to his chest as possible. I never really understood why, though. But, in the end, I came to trust his judgment. I don't think things would have turned out well if I'd had my way."

"You think things turned out *well*?"

"No . . . perhaps not. But it could have been worse. Much worse."

"Maybe." Arivana lowered her hand from the window. "I find it strange that you called her a betrayer. To betray someone, you must first give them your loyalty. *True* loyalty. She deceived me, deceived us all, but we were merely targets to her. We weren't ever really friends."

"Are you sure? It didn't seem that way. Looking back, she went far beyond what was needed to maintain her cover. She helped you, Arivana, in ways that might even be interpreted as contrary to her mission. She *cared*."

The queen stared, unblinking into the theatre. "A credit to her expertise, perhaps. Nothing more."

Tassariel averted her gaze. She didn't know what to say. Arivana seemed to need something from her: some assurance perhaps, or even just some empathy.

Whatever it was, Tassariel didn't think she could provide it.

How can I fill another when I myself am empty?

She'd come here to meet up with an old friend, only to find them both too changed, too damaged to give the other what they needed. Some small part of her might have hoped she'd find some service to provide, but she didn't know how to offer, and Arivana appeared too distracted to think to ask.

"I was told I could find you here."

Tassariel jumped, then turned to face the voice. Striding down the corridor towards her was a man who looked far more comfortable in the shadows than she would ever be. Smooth, ebony skin stretched over a muscular yet compact frame, all topped by short, spiky hair.

"Draevenus," she said.

"So you *do* remember me," he said.

"Was that ever in doubt?"

He shrugged. "Our one and only meeting was brief, amidst chaos. And—pardon me for saying—I don't think you were quite yourself at the time."

"No," Tassariel said, remembering the ethereal sensation as she surrendered control to Elos, watching from behind her eyes, a passenger in her own body. "But I was still able to observe everything that happened."

"I can't imagine," he said, echoing Arivana's words on the same subject.

"No. You cannot."

"I suppose you and I are, if not unique, then the same sort of rare. Not many get to speak directly with their god."

"The gods are dead," she replied. "If they were even 'gods' to begin with."

Draevenus clamped shut his eyes, holding his breath, and his body started to tremble, like someone suffering from an acute, powerful headache. Tassariel glanced at Arivana, who seemed just as confused by the reaction.

With a gasp, his strange state ended as quickly as it began. He took several calming breaths, then nailed her in place with his piercing brown eyes.

"Perhaps you're right," he said, inexplicably donning a smile. "If you'd like, we can discuss the nature of . . . higher beings later. If you accept my invitation, we'll have plenty of time to talk."

"Invitation?"

He nodded. "I've been asked to provide a unique service to the war effort, one which will take me deep into rukavi-held territory. However, given the nature of our enemy, it would be suicidal to go without the help of someone like yourself."

"You mean . . . a valynkar? But why me? There are plenty to choose from."

"None with your particular set of skills."

Tassariel swallowed hard, feeling something rise from within her. A sweet ache, indefinable. She didn't

even know what to call it, though, and her distrust
of abnormal impulses made her instinctively fight to
keep it in check. "My calling. It can't be *that* rare. I'm
sure—"

"I won't find another as able-bodied, or as experienced in their craft.

"Nor will I find someone so wasted in their current line of service."

"But—"

"Please, Tassariel. There is no other that can do
this task half so well. I *need* you."

The bubble inside her burst, and she realized, now,
what it meant. What it was trying to tell her.

*This is the purpose you've been lacking. This is what
you* need.

And yet . . .

"Behind enemy lines?" she asked. "Just the two
of us? Hundreds of leagues from anyone that could
come to our aid?"

"That's right."

"Sounds dangerous."

"Extremely."

Tassariel smiled. "Count me in."

Draevenus simply nodded, then turned around
to walk back the way he came. She hugged Arivana,
somehow even more fervently than their first, as they
both said their tearful goodbyes, then stalked off after
her new partner as he disappeared down the darkened hallway.

Vashodia took her eyes off the approaching daeloth to watch a snake as it slithered nearer. Fully elongated, it would barely reach from finger to outstretched finger, far too small to consider *her* for its next meal. Having done nothing to disturb its hunting ground, she couldn't think why it would advance on her with such obvious fixation.

"Perhaps you think me a kindred spirit?" she said, examining the scales adorning her arms. "But yours are too small, too square, too bright. And I, alas, do not have any kin. I'm the last of my kind. Unique. The rest of them were too short-sighted, fretting over the mostly superficial drawbacks, to fully appreciate all that immortality has to offer."

She squatted as it came closer still. A forked tongue flicked in and out of a wide head that stayed arrow straight despite its body's weaving. Eyes sharp as the diamonds suggested by its green-and-yellow pattern seemed to peer into her soul. She reached out a hand. The snake hesitated a beat, then crawled up her bare arm. Its smooth belly rhythmically scraped across her coarse, dry scales, coiling about limbs and torso alike until the last tip of its tail disappeared beneath her robe. Vashodia found the sensation . . . pleasing.

She straightened—not too quickly of course—as the daeloth pushed aside a hanging branch and came to stand beside her beneath a vine-choked tree.

"Good morning, Feralt," she said. "I'm so very glad you decided to keep our appointment."

"It was that or end up on your bad side," Feralt said, flicking back his perfectly groom hair. "Wasn't much of a choice."

"And what makes you think you aren't there already?"

He stepped back, eyes widening as he stuttered over a reply.

"Now, now," she said, "you're a pretty enough boy, Feralt—if far too old for my tastes—but wearing stupor so plain on your face ruins what little charm you have."

"I—I don't understand. I did everything you asked!"

"Everything?"

Somehow, he blanched even further. "Look, I tried, all right? It's not easy getting a virgin to open up her legs. And even if I could have forced the matter along, you told me explicitly not to. What was I supposed to *do?"*

Vashodia sighed. "Oh, nothing of course. The fault was as much mine as it was yours. Your success would have granted me an excellent means of control, but even your failure gave me key insight into her resolve. Into her—" Vashodia snorted "—passion."

Feralt exhaled deeply. "You're not mad at me, then?"

"Mad? No. But neither am I entirely pleased."

She shook her arm, and the snake poked its head out the end of her sleeve. She gripped it by the neck, holding it up before the daeloth's quivering face.

"A tool," she began, "is only good so long as it's in your grasp, carefully handled to prevent it from wearing out or being used for other purposes. Someone smart can deploy it any way they wish, over—" she touched the reptilian lips to Feralt's temple "—and over—" his cheek "—and over—" his neck.

She stepped back and began wriggling her fingers before the gaping yet immobile jaws. "But once you lose control—" She let go. The snake darted out, fangs puncturing through the meaty part of her hand, eliciting a gasp from her throat. "—even the best tools have a tendency to strike where you least expect."

She flung the snake away. It slithered into the underbrush, vanishing in beats.

Feralt wiped a hand across his forehead; it came away acrid and drenched. "Wh-what do you want from me?"

"Well, seeing as how you tried to curry favor by volunteering for an assignment—which you failed— it's only appropriate that you owe me a favor in return."

"A favor? Sure. Anything you want. Just ask and it'll be done. I swear."

Vashodia smiled. "Keep an ear out, then. You'll be hearing from me soon."

Feralt stood there a moment, too stupid to realize he'd been dismissed. Vashodia rolled her eyes and had to flick the backs of her hands at him twice before he got the hint. He spun on his heel, but paused before taking a step and looked back over his shoulder.

"Was that thing . . . venomous?"

A stinging, virulent burn was rising up her veins, only a few beats from entering her heart. "Quite," she answered. "And a flavor I've never tried before. What a productive morning it's been!"

Eyes flaring, he faced forward and ran.

Vashodia giggled.

Energizing, she probed her insides with dark power, surrounding and isolating the insipid liquid. She let it run its course as she analyzed the effects, savoring each wave of pain it delivered whilst keeping it away from anything vital. A most productive morning indeed.

With a sigh, she scoured the rest of it clean from her blood, lest it do any permanent damage, and began skipping along through the tangled jungle. Birds chirped and cawed in counterpoint to the incessantly buzzing insects, and a great cat growled in the distance. She was surprised at how wild nature was allowed to be, even here within a league of the city. An amusing dichotomy. And, to be honest, she understood the allure of surrounding oneself with danger on all sides.

No better way to feel alive.

She came clear of the stifling canopy, spotting the city filling half the horizon. Even from here she could make out the phoenix statue, ever shining, and the sphere of darkness blotting out its nose, which she'd left active in her absence. No point letting people know she was away from the nest.

Focusing her eyes on the sight, she shadow-dashed towards it.

Wind and cold and dark greeted her arrival, all changes that were welcome. The intruder, whom she noticed a beat later, was not.

Jasside raised an eyebrow, appearing not the least bit surprised by Vashodia's sudden appearance. "Busy morning?" she asked.

Vashodia smoothed out her robe, still unbalanced from the lengthy jump. "Perhaps. Are you checking up on me now?"

"And what if I am? You've haven't exactly been—" Jasside paused, inhaling deeply then softening on the slow exhale. "I came," she began again, "to see how you were doing. If you needed anything. I know I haven't been a very attentive apprentice lately, and for that I'm sorry."

"An apology? My, my. Someone must want a favor from me *very* badly."

"Not a favor exactly. Just wondering if you had any insights about the ruvak. Something that might help us fight them, or at least understand them a little better."

"And what makes you think I'd have anything of the sort?"

Jasside shrugged. "I've been too busy fighting, which—" She stopped herself again, flashing a tight, unhumorous grin. "Which doesn't allow much time for . . . meditations."

Vashodia returned an equally mirthless smile. Truth be told, she hadn't learned much about them at all, a faulty situation this morning's adventure would work to rectify. She couldn't tell Jasside about any of that, of course. No master—or mistress, in her case— ever wished to look less than efficacious in their pupil's sight.

And I certainly do not plan on starting now.

Dark chords struck inside her mind: her machines singing their song. Perfectly on schedule.

"I might have learned *one* thing," Vashodia said. "And a rather pertinent bit of news at that."

"What is it?"

"The ruvak are smart, it seems. They've figured out who controls all the little pieces of scattered humanity that dare to stand against them. They're on their way right now to eliminate those who hand out the orders."

Jasside hissed in a breath. "You can't mean they're coming—"

"Here," Vashodia said. "By this time tomorrow, a fleet larger than all the rest you've faced combined will be at Panisahldron's doorstep." She giggled. "I think it's about time we meet!"

CHAPTER 5

Arivana gave up trying to count the ruvaki ships after her head grew dizzy from the attempt. They would not keep still. Even estimates were useless as many held back, clustered one moment to appear as if a single, large vessel, then dispersed into dozens of individuals the next. And there seemed to be no logical transition between states. All she could tell for certain was that the horizon itself churned like an angry sea, marred and broken by their presence.

How can we fight something like this? How can anyone even try?

She'd listened to all the reports on them with a strong yet vague unease. The enemy seemed impossible to understand, but there had still been victory—if endless retreat could be called that. Now, seeing them herself for the first time, that unease snapped like a tautly pulled string. Fear of the unknown seemed preferable to this mad reality.

This city—my city—they have come to destroy it. And I do not see how we can stop them.

She glanced upwards at their defenses. Halumyr Domicile and the Baudone family greatship lumbered overhead, the former twice the size as the latter. Less than fifty other allied ships hovered at various points around the city, none larger than a sapling compared to those two ancient oaks, and themselves little more than aerial platforms, sparsely manned, mounted with her nation's famed sorcerous batteries. With but one small change: half were now powered by darkness. All the rest of the ships—those that could carry passengers—had a different task this day.

Turning to face the opposite direction, she switched which forearm held her weight against the balcony's polished, marble rail. She hadn't bothered to style her hair today, as all the servants had already been evacuated, allowing the breeze to push it forward, framing her view westward in flapping orange strands.

The shipyards were busy, as usual, but not with the same kind of activity.

Unfinished ships stood empty and abandoned. The rest of the launching platforms had been cleared of all tools for construction, and were now crammed with mobs of humanity waiting their turn to board the next vessel. Of which—by an order of magnitude—

there were simply too few. A compromise had needed to be made. Thus, each ship was filled far past normal capacity, then departed to drop off their passengers a hundred leagues out, at the very southern tip of the Nether Mountains. She could just make out the long, thin line, keeping low over the canopy, disappearing between distant hills to make their lengthy round-trip journey. They'd been rotating in and out ceaselessly for most of the last twenty tolls.

And still, massed throngs of refugees flocked through the streets. The crowd at the shipyards had not diminished in the least.

Too many had waited, she knew. Packing up valuables or just waiting for the foot traffic to thin. Or, like her, they'd been too skeptical to think the city might actually fall, considering themselves safe behind their guarded and gilded walls. Like they thought wealth was infallible defense against any sort of hardship.

A great many assumptions are going to be tested today. Even—perhaps especially—my own.

Ripping shrieks, as if the air itself had been sundered, blasted at her from behind. She tensed at the noise, then turned once more to face the ruvak with reluctance. Dozens of projectiles spun wildly towards the city from as many enemy ships that had swept near enough to fire. Closer they came, passing the farthest outskirts.

The great shields around the city activated. Darkness, then light. A double dome of protection that shimmered in opposing shades at each point the enemy blasts had tried to penetrate. It held.

For now.

Arivana felt a single thump of her heart throb within her chest.

Then the ruvak opened up in full.

The horizon blazed with sorcerous energy: light, dark, and chaos roiling together in a menagerie of wild violence. The salvo stretched on, unabated, for what seemed like tolls. At last, though, it ceased. And amazingly, the shields continued to hold.

But the ruvak formation had halved their distance to her city, spreading out in frenzied motion that made their previous condition seem crippled in comparison.

Arivana glanced down once more at the people fleeing through her streets.

Hurry, she thought, shaking at the sight of so many still exposed. *For the love of all the beauty left in the world, please, hurry!*

Gilshamed clenched his jaw at the sight before him, a swath of enemy ships unbelievable in its enormity. Yet it was the sight behind him that was even harder to believe.

Valynkar and mierothi stood, preparing for war. Not as foes, this time, but as allies.

The combined sorcerous power of his hundred

kin hummed bright within him. He had chosen only those least skilled in combat or the healing arts, both of which, he knew, would be in desperate short supply. The mierothi had done the same. Only thirty of them were gathered here on the leading edge of the domicile, mostly women, but he'd been told that number would be sufficient. The diminutive figure who stood at his side, holding the reins of the thrumming dark energy, had gone so far as to call it excessive.

"Lovely morning, is it not?" Vashodia said, pointed teeth peeking out between curved, parted lips.

Gilshamed swept his gaze around for a beat. "There are no clouds, at least. That will make it hard for them to approach unseen."

"Quite right, my dear old foe. Our only difficulty will lie with correct prioritization of targets. You did read the instructions I sent, right?"

Sighing, Gilshamed nodded. "We are to focus on the smaller targets. Our batteries and ships are not accurate enough to hit them anyway, and will be occupied by the larger enemy vessels. Darkness leads to attune their defenses, while light strikes for the kill."

"Very good! It makes me so *very* happy to see that you've put aside ancient grievances at last."

"Perhaps," Gilshamed said. "But do not think that means I like you, let alone trust you."

Vashodia flipped her hand in a dismissive manner. "Naturally."

Gilshamed shook his head, unable to convince himself to be comfortable in the creature's presence.

Looking over his shoulder, he made eye contact with Lashriel, standing foremost among the other valynkar. She gifted him with a secret smile, a knowing smile. A smile that gave him strength. He knew that he was in the right place, doing exactly what was needed, for both the world and for himself. Because of her, he could tolerate any amount of distaste so long as it aided the right cause.

Through you, my love, I can do anything.

He faced the horizon once more, ready for whatever might come, just as the first ruvaki ships dipped their noses through the dome.

"All right," Vashodia said, folding her hands into her sleeves. "Let the fun begin."

Floating three stories up on the arrowhead-shaped platform—which she'd constructed herself—Jasside surveyed the broad arc of the allied fortification that protected Panisahldron from ground attack.

It seemed pathetically thin.

Sceptrine heavy infantry stood ready along the foremost line, their armor, slanted caps, and oddly curved shields all dulled to look like stone. Panisian shock-lancers, in mirror-shined plate, were spaced between every fifth man to better spread out the potential impact of their magically forged weapons. Behind them were three more rows holding pikes, like a strip of bristling needles almost twice the length of a man. Soldiers with crossbows, mauls, maces, and two-handed axes came next: specialty troops to counter the enemy heavies. Phelupari skirmishers, with spear and buckler, acted as a screen for the missile troops, which had only one wrath-bowman for every ten mundane archers. And bringing up the rear were the milling, disorganized reserves: surviving soldiers from Corbrithe and Kavenmoor, Panisian regulars, and a militia made from anyone willing to hold a weapon in defense of those who could not.

Half a million troops in all.

Jasside didn't know if it would be enough.

Panisahldron had no formal defensive wall, so they'd built their barricades here, along the front edge of the outer city, not a tower in sight. A thousand paces of open ground, much of it cleared quite recently, spread outward from their position. A killing field more than twice as wide as necessary—for a normal enemy, that is. Against the ruvak, she wasn't sure it was wide enough.

"Drinn, Tarlene," Jasside said, pivoting in the small space her platform allowed. A boy and a girl, twelve and thirteen respectively, sat strapped in seats along the miniature vessel's back edge. "Get a ready check from every commander. Based on the activity up top, we should expect contact soon."

"Aye," Drinn said.

"As you wish," added Tarlene.

Jasside frowned as the two escaped into commune, wondering—and not for the first time—if it was a mistake to include them. Drinn, a daeloth, and Tarlene, a daughter of House Faer, had been the best of the candidates she'd interviewed. They both understood orders without the need to repeat them, operated quickly within commune, and handled pressure well for their age. But *age*, itself, was the problem.

God forgive me for allowing children to go to war.

Though she didn't plan on entering the fray herself, her mere proximity to the action put them in harm's way. It couldn't be helped, though. Every able adult caster had more important, more dangerous tasks to fulfill this day. It was a weak argument, she knew, and did nothing to lessen her hatred of the ruvak for putting them in this position.

But war is war, and we can worry about right and wrong when and if we survive.

"All commanders report ready, Lady Anglasco," Tarlene said.

"Same here," Drinn said.

Jasside nodded. "Thank you."

One ranking daeloth and a Panisian sorcerer-commander were embedded in every company, each overseeing their dreadfully small cadre of casters. King Chase, much to the chagrin of the city generals, had been placed in command of the troops, while

Jasside had charge of the sorcerers. She'd need constant manipulation of her magical assets to keep them both from being overrun.

She turned around, facing northeast once more. Less than a mark later, the edge of the surrounding jungle trembled, and ruvak infantry glided out from under the canopy, as far to each side as she could see. Rank after rank after rank after rank . . .

. . . her breath froze in her throat as she tried to make count of them.

Jasside closed her eyes, filling her lungs to bursting, then let it out over the span of ten beats. An exercise in patience, calming her.

"I hope you're ready," she said, as much to herself as to the two youths behind her, and was glad to hear no tremor in her voice. "We have a city to save."

"Your Majesty, please! I *beg* you to reconsider."

Arivana turned her head slowly, glancing over at the only other occupant on the slowly descending lift. "I've made up my mind, Claris. Do not try to dissuade me."

"But this is madness! You'll be in danger every step of the way—and for no reason!"

"I have a *very* good reason. I'll also have you at my side. You were the Minister of Dance once, at the supposed pinnacle of your trade. Did the deep cells cause your skills to atrophy so far that you now doubt your ability to protect me?"

The lift came to a stop and the door rotated open. Arivana stepped out, eyes forward, missing whatever reaction might have shown on the woman's face at the remark. She heard only silence, not even a breath. The fury was implied.

The long receiving chamber passed by in a blur, the expensive decorations seeming even more gaudy now, considering what was going on outside. Their footsteps echoed off the empty walls, a sound as lonely as death.

"Look," Claris said, her voice under strained control. "Let me send a message, and I'll have a skimmer here in a mark or two. It can get you to your royal skyship quickly, and safely. There's no need to take such risk."

Arivana stopped, gathering her breath and her thoughts. Claris nearly bumped into the back of her. "How many times have I told you that I intend—no, that I *am* the queen. And as queen, I will be not only what my people *expect* of me, but also what they *need* of me. This, Claris, right now, whether you see it or not, is nothing more than that. It must be done. It *will*."

The woman, at last, bowed her head, having at least enough respect to conceal her sigh. "Very well, Your Majesty. Please forgive my impertinence."

"Given. Now, are you going to be willing participant, or must I swing you by the ankles?"

Claris twitched. It had been something she'd done to Arivana—against her will, though playfully—when she'd been just a little girl.

"No need for that, I assure you," Claris said. "However—if you'll allow me—I could better protect you if I took the lead."

Arivana acquiesced, gesturing forward and flashing a grateful smile.

They continued down the vast receiving chamber. Nearing its end, they stepped around the throne platform and came in sight of the massive double doors that marked the official entrance for royal guests. Four men snapped to attention, drawing her to a halt.

"Guards?" Arivana said, glaring at Claris. "I ordered the tower empty a toll ago. Why are they still here?"

"If it pleases you, Your Majesty," said one of them, "we volunteered to stay behind."

"And why would you do that?"

A confused expression painted across his hard, young features. "Because you were still here, Your Majesty. No way this side of the abyss we were going to leave the ground-level doors unguarded. Not while you remained."

Arivana nodded slowly, touched by the gesture. She'd been told, of course, that she was popular with the people, but only by those who sought her favor. To see evidence, firsthand, of such loyalty threatened to bring tears to her eyes.

"Thank you," she said at last. "There are other entrances. How many more of you are there?"

"Twelve, Your Majesty."

"Gather them up, if you would. I'm . . . going for a walk. I do believe I'll be needing an escort."

The guardsman gestured to his three compatriots, who took off in different directions at a run. It wasn't long before they returned with the full dozen as promised.

"What is your name?" Arivana asked the one who'd spoken to her.

"Richlen, Your Majesty. My friends call me Rich."

"That you are, in manner and wisdom, if not in material possession. Though I don't think many will be able to claim the latter in the coming days."

"Right you are, Your Majesty. And . . . thank you for saying so."

She smiled at him. "Now . . . Rich . . . please open the doors."

Without a word, the guards snapped into a square formation, four on a side, around her and Claris. One pulled a lever, and the way outside revealed itself in a split ten men high. They marched forward as one.

Claris bent close as they descended the great steps

leading up to her tower. "You were right, of course. This is exactly what the people need. I never should have doubted your judgment."

Arivana nodded, swelling with pride inside, yet forcing the reaction to keep clear of her face. "We can pat each other's back once we get out of this. But . . . thank you. Despite everything, your opinion still matters a great deal to me."

Two guards rushed ahead to open the mostly ornamental gate. Once through, only a few short steps separated them from frantic press of the street.

The crowds stopped, staring with wonder at her arrival.

Arivana held her breath.

From somewhere across the broad avenue, a voice called out, "The queen walks with us!"

The words were repeated, just a murmur at first, yet it quickly surged into a cry, then a cheer, then a chant that seemed to rock the very foundations of the towers around them.

"The queen walks with us!"

"The queen walks with us!"

She pointed westward, waving with her other hand. "To the shipyards," she said. Rich led his men onwards, their backs, perhaps, a little straighter than before.

I walk among my people in their toll of need . . . and they rejoice at my coming.

Arivana allowed herself, now, to shed a single, grateful tear.

Vashodia's heart pumped black blood through her veins, with an urgency she'd not felt in years, as she watched the last enemy ship this wave turn into a tumbling, molten slag.

"I'd forgotten how exhilarating this could be!" she said. "I really must remember to do it more often."

Gilshamed dropped his arms to his sides, exhaling in relief. "We could . . . certainly use you."

Vashodia giggled. "That must have taken a lot out of you to admit. Tell me, how much of your soul withered away just now?"

"None," he said, oddly granting her a grin. "You said yourself we should put old grievances aside. I like our chances better with you taking a more active role."

"Have no fear about my level of contribution, dear Gilshamed. Just don't expect it to always take the shape you crave."

"With you, Vashodia, I expect nothing."

"Then we've reached consensus at last!"

At this, he only shook his head, a motion that froze midswing as his eyes locked on something in the distance. "Another wave is approaching," he said. "One far larger than the last."

Vashodia took her own gander, assessing the incoming ruvaki over the span of two beats. "I'd say they're four—no, five times as numerous as what we've seen thus far, and almost entirely composed of smaller ships. A full quarter of their entire remaining force."

"You can *count* them? With accuracy?"

She shrugged. "It's really only a matter of peering past the point of focus. *Seeing* without looking. It was a beguiling thing to unravel, but in the end, just a simple trick. Sorcery that can play with an observer's expectations—quite the novelty, wouldn't you say?"

"A novelty. Sure." He raised his arms once more. "We had best get ready."

"Oh, of course. But, do you think we could switch roles for a bit? I fear the thrill of holding the enemy while you get to melt them will soon start to wane."

He glanced behind her, raising a golden eyebrow at the relatively small grouping of mierothi. The *new* version of them, anyway.

"Yes," she said to his unasked question. "I have enough power for the task. More than enough."

"Very well," he said. "I will do my best to keep them attuned as long as possible."

Vashodia smiled. "Just try not to make me wait."

She turned to face the enemy as they came, like a vindictive hive of wasps, through the protective shroud.

At her side, Gilshamed lashed out, blindly firing rays by their thousands. Some, inevitably, latched on to ruvaki vessels, attuning them to light. Making them vulnerable.

Sucking in power through the mierothi, Vashodia struck.

Tight, black beams shot out, aimed for nothing so large as a ship, but for the source of chaotic power resting near each of their centers. Quick, precise, efficient—Vashodia aimed for the heart.

Fifteen enemy vessels tumbled down towards an empty section of the city, mostly intact, ensuring Feralt would have plenty of opportunities later to fulfill her most sensible request.

Gilshamed lashed another group, and Vashodia repeated her surgical excision with the kind of glee most adults had forgotten. Not that she was mad at the ruvak. Not really.

She'd practically invited them here, after all.

Another group, and another, and another. Vashodia destroyed them faster than Gilshamed could latch on, long before most were even able to get off a single volley of chaos. She ignored what few projectiles of theirs did make it to the air. The domicile shook constantly from impact, but only to minor effect. Most expended their energy shredding empty buildings below.

She couldn't care less about those.

Her next breath began with all the joy she'd been aching to find . . . but ended buried beneath something she did not expect. Something she thought she'd rid herself of centuries ago.

Dread.

The remains of the wave, the latter half they had yet to destroy, morphed before her eyes, in a manner the ruvak had yet to show. A trick so simple, yet so devious, it had gotten past even *her* attention.

Each ship split in three.

"Shade of Elos, did you *see* that?" Gilshamed asked.

Vashodia shrugged to mask the shudder threatening to expose her. "It's no illusion. The extra ships were dormant, unpowered, connected by purely mechanical means to their host. Can you divide your rays any smaller?"

Eyes wide and jaw tight, Gilshamed began flexing his fingers. "I will certainly try."

Jasside braced herself as the first rank of heavy ruvaki infantry crashed into the Sceptrine shield wall. Fifty thousand within the span of a beat. The concussive blast, splitting the air like thunder, nearly knocked her off balance. The thin, human line took one step back.

Then another . . .

Then held.

Swords and pikes and cones of lightning thrust out from her side, while enemy soldiers chopped with blades attached to their outer forearms, so wide they could double as shields. Her allies gave far better than they got, adding more ruvaki bodies to a field already littered with them. Wrath-bows, war engine support, and direct magical attacks had turned the thousand-pace gap to the jungle into a wasteland of blood and death, every bit of it pocked and pitted by sorcerous impact, and filled with as many enemy corpses as there were living allies.

Yet the ruvak still outnumbered them more than two to one.

They reeled back, their nose well-bloodied, then charged forward again. Only this time a rank of lighter skirmishers leapt over the backs of their front line, swinging hooked blades attached to the end of chains. This time the pikemen were ready for the unorthodox maneuver, and caught most of them on their long points. Even so, the mere weight of so many writhing bodies and sharp-edged hands caused havoc among the lines, and Jasside saw multiple places along the shield wall buckle. Enemy heavies poured through the gaps, shrieking wildly as they hacked away at the less protected troops behind.

Jasside held her breath, thumbing the pouch at her belt.

She was proud to see the line didn't panic. Instead, at each breach, the pikemen parted to make way for the planned response. Crossbows snapped, thinning the intruders, and the specialty troops surged to meet them, crushing armor and flesh alike with massive, two-handed weapons. Able soldiers then stepped to the fore, picking up the shields of the fallen, and the wall was made whole once more. Less than a mark after they first appeared, the last breach was sealed.

She exhaled, then turned to Tarlene. "Half your casters, break rank and attend to the wounded."

The girl dipped her head, already entering commune.

Jasside thanked Chase in her mind for his forethought. His strategic ability approached the level of genius, seemingly having found a counter to anything the enemy might throw at them. Still, she couldn't stop herself from worrying. Of the three types of enemy ground troops that they knew about, thus far today they'd only seen two.

A glimpse across the killing field, however, changed that fact.

Out of the jungle they came, a single, widely spaced line. They bore no visible weapons, wore no armor of any kind she'd ever seen. Instead, metallic strips coiled about their bodies like swarms of misshapen snakes, covering them from neck to wrist and ankle.

A thousand of them began glowing, a sickly green hue surrounded by whorls of every color and none, all of which straddled the line between darkness and light. They were, in essence, the embodiment of chaos.

They took a step, then another, each time covering forty or fifty paces. Never in a straight line, they jumped in jagged, jerky fits, sometimes appearing to move sideways or even backwards one step to the next. But always, inexorably, closer.

"All casters, double shields," Jasside said. "Now!"

Her messengers relayed the order behind her, and Jasside counted off the beats until it was obeyed, each abstract tick accentuated by the enemy casters' advance and her own quickening dread. She'd never faced them this close before, always striking from afar at larger targets. She did not know what to expect.

There was some debate among those she'd talked to, about whether these troops were casters themselves, or if their strange suits provided their power, like a wrath-bow worn. Either way, they'd proven savagely efficient at dealing death.

Scanning up and down the formation, she saw shields finally begin to spring up, layered spans of light and dark, spun like gossamer across the front of each company.

But not quickly enough.

The third enemy type—conduits of chaos, she named them—finally made their presence felt.

With choreographed precision, gaps opened in the ruvaki horde through which the conduits launched spinning orbs of chaotic energy. Most of the companies had their protection in place, and the orbs crashed against the shields, releasing a noxious, guttural wave that scraped raw every sense. The rest were . . . not so fortunate.

Drinn grunted as if stuck in the gut, and Tarlene screamed. Both reactions were familiar to Jasside; it hurt trying to commune with the newly dead. Steeling herself for the worst, Jasside surveyed the damage.

Twenty-nine of the five hundred companies had been hit. It was easy to count them. Paths carved through her allies' lines, filled with the shredded remains of flesh and steel alike. Thousand-man units reduced to a hundred or less in an eyeblink.

The conduits moved. New lanes for attack opened before them.

"Extend shields over the exposed companies," Jasside said. "And get reserves into those gaps!"

"Third army requests assistance," Drinn said.

The third army was their center. *Not good*.

"Where?" she asked. But looking down, she had her answer, and saw right away why they needed help so desperately.

Whereas the rest of the afflicted companies had been spaced out along the line, on the left side of third army there had been three all right next to each other. Her allies had been unable to plug up the hole in time. Ruvak now held the ground—including a pair of conduits—and were ripping into the surrounding human troops, widening the gap with each beat.

She could no longer wait. Jasside flipped open the pouch at her side, pulling out two metallic spheres. She popped the clasps. Darkwisps swarmed into the air all about her.

She energized.

"Brace yourselves," she said to her young charges.

She released a wave of shapeless darkness. It crashed among the interposed ruvak, then morphed into a dozen discs, razor sharp and spinning, black blades whirling from which no one could escape. She directed them, mowing down hundreds every beat. With the press of flesh both living and dead so thick, even the conduits were caught and churned into little, bloody pieces.

A red, silent circle now lay where once had been ten thousand souls.

Jasside shook, as much from the effort as from the weight of death now pressing on her shoulders. She could smell the blood, the excrement of vacated bodies. She could taste it.

Too close. Even for me. I can't imagine what this is doing to . . .

A child vomited behind her. She didn't turn to see which it was.

Directing the platform, she floated back and away, putting distance between them and the scene. Her only consolation was that she'd managed to keep her messengers from harm's way.

"Transfer reinforcements from armies one and five," Jasside said, turning to grace them with a gentle, reassuring smile. "Half their troops, casters included, are to reinforce the third. The ruvak are pressing most heavily in our center. We can't afford to lose it."

The two gave her small murmurs of assent, and she was proud—and a little disturbed—at how quickly they were able to press on through the horrors of war.

"Also, contact the commander of the city war engines. I don't care how close the enemy is, we'll be overrun without their support."

"W-we can't," Tarlene said, tears brimming in her eyes. "I meant to t-tell you . . . but . . ."

"It's all right, child. What happened?"

The girl only shook her head and pointed behind them. Jasside felt her eyes widen as she took in the sight.

Abyss take us . . .

Panisahldron, jeweled city of the world, was in flames.

Arivana tried to keep her panic subdued as she fled the fires building up behind her. The tension in the air had become palpable, marked by frequent wide-eyed glances over shoulders, quickened steps that only served to further jostle an already crowded street, the raised pitch and volume in every throat that called out to strangers made siblings by their shared trial, and the sharpened reek of sweat and tears from children frightened by things they did not understand and from parents frightened by things they could not believe.

Five thousand years of history, going up in smoke.

Just buildings, she tried to tell herself. *Just wood*

and stone, cloth and steel, and far, far too many glittering things. Panisahldron is its people. So long as we live on, our nation, our legacy, will endure.

But even the combined might of humanity—mierothi and valynkar included—didn't appear capable of standing up to these ruvak, these invaders from the void. *Living on* might soon become a rare commodity in a world with no place for even simple luxuries.

"I've got an idea, Your Majesty, if you'll hear it."

Arivana blinked, returning her focus to her immediate surroundings. It was Richlen who'd spoken.

"Yes?" she said. "What is it?"

"If you'll look ahead," he said, pointing forward, "you'll see the road splits. Everyone is going right, for that's the shortest path to the shipyards, but the crowd gets so thick there it's barely moving at all."

"I take it the left route doesn't connect?"

"Right you are, Your Majesty. If you stay on the street, that is."

Arivana felt a hopeful pang take hold of her chest. "You know a shortcut?"

"I do indeed," he said, smiling. "Used to live in these parts. We'll have to cut through a tenement and a few narrow alleys, but I'll bet my next month's pay we'll get to the launching platforms in a fraction of the time."

"We'll have to keep an eye out for looters," Claris interjected. "But I think we can handle them."

"Looters?" Arivana said. "How can anyone think of theft at a time like this?"

Claris shrugged. "People with nothing—and nothing to lose—will take any opportunity to increase their position in the world. Especially when the odds of facing recourse is nil."

Arivana felt a bubble of fury begin to rise within her. Then, she remembered the secret stroll she'd taken through the outskirts of her city over a year ago, and the quiet, forceful sense of desperation that seemed to salt the very air.

A memory sprang to her mind of something her father had once said. Though the context was lost, the words sounded in her mind with rare vividity.

"When you're in a bad situation, it always seems like you have nothing but bad choices to make. Don't judge someone until you at least make an attempt at understanding them."

She supposed he would know. He'd been a commoner before marrying into the throne.

"Very well," Arivana said at last. "Please, Rich, lead the way."

The guardsmen pushed gently across the crowd that separated them from its edge, allowing their formation to break off into nearly deserted streets. The sudden loss of pressing bodies felt like rising up from being too long underwater and taking that sweet, first breath.

True to his word, Rich led them down an alley with their first turn. The guards, wearing thick pauldrons, had to turn sideways to fit through, and the sound of steel scraping against stone shrieked like a menagerie during a storm. But they were moving at least. They emerged from that narrow space for a handful of beats before diving straight through a ghostly, creaking tenement. Something foul assaulted Arivana's nose.

"What is that smell?" she asked.

"You don't want to know," Claris said.

Arivana gritted her teeth. "If I hadn't wanted to know, I wouldn't have asked. Stop trying to protect me from truths you think too ugly for me to handle."

With a sigh, Claris nodded. "I believe someone left a cook pot on, and it has now boiled over."

"A cook pot? You can't mean people eat something that smells like . . . *that*."

Claris shrugged. "Not everyone gets to dine on stuffed crocodile and peacock eggs."

Stung by the rebuke, Arivana hung her head. "I suppose not."

They exited what she now knew to be the front door of the shared dwelling, stepping onto something almost meeting her expectation for a street.

"Not long now, Your Majesty," Rich said. "Just a few blocks to go, then one last alley. You'll be flying out of this mess in no time."

"Thank you," she replied.

After a mark of quiet walking, Arivana peered back over her shoulder, surprised to find the street behind them filled with hundreds of civilians. There'd been none when they'd first arrived. Most, as far as she could tell, seemed to be coming from the same building they'd passed through in a steady stream.

"It looks as though we've started a trend," she said, gesturing towards them.

Claris turned her head, then flashed a wry grin. "Those along the edge of the crowd must have been eager to follow their queen."

"Is that it, you think?"

"Most definitely."

"Well, then, I'd better lead them as best I can."

Rich held up a fist. "Halt!"

Arivana peered forward as they stopped, wondering what obstacle might now stand in their way. But even a careful evaluation of the street ahead revealed nothing.

"What is it, Rich? What's wrong?"

He pointed straight down the lane. "Do you see that, Your Majesty?"

"See what? There's nothing there."

"Exactly. And that should *not* be the case."

Claris stepped forward. "What happened to the barricade? Where are all the guards!"

"No idea, Lady Baudone. On last checks this

morning the garrison commander reported all the outer posts were fully manned."

"I don't understand," Arivana said. "Did they desert? Or take to looting as you feared?"

Claris raised a hand, spinning light before her eyes—a far-vision spell Arivana had seen often before. After only a beat of squinting evaluation, she jerked her eyes towards Rich.

"Blood in the street."

Sixteen swords wrenched free of their sheaths in an instant, filling the air with an echoing ring.

Claris grabbed Arivana's arm. "Stay behind me," she hissed.

Arivana began shaking as the guardsmen formed a line across the breadth of the street, unable to banish from her mind images of the last time loyal soldiers had jumped to her defense. Only then, it had been in the garden . . .

. . . and Claris had been the one leading the ambush.

"Wh-what's happening?" she asked.

A moment later, the question was answered, but not in words.

In screams.

Claris spun around her. "Behind us!"

The guards pivoted, stepping past them back in the direction they'd just came.

Arivana caught a glimpse of greyish figures leaping down from the low roofs of the surrounding buildings. Dozens of them. Crashing down among the milling, helpless civilians.

The enemy was here.

In the very streets of her city.

Breath and blood both seemed to freeze as she witnessed the slaughter unfold.

Richlen yelled something she couldn't understand, and the guards broke rank and surged forward. Claris, raising one glowing hand and drawing a slim blade, outpaced them.

The ruvak turned from their savagery, shrieking like raptors approaching prey.

One guard fell without a sound, his head impaled on a hooked blade swung on the end of a chain.

The rest ducked behind shields and slammed into the ruvak.

Bodies tumbled. Flurries of stabbing steel were punctuated by gasps and grunts and cut-short screams.

Scorching light lashed out from Claris, snapping across inhuman faces as she danced between their attacks and snipped with precision at exposed bits of waxy flesh.

After an instant or a toll—she wasn't sure which—Arivana felt her pulse return and filled her lungs with air that felt too sharp. It was over. Two guardsmen lay still upon the ground, and five others moved with pained expressions, leaving dark smudges in the dirt-filled street wherever they stepped. The civilians . . .

Arivana rushed among them, helping find the few left living among the steel-shorn dead. She soothed children and reassured mothers and smiled with determination at the men. Claris began healing those who still clung to life.

"We need to warn them," Arivana said.

"Warn whom?" Claris asked.

"Everyone!"

Lifting blood-soaked hands from a woman whimpering in pain, Claris nodded.

Gilshamed coughed. It was difficult to avoid doing so. So much smoke and ash rose from the city below it had become impossible to even see, much less breathe. It did little to diminish his effectiveness, however; due to the enemy's nature, he had already been fighting blind.

"That's the last of them," Vashodia said. "From this wave, at least."

He nodded, coughing once more. As much as the destruction below chilled him, it was her voice that drove real shivers through his bones. Gone was the arrogance, the unflappable bravado, the confidence that knew no bounds.

He *knew* her. Better, perhaps, than all but a handful in this world. She planned for everything, calculating with forethought that would give even the dead gods pause. Whatever was happening now had strayed, somehow, from her impeccable vision of the future.

The weary blanket of hesitation as she'd spoken was the most frightening thing he'd ever heard.

Gilshamed felt his balance challenged as the domicile listed to one side again. Not all the damage had been sustained exclusively by Panisahldron.

"Are you ready to continue our defense?" he said, peering down at the darkly robed figure at his side. "That will not be the last attack to come today, nor have we seen, I'm sure, every tactic the ruvak have to offer. We must be prepared for anything."

Smoke whirled around her head, but she did not seem affected by it. "Yes," she said. "I'm ready."

Gilshamed shivered.

"They approach," Vashodia said. He no longer questioned how she knew. "Six ships, this time."

"Only six?"

"Yes."

"Not much of a challenge after that last group."

"It might be when each of them have twice the mass of all those we've faced combined."

He cringed, then looked below. Most of the ground-based war engines had been destroyed in the last wave, and over half of the fifty escort ships had been shot from the sky. Even with the valynkar and mierothi and the House Faer greatship still in the fight, their combined defensive power had been severely curtailed.

Steeling himself, Gilshamed straightened his back. He began pulling in more power through his kin, feeling their exhaustion and their resolve as surely as they felt his.

"We are not done yet," he said.

"No," she replied. "Not yet."

He raised his arms, ready to face whatever may come.

"Councilor Gilshamed!"

He turned at the high-pitched voice and saw a valynkar boy, no older than thirty, coming towards him at a run.

"What is it?"

The boy came up to Gilshamed, bowing breathlessly and nodding. "It's from the queen through her advisor, councilor. She says the city is breached."

"Breached?" Gilshamed furrowed his brow. "That cannot be. We would have had word from Jasside, or someone else along the front. You must be mistaken."

"No, no!" the boy said, shaking. "The front is to the north and east. Lady Baudone said they've taken out the guard posts and infiltrated from the south!"

Dread filled him like a wave. They had erected only minimal defenses along that edge of the city, sure the harsh terrain in the surrounding countryside would prohibit ground attack.

It appears that we were mistaken.

"The queen requests immediate assistance," the boy continued. "Whatever assets you can spare."

Vashodia laughed, a sour sound lacking even hints of her usual mirth. "And so we come to it again."

"Come to what?" he asked.

"Choosing which is more important—life . . . or victory."

"You honestly still think we can win this battle?"

"I do. But not if we let ourselves become distracted."

"Protecting innocent lives is not a distraction!"

Vashodia sighed. "A point on which the world and I seem to differ."

Gilshamed shook his head, then gestured to the figures huddled nearby. "Then we shall let *them* decide."

The valynkar and mierothi all turned attentive faces towards him.

He cleared his throat, lifting his voice. "If you think the battle still has a chance to swing in our favor, then stay. But hundreds of thousands, if not *millions* of innocent people are sitting exposed to the enemy, with little to stand between them and certain death. And is not the whole point of defending this city to safeguard the lives within it?

"If you think those people are worth saving, then divide yourselves, every other one . . . and go help them."

A span of only ten beats passed before half of each group had separated themselves and dove, wings spread, from the domicile's edge. Lashriel gave him a quick smile as she followed.

"I hope you're happy," Vashodia snarled. "You've just ensured our defeat."

Gilshamed felt the absence of half his kin's shared power. He could only grit his teeth and turn back to face the approaching enemy, and glimpsed, through the smoke, six massive ships begin to shove past the city's shield.

"Nothing is assured," he said. "Not even your plan. Most people, however, choose humanity over monstrosity."

"We'll see about that."

Jasside watched the Phelupari go. She and Chase, conferring briefly, had agreed that it was the only logical thing to do. The fleet-footed soldiers, now sprinting fearlessly through a burning city, were best suited to help the situation on Panisahldron's opposite end.

But with their departure, she could now clearly read the writing on the wall: the situation was hopeless. They couldn't win, but neither could they pull back without disaster. Not with so many of those conduits of chaos still to contend with.

Jasside knew what she had to do.

She turned to her two young companions. "Stay here," she said. "Stay safe. You remember how to use the controls, right, Drinn?"

"Yes," he said. "But . . . why would I need to?"

She gave him a tight smile, then shadow-dashed off the platform.

Smoke and scorched ruvaki bodies surrounded her as she landed. She turned to face her enemy, peering upon the back side of their frothing ranks.

Don't get carried away, she told herself. *You just need to buy some time.*

Jasside energized, pulling power through the darkwisps that still surrounded her. Several conduits turned to face her, which was pleasing. She had not meant to be subtle. Nor did she mean to let *them* dictate the encounter.

Two of them stood only a few paces apart, still apparently deciding how to deal with her. She didn't give them the chance. Dashing, she landed between them, releasing an explosion of darkness that consumed everything within reach. Two down, along with hundreds of nearby soldiers. Not even their screams survived.

Without pausing for breath, she sought out her next targets.

She dashed, sweeping a black beam across three conduits. Dashed again before their wrecked bodies even struck the ground, sending dark lightning that arced towards a pair of metal-wrapped figures.

Another dash, into the air this time. A beat of free fall, scanning. Eight targets in range. Swirling orbs, in dark mockery of the conduits' own favored attack, plunged outward, homing in unerringly onto inhuman flesh.

She dashed back to the ground, turned and dashed back the way she'd come. Green chaos writhed towards her now. She quickly erected a shield, which absorbed the blasts, but found herself dizzy from the chaos's unholy stench.

No more of that. Only dodging from now on.

She dashed among another cluster of conduits, forming black razor-whips in her hands. Four swings at four enemies. Eight half-bodies slumped to the ground.

Looking up, she sought more targets.

But they had at last awakened to her presence, seeking her in return. Instead of being nervous, though, she grinned.

Let them come. I am ready.

The next few marks became a blur of constant motion, never staying still for more than half a beat at most, as she struck back at the dozens—then scores; then over a hundred—conduits that came at her, a task made more difficult as they began to adapt to her frenetic motions.

They changed their attacks, seeking her out with lashes of chaos that threatened to hold her in place. And with their numerical superiority—and despite dodging them for a time—they eventually succeeded.

Of necessity, she gave up her just-made vow to avoid shielding herself. She poured more and more energy into that personal bubble of protection, but every beat added another latched attacker, deepening the strain.

They had her pinned.

A quick glance around her, however, revealed that her enemy was likewise locked in place.

I can't hold back their energy for much longer. But that doesn't mean I can't . . . redirect.

Natural darkness ever flowed just beneath the surface of all things, that layer beneath which light never touched. Of that, needing only the tiniest sliver of power, she carved channels that ran underground out from where she stood to the position of each assailant. Once formed, it was only a matter of cradling the chaotic energy they flung at her . . .

. . . and pushing *down*.

Reality itself seemed to warp around her as every last one of them exploded, torn asunder by their own power.

Jasside sagged herself, drained to the point of collapse by her ordeal. It had been worth it though, she reckoned. Enough of the conduits had been destroyed that her allies could now begin the next phase of the battle, no matter how distasteful it might seem.

She spied her platform, distant now, but still hovering just where she'd left it. Focusing in on the small surface area, she made one final shadow-dash.

The thing lurched as she landed, and both of her messengers squeaked in surprise.

"Get in touch with King Chase's messenger," she gasped. "Tell him it's time to begin the retreat."

Arivana clutched the crossbow in shaking arms, cranking tension into the string once more. Three times they'd encountered ruvak. Three times she'd pulled the catch. She didn't know if she'd hit anything, and a small part of her hoped that she hadn't. The thought of taking a life, no matter that they were an enemy bent on wanton slaughter, made her stomach roil. She didn't know if that made her a coward, or worse, a hypocrite, sending countless numbers of her own men and women to fight when she could not.

She retrieved a bolt from her waistband and attempted to place it in the slot. It slipped from shaking fingers, twice, before she managed to complete the task. She wasn't the only one holding an unfamiliar weapon. Over a score of civilians bore arms of some kind, most pilfered from the silent guard posts they'd visited or from the plentiful enemy corpses. Several more brandished the sword and shield of a royal guardsman.

Light flashed in her peripheral vision, and a man gasped. Arivana turned to see Claris rise from the side of her latest patient. The woman swept her gaze around, locked on to another bleeding man, and began to step towards him.

Rich grabbed her arm, stopping her.

"We need to move," he said quietly, though Arivana could still make out the words.

Claris shot him a look of plain fury. "There are still wounded, and we've a responsibility to—"

"My responsibility is to the queen! As should yours be. Once we get her to safety, we can . . . consider . . . coming back for any others."

Exhaling through clenched teeth, Claris nodded. Arivana felt she should say something, but no words would come.

Rich began ordering his remaining men into motion, as Claris directed the lifting and transport of casualties. Over a dozen, though, were simply too injured to move.

Surrounded once more by flesh and steel, Arivana let herself be led onwards. Her soul plodded numbly, every step tense with the expectation of ambush. She couldn't stop from scanning the lip of every rooftop crowding in the sky, just waiting to glimpse another line of ruvak faces peering down with murderous intent.

After some time, she knew not how long, the air before them brightened and the men around her all seemed to sigh in relief. Glancing through them, she could see why.

"The shipyards," Claris said. "We've reached them at last."

Only three hundred paces separated them now. The open ground was the most welcome thing Arivana could remember seeing.

Without further delay, they began trotting across the gap. She saw a loaded ship take off, and another slide into its place only beats later. The crowd waiting to board had thinned since she'd last viewed it from atop her tower, but still stretched back among the outer city, fifty thousand at least. Based on the rate of incoming vessels, it would be a miracle if the ramps cleared in less than two tolls.

I don't know if we have that long. Not with the enemy already inside the city, able to strike from anywhere, at any time.

Coming close to the thin line of defenders, she could see that they already had. Irregularities along the ground, which she'd dismissed at a distant glance, turned out to be a blanket of piled bodies. Though most belonged to the ruvak, far too many bore human faces.

Rich sprinted ahead, finding and conferring with the supposed leader of the defenders. By the time the rest of them arrived, it appeared they'd already come to some decision.

"This way, Your Majesty," Rich said, waving her after him. Not, however, in the direction of the nearest ramp.

"Where are we going?" Arivana asked, following him.

"The ramps are too clogged, Your Majesty. It would take a quarter toll at least to clear you a path. But there's a service staircase along the side of the platform. Three marks and I'll have you on the very next ship out."

Arivana stopped in her tracks.

Claris bent close a concerned visage. "Is something wrong?"

Arivana peered across her gathered people. The masses waiting for their turn to board, her makeshift retinue bearing weapons that didn't belong to them, the too few soldiers standing between them and whatever savagery might come, ready to fight through the exhaustion—physical and otherwise— that loomed large in their faces.

"No," she said at last. "I cannot go yet."

"Why the abyss not?"

"We don't know how many more ruvak are coming, nor how long it will take for help to arrive. Look at them!" She pointed to the weary defenders. "Does it look they could withstand another attack?"

"It's their—!" Claris paused, lowering her voice. "They are brave, Your Majesty. You need not be."

"Perhaps. But bravery without hope only creates dead heroes. If there's even a chance I can give them the latter, a delay in my own safety seems a small price to pay."

Wincing, Claris nodded at last.

Arivana turned to the crowd, then quickly glanced over at Claris. "Make them hear me," she whispered.

Claris lifted her hands, conjuring waves of invisible power. When Arivana next spoke, every soul within five hundred paces could hear.

"I know most of you just want to get to safety—and who could blame you?—but too many of our soldiers have fallen to protect you for much longer. If any among you are capable, I urge you to consider taking up arms and standing with them. Stand in defense of your children, your elders, your neighbors. Stand in defense of humanity!"

She paused, pointing at the pile of human and ruvak bodies. "There are plenty of weapons to choose from. If you are willing, please, pick one up."

Of those who had accompanied her through the alleyways, all who were already armed took position, and after a short moment of hesitation, many more stooped to collect swords and shields, bows, and spears, along with the chain blades and cruel-looking metal claws of the enemy.

Mere heartbeats later, hundreds more surged out from the crowd.

Arivana smiled. It seemed a small victory in the grand scheme of things, but it warmed her to see that humanity still knew how to cling to hope even when all seemed bleak.

A victory, it appeared, that was to be short-lived.

Out of the alleyways and side streets, and from around the edge of the shipyards, ruvak swarmed in force. Hands still becoming accustomed to new weapons would now put them to immediate, deadly use.

Arivana lifted her crossbow, aiming down the sights.

She did not think she would miss this time.

Gilshamed cursed as the ruvaki ship ducked back and the lance of energy he'd cast at it scattered across the inner face of the dome.

Another one poked through, firing off a massive bolt of chaotic power. He thrust forward, emitting a tight beam that struck the ship's nose. But only for a moment. It, too, retreated, long before he latched tight enough to hold it either attuned or in place. Unable to dissipate the enemy's attack, and too weary to absorb it, Gilshamed swept light across its path, driving the bolt down into an already ravaged portion of the city. A burst of fire and smoke that was lost among countless others.

Two more of the massive ships approached the city shield. He knew by now that one would only feint while the other dipped in, but was unsure which would do what. Taking a guess, he launched a beam for one of them, a small surge of hope welling within as he turned out lucky. Fire scraped the front edge of the enemy ship, and its shield became pearly and bright; a sign that it was attuning to light.

But it withdrew before the effect could fully en-wrap it.

He cried out in frustration, then peered down at Vashodia. "Are you planning to help anytime soon?"

She blinked once. The first thing she'd done in the last mark. "Patience, dear friend. I am about to. I was just waiting until the right fish swam into my net."

"The right . . . ? What the abyss are you babbling about?"

"Observe."

Darkness snapped in a wide sphere directly in front of the ruvaki vessel nearest the dome. As if pulled by invisible rope, the skyship rushed forward, fully inside both shields in an eyeblink. The sound of rushing, sucking air crashed across Gilshamed, and he nearly toppled over backwards.

He recovered quickly, however, and eagerly blasted it with light. The attunement took hold even before the enemy had begun to pull back.

Vashodia cracked it open with black rays, then ripped out its heart. The ship fragmented, fell, and crashed among the city's outskirts, expelling a cloud of dust and ash that darkened an already murky sky.

Gilshamed glanced down at her once more. "What was that you just did?"

"What? Oh, that. It was nothing, really. Just taking advantage of one of the more obscure natural laws."

"Meaning?"

"I removed the air from in front of the ship, creating a fully empty space, and it simply could not help but leap to fill that sudden void."

"Can you do it again?"

"Yes, but it's . . . difficult to do. Time-consuming."

Gilshamed shrugged. "With this fickle dance they're doing, time seems to be a resource we actually possess."

"As you wish, O wise master of war." She chittered, as if she'd made a joke; though it was not one Gilshamed understood. "It will be another mark or two before I'll be ready. Do kindly keep them—"

Words were lost as the domicile shook, and a sky-splitting crack wracked his ears. He fell to his knees, pressing palms to each side of his head. Pain throbbed through his skull. Turning, he faced towards the center of the floating city. His heart shattered at the sight.

Like a log taken to by an axe, the domicile had been split.

Motion above drew his sight. Two, three, four enemy ships careened straight down from on high, barely visible through the ash-filled sky. They crashed into that rift, widening it. The crack spread across the entire breadth of the domicile, sundering it in two, and Gilshamed felt the edge upon which he stood tilt down at a dangerous angle, farther and farther, until it became clear that it had passed any hope of recovery.

We have been fooled! Blinded by smoke and distracted

by those six dancing ships, they struck where we did not think to look. The ruvak already best us in savagery and numbers. If they now prove superior in cunning . . . then we are truly lost.

He broke harmony with his remaining kin as the surface began separating from his feet. Unfurling in a splash of golden light, he shouted to those standing behind him, "The domicile is broken. Fly free!"

Wings sprang forth from the gathered figures: black from the mierothi, and all shades of the rainbow from the other valynkar. They each took flight and dispersed.

He watched Vashodia descend, free-falling with the ruined structure, and considered swooping down to catch her. A moment later, though, a streak of darkness shot out from where she'd floated, quickly lost among the shattered towers below, and Gilshamed knew she would be just fine.

An idea came to him, then. He peered up towards the other gargantuan vessel hovering halfway across the city. *The Panisian greatship! If we can make it there, we can add our strength to their casters and continue the fight. The day is not yet . . .*

But then he spied rocky shapes curling down upon the vessel's head, and could only watch it succumb to the same shattered fate as the domicile.

The entirety of the remaining enemy fleet swarmed in through the shield dome.

Jasside sought those points spread out among the outer city buildings like beads on a string. Each of them, over a hundred in all, throbbed with preemptively gathered energy. She held them ready, waiting until the last human soldier had passed the designated line . . .

Not yet.

Not yet.

Now!

. . . then released.

The buildings imploded, collapsing within clouds of cold dust. Rubble filled every street and alley, mountains of it, forming a barricade that would prove treacherous to any that dared try to cross. Unfortunately no ruvak were caught by tumbling debris, this time; they'd learned to keep their distance after the first.

Jasside pulled her platform back another block, keeping her eyes peeled on the approaching foe as she gathered up the next batch of prepared detonations. The remains of the army—far too few in number—fled into the city; she alone guarded their retreat. Even now, ruvaki infantry began climbing over the barriers she'd made, often screeching in terror as the footing shifted beneath them, pulling them down into a crushing, choking end.

The gap between the two forces widened by the beat, but Jasside kept piling more obstacles in the way. The wreck that had become of Panisahldron promised to slow her allies' escape, and she knew they would need every possible moment she could give them.

She passed suddenly between two of the outer-most towers. These ones, at least, were presently free of damage. Still facing outward, Jasside addressed her messengers. "I want check-in reports from command-ers every five marks. I don't want anyone getting left behind in this mess."

"Aye," they both said.

Despite everything, Jasside allowed herself a small smile at that. The girl was finally catching on.

Jasside waited until she sensed them return from commune. "One more thing. Make contact with King Chase. Ask him what he wants to do about—"

Power erupted. Green fire filled the sky. The top half of the tower beside her disintegrated, flinging debris. Jasside desperately tried to throw up a shield, but a chunk of stone crashed into the platform before it could fall in place.

Breath fleeing as she fell, Jasside glimpsed the enemy ships raking along her army's line of retreat, and wondered, for a moment, what had happened to her allies in the sky.

Blood sloshed against Arivana's feet as the defend-ers put down the last few ruvaki warriors. Every place she could step was soaked in one rank fluid or another, but she was long past sensing the foulness around her. There was nowhere to look where it didn't wholly dominate.

She was just about to breathe a sigh of relief, when another horde of enemies surged into view.

Though the defenders still outnumbered this wave, the margin was slim. Few were left who had any sort of combat training, and the difference in skill was telling; each subsequent attack had felled more humans than the last.

Fingers now well-practiced, yet cramped from overuse, she began cranking her crossbow once more. Men and women around her picked themselves back up, forming what only vaguely resembled a united front as the enemy closed, screeching and frothing in rage. She pulled a bolt from her waistband, realizing it was the last one she carried.

If we don't get help soon, this may very well be our end.

The gap between species closed. Arivana lifted her weapon.

Jets of fire and spikes of freezing darkness ripped across the ruvak . . .

From *above*.

Arivana craned her neck, watching dozens of valynkar and mierothi swoop in as they rained down sorcerous destruction. She gasped for joy, tears flowing freely.

The enemy retreated, only to run into the waiting spears of Phelupari soldiers, who had flanked them from behind. More of those island warriors sprinted into place between the civilians and the ruvak, trapping them as surely as a set of closing jaws.

It took less than a mark for the last foe to fall.

A bright violet light descended, touching down gently next to Arivana. She squinted through the glare, but was only able to recognize the woman once she dismissed her wings. The resemblance to Tassariel was evident.

"Lashriel, isn't it?" she asked.

"Yes," the woman answered. "And you must be Queen Arivana. A pleasure to meet you."

"Pleasure doesn't even begin to describe what I'm feeling right now. I can't thank you enough for arriving as you did."

"I'm only sorry we could not get here sooner. The streets were riddled with ruvak, and we thought it best to engage rather than leave them unchecked at our backs."

"A wise decision," Claris said, stepping over corpses to reach them. "Though difficult to make, I'm sure."

Lashriel shrugged. "I'm just glad to see we were not too late."

Almost, you were, but I will not hold that against you.

"Come," Arivana said. "Let's get the rest of these people to a ship."

"You especially," Claris barked, pointed an accusatory finger.

Arivana shook her head. "Not until the last citizen is gone. Thankfully, that won't be very long."

The crowd waiting to board had dwindled to almost nothing, the last in line already halfway up the ramp. Even now they crept farther forward as another flock of evacuation ships set down and opened their doors. The nightmare's end was in sight.

"I wish you well," Lashriel said. "But our kind still have work to do. I just received word that the defenses have failed."

"Failed?" Arivana said, swinging her eyes back over her city. "How can that—"

The domicile . . . the house greatship . . . they were missing from the sky. All shapes that filled it now were of ruvak design.

Crushing weight. Cold below the waist. Numb. Head spinning, sitting in something wet. I can still breathe, though, even if it feels like my lungs are full of ash.

Jasside opened her eyes. Her initial self-examination complete, she now needed to take stock of her surroundings. She turned her head and was immediately struck by a hoarse fit of coughing. She cleared her throat and spit.

A wedge of stone lay atop her, pressing her hip bones into the cobbled street. With far more effort than it should have taken, she energized. Soft licks of power cradled the weight and lifted it off her. She swept it away with a bit more force than was necessary, then regretted it instantly as the world began swirling without mercy.

Got to take it easy.

Jasside turned her energy inward, probing herself for injury. Two ribs and her left forearm were broken. The back of her head was split. Too many small lacerations to count. Clenching her teeth, she got to work repairing the damage.

Three marks later, it was done.

Maybe not good as new, but right now I'll settle for being able to move.

Groaning, she got to her feet. She lifted her head to try to locate her missing messengers. They couldn't have fallen far. If they were still alive—

No. Not if. I will find them and bring them to safety. Or die trying.

She dusted off her leather outfit, then began clambering over the scattered debris. Straining with each step, she picked her way in the direction most filled with heaps of stone, where she thought them most likely to be found. Sulfur rasped against the inside of her nose and throat, lingering residue from the ruvaki attack, and the sound of enemy screeching echoed faintly between buildings. She estimated they were still several blocks away.

Coming around a corner, though, proved this guess dead wrong.

Hundreds of ruvak leapt into sight, just fifty paces

away. Beneath one cluster of them lay what she took to be two bundles of bloody rags.

A closer look revealed the sordid truth.

Drinn . . . Tarlene . . . I'm . . .

Sorry just didn't seem to be enough. Nothing would make up for this.

Nothing.

The enemy spotted her, including five conduits. Chaotic orbs swirled towards her as the foot soldiers rushed forward.

Numb and weak, and eyes filled with shameful tears, Jasside turned and shadow-dashed away.

"They're getting closer," Claris whispered from over Arivana's shoulder. "Soon we won't even be able to bring in additional ships. Please, Your Majesty. Get *on*."

Arivana guided the line of frayed humanity up the steps of another ship, giving and receiving blessings with all that her heart could bear. "If that happens, I will march out with the soldiers."

"That's mad—!" Claris clamped her jaw shut, practicing control of her breathing. "That course of action is *not* advised."

"Duly noted. Now, if you don't mind, I'm trying to help these people board. Lend a hand or get out of the way."

Claris sighed, then moved away. After a moment,

Arivana looked over to see the woman aiding those in line for the next ship over.

At last, something to smile about.

A flash of sorcerous energy snapped nearby, causing her to jump. The fighting was indeed getting closer. Wings of valynkar and mierothi, along with the scant remaining combat ships, waged a frenzied, hopeless battle against those ruvaki vessels that had penetrated this deep into the city; few so far, but growing more numerous with every passing mark.

"All full!" a voice called from the ship. Arivana regretfully halted the line, urging the rest back a ways to leave enough room for liftoff. Thankfully, though, there were only a handful of people left.

Sparing another glance behind, Arivana saw a welcome sight.

The army, marching clear of the city.

As glad as she was to see that they'd at least made it this far, there didn't seem to be enough of them. Over half a million soldiers had been tasked to stand in the city's defense, but even her most generous estimate couldn't pretend to number them greater than three hundred thousand.

So many lost. Dead in numbers I can't even fathom. And their sacrifice did not even buy us victory.

Arivana shook her head, fighting tears as she watched the evacuation ships depart. She didn't see any others flying in to take their place.

"Claris? Please tell me that wasn't the last of them?"

"I'm sorry, Your Majesty. I don't sense any others approaching. I'm afraid we'll have to—" Her eyebrows lifted. "Wait! Look!"

Arivana swept her eyes to the west, out away from the city. A single vessel, relatively small, darted out from the hills. As it neared it became clearer, and she at last recognized the shape of it.

It seemed fitting that the final rescue vessel should be her own royal skyship.

The tension in the remaining crowd bled out as the ship made its descent, the last exhale of people who'd seen more horror in one day that any lifetime should have to bear. A rush of air announced touchdown. Those waiting began ambling forward even before the short stairway had slid into place. Arivana stood by the entrance, guiding them on as before.

She knew her skyship, however; knew its limitations on deck space. Those still left to board thinned to almost nothing, but available room grew thinner still. It soon became apparent that not everyone would make it on.

Several men volunteered to get off to make room for the last of the women. Claris sidled up to Arivana's side.

"Please tell me there's no reason now to object?" the woman said. "Whatever hope you might have inspired in your people by your actions today will be undone, and then some, if you don't see to your own safety. As much as I hate to say it, some lives *are* more important than others."

Arivana glanced around at the few people left. Although she knew the loss of those holding important positions would be detrimental to a nation, she had a hard time valuing any one life above another. Even her own. Perhaps it was naïve or idealistic of her—perhaps it was the last part of her childhood that refused to die—but she'd rather live in a world where each soul was considered precious than blindly accept an alternative reality.

An oddity struck her vision, and she sent seeking glances to find it again. There, hiding behind the legs of some of the men, stood a child: a boy no more than five. Arivana ran and knelt before him, peering into his eyes. Long-dried tear marks streaked down dirt-covered cheeks. His gaze didn't seem able to stay focused on anything around him. Blood—both orange and red—speckled the sleeves of his shirt.

"I don't think you're right," Arivana said, glancing over at Claris. "But if you are, then lives such as these are the ones *most* worth saving."

She picked up the boy. After a moment where his limbs dangled numbly, he seemed to grasp the fact of human contact and wrapped both arms and legs around her tightly. She brought him to the ship and looked up at the cramped deck, making deliberate eye contact with a pair of women pressed closest to the entrance.

"He won't take up much space," Arivana began. "Surely there's room for just one more."

The ladies reached down without a word and, after the few beats it took him to let go, pulled the child up into their arms. Arivana stepped back, watching as the stairs retracted and the ship made ready its departure.

"You keep surprising me, Your Majesty," Claris said. "But I think I'm starting to catch on to just who you are, and what kind of queen you will become. I can only imagine what the history books will say."

"I do not care about my legacy, Claris. I just want to do what's best for my people. For *all* of humanity."

Claris chuckled. "Thus are legends born."

Sighing, Arivana dropped her eyes. The army now marched around and past the launching platforms, heading out towards the jungle and the long, dangerous trek ahead. She didn't exactly look forward to traveling with them, but neither would she deny herself any hardship others were forced to undertake.

Only Claris, six male civilians, and Richlen—along with five surviving guardsmen from the palace—stood with her still. She graced them all with a queenly, heartfelt smile.

"It looks like we have a march ahead of us," she said, then swept an arm across the surrounding army. "But at least we won't lack for company!"

Despite the day's trials, the poor attempt at humor managed to draw a laugh from them all. With Rich taking the lead, the company took their first, final steps out of the city together, angling to join the nearest formation of soldiers.

We mustn't lose hope. No matter what. Even if I'm the only one still clinging to it, I'll do everything in my power to ensure it never dies.

Her skyship at last took to the air. Arivana looked up and waved. Nearly everyone along the nearest edge, peering down over the rail, waved back, including one small boy whose name she didn't even know. It was well, though; they had escaped the slaughter at last.

A misshapen object smeared across the sky, just above and beyond the retreating royal skyship, with a wing of mierothi and valynkar close behind in pursuit. Darkness enfolded the enemy vessel, and light blasted it apart. Like a rock, it began to fall.

She felt time stand still.

With an ache that knew no limit to its depth, Arivana watched the ruvaki vessel crash into the ship she once called her own, exploding with virulent, grim finality.

She fell to her knees and screamed in terror. Even as the soldiers—upon Claris's orders—picked her up and hurried her from the city, she continued to wail, in disbelief, in rage, until her voice went hoarse and she could scream no more.

In an abandoned tower along Panisahldron's southern edge, Vashodia waited. She watched over the burning city, counting the thump of footsteps as they ascended the stone staircase behind her. The door creaked open at her back, but she didn't turn.

"Only six, Feralt?" she said. "A bit of a light catch, wouldn't you say? I expected better of you."

She heard his shoulders rise in a shrug. "Times have gotten . . . uncertain . . . as of late. Risking one's neck for a favor is a bargain most aren't willing to make. Even if the favor is from you."

"A pity, then. Looks like my rewards will have to be spread deep instead of wide." She spun to face him and flashed a sharp-toothed grin. "Perhaps that's what you had in mind?"

Feralt shook his head. "I didn't have much time to go fishing. This lot—" he jerked a thumb at the six other daeloth behind him "—were the only ones to bite."

Vashodia giggled. "Very well. I have no problem seeing that you all get your just due. Provided," she said, lifting a finger, "that the service does not suffer."

"We'll get the job done, all right." Clearing his throat, he leaned forward and added, "You . . . uh . . . ready to tell us what it is?"

"In a moment." She twisted back towards the city. "First, observe."

Vashodia energized, reaching out with her power to stroke the mechanisms that sustained the protective domes over Panisahldron. A few flicks of energy in just the right place, and their purpose, their functionality, changed.

The shroud of darkness began collapsing.

And the one formed of light? Why, it was inside the other and had no choice but to do the same.

All that leftover energy, and all those ruvaki ships—I can't let this opportunity go to waste!

The twin shields fell over the city like a net, catching every last enemy vessel within the perimeter. Attuned to light, then smashed by dark, they fell from the sky like the hollowed-out rocks that they were. The daeloth looked on in wonder.

"Now," Vashodia said, as if nothing of note had happened. "I want each of you to first bring me back one prisoner. Alive, of course, with bonus points given for those recovered most whole."

"First?" Feralt said. "What *else* could you possibly want done?"

She smiled. "Why, once our new friends are gathered, we're going to go snare us a ship of course!"

CHAPTER 6

Yandumar was the first to step onto the beach. The tide shrugged up against sands baking in the desert sun, waves lapping at his boots as he surveyed the landing site. Empty of all signs of life, the beach stretched past the horizon to either side, bending out of sight within shimmers of heat and haze. The fine grains crunching beneath his feet swept upwards 150 paces from the waterline, then gave way to low, turbulent hills of orange clay. Leagues distant, he could just make out white, rolling crests of sand dunes.

Mevon leapt off the ship's grounded prow to splash down at his side. "So," he said, "this is the place."

"The land where my exile began," Yandumar said, lifting his arms in a mock embrace of the wasteland before him. "Welcome to Weskara, son."

It, of course, had not been the original plan to

come here. They'd receive word a week ago from Jasside, however, wherein she'd told them about the loss of Panisahldron, and the subsequent withdrawal from the southern nations. By the time his armada would have made it there, all friendly faces would have been long gone.

So they'd turned north instead, shortening the trip considerably, and now prepared to make landfall where two deserts, one massive mountain range, and a thousand leagues separated them from the bulk of their allies.

The war—if it could be called that—had not been going well.

Mevon bent down, scooping up wet sand, then squeezed his hand into a fist. A strange gleam dominated his eyes. It took Yandumar a moment to realize why.

"Foreign soil," Yandumar said. "I guess I'm the only one who *won't* be seeing it for the first time."

Mevon nodded. "Even with it here in my grasp, I have a hard time believing it. The Shroud . . . it just *was*, you know? As much a part of daily life as the sun." He grunted humorously. "I suppose we have your former employer to thank for taking it down."

"Ha! *Employer* indeed. Vashodia was the puppeteer, and I, just one more of her countless dancing dolls. You might almost call me lucky, though. She at least let me know she was nailing in the strings."

"Yes, but it sounds like Jasside is doing most of

the pulling nowadays. A change I think we can both agree is for the better."

"Aye," Yandumar said, even though he still wondered if hers weren't being pulled as well.

He'd never known Vashodia to bow out of any game, especially not one she started herself. Yandumar was certain she still had the biggest influence on the way things were playing out.

In fact, I'd bet my empire on it.

"Well," Mevon said, sweeping both arms along the breadth of the beach. "Will this do?"

Sighing, Yandumar nodded. He turned, tilting his neck to peer up at his flagship's prow where Orbrahn stood waiting. "Go ahead," he called. "Tell the armada to start the landing. I want every soldier on dry soil by nightfall."

Orbrahn cast an incredulous gaze across the horizon. "You certainly have the 'dry' part of that right, old man, but I'm not sure if any of this can rightly be called soil."

"Can't you just do your job without giving me any lip for *once*?"

Orbrahn looked skyward, as if in serious contemplation. "I don't think that's possible. In fact, I'm sure of it."

"If there are any delays, I'm docking you a month's wages!"

Orbrahn waved a hand dismissively. "I've been getting the reports from the front lines directly, you know. No one here will live long enough to receive a single coin from the Imperial treasury."

Yandumar glared at him. "Do it now . . . or I'll sic Ilyem on you again."

Orbrahn bowed his head in an instant, eyes closed to enter commune.

Within twenty marks, the remaining Imperial ships had dragged themselves onto the beaches. Rope ladders and wooden ramps came down, and soldiers of the Veiled Empire, blanketing the beach like ants, began their first ever invasion of a foreign land.

"Ol' Emperor Rekaj is probably spinning in the abyss right now," Yandumar said.

"Why's that?" Mevon asked.

Yandumar jerked his head towards his forces. "Nineteen hundred years is a long time for a conqueror to be sitting on his ass. If we hadn't stopped him when we did, he'd be the one leading this army, with all the mierothi and daeloth at his back. And not a soul outside the Shroud would have welcomed *that* sight."

One corner of Mevon's lips twitched up. "Well then, I suppose it was a good thing I slit his throat."

"That it was, son. That it was."

"Yandumar!"

He faced up towards the deck of his ship once more. Orbrahn flinched as Ilyem strode up beside him. She gave the caster a curious glance.

"What is it, Ilyem?" Yandumar asked.

Sunlight bouncing off her head like a round mirror, she pointed inland. "It seems we have company."

Yandumar spun towards the desert hills, looking to where she had indicated. Though distant, he could still make out the dust that was rising in a long cloud.

"Horsemen," Mevon said.

"Aye," Yandumar replied, then turned back to Ilyem. "Send down our mounts, if you would. I suppose we'd better go and meet them."

"Already done," she said.

He looked, and indeed two grooms now marched Quake and his own Silverburr—a beast with a gleaming grey coat, unmarked by any blemish—off the end of the nearest ramp. He stepped into the stirrup and pulled himself into the saddle with an audible grunt of effort. At least his head didn't start spinning again this time.

Wiping sweat from his forehead, he watched Mevon take one stride and leap wholly into his seat.

"Cheater," Yandumar said.

Mevon shrugged. "I didn't ask for these blessings, Father. But abyss take me if I won't use them."

Yandumar rolled his eyes, then looked over his shoulder. "You coming, Orbrahn?"

The boy furrowed his brow. "But . . . I don't have a mount?"

"Sure ya do. Just not one with hooves!"

Orbrahn's face drained of color. "It's not ready yet."

"Well then, you have until we reach our rendezvous to *get* it ready. And I expect to see you there."

Without waiting for a response, Yandumar kicked his heels into Silverburr's flanks. He and Mevon began trotting up the nearest hill. By the time they reached the crest, he could hear the pounding of approaching hoofbeats. He tugged gently on the reins.

"We'll wait here," he told his son.

"Why?" Mevon said.

"You'll see soon enough."

A dozen beats later, three riders appeared from over the next set of hills, just off to the west. The one in the lead, bearing a white flag on a pole, pointed towards Yandumar, then angled his horse's path to intersect. They rode down the short gulf between hilltops, then up again, slowing to a halt fifteen paces away.

Yandumar inspected them, memories surging as he took in their polished plate armor, tarnished by only the faintest traces of sweat and dust. All three lifted their visors to reveal young, pale faces.

But it was not at him they looked.

"Sweet bloody abyss," said the one on the left, eyes wide as he surveyed the armada and the Imperial army taking over the shore.

"Hold your tongue," snapped the center man, obviously the leader. Still, his jaw hung almost as low as the others.

Yandumar held his chuckle in check. "You boys the welcoming party?"

"Ye . . . Yes! We are. Sorry. We're—I mean, you're . . . who are you again?"

"Yandumar. Though some idiots insist on calling me Emperor Daere."

Their simultaneous, nervous swallows probably could have been heard from the deck of his ship.

"Look," Yandumar said, "I'm not nearly as used to this heat as you are, and I'm guessing there's a place nearby that can give an old man some shade?"

"Indeed there is, Your . . . *Imperial* Majesty."

"Then bother all the formalities and lead us on, boys!"

Snapping their visors shut, the three soldiers turned their mounts and headed back the way they'd come. Yandumar and Mevon followed. They rode at a canter—much faster would have been too taxing on their horses—going single file for a time, but once they began crossing the dunes switched instead to a five-wide row to avoid eating each other's churned-up dust. His son rode at his side, on the formation's far left edge.

"So," Mevon said, "the man we're meeting—you know him well?"

"I did, once. It's been a long time, though. People change—yes, even old men like me. I can only hope he's enough of the same man I knew to see the right path to take."

"Do *we* even know that?"

"Ha!"

It took half a toll, all told, until they crested one last dune and came within sight of their destination: a round tent, encircled by at least five hundred soldiers. He and Mevon dismounted, and their three escorts led them right up to the entrance without delay.

The lead man lifted up a flap and ducked his head in. "Your Majesties? They're here."

"Send them in," called a voice from inside, one Yandumar knew well.

Yandumar stepped in, blinking rapidly to adjust his eyes to the dim, candlelit interior. Two figures rose at his approach: one slim and tall and breathtakingly beautiful, even in the gloom; the other hunched and grey.

It was towards the second that Yandumar inclined his head. "Daryn Reimos," he said. "I see you finally decided to lift your fat backside out of your throne for a change."

"Yandumar? I was told I'd be meeting with an emperor, not some upstart mercenary far lacking in manners."

They both stepped forward, closing the gap between them with dangerous speed . . .

. . . then wrapped each other in a jovial embrace.

"You've no idea how good it is to see you again, Daryn."

"I think I might, actually."

"That's probably just old age playing tricks on you."

"Pah! It doesn't need to. I have my new wife for that."

Yandumar released his old friend, stepping back to get a better view of the queen. "That explains why your heart's still beating. I was sure Ellesia was going to drag you down with her into an early grave."

"My dear first wife—may she rest in peace—departed not three years hence. This one has proven quite the upgrade." Daryn leaned in close, lowering his voice to a whisper. "In many . . . interesting ways."

"Halice," the woman said, extending a hand.

Yandumar shook it tenderly, surprised by the vigor of her return grip. "A pleasure to meet you."

"I'd say the same, but you're old friends of Daryn, which means you're probably quite mad."

"Guilty as charged," Yandumar said with a grin. He turned to his son. "And this is—"

"Mevon," Daryn said, his voice shaking. "Yes, we know. A couple of fascinating young ladies came through some time ago and told us all about it." Tears now welled in the old man's eyes. "I'm glad . . . so, so glad . . . that you found him at last."

Yandumar clamped down on his own rising well of emotion as Mevon swapped greetings with them. "I take it those 'young' ladies were the reason you haven't driven the mierothi from your border?"

"That, and I didn't want to throw away half my standing army just to make the attempt."

"A wise choice. Trust me, they're better to have on your side."

"So I've gathered. But sides aren't really a problem anymore, are they? We've got bigger issues to deal with."

"So you've heard?" Yandumar asked.

"About the ruvak? The invasion? Of course I have. What do you think, I've been living under a rock?"

"Well . . ."

"Don't answer that. Just tell me you have a plan?"

Yandumar nodded. "Right now, it's just to go wherever the alliance sends us. We were hoping to march through Weskara. If you'd like, we can draft a treaty—"

"Abyss take all that. Your boys can walk wherever they'd like. I'll even send some of mine to join you."

Yandumar lifted his eyebrows. "Really? They'd have to share meals with casters daily. Are you sure they'll . . . behave?"

"Oh, probably not. But they'll learn quick enough once they've been put in their place a time or two."

"In that case, I'll welcome them. How many can you afford to lend?"

Daryn snorted. "Lend, huh? As if I'll ever get them back alive."

"You're not the only one to underestimate our friends," Mevon said. "Not even the first today. Trust me, no life will be thrown away, and none lost without good cause."

"Oh, he's a fiery one," Halice said. "I like him."

"Hands off," Daryn snapped. "Or have you forgotten your vows already?"

"Don't be vile, O husband of mine. I was just admiring his . . . spirit."

Yandumar couldn't help but smile. He raised a questioning eyebrow at the king.

"Right. Numbers," Daryn said. "Two hundred thousand is the most I can spare of the regulars. Any more than that and I won't be able to maintain order within my kingdom."

"A generous offer, thank you. And a significant bolster to our own troops. What of the border guards?"

"One company, and that only to guide you through our land. I'm still hoping they might be some use in keeping out these invaders."

"Not likely."

"Why's that?"

"You haven't heard?" Mevon said. "They have ships, we've been told—ships that can fly."

Daryn and Halice both shared a stunned look.

"It's true," Yandumar added.

"It's not that we disbelieve you," Halice said. "It's just . . . so . . . incredible to imagine!"

Daryn rolled his eyes.

Yandumar now turned his own stunned gaze on the king. "You married a *northerner*?"

"Eh, the good outweighs the bad. Most days.

When you get to my age—next month for you is it?—you'll appreciate a little vigor at your side."

Yandumar grunted. "Don't I know it."

"Poke fun all you want," Halice said. "I, for one, can't wait to see something like that in action. You think so too, right, Mevon?"

His son nodded. "Indeed."

Shouts rang out from among the soldiers outside, rising sharply into panic. Yandumar heard, very clearly, someone cry, "Look out below!" just before something large thumped into the sand.

He rushed outside, though Mevon beat him to it. The king and queen joined them a moment later, and together they took in the scene.

Orbrahn climbed free from the wreckage of his flying contraption, now little more than scattered, smoking scrap. He staggered forward, coughing, then laid a hand on Yandumar to catch his balance.

"I see you got it working," Yandumar said. "For a mark or two at least."

Mevon grinned. "I'd even call it an improvement."

"Abyss take you both," Orbrahn said, straightening with a groan.

"I missed it?" Halice said, face turning red with rage. "You had one here and didn't tell me, and now I just missed watching it fly!"

"I wouldn't worry about missing anything," Orbrahn said, finally able to summon his perpetual smirk. "We'll be seeing a lot more of that around here."

"What do you mean?" Daryn asked, his eyes narrowing.

"That's why I rushed here. I got a message, you see. A rather urgent one."

The boy began dusting himself off, obviously taking great pleasure in making them all wait. Yandumar had seen the routine before, and knew Orbrahn was just waiting for someone to ask—

"Well, what is it?" Mevon said.

"A change in our orders. They need help along some new line of conflict—Sceptre, the place was called—and can't wait for us to travel there. Not by *foot*, anyway."

He pointed towards the horizon just as five ships sailed into view, hovering above the dunes like a mirage.

"Impossible," Daryn said.

"Majestic," Halice said.

"About time," Mevon said.

Yandumar watched the wheels turn inside his son's mind, tactics and strategies for how to put his new toys to deadly use. He didn't question at all that it would be Mevon to whom they fell. It seemed inevitable. It seemed *right*. Where people were in need of saving, Mevon would go. Simple as that. He couldn't keep his son from throwing himself into danger any more than he could stop the sun from rising each morning. It was what he was meant to do.

And far be it from me to stop any man from fulfilling his destiny.

Yandumar grasped Mevon's shoulder, turning him around and embracing him, hoping it wouldn't be the last time, knowing that if it was, his son would meet his end as well as any man ever could.

"Send 'em all to the abyss, son."

"Without remorse, Father. Without even batting an eye."

PART II

CHAPTER 7

Rain pattered against the forest's broad leaves like millions of tiny drums all thumping to different beats. Petrichor dominated his senses as the thirsty soil drank in the much-needed moisture. The summer had not been kind to the land of Corbrithe.

In more ways than one.

Squatting on his heels, motionless, Draevenus peered out from beneath his cowl, focused on the backs of the retreating ruvak patrol. Tassariel was similarly postured, to his front and left, face angled past his as she scanned the enemy's back trail for stragglers. A spear rested across her knees, wrapped in white knuckles.

He waited until the sound of squelched breath and inhuman footsteps squishing in the mud faded from his ears before curling his pinky finger in the hand sign for a general query.

Tassariel pinched her brow in concentration, then signed back a moment later.

All clear.

Draevenus acknowledged with an extended thumb, then returned to his imitation of a statue.

Five marks later, he stood at last, then stepped off to resume their trek.

Their journey so far had been one of silences. What noise they'd heard had belonged to nature, to wind and thunder, tides and tumbling stone, angry predators, startled prey; and to the ruvak with their thrumming ships and screeching patrols. The silences, though, had been the more constant companion.

Silences belonging to humankind.

Villages, towns, even a few cities—they'd all been devoid of life. Some had fled, but most hadn't been so lucky. Not even bodies remained. He had no idea what had become of the Corbrithites; dead or alive, he didn't want to think what the ruvak might be doing with them.

The silence that embodied the absence of this land's native inhabitants was perhaps more chilling, but it was far less personal than the one that fell between him and Tassariel.

A twig snapped behind him. Draevenus spun, narrowing his gaze on his new . . .

Apprentice? Protégé? Partner? I'm not even sure what to call you yet. Except—right now—for careless!

Her eyes widened in fear. Not at the threat being discovered—she'd displayed a naked yearning for something, *anything* to happen—but of invoking his displeasure; which, try as he might, he couldn't keep from showing on his face.

She was, by all measures, a nearly perfect student of his art: flexible yet strong, quick of reflex and mind, skilled in all manner of armed and unarmed combat, and in absolute control of every muscle. If it wasn't for her regrettable valynkar height, and her inability to stay focused over long periods of dormancy, she'd make a fine assassin.

That, and her as-of-yet untested capacity to kill.

Draevenus forced his features to soften, almost smiling as he raised a questioning eyebrow.

Planting the butt of her spear in the ground, she shrugged apologetically.

Glancing around, he found a narrow gully only fifty paces away and gestured her towards it. He followed her in, then squatted until his head fell below the sharp rise on either side. She settled in opposite him, close enough that their words wouldn't travel more than a few paces, but far enough to where they could still watch over each other's backs.

You may still be learning, but you're catching on quick.

"Sorry," she said, beating him to the punch.

"It's all right," he replied. "Just try to keep your attention on where you step."

"I know. I *know*! It's just hard when I'm also supposed to be watching out for threats."

"Doing both at once is indeed difficult, but all things considered, you're doing quite well. It will come with time. And practice. And—"

"Focus. I know."

Draevenus sighed. "You know a lot of things, Tassariel. But that's only the first step. You must *do* what you know, over and over, until it comes without thought. Then—and only then—will you *be*."

She averted her gaze, clearly distraught by his words. Draevenus understood. When he'd first formed the adjudicators, the most difficult part of training his pupils had been getting them to overcome their reticence towards what they considered murder.

Unfortunately, there was only one way to hurdle that particular barrier.

"Look," he began. "We're deep enough in enemy territory now that we won't have to keep our presence hidden for much longer. In fact, it's about time to make it felt."

Tassariel shuddered, but nodded. "I understand."

"Good. Because there will be no going back once we reveal ourselves. We'll have to stay alert, day and night, as I've no doubt they'll bend any and every resource to hunt us down." He paused, allowing a wry grin to form on his face. "But if there's hunting to be done, it will be done by *us*."

She smiled as well; faintly, but it revealed a crack in her shell all the same.

He knew it wouldn't last after what he had to tell her next.

"I need to know that you're ready, Tassariel. I think it's time for your final test."

Her lips parted, expelling harsh, hot breath. If her mouth were going dry, the moisture gathering in her eyes more than balanced it out.

Draevenus furrowed his brow. "Are you all r—"

"I'm fine," she barked. "It's just . . ."

Tentatively, he reached out a hand and laid it on her shoulder, peering intently into her lavender irises. "Whatever it is, you can tell me. I hope I've earned enough of your trust for that."

"You have. I just don't know if this is what Elos had in mind for me."

"How so?"

"I mean, he called me his chosen. Shouldn't that mean something? Maybe it's just a child's wish, but I'd like to think he had a plan beyond the simple task he accomplished through me. Even if he's dead." She lowered her face. "Even if he wasn't really a god."

He squeezed her shoulder once then reached for his waterskin, taking a drink to try to hide his smile.

"Something funny?" she asked.

He cringed. *More observant than I give her credit for.*

"My sister had a similar theory about Ruul, calling into question his divinity."

"What about you?"

"What *about* me?"

"Everyone's heard the stories. They say you came to the battle in Fasheshe straight from Ruul's cradle. That you talked with him for days. Surely you have some insight into his nature?"

Draevenus closed his eyes, conjuring memories of his time there. He almost expected another bout of hidden visions to come floating to the surface. He almost wished for it.

But nothing came.

He sighed, glancing up at her again. "His nature? Ruul was powerful, possessing of more knowledge than any hundred lives could contain, and enough wisdom to know how to use it. He made mistakes— some that led to heartbreak beyond compare—but he always tried to do what he thought was best. And in the end, he sacrificed himself for a cause he considered greater than himself.

"I don't think it matters what label you place on Ruul or Elos. You just have to judge if their actions were worthy enough to call yourself their faithful."

"And were his?"

Draevenus shook his head. "Ask me later. Maybe then I'll know."

The look she gave him carried all the confusion he'd thought to expect.

"Come, Tassariel. Let's find some shelter for the night. I don't know about you, but I'm getting kind of tired of this rain."

Jasside couldn't believe her eyes. Despite seeing the sight every night for a week, she still had no way to reconcile it to what experience and probability allowed. From her vantage a thousand paces from the ground, on an upper balcony of the Vandulisar family greatship, she could see the world curve away in all directions. And everywhere she looked shone the refugees' campfires.

White stars hung countless in the void above, but it was the orange ones below that seemed to claim the greater number.

Dark shapes in the air ringed the sprawling camp: skyships, which she knew were friendly by the fact that they weren't swooping in to unleash devastation. The ruvak had ceased their attacks at sunset, as if to herald the promise of a peaceful, bloodless night.

Jasside knew such a promise would be broken.

A throat cleared behind her. She turned, glimpsing Gilshamed under the arch that led into the chamber adjoining the balcony. Beyond him, she saw that the others had finally arrived. She readied herself, attempting to reverse her slumped shoulders and eyelids hanging more than halfway closed, before marching past the waiting valynkar.

He grabbed her arm, gently yet forcefully, bringing her to a stop. She glanced down at the offending arm, then up as he bent his towering, golden-haired head towards her.

"A word, if you please?" he said.

"Your hand—"

"I apologize," he said, his tone indicating nothing of the sort. She didn't blame him, either—she'd have done the same if she thought the action necessary. Still, he *did* release her arm.

"Yes, fine. What is it?"

"First, I want to you to know that I bear no ill will towards you in regards to our reversal of roles."

"I didn't—"

"Let me finish, please."

Jasside dipped her head, gesturing for him to continue.

"Back during the revolution, I did not see your potential. No one did. However, all that has happened since the descent of the ruvak has made it clear to me that no valynkar can lead this alliance. We have kept ourselves separate from the rest of humanity for too long. And while we deal with the familiar with perhaps the best combination of wisdom and patience, this . . . conflict . . . is beyond unprecedented. As you know, my people do not have the best history with such situations."

"I see."

"I want you to understand that so long as it within

my power, I will provide whatever aid you need. But *you*, Jasside, are the center of all this. Every eye is on you. You are human. You feel. These are not bad things, but you must learn to guard yourself when among others, to keep separate the private self from she who would lead us all.

"It is a difficult task to manage, a trial of will and endurance beyond any other . . . but out of everyone available, I believe you can do it best."

Jasside nodded slowly. Though grateful for the praise and the advice, she didn't want to hear it right now. He wanted her to be strong, when all she wanted to do was curl up in her bed, to grieve for the lost and punish herself for the weakness that had allowed it.

Children are dying. And I may as well be the one thrusting the blade. What hope is there for the light in our souls when someone so broken is declared worthy to follow?

But she knew there was a glimmer—and with hope, sometimes that's all you got.

"Thank you, Gilshamed," she said at last. "I'll try to appear the leader everyone expects—everyone *needs* me to be." She straightened her posture, forcing regal composure into her face. "Better?"

Gilshamed nodded. "It will do."

Head held high, she finished marching past him, joining the others around a rectangular wooden table. Gilshamed stepped into his own position on her left. Jasside met Chase's then Arivana's eyes, projecting what she hoped was confidence. Little, if any, was reflected back. Though both looked like they were trying to hide it, she could tell they felt as hopeless as she did.

"I appreciate your coming," Jasside said, trying to mean it. "And my apologies for keeping you waiting."

Chase dipped his head. "I think we're far past the point of useless posturing. Let's just say what has to be said."

"Agreed," Arivana added.

She looked as if she wanted to say more, but didn't have the heart to voice it. Instead, she cast a crooked smile at Chase, who stared back with something close to compassion. Whatever coldness had once existed between the two rulers was gone. They'd realized, as had every person below, that all of humanity was in this together.

Small things. Small victories. Small bright points in an otherwise endless sea of shadow. That's all we can hope for anymore. I suppose it's better than nothing.

Jasside nearly laughed, struck by the contradiction of herself, a master manipulator of dark energy, clinging so desperately to every scrap of light.

She exhaled heavily, leaning forward and pressing her palms onto the table. "If we're going to speak freely, then I'll say what I know we're all thinking—humankind, valynkar and mierothi included, are now faced with the very real threat of genocide at the hands of the ruvak. Our defeat at Panisahldron made that perfectly clear. As hard is it might be to carry on, it seems the burden of responsibility has fallen to us. I, for one, don't plan to just roll over and die."

"Neither do I," Chase said. "But if we expect to survive, we need to come up with a plan."

"Exactly. Which is why we now need to take stock of the resources at our disposal."

"If you're talking about our fighting strength, I can give you only a rough estimate."

"Why is that?"

"We lose soldiers every day, which I'm sure is no surprise. But we gain some, too. The young and the old, mothers who've lost children, anyone who finally gets fed up watching people around them die without so much as a sword in their hand."

"I'd be surprised, then," Arivana said, "if our numbers weren't actually increasing."

"They have been," Chase said. "And significantly. But our forces are too vast and too dispersed to get a count that might be considered accurate. They're also not organized—or necessarily true soldiers. To be honest, I'm having a difficult time keeping track of everything that's going on."

"Perhaps," Gilshamed said, "I can be of some assistance in that regard."

"How so?" Jasside asked.

"I often find that visual representations help solidify things in the mind."

The valynkar lifted a hand and light poured

from it, gathering across the top of the table. After a moment, it shaped itself into a glowing map of the continent, complete with raised sections, indicating mountains, and different colors for the varied natural environments.

"Arivana," Jasside said. "You're the most familiar with these territories. Could you please orient us to the land?"

The queen leaned forward to extend a hand. "You know about Panisahldron, and Phelupar beyond that, in the south, so I'll start here in the northeast." She pointed to a large island, vaguely horseshoe-shaped, with a smaller speck of land dotting the interior of its curve. "This is Yusan. Directly west of it you have the Suwanea Mountains, which separate Sceptre to the north from the rest of the middle nations." Her hand ran down the eastern coast. "Here is Mataroa, and below it Corbrithe. This ring of hills in the heart of the continent surround Kaunax, which is bordered to the north by Tristelkia, to the south by Kaven-moor, and to the west by Tarliskan. In the northwest we have Dorgon and Ameb, and running along the length of the Nether Mountains, Fasheshe, whose southern border our group just recently crossed."

"What about our allies?" Chase said. "Where are they?"

Gilshamed lifted his other hand, and a multitude of new points danced across the map, clustered around five distinct locations. "This, as far as I can tell, is where all casters of light can be found. Their positions correspond with that of our main war groups."

The five spots lay in a crooked line, curving up from southern Fasheshe. One each was in the western end of Kavenmoor and Kaunax, with another in northern Tarliskan, and the last at the center of Dorgon. A week ago, they'd been moving south, towards Panisahldron. Towards what they thought would be a stronghold. They'd since changed direction.

Jasside glanced towards their new destination on the map. Where the Nether smashed against the Suwanea, and the borders of Weskara, Sceptre, and Fasheshe all came together.

The place the mierothi now claimed as home.

"This is . . . helpful," Chase said. "Very helpful."

"Agreed," Jasside said. "Now, about those rough estimates . . . ?"

Chase sighed. "Near as I can tell, we've somewhere between three to four million soldiers. Of those, as I said, maybe a third are actually trained fighters."

"Between the valynkar and the Panisians," Gilshamed said, "we have nearly six thousand major casters of light, and somewhere around thirty thousand of the minor."

"Of the dark," Jasside added, "there are five hundred eighty-six mierothi, and just over nine thousand daeloth. Our allies from the Veiled Empire will add twenty thousand more casters. Though the best among them are typically half as powerful as daeloth, they should still help balance out our sorcerous strength."

"A welcome addition," Chase said bitterly, "but they won't be in position in time to do any good."

He pointed toward the part of the map representing Sceptre, a place noted by its distinct lack of alliance forces.

"I don't like it any more than you do," Jasside said. "But the eastern half of your nation is the most sparsely populated region. Your people had only begun to move back in after . . ."

"My war," Arivana said, before the moment even had time to grow awkward. "It's all right, you can say it. No matter how unjust, we shouldn't pretend it never happened."

"Very well," Chase said. "But there are still tens if not hundreds of thousands of my people there. If you expect my cooperation, I can't stomach leaving them unguarded for long."

"Arivana," Jasside said. "You've taken to overseeing the day-to-day needs of the refugees. Can you guess how many there are?"

"At best estimate, our current group holds nearly six million refugees alone. If all five groups are the same size, that leaves us with somewhere around thirty million." The queen closed her eyes. "But before this all began, according to the most recent census, the middle and southern nations were counted at over ten times that."

Jasside hadn't known the exact numbers before, but hearing them now drove ice up her spine. She turned back to Chase. "Do you see now? Ninety percent of the population, dead or worse at ruvaki hands. *That* is what we are facing. The very survival of our species depends upon the choices we here in this room make. As coldhearted as it sounds, we have to protect as many people as we can, even if it means leaving some few unguarded."

She sighed, glancing down at the map. "Besides, the enemy incursion into Sceptre has been minimal so far. And I *did* allocate a small guard force. They should make first contact with the ruvak in days."

"Small?" Chase scoffed. "Five ships isn't small—it's an insult. These friends from your old empire fight may be good fighters, but they won't be enough to make a difference."

Jasside smiled. "You don't know them like I do. Trust me, your land will be as protected as they come. The very best men are on the job."

CHAPTER 8

"**A**re you sure about this?" Ilyem asked.

Arms crossed as he peered out from the skyship's edge, Mevon nodded. "There's only one way to find out, and I will not ask anyone else to do it."

"Others have volunteered. Many others, in fact."

"I won't submit someone to danger I myself am not willing to face."

She said nothing, but the slight pinch of her lips spoke tomes enough to him.

"You think I'm too important. That the son of the emperor shouldn't take any risk."

"Not unless it's necessary."

"You think this isn't?"

"I may command the Hardohl in title, but it's *your* example that we all seek to follow. Losing you would be . . . costly."

He grunted. "Then I'll be sure not to fail."

Her eyes tightened by a fraction. On anyone else, it may as well have been a full-faced scowl.

"Enough," Mevon said graciously. "We've waited too long to meet these ruvak. I won't delay for a point that needs no more debate. Lives are at stake. That is, after all, why we are here."

She must have realized the futility of further argument, for she merely inclined her head in acknowledgment—then leapt off the side of the sky-ship. Mevon glanced down, watching as she landed in a crouch on the deck of the other vessel hovering thirty paces below.

Leaving him with just the pilot of his skyship for company.

Mevon gestured forward. The man sitting at the controls knew what was expected. The skyship lurched into motion, gliding around the stone-spiked hill they'd been hiding behind.

They emerged into a broad valley freckled by boulders amidst stubbly grass, whose sides sloped up into sharp, snowcapped mountains. Fog hung below grey clouds, making the bowl of land seem closed off from the world, its own private pocket resting in serenity.

In the days they'd spent crossing Sceptre, Mevon had found it to be beautiful and rugged, both quali-ties he could admire. He'd always have fond mem-ories of home, but the Veiled Empire was a broken land, still recovering from the Cataclysm all those centuries ago, with signs of its struggle to adapt apparent wherever you looked. This place had no such hindrance, reveling in untempered wildness. Even the cities, what few he'd seen in passing, paid tribute to their surroundings, being built of the same wood and stone that thrived just outside their walls. It was, all things considered, a land worth fighting for.

But it's not the land I came here to save. It's the people.

People now visible through the fog at the far end of the valley. Ten thousand of them, in wagons and on foot, fleeing the invaders.

Eyes narrowed, Mevon took in his first sight of the foe he'd been sent to contain.

A frothing mass, a thousand strong at least, bearing armor and weapons neither burnished nor dull, snapped at the heels of the refugees. Only a thin line of outnumbered defenders stood in their way. In garb that suggested they were farmers, or miners, or shepherds, the humans fended off the ruvak with staves and slings, picks and axes; a desperate, reeling defense that could only succeed in buying time, and not even that much of it. A brief examination of the enemy's movements revealed that they were only toying with the Sceptrines, like a cat that claws off a bird's wings, watching it flop around helplessly for its own amusement before moving in for the kill.

Mevon felt the storm surge to the point of breaking.

Just hearing the stories was not enough. I had to see your heart with my own eyes. Thank you for so quickly telling me everything I needed to know.

He clenched his jaw, fury he knew without doubt to be righteous cascading through every pore. Today, here, against this foe, he would have no trouble unleashing the fullest measure of himself. Jasside's instructions had been to find the enemy, wherever they might threaten the innocent. Find them . . . and destroy them.

In this, he did not plan to disappoint her.

He lifted his gaze past the troops on the ground. He had a secondary mission, at least to begin with. The whole reason he was here, at the fore, alone. An important test that would determine how effective he and the rest of the Hardohl would be as they alone stood in defense of Sceptre.

Two enemy vessels, their hulls like masses of rough-hewn blocks smashed together and held by mud, swam through the sky like sleeping fish. As his own skyship drew near, however, they awoke quickly enough.

Mevon shuffled forward, poking his boots over the foremost point of the arrowhead-shaped transport. The enemy ships began glowing a muted, warbled green, angling their noses towards him. A moment later, twin energy beams shot out like javelins.

Mevon stood firm as they struck . . .

. . . and did him no harm.

When voiding darkness or light, Mevon had only felt a tingle of energy, a small wash of cool or warm air as the sorcery vanished. The caster would typically reel from the backlash, but most would recover unharmed within beats.

What happened now was . . . not so gentle.

Something shrill rasped against every sense as the energy around him spiraled back to its source, surging into and through those two enemy vessels. Like blocks of soft cheese struck by a hammer, the ships ruptured, expelling rocky chunks in all directions with galewind force.

Eyes flared, all Mevon could do was stare. *That was* not *the reaction I was expecting.* A smile crept into his lips.

Though it's a surprise I certainly welcome.

His first task done for the day, he spun to see about the next.

The four remaining ships in his party swept low over the refugees' heads. Eighty-four other Hardohl, all who had volunteered for the expedition, rode poised along their starboard edges. The rest of the deck space was filled with the eight-score members of the Imperial Guard.

Mevon watched as his skyships came abreast of the harried human defenders. Their noses angled left and their back ends curled forward as they braked hard, losing almost all speed in an instant.

Carried forward by momentum, his peers leapt from the decks. *Andun* gripped in eager hands, they sailed thirty paces through the air, barreling through the wedge of ruvaki troops like hawks swooping down on prey.

The Imperial Guard unloaded in the next instant, placing themselves in a line before the Sceptrines in formation, two ranks deep: the front bore heraldic shields and longswords, while the rear wielded heavy crossbows.

Faced on one side by a wall with teeth, and on the other by whirlwinds of death, the enemy force dissolved into chaos.

Mevon smiled. *How . . . appropriate.*

Even outnumbered more than four to one, it was his allies who closed on their adversary, clamping shut the trap like jaws. Still, somehow, a group of perhaps forty or fifty ruvak managed to squeeze out and made to run for the hills.

The skyship beneath him was merely a transport, mounting no weapons of its own.

I guess I will just have to do.

He pointed towards the escapees. The vessel veered, sweeping towards them twenty paces above the surface. Mevon reached behind him, lifting Justice from the hooks holding it to his back. Twin black blades, bent back onto themselves like the outline of a diamond, jutted from either end of a steel rod carved with thorns. He spun the *Andun* once for good measure.

He gauged distance and speed, waiting until directly above the enemy before simply stepping off the deck's edge.

Falling, he unleashed the storm.

Time slowed. He examined his enemy, close now for the first time. He noted weak points in their armor, the length and manner of their weapons, the quickness of their limbs, how many of them—or, rather, how *few*—lifted chins to acknowledge his descent.

He spread his feet to contact two heads as he crashed to the ground. Inhuman skulls squashed beneath his boots. The impact sent out a shock wave that toppled the surrounding enemy troops, and raised a panicked shriek from the rest.

Mevon swung one blade in a wide arc. Blood spat from half a dozen fatal wounds, filling the air with thick orange mist that coated him entirely in a beat.

He had space now: two or three paces on all sides, filled with a convenient barrier of dead or dying ruvaki bodies.

The next layer of his foe turned inwards, lifted blades, and converged.

Mevon punctured the largest one in the chest, then swept his *Andun* with the enemy soldier still attached. Half his would-be assailants tumbled after contact.

He extracted the blade, then spun, lifting Justice as three hooked blades swung down at him from the end of chains. The middle one slashed down his cheek, spilling the first red blood of the skirmish. All three, though, wrapped tightly around the rod.

Mevon smiled . . . and yanked backwards.

A trio of inhuman bodies, shrieking in surprise, careened towards him. He thrust forward again, decapitating the outer two. He rammed his forehead into the third's face, eliciting a wet, satisfying crunch.

Metal whistled through the air behind him. Mevon swung blindly. Head turning to find his target only a quarter beat later, he saw the wide, tapered blade, attached to the outside of an arm, reeling back from the parry. He followed through with his other edge, entering at the ruvak's hip and exiting at the opposite shoulder.

Mevon jumped amidst the pile of those he'd knocked over before, who were just now attempting to get back to their feet. Justice stabbed down, precisely, again and again, delivering its namesake.

Chest heaving from exhilaration, Mevon peered all about him, disappointed to find no more opponents bearing down.

No surprise, really. They've already proven themselves cowards by running once. Why should I expect them make a stand now?

A broad arc, some twenty strong, fled out from his position like a wave.

But not nearly fast enough.

It took him four marks to chase down the last of

them. By the time he was finished, so too was the battle.

He found Ilyem, who was conversing with what he assumed were the makeshift commanders of the refugee defenders. He waited nearby until she finished relaying her instructions.

At last, she dismissed the Sceptrines, then marched over to his side.

"Losses?" he asked.

"No Hardohl, but three of the guard," she said. "They have the enemy's measure now, though, and first blood out of the way. They won't be so careless next time."

"And what of yourself?"

"I am well. As you can clearly see."

"Yes, but does your moniker still stand?"

"My reputation is . . . intact," she said with forced modesty. "I do not plan to stop being called Ilyem the Uncut anytime soon."

Mevon nodded, smiling, then gestured towards the refugees. "What about them?"

"They're grateful for our rescue, of course, but surprised that it was necessary. No other ruvaki force has penetrated so far westward into their land."

He grunted. "That means we're on the right track. Any chance they know where more of them might be?"

"East," she said. "And in far greater numbers."

Sighing, Mevon rubbed his jaw. "We'll need help,

then. Send four of our ships back to pick up more of the Imperial Guard."

"What about the last? It can't carry us all."

"No, but it can scout out for the ruvak, then ferry back and forth to bring us all close enough to attack."

"I don't like the idea of limiting our mobility so much."

"If the enemy operates in larger units than what we faced here today, we'll have to dictate each engagement. And until we get more reinforcements, those will, by necessity, have to be carefully planned raids, rather than chance rescues like this one. The people of Sceptre need an effective deterrent against anything the ruvak can muster. We're simply not enough as we are."

At last, she nodded. "I'll see to it." She walked off to begin issuing the order.

"Oh, and Ilyem?"

She halted, turning her head. "Yes?"

"This feels good, doesn't it? Protecting the innocent. Like we're finally doing what we were meant—what we were *born* to do."

Though it lasted less than an eyeblink, Mevon swore he saw her smile.

"They have assembled," Claris said.

Arivana placed the stack of reports she'd been reviewing on the bench next to her and rose. Hunched to avoid brushing her hair against the wooden supports and weather-beaten canvas that stretched overhead, she moved to the back end of the wagon and descended the three steps that led to the ground.

Boots crunched against what had once been soft, powdery sand.

The Fasheshish desert was no place for traveling across open terrain, but the few trade routes leading north weren't wide enough to contain the massive, rolling camp of refugees. Casters—those too young or too frail for combat—had been forced to rove ahead of the formation and blast the sand until it had hardened enough to allow passage.

Just one more headache on the long list of logistical nightmares.

The thought made her pause. She turned back to the wagon and reached for the sheet lying atop the pile of reports. Anything to help get the point across.

With Claris guiding, and Richlen and his men in a protective ring around her, Arivana marched to the latest of an endless series of appointments, squinting against the harsh, orange glare as the sun rose in her face. A breeze swept by, raising chilled prickles on her arms. Though afternoon would see her drowning in her own sweat, this late in the year the desert failed to hold heat throughout the night.

She didn't mind the cold, though. For her task today, it suited her mood perfectly.

They came shortly to an entrance guarded by the

wardens, passing between them into a temporary square, two hundred paces across, lined on all sides by rudimentary tents. Claris gestured towards several crates; three were stacked up like stairs, leading up to the last, largest one. Without hesitation, Arivana mounted her makeshift podium, then surveyed the crowd arrayed before her.

Rows and rows of haggard, unshaven men, wearing little more than sandals and sweat-stained tunics, peered intently towards her. The odor that rolled over the heads of the wardens standing guard before her might have made her gag, not so long ago. But no one—not even her—was smelling the least bit fresh these days. From the men, no sound was made except the occasional cough . . .

. . . and the rattle of the chains that bound them.

I could look for a hundred years and never find a more captive audience.

The thought should have held humor, but failed to elicit even a private smile. Arivana shook her head, clearing her throat to begin.

"Prisoners of Panisahldron," she said. "You're probably wondering why you're all here. I'll keep this simple. Since the merging of our war group with the one from Kavenmoor, we are now tasked with protecting, feeding, and otherwise caring for, thirty-nine million souls."

Arivana held up the slip of paper in her hand. "This is a list of the dead." She lowered it before her face and began reading. "Dehydration, eleven hundred. Malnutrition, eight hundred. Exposure, thirteen hundred. Injuries and illness, nineteen hundred. Combat related, twelve thousand. Unknown causes or missing, five and a half thousand."

She let her arms hang, limp fingers barely holding on to the sheet in the breeze.

"Realize two things," she continued. "One, that these dead are women, children, innocents who have committed no crime, except that of being human. A crime for which the ruvak have condemned us all. And two, this list does not chronicle those lost on the exodus as a whole . . ."

Arivana paused, feeling the tremors start again.

"It is from yesterday alone."

The wind finally won the battle, and the paper fluttered away. No one seemed to notice.

"The truth is this, we cannot afford to feed those with idle hands. There is simply too much work that needs to be done to keep us moving towards safety. It comes in many forms. Each of you will get the opportunity to choose the new manner in which you will serve your remaining debt to society. Like it or not, your days and nights spent doing nothing more than marching are over.

"I have good news, though. Anyone who chooses to take up arms in defense of our species will have the remainder of their sentence rescinded once this conflict is over. On that, you have my word."

Arivana looked down at those closest to her. "Wardens! Get each prisoner's pledge. Then put them to work."

She spun and stepped down from the podium without another word, joining her entourage as they departed the mobile prison camp. Claris waited until they were both seated once more in the wagon before opening her notebook and scanning for the day's next scheduled activity. The woman winced.

"What is it this time?" Arivana asked dourly. "More mothers concerned about their missing children? The once-affluent complaining about their rations and labor duties? People begging for a nonexistent berth on a skyship? *What?*"

Claris raised an eyebrow. "Perhaps it's best to cancel the rest of the day's appointments?"

Arivana sighed, shaking her head. "No. I made a promise to take care of the people, and it's one I don't plan to break. I just didn't anticipate their needs being so . . ."

"Petty?"

Arivana almost laughed at that. Almost. "Consuming."

"Of what—your time?"

Arivana dropped her head in half a nod. "Among other things."

Claris snapped shut the leather-bound book then forced a smile Arivana's way. "Well, at least you have this morning's business taken care of. Putting them to work with the promise of freedom for their cooperation is the best way to handle all those prisoners."

A vise seemed to grip her heart, spinning tight. "Not *all* of them."

"No," Claris admitted, after a moment. "But we can't very well set *her* to stirring a cook pot or bandaging the wounded, now can we? Putting any ruvak in the public eye would be worse than a death sentence. They'd rip her to pieces."

"Of course we can't. I know that. But keeping her hidden and isolated hardly seems a better situation than simply handing her over to Vashodia for . . . testing."

Claris looked away, pursing her lips. "That is no longer an issue."

Arivana pinched her brow.

"I'm sorry for not bringing it to your attention before now," Claris said. "I would have told you sooner, but I only found out recently myself."

"Found out what?"

"Vashodia obtained new prisoners after the battle for Panisahldron, along with a mostly intact enemy vessel. She has, apparently, been studying them both quite extensively—and quite secretively—the whole time we've been on the march. I don't think you need to worry about her trying to snatch Sem Aira away from us anymore."

For several long breaths, Arivana lost focus on the

world around her, caught in the throes of a powerful, yet strange sensation.

She was . . . relieved.

Then, a moment later, disgusted. With herself.

And then confusion at her mixed emotions.

They are all enemies. Why do I care what happens to one over the other? Shouldn't I simply hate them all?

Hunching over, Arivana wrapped her arms about herself, feeling the chill with sudden acuity. She didn't want to hate anyone. Not even those who slaughtered her people indiscriminately. There had to be some misunderstanding, some lie or twisted truth, some essential barrier to communication between the species.

If only we could overcome it . . .

Sighing, Arivana straightened once more, calmly sliding her hands to the ends of each knee. Such a notion belonged to the child she'd left behind—that she'd *thought* she'd left behind, anyway. A queen had to deal with realities, not the impossible dreams of an undeveloped mind.

"Let us continue on, then," Arivana said flatly. "Our next task of the day awaits."

Jasside eased down her platform onto the grassy knoll outside the residential district of Loranmyr Domicile. The two ancient women—one a Corbrithite, the other a daeloth—stepped off first. She hadn't learned her new messengers' names.

She didn't want to get too close.

As much as their old bones crackled as they touched down, it was Jasside who felt as if her knees were about to buckle. The ruvak had been relentless today. With no food since morning, and almost twelve straight tolls spent channeling energy that seemed increasingly difficult to control, she felt on the very edge of her limits. And each day spent testing them didn't seem to push the boundaries any further.

If Vashodia would take over duties for just one *abyss-taken day . . .*

But Jasside knew she wouldn't. Her mistress was much too busy experimenting with her new playthings. For all the good that had done.

Not for the first time Jasside considered putting a stop to such activity. Or, at least making the attempt. There'd been a period, back when they were still trying to end the violence between Sceptre and the southern nations, when Vashodia had seemed receptive to, for lack of a better term, *correction*. She had a soul that was forever closed, yet somehow, the door had finally cracked open.

Only to slam back shut.

Since the descent of the ruvak, her mistress had regressed, becoming not just closed, but locked, as well. And Jasside had been far too occupied to even begin looking for a key. She knew one existed, but also knew the search would consume her wholly. As important as such a task would likely prove, too many lives hung in the balance to allow herself distraction.

Twin bright lights, glowing violet and gold in the evening gloom, preceded the descent of two figures. Seeing them reminded Jasside of a different type of distraction. A kind she craved.

Gilshamed and Lashriel touched down lightly at her side. They dismissed their wings—and the glow that came with them—sinking the knoll in shadow. Jasside felt better at once. She'd worked with darkness so long it had become more comfortable to her than light, but that wasn't the real reason for her relief. Shadows did a better job of hiding the fatigue.

As the couple clasped, winding around each other as if they'd been created for that very purpose, Jasside found another reason to embrace the darkness.

It masked the ache she couldn't keep from blanketing her face.

"My apologies," Gilshamed said after a moment. He disentangled himself from Lashriel, yet still kept hold of one of her hands. "I did not mean to make you uncomfortable."

Maybe the shadows aren't as deep as I thought. "Nonsense, Gilshamed. You don't have to apologize for being happy. Especially after what *you two* have been through. I'd be ashamed to know you if you ever let go."

The pair brought their eyes together, love enough to overcome anything writ there as plain as day. But in Gilshamed's eyes was also something else—the barest twinge of what could only be guilt. Though it was gone just as quickly as it appeared, Jasside remembered the last time she'd seen it on his face: when the revolution decided to diverge from his vision, to step down a path they *had* to take that came with a high probability for failure.

Not long after, he'd abandoned them entirely.

Is that where your guilt stems from, then? Not from enjoying love amidst so much death, but from fighting the desire every day to take that love and run away from it all.

Jasside cast her gaze over the northern horizon. Towards Sceptre.

Towards Mevon.

Not that I can blame you. It's an urge I understand all too well.

"Well," Lashriel said. "It's been a long, trying day. I think we could all use as much rest as our adversary will allow."

"Agreed," Jasside said.

The two valynkar bowed their heads to her and began strolling off.

"Before you go," Jasside added, bringing both their heads around, "I just wanted to say . . . you don't have to feel guilty for having found love in a time of war, you know. If anyone has earned it, it's you."

Grateful smiles made each of them seem to glow, far brighter than had their wings.

Jasside lingered after they'd gone, exhaling deeply

to release at least *some* of the day's tension. She pulled her braid over her shoulder, loosened the tie, and began unwinding the long, blond threads.

"Does that statement apply to you, as well?"

Her heart skipped as she swung around. Insensate from the day's battles, she hadn't noticed anyone approach. And the voice that spoke was one, she now realized, that she'd been dreading to hear.

"Daye," she said. "I . . . was not expecting you."

He smiled at her. "I've learned how to lighten my steps. Helps that I've lost so much of myself since the invasion began."

Jasside studied his frame, obviously much leaner than the last time she'd seen him. Not a surprise, considering most soldiers were engaged in combat daily. While his face sported slightly sunken cheeks and dark circles under his eyes, it still appeared quite inviting, quite kind—and quite obviously happy to see her.

"No," she said. "I mean, I thought you were leading the ground defense of the Kaunese war group."

"I am. We're a week out still, but I rode ahead to confer with my brother in person about merging forces. Chase said you liked to land here after a sortie."

She flung her mess of hair back over her shoulder. "Why are you here?"

"To see you, of course. See how you were holding up. I heard you hadn't gotten any rest since all this began, so I came to ask if there was anything you wanted, or *needed* me to do for you. Anything at all."

The offer was made with innocence and sincerity, neither feigned, and he'd long ago proven a gentleman in most respects. It was a gift without strings. Even so, it still implied the possibility of things to come. Things she might have welcomed, once.

Things she almost *had*.

"Thank you, but I'm fine," she said. "I'd be lying if I said I wasn't weary, but there are few among our race who can claim otherwise. You're better off putting your energy towards your duties."

She hadn't meant the words to be harsh, but knew she'd failed by the grimace flashing across his face.

"Sorry," she said, much softer this time. "You . . . didn't deserve that."

"It's fine," he said, smiling in an attempt to look like he meant it. "I suppose that means I have your answer."

"My answer to what?"

"To the *first* question I asked."

She had to think back, past the startlement of his appearance, before conjuring up what he'd said. Then, even further back to glean what he was referencing.

"No," she said at last. "It applies to me, as well. To everyone in fact."

"Everyone but me, you mean."

"It applies," she continued, "to those who choose each other."

"You know who my choice is."

"Yes."

When she said no more, he averted his gaze, sighing. Joy bled from the cuts she'd given him, supplanting his handsome features with pain. Even knowing who awaited her, she still fought the desire to plunge herself into his arms, to touch his face and see the wound reversed, to cleave herself to a man worthy of any woman's love . . .

. . . *any woman but me.*

"He must be something special," Daye said. "This . . . Mevon Daere."

Jasside cleared her throat. "Yes, he is."

Daye turned half away from her, giving her a clear view of his jaw as it worked back and forth, grinding his teeth together so that she could hear it.

She felt, for some reason, as though she owed him an explanation. That she and Mevon had met during a tumultuous time in their lives. That they were both broken, but gave each other their imperfect hearts anyway. That what they found was more than either of them had ever hoped for. And that the only reason they weren't together now was that they both thought the other dead.

That we both turned out to be wrong, well, I have to believe that means something.

At last, Daye sighed. "I guess love doesn't work like they say in all the folk tales."

Jasside furrowed her brow. She was unsure exactly what he meant by that, but it didn't seem a good time to disagree. "No, it doesn't."

"And I suppose, in times like these, we can't allow ourselves to become divided over something so . . ."

He paused, and in that momentary silence, Jasside couldn't help but complete his words with one of her own.

Meaningless.

"Something," Daye continued, his inflection grown stale, "that doesn't pertain to our survival."

He turned without another word, without glancing back even once, and disappeared among the domicile's streets. Just another soldier doing what was expected of him, no matter how much it might hurt.

Jasside wished she could have put it in a way that didn't cause such pain, but knew, no matter how gentle she might have been, that there was no easy way to accept rejection.

CHAPTER 9

The ruvaki vessel loomed three hundred paces in front of Tassariel's hiding spot, blocking out half the stars in the sky. Lit from below by bonfires, its bulbous, multifaceted skin appeared like an amalgamation of horrors pulled from her worst nightmares.

But it was nothing compared to what had been happening on the ground.

Hundreds of humans, of every shape, age, and sex, encircled each of a dozen pits of burning wood. Stripped of every scrap of clothing, most sat or lay in awkwardly hunched positions: modesty fighting with the need for warmth.

She'd been watching for the better part of a day now, and had yet to see them be fed. Their only source of water was a single wide trough that had looked, in daylight, more brown than clear. A ring of feces had sat around them until the ruvak guards made them start throwing their waste in the fires, which, if anything, had only made the redolence worse. And every so often, someone would get pulled from the group and marched up into the waiting bowels of the skyship.

Not a one of them had returned.

"It's time," Draevenus said, crouched at her side. "Are you ready?"

Tassariel nodded. "More than ready."

"You'd better be. This was *your* idea."

That the ruvak were taking prisoners was itself a shattering discovery. Draevenus had reported the fact to his sister through commune, but that hadn't been enough for Tassariel.

If it is time to make our presence felt, what better way than to rescue those caught by the enemy? she had said.

What good would it do? Draevenus had replied. *We could free them, true, but what then? We can't escort even one group back to safety. And gods know how many others there might be.*

They could travel in small groups, keeping to the hidden paths like we have. It's not much, but it has to be better than simply leaving them to this!

In the end, he'd agreed. As much because it seemed the right thing to do, as it was a perfect opportunity to take the next step in her training. She didn't care about his reasons, though. She just cared about doing the one thing that made sense to her.

Tassariel swiveled her knees and took a single crouching step down the path they'd already determined to take.

Draevenus laid a hand softly on her forearm, stopping her from taking a second.

"Leave the spear," he said.

She pinched her face up, to keep from yelling out. He knew it was her favorite. But with a sigh she backed up, then slid the spear under the pile of branches concealing their packs. "Anything else?"

"The rest of your large weapons. You won't need them."

"Only if things go perfectly. And do you really expect that on my first time?"

After a moment, he dipped his head. "You can keep your sword in case we run up against the unexpected. But lose the rest. They'll make too much noise where we're going."

Regretfully, she loosened her weapons belt, removing the laden sheaths for her axe, hand scythe, and morningstar, then retied it with only the sword scabbard still in place. Under the leaves they all went, as well.

"Good," Draevenus said. "Now check your knives."

"Again?"

"Constantly. You have to keep them oiled and loose in their sheaths so you can extract them in silence the instant you need them. Of course, the drawback to this is they have a tendency to fall out if you're not cognizant of your movements. Again, though, that's why you must always be checking them."

"Understood." She began patting herself down. Two thick-bladed daggers on her hips, a pair of stilettos strapped to her calves, four throwing knives on the inside of her forearms, and the sheath planted in the small of her back, which held what Draevenus called the *last dagger*—for when all other plans have failed.

The last one was empty.

Just when she was about to panic, she saw him twirl a small blade across his knuckles. Flipping it up, he snatched it by the point and thrust it towards her.

"You knocked it out when you were taking off the axe," he said.

She grasped the handle with a sigh and placed it back where it belonged. "Lesson learned," she said.

His black face unreadable in the darkness, he nodded. "Let's go."

Tassariel trailed behind Draevenus several paces, crouching low—if not quite as low as him. They swept around in a broad, jagged arc, moving slowly. He paused every score beats and listened intently, yet briefly, before continuing on. Her own breath seemed the loudest thing, drowning out the crackle of the bonfires and the faint scuffle of her feet through the underbrush. From Draevenus, she heard nothing.

It's not often that you get to see a master at his craft.

Pay attention, and learn all you can. Lives are depending on it. Those to be saved . . . and those to be taken.

She shuddered but pressed on, putting aside her reservations and fears for another time. She could deal with them later, after all this was over.

At least she hoped as much.

After almost twenty marks, they had finally circled around, crawling the last thirty paces until right under the vessel's belly. The ramp leading into the ship lay just beyond what her fingertips could reach. Prostrate, yet ready to pounce in an instant, she waited. They'd both memorize the guard schedules.

Any beat now . . .

A squad of ruvaki warriors, chittering in that strange speech of theirs, came clomping down the ramp. Before the last foot had even left it, Draevenus lunged to the other side of the ramp.

Tassariel sprang up, hurdling the ramp's side and landing *almost* as quietly as the mierothi opposite her. Convinced the bonfires would keep all those outside blind, they stood and walked into the enemy skyship. Comparatively, it felt like a stroll.

When they'd been making their plan, Draevenus had told her to be ready for anything once they got inside. Now, she could see why.

At least eleven different passages led away from the small entrance chamber. Four, branching out in cardinal directions, were tall and wide and glowing green, with flat floors and smooth walls. The rest had had portals set well above the floor, leading into narrow, rough-hewn passages that twisted around bends into shadow.

It was no surprise when Draevenus crawled into one of the latter.

Clenching her jaw, she went in after him.

The next half toll was an agony of scraped knees, bumped elbows, and a back bent in no natural way. Her sword had made a seemingly permanent impression against her thigh. She was glad Draevenus convinced her to leave the rest of the weapons behind.

Thrice they had to scuttle into side passages or darkened alcoves as small ruvak—what they took for maintenance workers—whisked by. Draevenus stopped at every hatch they came to, pressing his ear to listen for what might lie beyond. She counted sixteen of them before he turned and waved her close.

Kneeling, she bent her head until it was nearly touching his. "What is it?"

"We're here."

She exhaled in relief that their cramped crawl was over.

But her next inhale brought a whole different set of tensions.

"What is my . . . target?"

"There will be six guards in the room. I'll take care of those. This passage will lead out just behind the crew controlling the ship. Five of them. You'll need to take them out quickly."

"Why is that?"

"Because if they sound any kind of alarm, it will make getting out of here a much more hectic experience."

"I'd almost prefer that to all this sneaking around."

He paused, though for what reason she did not know. It was too dark to read his face.

After a while he sighed, then gently took her hand and guided it down to the hatch. "You feel that?" he asked.

"Yes. A handle of some kind?"

"Turn it top side right a quarter rotation, then pull. There will be a short passage beyond, then a second hatch, identical to this. Give me until the count of one hundred to get into position."

"Understood."

He turned, bracing his arms against the passage walls. "Timing is critical. Once you get to zero, commit yourself to the action. In this business, the hesitant don't usually get a second chance."

"I . . ." She swallowed the lump in her throat. "I will try."

Again he paused. She could almost feel the tension surrounding him, something he wished to say but could not. Or would not.

"Start your count . . . now."

One . . . two . . .

He was out of sight down the tunnel before three.

Tassariel watched down the shadowed passage for

perhaps a bit too long. Some small part of her willed him to come back to her.

She couldn't remember ever feeling quite so alone.

Around the count of twenty, she turned the handle and pulled opened the half-oval hatch, noting the hiss of released air. She slipped down, gripping the regular handholds carved into the rocky walls, and closed—but did not latch—it behind her. Drae-venus was right. The passage was not long.

At fifty, she descended to its end, and pressed her own ear against the hatch leading into the chamber beyond. She heard nothing but muffled voices speaking words she did not understand, and a low but constant hum.

This must be it. Are you ready to kill again?

Her breath became labored at sixty.

Sweat drenched every crevice by seventy.

Her pulse pounded like drums in her ears at eighty.

At ninety, she gripped the handle with tremulous fingers. Turned it. Regretfully grateful for how little sound it made and the darkness around her exit point. She stepped out, able to straighten for the first time since she'd entered the vessel, and peered about her. Nothing appeared to make any sense, but there was a door just off to her left—the only normal thing she could see.

Ninety-eight . . . ninety-nine . . .

Breathing deep, she pulled both daggers from the sheaths at her hips and pushed through.

A ruvaki man sat directly before her, the back of his neck less than an arm's length away.

Exposed.

Oblivious.

All time and all sense seemed to stand still as she lifted her blade-laden hands.

Unbidden, memories sprang forth in her mind, taking hold.

Bitter drink, hands on my thighs, a god gives me strength but far too much.

Bones snap, blood sprays, steel flashes, my own flesh chars.

Dagger falls with finality.

Silence wracked by pain.

I don't dwell about what I've done then, no, I lock it all away never to think about again, until . . .

Now.

And, as it turned out, it wasn't *time* that had been standing still.

It was *her*.

The target now faced her, on his feet, fist flying towards her face.

Instinct and training finally kicked in.

But too late.

Hard knuckles slammed into her jaw, a moment before her block struck home. Her head snapped back, white filling her vision.

She staggered. Screamed.

Energized.

Fueled by rage and pain, both new and old, she cast aimless light in all directions. Screaming still, she blinded all around her—including herself—poured all the energy she had into that brightness that now filled, now saturated, now *scalded* every pore of flesh and stone and metal in the chamber.

It lasted for beats or marks or tolls, consuming all sense as self-hatred overcame even hatred for her foe. Hatred for what she'd done, what she'd been about to do, hatred for hate itself and all the things it put people through.

A cold, dark bubble began warring with her light, and she hated that too. She fought it, concentrating her power to smother it before it could grow, but it slipped away from her again and again, until a hand gripped her throat and pushed and slammed her head into something hard behind her.

Power and light evaporated as the world seemed to spin. She fell to her knees, gasping for breath, and clawed away from the darkness creeping in, even though some part of her welcomed it.

After a time, though she did not know how long, she finally felt as if she'd regained control of herself. Enough, at least, to try to make sense of what had happened.

She lifted her head to examine the scene.

Eleven ruvak bodies lay sprawled and bleeding and still, in a chamber where every surface yet shimmered with the heat that she'd poured out in her insensate fury. Charring scoured her nose as she inhaled.

A darkly clad figure stood before her, breathing hard.

"What the abyss was *that!*"

A cold stone took hold of her chest as she peered up at Draevenus. "I'm sorry," she said. "I . . . I don't know what happened."

"You panicked, is what *happened*."

Lowering her face, she nodded.

He bent down, sighing, and wiped orange blood from his blades on the sleeve of the nearest dead ruvak. The first she'd seen. Her target. Her failure. After replacing his own weapons, he reached down and plucked her two daggers from the metal floor. She didn't even remember dropping them. Gently, he stretched around to both her hips and put them back in their sheaths.

Before he could withdraw, she snapped her hands up and clutched him by the upper arms.

"I know," she began, struggling not to sob, "you want me to say that it won't happen again. I do too. But I don't like to make promises I'm not sure I can keep."

His brown eyes flickered up only briefly. "I understand."

"I'm sorry. I really wish—"

"Don't," he said. "This is my fault, not yours. I should never have put you in this situation. Not everyone is cut out for this line of work. I should have seen that long before now."

He stood, pulling her up after him. She released him and stepped back, embarrassed at their proximity. Even so, she was glad for that embarrassment; something so normal, so innocent—or, perhaps, *not* so innocent—helped to bring her back to reality. A reality that the chaos around her had threatened to dislodge.

"Come," Draevenus said. "Our work is not yet done. But, at least, the hardest part is over. They didn't get off an alarm, as far as I can tell. Do you feel up to freeing some innocent people from this abyss-taken hole?"

She burst out laughing, uncontrollably, feeling hysteria rise even as tension seeped out. When at last she got herself under control, she felt much, much better.

Tassariel nodded to Draevenus once. "Let's go."

Arivana held the leather-bound stack of reports against her chest with one hand, and swept the other across the door chimes. Alone, she stepped back to wait, thankful for the heat rising from the silverstone streets. Every day brought them farther north, and one day closer to winter. And here, high above the surface in the domicile, with dawn half a toll away from breaking, the wind cut more sharply than ever. Her chills had only gotten worse.

But not always from the cold.

The door slid open at last, revealing a groggy-eyed Jasside, who leaned against the frame, barely contained in a rumpled shift. "Arivana?" she said, blinking eyelids that spent more time closed than open. "Is something wrong?"

"You might say that," Arivana said. "May I come in?"

Jasside backed up into the dwelling the valynkar had gifted her, and waved inward. Stepping softly, Arivana entered after her.

"Tea?" Jasside asked between yawns.

"Since it looks like you could use some as well, I can't possibly say no."

Jasside was already crushing leaves into a small, black kettle. She filled it with water from a spout running down the wall, then set her hand beneath it. Steam began rising within beats.

"Make yourself comfortable, please," the woman said, gesturing to a pair of cushioned seats. "This will be ready shortly."

Arivana smiled tightly, then nestled down into the chair nearest the door. As her host collected two porcelain cups and a silver tray to contain their repast, she studied the woman's movements. Disheveled didn't even begin to describe them.

"Rough night?" Arivana asked.

"You might say that."

"What happened?"

"Are those the death reports you have there?"

"Yes."

"Let's just say they're now woefully incomplete."

Arivana cringed, outwardly at least. "How bad?"

Jasside sat opposite her, laying the tray on a round table situated between them. "One of our units got caught out of position. Bad terrain. A new commander. Darkness. The ruvak swept in . . ."

"Gods, how many soldiers did we lose?"

"None."

"But I thought you said—?"

"The ruvak passed *through* the gap that unit was supposed to protect . . . and came into the camp unmolested."

Jasside tipped over the kettle, pouring hot liquid through sieves placed atop each cup. "If you're looking to count the lost in your reports, you might as well mark down an additional fifty thousand souls."

Arivana placed the ledger in her lap, then reached to accept the proffered cup. She blew, sipped, and wondered why she didn't feel anything more than a faint twinge of regret for the fallen.

New nightmares pile atop the old every day, so many now you could make of them a mountain. If horror has a limit, I have surely reached it.

Still, she didn't consider herself completely numb to suffering. It was, after all, why she was here.

"Oh!" Jasside said. "I completely forgot to offer. Would you like some honey? Or some mint? I've not much of either, but I grow the latter here myself."

"No, thank you," Arivana said. "But I'm glad you brought it up. It touches on my reason for coming."

"Oh?"

"Yes. You see—" Arivana separated the leather covers, and pulled out the top sheet "—while I'm sure you've been monitoring combat-related casualties, I've kept careful track of those with no connection to ruvak activity. At least not directly. Fifty thousand in one night is terrible of course, but we lost just as many to other causes. Namely . . . starvation."

Arivana handed the page across to Jasside, who took it and began reading the tally marks.

The cup in her hand soon started to shake.

Setting down both report and tea, the woman hung her head with a sigh. "I should have seen this sooner."

"I didn't come to cast blame," Arivana said. "Abyss knows I've failed every day at foreseeing what troubles the refugees might face. I only came, now, to ask for your help. I heard that you were more than competent at growing food."

"Oh, of course I can help. We'll have to convert some of the transports to mobile fields, but I'll have new crops ready in four days, then twice every week after that."

Arivana finally had her first real surprise of the

day. "So quickly? I was told you had a way to speed up harvests, but that's beyond anything I could have imagined."

Jasside nodded. "I just need soil, all the seeds you can find, a few thousand workers to get everything set up and maintained—" she leaned back, exhaling loudly "—and for the ruvak to let off their attacks for a day."

"I can help you with all requests but the last. As important as you are to our defense, you *are* just one woman. We may suffer temporarily for your absence from the front lines, but in the long run, I believe we'll save more people than otherwise. Far more."

"You're right. I *know* you're right. I just wish we'd thought of this sooner."

"I wish a lot of things had happened differently. I wish my family hadn't been murdered to spark a war. I wish my advisors had tried to resolve things peacefully, instead of working the conflict for their profit. I wish . . ."

I wish Flumere had remained just Flumere.

I wish I'd never heard the name Sem Aira Grusot.

Arivana lowered her cup to her lap, sitting rigid to hide the tremble that threatened to overwhelm her. "May I ask you a personal question, Jasside?"

"Feel free."

"Do you think it's possible to love someone you have every right to hate?"

Jasside sat forward, smiling, and reached out to place a hand over hers. "Oh, Arivana. Sweet, young Arivana. Love doesn't always make sense. But then again, what would love even be if we could predict it? If it was governed by a set of rules anyone could follow?

"Is it possible? Of *course* it is, my queen. Of course it is."

CHAPTER 10

Mevon was careful to keep clear of the humming circles as he hung, one-handed, from a handle on the underside of the skyship. Those sorcerous engines were all that kept them airborne. The slightest touch from him, or any of the other Hardohl, who were dangling in a similar manner, would turn their already rapid descent into an uncontrolled spiral, one that would only be stopped upon impact with the ground.

Not, in fact, the way I'd prefer to die.

For the past week, his strike force had wreaked what havoc they could among the enemy. They had baited the ruvak into traps, sprang ambushes, raided camps, and met small enemy squadrons in open combat wherever they threatened groups of refugees. But with four of their five skyships away, they had been able to do little more than run from the largest enemy fleet operating in Sceptre.

Now those skyships were back, with reinforcements enough to more than double their Imperial Guardsmen. And with the added mobility, they had the ability to launch complex attacks against a far superior number of foes.

Wind rushing by as his skyship swooped down from the clouds, Mevon saw their two score vessels spring into view. And beyond them, twenty-five thousand ruvaki infantry raced down a broad yet steep ravine. They closed in on another mass of desperate, fleeing refugees, screeching in anticipation of an easy kill.

Mevon gritted his teeth. *Not today.*

His men had scouted thoroughly. Everyone knew the plan. It was only a matter of . . . execution.

The enemy skyships grew in his sight with every passing beat, larger and larger, until the whole of the sky below him was filled with their scattered hulls. Still distant, as testament to their size, they finally began angling their noses up in response to the five tiny vessels that dared approach them. More than half began glowing in preparation for attack.

Mevon smiled.

Twelve beams shot upwards, connecting with his or one of the other four skyships.

Twelve enemy vessels exploded.

Impossibly, two more fired upon them a moment

later, to the same result; either too late to pull back their attack, or they simply hadn't seen what had befallen their comrades. Whichever it was, the reduced number of them meant he and his allies could change tactics.

"Twenty-six left!" he yelled over the wind to Ilyem, who dangled at his side.

"I saw!" she replied. "That means we go to three per, instead of two!"

"Are you ready, then?"

In answer, she bent her right arm until perpendicular to itself, then clenched her hand into a fist: the Imperial salute.

He returned it.

The remaining ruvaki skyships began maneuvering erratically in what he assumed was an attempt to evade. But their bulk made them slow, and his five transports were more than quick enough to catch them. A single Hardohl stood up top, directing the pilots. The enemy sorcery made it difficult for normal people to keep track of them, apparently, but voids seemed to suffer no such limitation.

Darting like sparrows against the backs of lumbering beasts, the five skyships under his command scraped across the top of the ruvaki vessels, dropping a trio of Hardohl onto each one. They planted a red flag, to let others know it was already being taken care of, before cutting open a hole and plunging inside.

Soon, it was only him and Ilyem left dangling. And only one enemy skyship as yet unmarked.

"Ready to nail the last plank on this bridge?" he said.

"Even when it's burning," she replied.

"Good. Though, I'm not sure it counts when we're the ones starting the fire!"

They came above the last enemy vessel, their own slowing by a fraction.

Mevon let go.

He fell forty paces, thumping down onto the irregular hull. Ilyem landed at his side a half beat later with only the faintest sound. They each retrieved their *Andun* from their backs, located the nearest hatch, and began stabbing downward, grinding steadily through the stone. A hole was opened before them in less than a mark. Ilyem bent down and wrenched the remains out of the way, while Mevon made himself as thin as he could, holding Justice vertically against his chest, then dropped through into darkness.

Two blades cut him even as he fell.

The first punctured his left hamstring, then slashed up and away through his buttocks as he finished his descent. The second snagged between his lower two ribs, piercing his right lung.

Pain washed through his body like magma.

The storm within him broke.

Mevon spun on his good leg. His *Andun* found his two assailants, separating the upper and lower halves of their bodies, and then two more who had been readying additional strikes. He spied more ruvak to either side in the cramped, dim hallway.

He lunged in one direction, sucking in a breath.

And collapsed.

Between his deflated lung, and the severed muscles in his leg, his body did not respond as it should have. Clutching at the blade lodged in his chest as he knelt, Mevon could barely make out the figures converging from both directions, screeching in fury.

Light feet touched down at his back.

Unconcerned with those behind—even now he heard their death cries—Mevon focused on keeping those before him at bay.

One-handed, he stabbed at the first to approach, then tugged free the metal from between his ribs and hurled it at the next. More of them rushed in. He aligned Justice horizontally and pushed. Between the slick blood and the corpses already covering the floor, the entire press tumbled backwards.

Mevon struggled for breath.

"Down!"

Obeying instinctively, he ducked, feeling a slight breeze as Ilyem sailed overhead. He kept his face to the floor, allowing his blessings the time they needed to work as she engaged. The sounds of splashing blood and crumpling flesh soon overtook the shrill cries of their enemy, and in no time at all, the hallway fell silent and still.

It was another mark before Mevon could stand or fill his lungs without agony. Peering over a blanket of shredded bodies, he made eye contact with Ilyem, who was covered head-to-toe in blood. All of it orange, of course—the only red he saw was his own.

She lifted an eyebrow.

Mevon nodded.

They ran through the twisting corridors, spiraling down towards the vessel's center. Excluding the occasional unarmed crew member, whom they ignored, they encountered no resistance. All the guards aboard must have faced them at their insertion point, hoping to cut them off before they penetrated any deeper into the skyship. A good tactic, all things considered. Had Hardohl been lesser warriors, it likely would have worked.

All paths eventually converged on the heart of the vessel, and they soon found themselves standing outside a half-oval door. Ilyem pressed the button, which should have opened it, but nothing happened. Mevon slammed his shoulder against it to no avail.

One shared glance, and they both lifted their weapons towards the door.

It took a bit longer than had the hatch, but they eventually loosened the stone surrounding and binding the frame in place. Reaching each to a side, they fitted fingers into the crevices they had created and pulled. Twenty beats of strain, of stone and metal grinding one against the other, and space enough had cleared for them to be able to slip inside.

"You first, this time," Mevon said.

"What a gentleman," Ilyem replied dryly. But she seemed more than eager to dash in ahead of him.

He stepped in after her, then stopped short. She stood just inside the portal, tilting her head quizzically. Mevon glanced past her and saw why.

Five crew members stood before them. They were taller than most that they'd seen, if not so bulky as the warriors, and on each of their right hands were coils of metal, wrapped up their forearms like a gauntlet.

The ruvak in the middle lifted her arm towards him and Ilyem. A beam similar to the kind fired from the nose of their skyship shot forward, filling the air with acrid fumes as it made contact with Ilyem . . . then vanished. The metal glove on the ruvak woman's hand shattered and its bearer screeched in pain.

"They *still* haven't learned," Mevon said, shaking his head.

"A stubborn race," Ilyem said.

He grunted. "Not the first we've seen."

"Aye."

Dripping orange blood from a ruined hand, the lead ruvak chittered at her comrades. They, too, lifted their sorcerous gauntlets, aiming not at him and Ilyem—but at the rectangular box in the center of the chamber.

It exploded as all four beams hit simultaneously.

Mevon felt the floor beneath him lurch. The vessel began falling from the sky.

The five ruvak dashed away, out a door on the opposite side of the room. Ilyem tensed to lunge after them.

"Let them go," Mevon said, bringing her up short. "We've got to get out of here. They did our job for us."

Ilyem hesitated half a beat, then nodded.

They sprinted through the corridors, retracing their steps with haste, often simply flying as gravity shifted towards the skyship's front end, and *forward* instead became *down*. They made the hatch and jumped up through it, grabbing on to the lip to avoid a meeting with open air.

Mevon took in the battle at large.

Every enemy skyship was either falling or already down. Many, he noted with satisfaction, had crashed among the bunched ruvaki infantry. The Imperial Guard were lined up three thick before the massed refugees along the entire breadth of the ravine. But they weren't alone. Thousands of Sceptrines backed them up, forming a wall that, though hard-pressed, he knew would never break. His own skyships swept along the battle's edges, filled now with native defenders who slung stones and axes, and whatever else they had to hand at the ruvak trying to flank—or escape, more likely—along the steep ridges to either side.

Fellow Hardohl raced towards their secondary objectives. Half sprinted to the rear to cut off the ruvak from escaping. A quarter cut their way to the front, to reinforce the line. The rest moved across the battlefield, hunting down those so named by Jasside as conduits.

Looking down now, he watched the ground rush up to meet them.

He and Ilyem slammed their *Andun* into the hull.

Impact.

Feet and blades scraped across the vessel's skin: a vain attempt to slow themselves. The vessel crumpled and bent below them, and Mevon soon found himself hurtling through the air. He crashed down, rolling through dirt and stone and debris, breath purged from his lungs as the sky above him twirled, darkening.

Eventually, he regained his feet, coughing, and peered about him. Ilyem stood ten paces away, wiping dust from her eyes with one hand. The other hung limp at her side.

"You all right?" he asked.

"Fractured arm. I'll be fine in a moment."

"Did it break the skin?"

"No."

"Still the Uncut, then?"

"Still the Uncut."

Mevon nodded, then cast about, looking for Justice. Spotting it, he retrieved it from under a slab of metal cast off from the wrecked vessel behind them, then straightened, surveying his foe in their frenzied scramble to escape the trap.

"This," he said, as Ilyem stepped up to his side, "is what I call a target rich environment."

"Aye," she replied, with more than a hint of eagerness.

Both hefting their *Andun*, they sprinted off towards the nearest ruvaki formation.

The babe's soft, delighted squeals were the most threatening thing Jasside had yet faced. Innocence incarnate. The very thing she was trying to protect. Yet, she had not the heart to face it directly—not and still cling to that hardness, that solid core of herself that she could never allow to break. The self she had to be to in order to face the ruvak, day after day, and never falter in her defense.

"Would you like to hold him?"

Angla held her child gently cradled in one arm. His grey skin, shaded with spots of red in his cheeks, marked it not of pure blood, but still, he was the first one conceived of a mierothi without the need for complex rituals and the sacrifice of the father. The first natural birth in almost two millennia.

Jasside shook her head. "I'm afraid I'll break him."

A lie, she knew.

I'm more afraid that he will break me.

She and the other leaders had recently decided to start bringing a second to meetings. They had found themselves increasingly fatigued, and increasingly likely to overlook things that should have been routine. Thing upon which lives depended.

She was now starting to regret her choice.

"Nonsense," Angla said. "He's made of pure stone, is my little Traevan."

"A good name," Jasside said. "Was that your choice? Or your husband's?"

"Oh, Harridan wanted to name him a Ragremon name—Ganar, or some such—but I overruled him. If I carry a child inside me for eight months, I can call him whatever the abyss I please!"

Jasside smiled. Beset by curiosity, she asked, "Was the labor difficult?"

Angla snorted. "It sure wasn't easy."

"Oh, few of them are. Or so I've been told. But I know the valynkar go through more extreme distress than humans—regular humans, that is. More of their mothers pass than not when giving birth."

"Nothing of the sort for me. In fact, if memory serves me right, it was the easiest of the three."

"Let me guess—Vashodia was the most difficult?"

"Ruul's light, no! She couldn't *wait* to get out. Draevenus, now, he was a little too . . . patient for my tastes."

Jasside laughed. She was glad the conversation had

steered the woman's mind with so little effort; Angla hadn't tried to get her to hold the child again.

Her mirth vanished, however, as she realized who she was mimicking.

The grand mistress of manipulation herself.

"Come, Grandmother," Jasside said, nearly shivering at the coldness in her own voice. "We shouldn't keep them waiting."

They walked into the conference chamber together, Angla cooing at her giggling infant, Jasside wondering if she was even cut out for motherhood.

Wondering if she would ever get the chance.

She joined the others around the table, unsurprised to see who each had brought as their second. Gilshamed stood at Lashriel's side, their hips pressed together with envious familiarity. Arivana spoke softly to Claris. And Chase . . .

Of course he brought Daye. Who else would it have been?

The brothers Harkun, king and prince, looked crisp in their dark, military uniforms. Daye's eyes grazed past her a few times, but he could not maintain contact longer than a beat before glancing painfully away. Though she understood why he was here, she knew this meeting would be more comfortable for them both if he wasn't.

"I know we're all very busy, so let's keep this short," she said perfunctorily; they'd dispensed with even informal introductions weeks ago. "You all have the reports. There's no need to repeat what's in them. If anyone has anything to say that is not already written down, or if you have insights or concerns that mere words on paper cannot address, please, feel free to speak up now."

No one spoke openly for several beats, as each leader in the room conferred with their partners. Gilshamed and Lashriel whispered with cheeks pressed together and lips practically tickling each other's ears, their faces plastered with ever-present valynkar serenity. Arivana gazed inward in thought as Claris spoke softly over the queen's shoulder. The brothers put their foreheads close in a clipped, terse exchange. Chase pulled away from Daye only moments into their conversation, cutting the air with a hand to signal an end to debate. Neither of them looked happy, the prince least of the two.

They straightened, turning towards Jasside, but said nothing. It was Arivana who spoke first.

"I did not put it in the report," the queen said, "since projections are still in flux, and optimistic at best. But since the modification of the new crop barges, casualties unrelated to combat have dropped almost ninety percent. It appears we will have enough food for full rations until we reach the mierothi colony."

"That is good news," Jasside said. "It's nice to hear some, for a change."

"Yes," Gilshamed said. "It is welcome indeed. But

those facts only apply to the four war groups that have merged together under our guidance. The last, the most northern one, tells a different tale."

Jasside furrowed her brow. "Are you sure? The reports indicate difficulty, but nothing worse than what we are facing."

"The reports do not portray the full situation. Especially considering the main forces involved in that group's defense."

Jasside tried to conjure up the names of nations she'd never visited, and people she'd never seen. "Tristelkia and Dorgon, correct?"

Gilshamed nodded. "And as Queen Arivana here can likely attest, the temperament of those two peoples, especially in relation to each other, does not lend much credence to their honesty."

"Are you telling me they're lying?"

"Embellishing, perhaps," Arivana said. "Those two have long been in competition, each trying to outdo the other in whatever contest might present itself. Neither is likely to report failure, or ask for help. They think doing either is the same as admitting defeat."

Jasside leaned forward onto the table. "We've enough to deal with without ego getting in the way of things."

"Oh, child," Angla said. "And you're Vashodia's apprentice? You of all people should know that few things are more difficult to put aside, regardless of what's at stake. For some, when all they have left is their ego, their pride, they cling to it all the more tightly. Even unto their own doom."

Jasside well knew the truth of it. But hearing it said aloud still stung, and bitterly. Just one more reminder of her failure to fulfill the promise she made to herself, so long ago. A promise to heal the darkness within Vashodia, a task upon which the world very well might rest.

Appropriate, then, that you speak of doom.

"Very well," Jasside said at last. She fixed Gilshamed with a pointed stare. "I assume you brought this up for a reason. Have you evidence to refute the reports?"

"Yes, unfortunately," the valynkar said. "My kin standing with their defense tell me a much different tale. To keep it brief—they are hard-pressed, day and night, and their defenders have been ravaged by the ruvak. If they do not receive aid soon, they will be overrun."

"How far out are they from the main group?"

"Two weeks' march," Chase answered.

"They cannot hold that long," Gilshamed said.

Jasside sighed. "Then our reinforcements will not travel by foot. Our position here has been harried of late, with few decisive engagements by the enemy. We can afford to give up a fleet of skyships to transport an army to the north in haste."

"May I make a suggestion?" Arivana asked.

Jasside gestured permissively.

"Whoever we send needs to be able to take command immediately. Someone who can force the Tristelkians and the Dorgonians to work *together*, rather than in competition with each other. Someone for whom they both have respect, and maybe even a little bit of healthy fear."

Jasside immediately conjured a name based on the queen's suggestion. And the fact that she needed distance from a certain someone had, she told herself, little bearing on the eagerness with which she made her choice.

"Daye," she said, looking at him as calmly as she could. "Will you lead a force north to relieve our allies?"

His jaw tightened as he locked furious eyes on her. But just as quickly as it appeared, the anger vanished, and his face became set in determination once more. The face of a soldier putting duty above all else. "It will be done," he said at last.

"And if there's nothing else," Chase added, "I suggest we end this meeting now. We have preparations to make."

"Agreed," Jasside said. "Until next time, then."

Daye was the first person out of the chamber, his steps louder than those of the rest combined. Gilshamed and Lashriel strolled out next with intertwining fingers, followed by Claris and Angla, who was soothing her fussy infant. Only Arivana remained.

"Is everything all right?" the queen asked.

"What? Yes, I'm fine. It's just . . ."

"Just what? It okay to tell me . . . unless you don't think I'm worthy of your trust?"

"No. *Abyss* no. I trust you completely, Arivana. But Daye? Well, I've never known a man who took rejection well."

"Rejection? You mean, you two were . . . involved? Romantically?"

"Almost."

Arivana raised an eyebrow.

Jasside sighed. "It's a long story."

"He seemed angry."

"I suppose he has a right to be."

"Because you refused him?"

"No. Because, from his perspective, it must seem like fate conspired against him. Against . . . us. But it's not. Daye is a good man—one of the very best this world has to offer—and there is every conceivable reason for me to give him my heart. I remember you asking if it was all right to love someone even when it didn't make sense, and I told you it was. There is another part to that, as well—it's also all right *not* to love someone, even when it *does* make sense. Love is a choice. And I?

"I chose . . . differently."

CHAPTER 11

Draevenus hung from the eaves of an inn ruined by more than just fire, watching the sentries kick up dust on the street below. With no human feet, no carts hauling produce, no hooves clopping by day after day, the roads had lost their hard-top layer, growing brittle with misuse. Growing dead. Ash choked him with every breath, and he had to fight both nausea and the rising urge to cough, to spit, to rid himself of the intrusion that cloyed body and mind alike. He'd seen the pyres at every intersection. Old, now. Cold. But still thick with char, and littered with what appeared, in the moonlight, to be scorched branches, splintered and tossed together like refuse. Draevenus knew better, though.

Not just wood had burned when the ruvak took the city.

They'd crossed the border just days ago, coming into Mataroa. After Yusan, it had been the first nation to face the invaders. Not having heeded his sister's advice, however, it wasn't much of a defense. The ruvak had had plenty of time to get . . . comfortable.

But not for much longer.

He tracked the two sentries as they passed behind what remained of the inn's stable. It was not difficult. Their armor wasn't as polished as a Panisian's, but on the night of a full moon, as that lone orb arced across the sky unobstructed by clouds, they may as well have carried lightglobes strapped to their backs. He saw flashes of them through the stable's ruined roof, progressing exactly as he expected.

He loosened his feet from the boards behind him, even as he tightened his fingers on the one in front.

Breathe even. Count the steps. Ready the angle and distance.

Execute.

He swung forward, releasing as his body became vertical. He flew straight, hands empty, finding the closest sentry in the instant his path crossed the narrow space between inn and stable.

Colliding.

Controlling.

Draevenus wrapped his legs around his target, hands grasping the slack shoulders, guiding them both as they struck the ground. Tumbled. Raised clouds of dust into both their faces, though neither of them coughed. Draevenus held his breath. The ruvak beneath did as well, though only because of the arm clenched tight about his throat.

Between surprise and Draevenus's centuries of practice, the chokehold did its work flawlessly: his opponent went limp in fifteen beats. And all without making a sound that could be heard as close as the next street over. Which was more than sufficient; the enemy's makeshift fortress began half a dozen blocks away.

He pushed off from the unconscious body and turned around, searching for the second sentry.

Tassariel was already standing and dusting herself off, one foot propped on the ruvak's back, just to make sure he didn't try squirming away, most likely.

"Nicely done," he said. "I didn't even see you."

"I waited for you to strike first, as was the plan. And you were a little busy when I made my move."

"True. I'm just glad to see you were so decisive."

"Glad I didn't *hesitate*, you mean."

"No, no! I don't—"

"It's fine. Really. It's a valid concern after my last performance."

Draevenus sighed. "I'm sorry. How do you feel, though?"

She shrugged. "The quiet approach still isn't my preference, but it *is* easier with empty hands."

"Right. About those hands . . ." He pulled the thin

rope from his belt. "Time to make sure ours are the only ones that can move freely."

Tassariel knelt, removing her own rope, and set to work binding her prisoner. Draevenus trussed up his own by reflex, keeping his eyes on her. Not that he doubted her ability, but he did like to see his instructions put to the test. He'd made her tie himself up five times, each tighter than the last, until he couldn't so much as budge. It seemed a gentler sort of training than the last he'd tried to give her.

She'd become withdrawn, turning to the softer side of her nature after he'd asked her to kill in cold blood. After she'd failed. A part of him understood the reflex—even cherished that about her—but he still needed her help if their mission was to be anything more than a nuisance to the enemy. He needed the warrior that he knew she could be. Tassariel had the potential, in some ways, to surpass even himself. So, as much as he hated to do it, he'd forced himself to begin killing the softness within her.

Slowly, though. Gently. And perhaps, if I'm very good—or very lucky—I won't need to slay it entirely.

He watched her finish the knots, satisfied by their placement and tightness, and offered her an affirmative gesture as she looked his way. They each grasped their prisoner and hefted them up on their shoulders. Draevenus led the way to a secluded spot they had picked out during their reconnaissance.

They would need some privacy for what came next.

In only a few marks, they were gliding down into the dark of a butcher's cellar, one of the more intact structures left standing, even if the shop above was ruined. The left behind tools would also prove useful.

When the two ruvak next opened their eyes, they both glanced around dazedly, terror soon overcoming all else as they realized their predicament.

Captured.

Bound and gagged.

Facing each other as they dangled on creaking chains.

Held off the ground by meat hooks.

Draevenus stepped between them, into a shaft of moonlight coming in through a rent in the ceiling. He hadn't asked Tassariel to participate in this. Only to watch.

Only if she could.

My own soul is stained enough. But not so stained that I would wish to share it.

"I have some questions," he said, looking them each long and deep in the eyes. "The speed and accuracy with which you answer will determine how swiftly I will allow you to die . . . and how much of you will be left, at the end."

He watched closely, gauging for a reaction, and found . . .

Nothing.

This was his first time dealing with the ruvak—in something other than death, that is. Perhaps it was their inhuman faces that defied his scrutiny. Perhaps some training that worked to defeat interrogation.

Or perhaps they simply need a different form of motivation.

He flipped daggers into both his hands. Snapped the points up to tickle their chins.

"I'll let only *one* of you speak. If you wish to be whole upon your death, I suggest you make your intentions plain."

He moved the edges to their necks, felt pulses shimmer up the steel as not-quite-similar blood flowed in not-quite-similar veins.

"If you wish to be heard, nod your head now and I'll remove your gag. I won't ask nicely a second time."

Again, he watched. And again—other than a slight deepening of their fear—there was no obvious reaction. No . . . comprehension.

"Stop," Tassariel said forcefully, stepping into the light opposite him. "Don't you see what's happening?"

"I don't see *anything!*"

"Neither do they."

She moved between their prisoners, forcing him to either back up or get pushed out of the way. He retreated a single step, lowering, but not replacing, his blades. Lifting hands to both faces, she pried out the gags from their mouths. The cellar filled with ragged screeches in an instant.

All of it completely incoherent.

"Listen!" Tassariel said. "We just have some questions. Will you please answer? Do you even understand me at all?"

Their unintelligible sounds continued unabated. If anything, they grew louder and more nonsensical.

"This," Draevenus said, "is not what I expected."

Tassariel put the gags back in, tempering the cacophony. "Why wouldn't you? Have you ever heard a ruvak speak in words you understood?"

"Yes, actually. And so have you."

"What are you—?" Her eyebrows rose. "Oh. You mean . . . Flumere."

He nodded. "If she could communicate with us, I thought they all might be able to. An incorrect assumption, I now see. Trying to interrogate them was a waste of our time."

"There's no need for that. At least now we know for sure. I imagine only the spies took the time to actually learn our speech."

"I suppose. But I wouldn't call this night a victory yet." He glanced at both prisoners, then at her, then back at the prisoners. "We move on to the backup plan."

She took a deep breath. "I'll go get my things."

Draevenus waited until her back was turned.

Then drove a dagger into each prisoner's heart.

The slightest creak in the chains as the two suddenly limp bodies swayed from the impact.

It was enough of a warning.

Tassariel spun back around, eyes wide. Though with what, he could not tell. A mix of things, it seemed, all fighting for dominance: surprise, anger, sorrow . . .

. . . relief.

Another mark and she would have begun asking what they were going to do with the prisoners. Once the concern was raised, he knew she would never have allowed him to do as he just had. To do what was necessary. And despite her inevitable protest, he knew he would not have done any differently.

I saved you that, at least. I didn't give you a chance to take the burden of their souls upon your own. As your nature demands.

He didn't know if everything within his mind was conveyed in the look he gave her, but she said nothing and turned away once more. She moved to the rear of the cellar and began retrieving her weapons, strapping them back into the sheaths beneath her cloak with exaggerated, careful motions. Taking time to gather her thoughts, most likely.

He didn't blame her. He wiped his daggers clean on the sleeve of one dead ruvak, then looked down to watch each sliver of black steel slide home, himself moving with equal lack of haste. She could have all the time she needed.

Draevenus lifted his head to find her standing only

half a pace away, clutching her spear beneath white knuckles.

"It's not the killing," she said.

"What do you mean?" he asked.

"We're at war. The ruvak are trying to wipe our kind from the surface of this world. And they've been *succeeding*. I just wanted you to know that I'm not opposed to fighting them. I never have been. But this . . . talent of yours. Assassination. I don't know if it's necessary or not, but to me it just feels too cold. It feels . . ."

"Inhuman," he said.

Gulping, she lowered her eyes and nodded.

Draevenus sighed. "Maybe you're right. I've been around war for far too many days of my far too long of a life. I'd like to say I tried every alternative, but too many moments were never committed to memory, too much of it lost for me to say for certain if that's true. Maybe my life's been too stained by blood to see any other way."

"Then why don't we try a *different* way for once? Just to see what happens."

"What did you have in mind?"

She twirled her spear. "I'll show you when we get there."

In moments, they were on the rooftops again, hopping from one to the next with only a faint whisper of wind, the slightest scuff on crumbling structures to mark their passing. He was surprised, happily, at how little disturbance Tassariel made. For all her resistance to his methods, she'd progressed in matters of stealth quite nicely.

Like wraiths, they dashed from shadow to shadow and came within sight of the stronghold unseen.

They crouched, shielded from the moon's silver glare by the wreckage of a belltower that had once stood above their position. Two stories from the ground, he could just see over the wall opposite them and into the sprawling grounds of the estate that the invaders had taken as their own. No one living was left to debate their claim.

"All right," Draevenus said. "What's your plan?"

She pointed to the mansion sitting at the center of the compound. "Since we can't speak with them, there's only one way to uncover what's going on in that house."

He peered towards the structure, four floors tall and two hundred paces on a side. Ruvak caravans had been bringing prisoners there from the surrounding territories. He and his apprentice had come to find out why.

"Go in there ourselves?" he asked.

"Precisely."

"That won't be easy. There's four groups of guards, each twenty strong at least, around all four approaches to the building. I can't see a way to eliminate any of them without alerting the others," Draevenus said.

"Then we alert them."

"Are you mad?"

"We're trying a different way, remember? *My* way."

Draevenus sighed. "Right. Sorry. Please, continue."

She pursed her lips, narrowing her eyes as she gazed on the scene below. "There's nothing else to it, really. I don't want to overthink things. Just stay in the shadows until it becomes . . . opportune."

Draevenus opened his mouth to ask what she meant by that, but didn't get the chance to say it.

Tassariel stood. Shed her cloak and let it fall. Energized. Unfurled her wings.

Draevenus squinted, blinded by the lavender flare. Heard the rush of air as she stepped off the roof and glided over the wall across the street. He blinked until his vision cleared, and saw her standing in the estate's courtyard, wings now tucked safely away.

In full view of two sets of ruvaki guards.

For what seemed an eternity, no one moved, each of the forty or so ruvak studying her with the same wide-eyed astonishment as any human. And Tassariel? She glared right back, completely lacking any apparent fear.

Draevenus felt enough of it on her behalf.

She planted the butt of her spear between the pavestones, leaning the sharp end against her shoulder. Lifted her arms one to each group. Beckoned tauntingly.

The ruvak screeched curiously. Fury filled those

voices, but also amusement. They began sauntering close, forming a haphazard ring around her as they readied weapons in loose hands.

Draevenus felt a surge of energy explode from her position, but saw no visible effect. A self-blessing, he guessed.

When next she moved, she moved like lightning.

Her spear thrust out three times in a beat, taking a trio of ruvak through their chests. Their bodies were still falling as she cartwheeled across the line, smashing two faces with her booted feet, landed and swept a leg to knock down two more, parried an attack with her spear in one hand and stabbed a dagger into the throats of those she'd toppled with the other.

She pounced upward, kicking out to both sides. The two ruvak catapulted backwards, bringing half a dozen others with them to the ground. She threw her spear forward like a javelin, impaling the largest ruvak of the group, then withdrew her axe and morningstar all before touching down.

Twirling, she crushed those who tried to parry and chopped through those that didn't. Six more fell in the span of a breath.

The ruvak as a whole withdrew several steps, fury having fled from their voices along with their previous amusement. All that remained was dread.

Tassariel put her weapons away. Lifted her hands again, pulling in more energy . . .

The courtyard around her erupted in fire.

Spellbound by the flames, licking flesh that began cooking in scents all so sickly familiar, Draevenus nearly missed his cue. Out of the shadows on the periphery of the fight, the other two groups of guards poked their heads around the corner of the mansion. They took in the scene for a beat, then all began rushing in to join the fray.

Opportune, she said. *I'm fairly certain this counts.*

Draevenus stood, flexing his back, groaning on the edge of ecstasy as his own black wings sprouted from his spine. He leapt off the roof, feeling gravity threaten to claim him—but fail.

On wings that seemed as if they'd been a part of him his entire life, Draevenus soared above the battle. He reached into special slots sewn into his cloak and retrieved four daggers that he'd prepared ahead of time. Aiming at the rightmost group of ruvaki reinforcements, he thrust his hands forward. Two pairs of metal spun down, glinting in the moonlight.

Energy exploded upon contact, the cold antithesis of valynkar light.

The dark that scythes.

The groups reeled, cut down to manageable numbers, and those that remained were dazed by the onslaught. Draevenus turned to the left.

Energizing, he dove, blessing himself—as his partner had—just before landing in a crouch at the second group's back. His pulled his thick-bladed combat daggers from their sheaths and danced forward through their formation.

Everywhere he moved, he cut.

Blinded by the fire in front of them, they had little chance of finding—much less facing—the shadow from behind. Tassariel could fight in the light all she wanted.

This is where I belong.

It seemed only beats later that the enemy around him thinned. Half were down, if not dead, and few had made it to engage the valynkar. The rest had scattered. He spared Tassariel a glance, found her fighting now with her sword, using the flaming bodies around her as obstacles to keep her foes from swarming and countering every attack against her.

He captured that image of her. Surrounded by foes and fire, effortless grace abundant in every motion, making her opponents seem slow and clumsy. A valynkar warrior unleashed.

Draevenus could recall few things more beautiful.

He swept his gaze around the surrounding darkness, spying those that had fled. He began shadow-dashing to each one, killing on the exhale, and streaking off towards the next on the inhale. Seventeen breaths later, those parts of the estate grounds less illuminated were empty of anything living but him.

When he came back around, Tassariel was waiting by the mansion's front door. Splashed by orange blood, her chest heaved as she cleaned off her weapons. Flames reflected off eyes wide with exuberation.

"So," Draevenus said. "*Your* way."

"What about it?"

"It has . . . appeal."

She smiled.

Then kicked in the door.

Together, they raced through the house as cautiously as they could, unknowing what dangers might be lurking within, or what they were even looking for, but still moving quickly. Though they encountered no resistance, their destination soon became apparent.

They just had to go towards the smell.

Following it down to the lower level, then again to a cellar—a strange mirror of their earlier activities—the odor grew increasingly rank. And Draevenus grew more certain with every step that at its source they would find no good thing.

At last they came to a sturdy door, from which the smell came. Locked tight. Tassariel kicked this one too, but it didn't budge. Something was propped up against the other side. Draevenus energized again and blasted the hinge and lock carefully with darkness. They pried open the ruined door, revealing what lay beyond.

Piled nearly to the roof were mutilated human corpses.

Tassariel spun away from the sight and sickened

onto the floor. Even Draevenus felt queasy, and he'd seen more death than any soul ought.

But very little of it like this.

He had only a moment to wonder what kind of person could cause such torments to victims that must have been living at the time, for he heard motion deeper in.

And a whimper.

He sped into the chamber, trying to ignore the crunch and squish that came with every step across a floor blanketed by discarded human flesh. He ran around the largest pile in the room's center, and saw an open doorway into an adjoining chamber. From there, he heard the whimper again.

Dashing forward, he stopped in the portal as he saw what lay on the room's far side.

A woman, strapped to a table, already ravaged in ways he couldn't imagine—but still breathing.

A ruvak man, slim and withered, standing over her.

A curved blade in his hand, which now began to fall.

No space to shadow-dash. The distance too great to run. Draevenus felt the world slow to a crawl as he surged forward, already mourning another life he failed to save.

He tackled the man a full beat after the ruvak had stabbed the woman through the heart.

Draevenus pinned him down, straddling the in-human chest.

"You *bastard!*"

The ruvak smiled. "You . . . not first . . . to call me that."

Jasside finally found the place.

The ruvak hadn't exactly given up the attack, but they seemed content to herd them as of late, never pressing for decisive actions. She'd used the extra tolls of each day to search for her erstwhile mistress. It hadn't been easy.

Vashodia been masking her signal, making it impossible to find her through commune, and she'd been keeping her physical location circumspect by changing it, supposedly, every day. With functionally infinite space in which to disappear, finding her had seemed a futile task.

But Jasside had long ago ceased being intimidated by infinity. After all, she had learned from the best.

She had been forced to follow the rumors of the woman's activities, which Vashodia hadn't bothered to conceal to those nearby. Stories of strange sounds emerging from a large, unmarked tent, which appeared one night and vanished the next, had led Jasside on a chase spiraling all around the rolling encampment, seemingly at random. Vashodia, however, was not ruvak; not a creature of chaos. Her life was defined by patterns, by logic, by making sense of things most would call senseless. Jasside, who knew her better than anyone else, living or dead, had been able to follow the signs, if not with haste, then with a certainty for inevitable, eventual success.

Her own signal masked to avoid spoiling the surprise, Jasside pushed through the tent's loose, taunting flap without making a sound.

"Good morning, apprentice," Vashodia said. "I've been expecting you."

Though the interior was lit only by what little sunlight could force its way through the thick canvas on all sides, Jasside's eyes adjusted almost immediately; another symptom of her dark energy use, so constant it sometimes seemed an addiction. Vashodia sat crosslegged on a cushion before a curtain that obscured the rest of the massive tent, concealing whatever . . . activities . . . she had been getting up to.

Jasside had half a mind to simply march past; an impulse more interested in how Vashodia would react than in what she might find beyond.

"Highly improbable," she said instead, answering her mistress. "I've been masking myself during my approach. And you told me yourself the technique cannot be defeated."

"Perhaps I lied. Or perhaps I've learned, since my lesson to you so long ago, a new way to detect that which wishes to remain undetectable." Vashodia giggled. "Or perhaps there are other ways than *commune* to keep track of who approaches."

Jasside began to sort through her mistress's statements, attempting to untangle the truth hidden somewhere among the skein of words. Vashodia was rarely ever apparent with her meanings, though she rarely spoke without them.

But then Jasside stopped her analysis. She had allowed herself to become distracted—and so quickly!—after promising herself she would stay focused on her task. Everything her mistress said likely held more weight than a lifetime's worth of words from a million other mouths, but today, Jasside had something of her *own* to say.

"It doesn't matter," Jasside said. "I didn't come to compare notes on sorcerous procedure."

"Of course not. You came to chastise me for my naughty behavior."

"I wouldn't bother. The only time you ever seemed receptive to criticism was back when we were freeing Sceptre from occupation. And then, only just. What changed?"

Vashodia scowled. "I came to my senses."

"It was intentional, then?"

"It was a mistake."

"I'm surprised you'd admit that. But then, not *that* surprised. I should expect that you, of all people, would view being *wrong* as a lesser fault than being *vulnerable.*"

"I like to conduct experiments. That doesn't mean I won't end one when I see results that point towards failure."

"Failure? Abyss take me, you were just starting to succeed!"

"Well then, it appears, yet again, that you and I have much different criteria for what constitutes a favorable outcome."

"Clearly."

Jasside placed her hands on her hips and began tapping a toe, searching for a way to come back to her point. Frustrated that she'd allowed herself to become distracted again.

Just say what you have to say, then get out before she can twist your mind in another dozen directions. You have too much responsibility to try to wrangle this maelstrom.

"Look," Jasside began, "I know you don't care about lives you view as pointless—I won't try to debate *that* with you again—but there are still so many that even *you* can concede are valuable. And they need your help.

"*I* need your help.

"People are dying every day. It takes all of me to stem that flow of blood, to make it a mere sprinkling compared to the raging torrent it would otherwise be. You know me. You know this is simple fact and not a boast. And you also know that there are none better at doing the job than me.

"None better . . . except you.

"I know you claim to have a plan for everything, and I'm sure you think you have everything under control, but we are in a fight for the very survival of our species . . . and we are losing! I've tried to imagine a scenario where you'd consider the eradication of humanity—in all its forms—to be a 'favorable outcome,' but even the darkest part of me can't believe that about the darkest part of you.

"That's why I'm asking you now to put aside your projects, your experiments, your distractions, and help us fight! Give me a *break*, at least, before I start making mistakes. Worse ones than I've already made, that is."

With all the haste of a flower unfolding for spring, Vashodia rose. Clawed hands began clapping as pointed teeth flashed towards Jasside in a grin; disingenuous both, and not bothering to hide it.

"My, my, what a touching speech," Vashodia said, mock emotion laced through her voice. "You must have spent all night rehearsing it."

Cold flowed down Jasside's neck. She wondered how she could have thought there'd be any other kind of response.

The mierothi ceased her feigned applause. "Really, child, what did you expect? I never do anything without reason, nor will I do things twice when once will do. I battled the ruvak at Panisahldron to get their measure. Now, I work to uncover other secrets they'd rather not have brought to light."

"What secrets? You haven't discovered *anything* useful!"

"Haven't I?"

Jasside furrowed her brow. "What are you saying?"

Vashodia shrugged. "Oh, nothing. Just that I may have chewed off a morsel or two. Most delicious. Would you like a taste?"

Jasside hesitated.

"As I thought," Vashodia continued. "You simply can't stomach the fact that my methods are effective. You'll even go so far as to refuse my information, due only to the circumstances of its . . . extraction. Pity. I once thought you had more sense than that."

"There is no sense in what you do. Only pain. Only . . . darkness." Jasside shook her head. "To think I was once so naïve as to believe I could save you."

"Save *me*? Oh child, I do not want to be saved, and certainly not in the manner you envision."

"The very fact that you think so only proves how desperately you need it."

"You are wrong," Vashodia said matter-of-factly. "Training such folly out of you is going to take some doing. I'm not sure you're up to the challenge."

"I have nothing to learn from you."

"You think you've surpassed me already? In just a few short years?"

"I'm not so vain as that. Besides, surpassing you implies I seek to follow in your footsteps. Nothing could be further from the truth."

Vashodia snorted. "If that is the case, then you can consider your apprenticeship terminated. To think *I* was once so naïve as to believe I could . . . groom you."

Jasside felt herself stepping back, gut aching as her own words were twisted back upon her. Coming here, confronting her mistress—she never expected things between them might come to an end.

Not like this . . .

"Once again," Vashodia continued, "it appears I'll have to do everything myself. Everything that matters, anyway. Try not to let any dust in on your way out."

Jasside shuffled her feet around and began trudging back towards the entrance. Even if she could have thought of anything to say, her mouth was too dry to speak.

Too many disasters. One right after another, unceasing. How many more until I break?

"Oh, and Jasside?"

She stopped. Turned. Stared.

"If I were you, I'd start keeping a closer eye on my men. They are, after all, such naughty little creatures."

Jasside pushed through the flap, head flaring with pain as the bright light of the sun seemed to slap her in the face. Ignoring it—just one wound among many—she energized and jumped into commune.

The realm of endless white surrounded her instantly. She turned north and flew, casting her metaphysical self through fields of dark stars, across a gap where none existed, then into another black cluster: the fifth war group, where the reinforcements had been sent. She looked about for the ones she sought.

But did not find them.

With the weight of inevitability crashing down upon her mind, she peered even farther to the north, into what would be, in the waking world, the land she had liberated what seemed an eternity ago.

Into Sceptre.

And found, at last, her quarry.

CHAPTER 12

Mevon tore a chunk of meat off the bone. The fire before him sizzled as a Sceptrine woman turned the spit and her husband cut off slices from the pig to ready another platter for any of the dozens seated eagerly nearby. Two full days since they'd last seen a ruvaki force, though not for lack of trying. All five sky-ships were currently roving, and hundreds of native citizens had volunteered to act as scouts, guides, and rangers. Mevon savored each moment where the innocent were not in danger almost as much as he did each greasy bite.

Almost.

Too much of him still yearned for action, for taking the fight to the enemy before they had a chance to regroup. But despite another round of Imperial Guard to reinforce them—along with the thousands of locals who'd chosen to fight rather than flee—there weren't enough troops with him to truly go on the offensive. To drive deeper east into Sceptre would leave those behind them exposed. Instead, they'd been coming slowly west.

"It's late."

Mevon peered over his shoulder to see Ilyem standing behind him. He quickly chewed and swallowed, washing his mouth out with a swig from his waterskin. "So it is," he said. "But this couple here told me they make the finest roast pig in all of Sceptre. I couldn't pass up the chance to test their claim."

"And?"

Mevon smiled. "I've yet to taste better. Want some?"

In answer she sat beside him on the log. The husband brought her a plate piled high with steaming meat, smiling and bowing enthusiastically. She ripped a piece from the slab with her fingers and plopped it into her mouth.

"Very good," she said half a mark later. "But I'm not sure it's worth losing sleep over."

Mevon grunted, flipping his wrist. "I'm too stirred up for that right now. I want be ready in case there's a sighting."

"All the more reason to get rest while you can."

"Maybe. But we've only had the upper hand so far because we've struck hard, leaving none alive to tell of our tactics nor allowing them a chance to rest. I don't like this quiet."

"Is that what has you so antsy lately?"

Mevon hesitated. "Of course."

"*Really*. So it has nothing to do with your upcoming . . . reunion?"

After a long pause, Mevon sighed, then dipped his head in acknowledgment. "That might also have something to do with it."

Two weeks was the estimate. Two weeks until all the refugees and war groups, those from Sceptre included, would at last gather at the mierothi colony.

Two weeks until I see Jasside again.

"I don't even know what I'm going to say to her," he said.

"Is that your way of asking for my advice?" Ilyem said.

"Well . . . no. But if you're offering—?"

"I'm not."

"I didn't mean . . . that is . . ." He sighed. "It's rude, isn't it? To ask one woman how to deal with another?"

"Probably."

"You don't know?"

"I'm not most women."

Mevon grunted, smiling. "My apologies anyway. I'm . . . no good at this sort of thing."

"That much is obvious."

"Thanks."

"But you are not alone among our peers when it comes to struggling with such matters. When you expend every effort towards making hearts stop, it becomes difficult to treasure them."

"That's one way of putting it. Though . . . I don't know how that helps me."

"I didn't say it would. Just trying to establish how rarely our kind make such connections."

"So, the more unique something is, the more it should be valued?"

She shrugged. "You're the one who keeps looking for a point. Make of it what you will."

Mevon turned back towards the fire. Stuffing his mouth as he stared into the dancing flames, he found himself obsessing over his future choice of words to a woman he could only hope held no hate in her heart towards him. Coming up empty, time and time again, he soon had to contest with terror that threatened to set him trembling.

You, Jasside, seem to be the only person capable of doing that to me.

When he heard the call to battle, sometime later, fear vanished in an instant.

The force loaded up over the next several marks as the skyships returned one by one: Hardohl to their harnesses beneath, Imperial Guard pressed close together on the deck, which they had since modified to contain more space. Weighed down far past their designed intent, the skyships lumbered through the air, heading—to Mevon's surprise—south. Only a few dozen leagues lay between their current position and the Suwanea Mountains, which formed Sceptre's border. He had thought the place well clear of enemy presence.

"What do we know?" he asked Ilyem, as treetops scraped by just paces below them.

"A mass of human civilians are fleeing a ruvak fleet," she said.

"That isn't exactly news."

"No. But the fact that both groups are larger than anything we've encountered before is."

"How can that be? The ruvak I can understand, but wouldn't we have noticed a group of refugees that large? Where did they come from?"

"The east."

"That . . . isn't right."

"I know."

Mevon let the winds of Sceptre's autumn chill flesh and mind alike as he fought the clenched feeling in his gut.

Such instincts, unfortunately, had rarely failed him.

Twenty marks later, they crested a hilltop, and the sight before them filled with a vast plain that swept towards the mountains standing dark against the stars. Fires glimmered on every patch of ground he could see.

"There's got to be two . . . three hundred thousand

at least," he said. "Far too many for us to even attempt to protect."

"We won't have to do it on our own." She pointed to the far end of the human mass. "Look."

Mevon peered across the distance, seeing little but shadows at first. Then, something else: torchlight flashing from steel in too regular a pattern to be anything but a military formation.

"Who the abyss is *that*?" he said.

"We'll soon find out."

Their skyships swept over the sprawling encampment, which showed signs of rousing: tents fell as figures around them yanked on ropes and pulled up stakes, campfires were doused, spitting steam towards the sky, and figures scrambled with more haste than night and the press of bodies could safely permit.

They should have known better than to expect the ruvak would give them a moment's respite.

At last they came over the far side to a gap between the civilians and the military force. The pilots nosed up to hover and begin landing. Mevon released his harness twenty paces from the ground. The rest of the Hardohl followed suit.

Marching closer, he could finally make out the brown-and-black uniforms worn over dull, stone-like armor, and saw the bear flapping on banner poles all across the formation. Though he hadn't see it before, he'd been in this country long enough to recognize the marks of its own flag.

Before he'd covered half the distance, one of the Sceptrine soldiers broke away from the rest. Taller and fairer than most locals Mevon had seen, the man bore a greatsword strapped to his back and carried himself with authority as he strode out to meet them.

He came to a stop. Folded his arms as he flicked narrow eyes between Mevon and Ilyem. "You must be the soldiers from the Veiled Empire."

"We are," Ilyem said. "I am Ilyem Bakhere, commander of the empire's Hardohl."

"Hardohl?"

"Voids."

The man's eyes widened as he scanned those fanning out behind them. "All of you?"

"Yes."

"But how can there be so many? I am one of only twelve known in my nation. Does your empire breed our kind like horses?"

"No. But our previous ruler knew how potent a weapon we could be. He wasn't one to let good tools go to waste."

"Not good enough, it seems."

"Strong words from a man who hasn't even told us his name," Mevon said.

The man sneered. "I am Daye Harkun, Prince of

Sceptre. And I am here to do what you could not." He gestured over Mevon's shoulder, towards the encampment. "I came to save my people."

"A noble cause, were *we* not doing just fine at the task . . . and were it not against your orders."

"How would you know what my orders are? Just who are you anyway?"

"I am Mevon Daere. Son of the current emperor. Slayer of the previous one. I was sent here by Jasside Anglasco, at whose side I fought during our empire's revolution, to hold off the ruvak as much as our small force could. The real question, then, is this—what the abyss are you doing here?"

Daye dropped his arms to his sides. "*You* are Mevon Daere?"

"Yes. What of it?"

The prince studied him, scrutinizing every detail, lingering long on the *Andun* poking up over his back, and longer still on his face. He must not have liked what he saw, for he shook his head and said, so softly Mevon knew he wasn't meant to hear it, "Of course it had to be you."

Before Mevon could even begin trying to figure out what that meant, a hand on his arm drew his attention.

"Incoming," Ilyem said.

Mevon looked past Daye to see the ruvak approaching, over a hundred small skyships swarming like locust.

"**D**o you feel that?" Draevenus said.

"Feel what?" Vashodia replied. "This is commune, dear brother, an unreality occupied exclusively by our minds. The only sensation to be had here is what you *want* to feel. What you expect."

He scanned the unbroken white around them, unable to shake the itch that told him something was wrong. "I know that, but this is different. I can't help but feel like I'm being watched."

"I feel nothing."

"And I suppose you think your perception is the only one that matters. That it might as well be reality."

"*Will* is reality, for those strong enough to shape it. Perception only confirms what you already ought to know."

"And that is?"

She smiled. "That I'm never wrong."

"Never wrong isn't the same as always right."

"Thus spake the fool."

"We share the same blood, sister. If I'm a fool, you can't be less than half one, as well."

"Why, brother, that almost sounds like wisdom . . . if only it weren't utter nonsense."

"Right. Next you'll try telling me blood has no bearing on a person."

"Oh, it plays a part in potential, probability, and predictable behaviors, but it's the experiences you have and the choices you make that truly define who you are."

"Well then, maybe I'll *choose* to give my reports to Mother, or Jasside, from now on. How would you say that defines me?"

"I'd say you're a man no good at making threats. Not with words, anyway. If I were you, I'd stick to making them with knives."

Draevenus sighed. "I've been doing more than enough of that recently, and even Tassariel hasn't objected. That's why I'm here."

"Discovered something tantalizing, did you?"

"You might say that."

"Do tell!"

Draevenus ran a hand through his hair, almost surprised to find that he'd remembered to conjure it. His first few times in commune, he'd summoned the old version of himself—scales and claws, and definitely no hair. "We captured a ruvak a few days back. Found him in a room full of human corpses— his test subjects—disposing of the last of them after Tassariel and I took out his guards."

"The girl is working out for you, then?"

"No. Yes. That's not the point."

Vashodia yawned. "Please get to it, then. Quickly. It's almost time for my beauty rest."

"Look, we could understand him, you see? Other than the spy, he was the first ruvak we'd found for whom that was true, after I'd almost given up finding someone we could actually question. And abyss take me did he have some answers."

"Regarding?"

"Voids, sister. He'd been torturing people for information about voids."

"What did he discover?"

"Enough. That's what I came to warn you about. I didn't get specifics, but he gave up hints about the trouble the ruvak have been having with the Hardohl up north . . . and about an operation they'd launched to wipe them all out."

Mevon grasped the front railing as he vaulted aboard his lead skyship, shouting at the pilot to launch immediately.

"What's the plan?" Ilyem shouted from below, even as he began to rise.

"I'll leave the ground fighting tactics to you," Mevon called back, then gestured to the four other skyships, two on either side, that were lifting alongside him. "We'll take out as many of them as we can, and try to screen you from aerial attacks."

"We have some ships of our own," Daye said. "And a few war engines that can strike at theirs from the ground. We can use them both to break the enemy center—"

"No. Protect your flanks. Keep the ruvak in front of you. And abyss take me, get those civilians moving! This plain is no place to stage a defense."

Daye clenched his jaw, but nodded. "Good luck, then."

Mevon returned the gesture. "To you, as well."

The vessel beneath him at last achieved altitude and surged forward, wind snapping his hair behind him. Mevon lifted his eyes once more to the enemy, whose vessels outnumbered his own more than twenty to one. Tearing through the air with shrill whines that seemed to split the sky, scores and scores of ruvaki skyships, each smaller than his own, bore down upon him, twisting over and around each other in almost choreographed motions.

Mevon gripped Justice and twirled it before him.

Let's dance.

He spared a moment to glance behind. The Hardohl were spreading throughout the Sceptrine formation. A good move on Ilyem's part. They'd be able to utilize their individual combat power to bolster each company they augmented, as well as providing a greater range of coverage against sorcerous attack—either from skyship or conduit.

The Imperial Guard divided to either side, extending the arc of soldiers protecting the civilians behind. There seemed far too few of them to Mevon, but he knew how critical it was to prevent the ruvak from flanking, and how staunchly those men could hold. Thin as they stood, there were none better for the task.

Still, it was difficult to judge their chances of victory. He knew how many ships the enemy had, but little else. How effective were Daye's soldiers? His skyships? His war engines? And just how many troops had the ruvak brought to battle?

This last question, at least, was answered a moment later, as the deck beneath him nosed over a shallow line of rolling hills, and he saw into the cup of land beyond.

Thousand-strong squares of ruvaki infantry stormed forward, twelve wide and eight deep—almost a hundred thousand in all—tearing gouts in the soil in their haste to cross blades with his allies. Even with the addition of the Hardohl and Imperial Guard, the human defenders would be facing more than four times their number.

The space between him and the ruvaki skyships had dwindled to less than half a league, now a quarter, now well within range of their weapons. Mevon edged closer to the forefront of the deck, keeping a wary eye out for the telltale mottled glow that announced a pending attack. He swept his gaze left and right, down and up, all across the swarming mass of vessels . . .

Yet saw nothing.

The distance closed to hundreds of paces, now scores, their buzzing movements filling the entirety of his vision . . . . and still the noses of the enemy skyships remained dark and dull.

A chill rode up Mevon's spine as he realized what was happening.

They've learned how to deal with us at last.

He turned to alert to the pilot, to tell him to disengage, to evade.

But the warning came too late.

Within the span of two beats, four ruvaki vessels slammed into his own, the deck lurching as wood and stone exploded in splintered fragments all around him. Mevon clung to the railing as his body and the skyship beneath him flew in suddenly opposite trajectories. But the section he grasped ripped away from the rest with only the barest resistance.

Mevon fell.

The total lack of surprise on his sister's face spoke more truth to Draevenus than scripture.

"You *knew* about this?" he said.

"Of course I did," Vashodia said. "It is my job, after all, to monitor all the fickle souls on this planet. Human and otherwise."

"How can you be so calm? By all accounts, the Hardohl have become our greatest weapon against the ruvak. We can't afford to lose them!"

"*Them?* Or is it one in particular for whom your concern is leveraged?"

"Mevon is a friend of mine, yes, but that doesn't mean I've lost sight of the greater picture. I may not be you, Vash, but I do occasionally think beyond what affects only myself."

"How noble of you. Unfortunately, however, such traits are like the voids themselves—painfully rare."

"But potent all the same. And it doesn't take many thinking the same way to make a difference that the world can feel. Even *you* can't argue against that."

"Of course not. If anything, I'm living proof of its validity."

"Or the exception that proves the rule."

"Stop trying to sound wiser than you actually are, brother. I can only cringe so much."

Draevenus shrugged. "Fine. But can you at least tell me what you're planning to do about the threat to the Hardohl?"

Vashodia snickered behind her hand. "Oh, it's already being taken care of."

"What do you mean?"

"Have you no faith? The gods may be dead, but *I* am still here. And I'm arguably more effective than they ever hoped to be." She sighed. "I haven't even demanded worship from the people I have saved."

"With that attitude, I wouldn't hold my breath waiting for them to start. But what about the situation? *What* is being taken care of?"

"A wayward child runs even now to prevent the annihilation of the voids, duty and desire aligning at last, even as she wars with her own joy at this fact. The only question remaining is if she'll be in time to save the one for whom her heart yearns. Then again, I'd not worry too much—he *is* rather difficult to kill . . ."

Mevon's eyes snapped open. Before him was nothing but a dark, swirling blur. His head felt as if pressed between two boulders clamping shut around his skull like hungry jaws. Pain would have been reassuring; all he felt was pressure, though, and numbness, a tenuous fiber threading body and mind.

Then, blessedly, came the burning.

It scorched most potently in his back and hips and legs, places most likely shattered by the impact and now mending. He'd fallen before, but never from such a height. He could only wonder how close to that edge he'd come, how near to death. If he'd been another few paces high he might have tumbled fully into that chasm, from which no blessing, however potent, could retrieve him.

The thought of such a death angered him.

I've come too far to die by anything other than an enemy's blade.

Darkness came and went, making mockery of his attempts to gauge time, or to infuse will into his recovery. Eventually, the weight from his head subsided and the world ceased its nauseating spin, resolving above into that black blanket of the night sky scattered with glimmering stars. Pain still blazed throughout, but he felt well enough, whole enough, to attempt sitting up.

A new sensation gripped him when he rose, the same that always did after he'd healed from a grievous wound.

Mevon was starving.

He hadn't brought any food with him, but he withdrew his waterskin from his belt. With shaking fingers he upended it over his mouth. He felt better after downing it, and the gnawing void in his stomach subsided. But not entirely. He groaned getting to his feet, and the world began spinning again. He leaned over, propping elbows on knees to steady himself, and took deep, slow breaths until the dark around his sight began creeping out instead of in.

When he righted at last, he peered around to search for Justice.

What he found instead were the ruvak, surrounding him on all sides.

He hadn't even heard them approach.

If you think you've sealed my fate, then you still don't understand the Hardohl.

Spotting a glint of dark steel in the grass nearby, he dove for it, wrapping his hands around that familiar, thorn-studded rod just as scores of shrieking, inhuman warriors converged.

"I don't know if I've said it aloud to you before," Draevenus began, "but the way you use people sickens me."

"You wound me, brother."

"You have to have feelings to experience hurt, sister."

"My, my, the filters are off today, aren't they." Vashodia giggled. "Why the change of heart after all these centuries?"

"Maybe I've finally realized how pointless you are. What have you actually done that's made the world a better place?"

"Better is such a *subjective* word."

"Answer me!"

"Patience, dear brother. My plans haven't yet come fully into bloom. And as they say, good things come to those who wait."

"What idiots said that?"

"Those long dead, though still wise despite their hubris."

"I'm not sure many would agree. Just look at Mevon and Jasside. You've used those two far more than most, breaking every facet of them both just to further your own gains. And for what? Bringing the ruvak down upon our heads? *What possible good can come from that!*"

"You'll see, in time. Or, we'll all be dead. One way or another, we will at last have peace."

Draevenus sighed. "You know, before, I wasn't

sure if you were mad or simply arrogant beyond compare."

"And now?"

"Now, I know you're both."

Mevon skated backwards, nearly tripping on a thick tuft of grass. He righted himself just in time to parry a slash aimed at his head, then reversed his stroke to slice his other blade through his assailant's chest. He repeated the move as another ruvak warrior lunged at him from the other side.

Two more approached from the front. One feinted high, then spun in low. The other leapt over Mevon's head.

He stabbed his *Andun* into the dirt, blocking the ankle chop, then bent down and grabbed the ruvak by the wrist. He surged around, wielding his enemy like a club, and battered the leaping warrior away. Bones crunched, sending shivers up Mevon's arm.

Releasing the crumpled, insensate figure, Mevon spun to face the rest of his attackers. Vision blurred as, breathless, he tried to count them.

Eleven . . . I think. As many enemy left as there are cuts I've already taken. This shouldn't be too h—

His knee buckled as he took a step towards them.

He stared down at the blood oozing from a deep gash in his thigh, the wound afire with pain, yet cold all the same.

I've lost too much, too quickly. If they knew how little I had left, they wouldn't hesitate as they do now.

But they did. The eleven half ringed him, no less than ten arm's lengths away. One, the largest left of the bunch, squawked at the others, gesturing behind them. Dozens of ruvaki bodies, slashed to ribbons by Justice, marked the path of his frantic, fighting retreat. Another argued with the first, pointing towards Mevon—highlighting his weakened state, no doubt—but the first ruvak seemed disinterested in testing him.

Unsure if he was grateful or not, Mevon stood his ground as they turned their backs and ran. Less in flight, perhaps, than it was in search of easier prey. He gave only the barest thought towards giving chase.

All he could think about was the possibility that those he'd already slain might have something on them he could eat.

Mevon spent the next several marks rummaging through the pockets of warm corpses, finding more than a few still breathing: further evidence of his weakened state that he'd been unable to do more than wound. He left them, not knowing if it was mercy or not to let them bleed out. What he did know was that he didn't have the energy to finish them off.

He gathered several armloads of a bread-like substance, tasteless and crumbly. After the first bite, it seemed the most delicious thing in the world. He washed it down with a borrowed canteen, secured two more, and thrust as much of the bread-stuff into his pockets as would fit.

Then, finally, he took stock of the situation.

The clank of metal, screams and shrieks of the dying on both sides, and rattling thumps that could only be conjured by sorcerous sources indicated the direction of battle. West. He'd fallen behind the ruvak, then. Those that attacked him must have broken off from the rear of their formation after seeing his crashing descent.

He had a choice to make, then: return to the battle, or search for the five pilots and four other Hardohl who had joined him in the fateful aerial assault.

Mevon closed his eyes, sighing as he realized the only logical course of action.

Even if I could find them in a timely manner, there's no guarantee they survived the crash, or the attack that likely came after. And there's not much I could do for them in any case.

Feeling revitalized, somewhat, by the food and water filling his stomach, Mevon took off west in a run. He found seven human bodies along the way, two of them his peers, which helped justify his decision.

What it didn't do was temper his rage.

"**F**unny you should mention doubt," Vashodia said. "It is, after all, one of the more powerful tools at my disposal."

"To you, *everything* is a tool," Draevenus replied.

"You say that like it's a bad thing."

"Only the blind could think it's not."

"There you go attempting wisdom again. Like a marmot struggling to escape once clutched in an osprey's talons—a valiant effort, yet, ultimately, a bit sad to watch."

"Don't speak to me of sad. Tell me one person in this world who would call you friend. One person who, without threat or promise of favors, would do *the smallest thing* for you. Tell me that, and you can call me 'sad' all you want."

Vashodia glowered. "Friends are a weakness those in power cannot afford."

"What about love?"

"Love?" She shook her head. "Love is a tool, as well. When harnessed correctly, it can be even more powerful than doubt. More powerful . . . than *anything*."

"How can you possibly use what you don't understand?"

"I can understand perfectly the way magma flows beneath this world's pathetically thin crust. That doesn't mean I'm foolish enough to let it touch me."

"Not everything can be mastered through observation alone, Vash. Sometimes you have to dive in, headfirst, before you can truly see what something is all about."

"Are we still talking about me? According to

my . . . observation . . . that statement sounded a bit too personal."

Draevenus shrugged. "What does it matter? You'll either have your way . . . or have a fit. Just like the child you appear to be. The only difference is when *you* throw a tantrum, every mother in the world hears the screams."

Mevon screamed in fury as he chopped his way through the ruvaki lines, the storm unleashed in full. Bodies pressed close on all sides, shrieking in counterpoint. All fell as quickly as they came in range of his blades, spinning without end, without mercy. Orange blood filled his sight, misting in the air, splashing across his face, weeping from wounds in waxy flesh that gaped open everywhere he looked.

Justice . . . delivered.

He didn't bother trying to count the corpses he created. He was too busy making more.

"*Is this all you have!*"

Chop, twirl, slash.

"*You come to our world—*"

Step, twist, stab.

"*—you place your cowardly blades upon the necks of our children—*"

Sweep, crush, parry, sever.

"*—invoking the wrath of this world's defenders—*"

Batter, break, eviscerate.

"—and this *is* the best you've got!"

Kill.

Kill!

KILL!

Tides of blood flowed and Mevon allowed himself to be carried away, swimming with the currents ever deeper into rage. No part of him wanted to return to the surface. The quiet voice in his mind, which normally sang of sanity, called out encouragement along with all the rest.

He saw no need to disappoint.

"Mevon."

The voice, soft yet firm, began sweeping away the haze consuming him. He looked about him, seeking more ruvak to kill. Froth flew from his lips as he found none in range.

"Deep breaths."

The dappled surface seemed just above him. Mevon, regretfully, obeyed, filling his lungs with copper-tinged air.

Things quickly came back into focus.

But chaos still surrounded him on all sides.

"Are we winning?" Mevon asked.

Ilyem, standing close—but well out of blade's reach—shook her head. "Many of their skyships crashed into our lines, forcing us to disperse in order to mitigate the damage. When their ground troops arrived, we were in disarray. We've lost half our troops already and barely bloodied their nose."

Mevon blinked, shedding orange blood from his eyelashes. He spun his focus outward and could see the truth of her words clear enough. Decimated Sceptrine troops and Imperial Guard staggered backwards in ragged retreat. The other Hardohl bought them precious beats in which to drag free their wounded before themselves dashing back to avoid the surging enemy onslaught. The remaining allied skyships traded spats of sorcerous energy with the far more numerous enemy vessels above them.

Defeat seemed but a breath away.

Unacceptable.

"What do we need to do?" he asked. "How can we turn this battle around in our favor?"

"Ask the gods," Ilyem said. "They're the only ones that can help us now."

She jogged off, and Mevon followed, nearly replying that the gods were dead.

Which, he soon realized, was likely her point.

They joined the retreat, marching within a moving bubble of serenity beset on all sides by savagery. None challenged them directly. Confused, Mevon peered behind him and quickly saw why. The trail of destruction he'd left behind split the enemy formation like a scar, each ragged seam a ruvaki body ravaged beyond recognition. For all that the images of his attack seemed ripe within his foes' minds, Mevon recalled only flashes.

He didn't know who held the most fear of him: the ruvak . . .

. . . or himself.

He surveyed the situation, reading the outcome as if it were already carved into stone, and knew that nothing short of a miracle would see them through the next dawn.

"When we fall," Mevon said, "it *will not be* from a blow to the back."

Ilyem pondered his statement for three beats in silence. Then, without a word, she lifted her weapon, spun, and pointed a blade back towards the enemy.

The Hardohl responded immediately, with the Imperial Guard following soon after. The Sceptrines were slower to catch on, but he saw Prince Daye waving his greatsword and heard him shout, "We hold here, my brothers! We hold here!"

The rout reversed in moments, and Mevon swelled with pride that at the side of such souls he had the privilege of waging righteous battle.

Even if it would be his last.

"I never did ask," Mevon said, "but what did you name your *Andun?*"

"That's a bit personal, don't you think?" Ilyem said.

"Yes."

She smiled. Fully. The first time he'd ever seen her do so.

"I call it Balance. And you?"

Mevon returned the smile. "Justice."

"A good name."

"As is yours."

He faced the ruvak, the once-empty sphere around him collapsing as their own momentum drove them inexorably closer. A change he welcomed.

Ilyem hoisted Balance. "It will be a pleasure, Mevon, to die at your side."

"Likewise," Mevon replied. "What do you say to taking as many of these rabid bastards down with us as we can?"

"For the sake of our blades?"

"For the sake of our blades."

Summoning the storm, Mevon led the charge.

The night wore on, every beat drowned in untold oceans of bloodshed. The human defenders engaged their enemy in a manner that left no room for retreat, matching them in savagery even as they managed to hold off their inevitable defeat for just one more mark. Then another. And another.

But no amount of valor could account for the disparity in numbers. Though the greatest warriors any world would ever see fought on, even they knew that their limbs would grow weak long before they'd run out of foes at which to swing. But fight on they did. And even if they knew they couldn't win, they were giving the ruvak a fight to remember. A fight that would open their eyes.

With their numbers dwindling, and energy all but spent, the human defenders soon saw something that none of them had ever expected to see again. The eastern sky had lightened, and the first sliver of sunlight rose over distant mountains, nearly blinding them with sudden, burning brilliance.

They'd made through to the dawn.

Though it had no real reason to, this fact filled each of them with unmitigated hope.

A hope that only grew as they saw what else the new day had brought.

A line of dark spots darkened the face of dawn. The spots became spheres, then hazy figures, then individuals hundreds and thousands strong.

Valynkar and mierothi, approaching in battle formation.

And at their center, outpacing them all, came a single woman; the only one among them who did not fly on wings.

Darkness and light in equal measure crackled outwards from them all, batting down the ruvaki skyships like flies and crashing through their infantry in waves of ice and fire. Half their remaining troops were engulfed in less than a mark. The rest, sensing their doom, gave up the fight and fled.

But not very far.

Killing magic rained down everywhere they went. The same plain that made protecting the refugees a suicidal task provided no cover for the fleeing ruvak.

Some, through sheer numbers alone, managed to escape the initial barrage, but the floating figures broke ranks and scattered, diving in every direction to begin their hunt.

All of them . . . but one.

A small metal platform descended into the space recently vacated by those that would have been Mevon's end. Glorious though it may have been, he would trade it for this gladly.

Jasside leapt from her ride, lips parted ever-so-slightly, brown eyes wide and fixed on him. Blond hair fell past her waist in a braid, shimmering in the same sunlight that framed her face from behind like a portrait.

Exhaustion forgotten, Mevon dropped Justice and took a tenuous step forward, wiping away the blood half-moist, half-crusting upon his face. He was still unable to think of anything to say, so instead . . . he smiled.

Blessedly, Jasside smiled back.

"Hello," she said.

Mevon's heart skipped at the sound. "Hello."

Without another word—for indeed, no words seemed worthy enough to express what he felt—they rushed into each other's arms, both gasping as they pressed their lips together for the very first time.

"**T**here's . . . one more thing, sister."

"Done with your pointless bickering so soon?"

"You must promise me—promise me!—that you'll pass this information along to our allies. Can I trust you to do that?"

"How could you not?"

"No more games. This is too important."

"Oh, very well. I *promise*. What's the big news, then?"

"It's about the ruvak themselves. I found out—" he swallowed "—I found out where they came from. Why they're here."

"Did you now?"

"Yes."

"Well, don't keep a girl in suspense. Out with it!"

"They came from *here*, Vash. This was their world once, until Ruul and Elos took it from them. And now . . . they want it *back*."

PART III

CHAPTER 13

The combination of rain and wind was enough to make any stretch of exposed skin turn blue in marks. Yandumar, however, felt none of it. Orbrahn maintained a shield of some kind around the welcoming party, keeping them all dry and warm despite the deep hold of autumn in these foreign, forsaken mountains. A place that would soon be sanctuary to the tens of millions who had survived the exodus.

Never thought I'd see the day the mierothi, of all people, would be who humanity turned to in its most desperate toll.

It had been a skeleton crew that greeted him when the armies of the Veiled Empire first arrived a month ago: a few pregnant mierothi and their husbands, a hundred or so daeloth who were too old or too young to participate in the fighting, and the scant number of humans from the surrounding nations enterprising enough—and brave enough—to set up trade posts among their new neighbors.

His troops and engineers had kept busy in the meantime, but the nebulous shapes pushing closer through the clouds promised to make it a whole lot more hectic very, very soon.

"Light the beacon, Orbrahn," he said. "Wouldn't want 'em getting lost."

"I don't know about *light*, old man," Orbrahn said, "but I can certainly ignite it."

The boy lifted an arm. A pillar of blue flame five paces wide jetted towards the sky, visible even through the thickest thunderhead. Within moments, bright spots appeared on the horizon, separating from the lumbering hulks now dipping low through the murk. Foremost among them, a figure whom Yandumar recognized by his wrapping of golden light.

Three marks later, Gilshamed touched down gently before him. At his side, a woman whose wings were wreathed in violet.

"Yandumar," Gilshamed said, as both valynkar dismissed their wings. "Old friend."

The last two words almost sounded like a question.

Gilshamed turned to the woman. "Let me introduce—"

"No need," Yandumar said. "I've heard enough of your stories to know exactly who this lovely lady is."

She whispered in Gilshamed's ear, to which he

nodded in response, then she stuck out a hand as if to shake.

"Abyss take me," Yandumar said. "I'll have none of *that*."

He lunged forward, closing the gap in an eye-blink, and wrapped an arm around both of their waists, lifting them off the ground in his embrace. Though neither lacked in height, and his arms weren't as strong as they used to be, he wasn't going to let such trivial facts stop him from showing them his enthusiasm.

Yandumar set them down after a twirl or two. Lashriel tittered melodically. Gilshamed, though looking chagrined at so public a display, still couldn't help but show the ghost of a smile.

"Ah, Lashriel," Yandumar said with a sigh. "It's good to finally meet you."

"Likewise, Yandumar," she said. "Gil has told me so much about you."

"Not *too* much I hope."

"Oh, he has been very thorough. Telling *his* side, anyway. If you have some time, I would love to hear yours."

"Ha! He'd never forgive me if I told you the half of it!"

"Nonsense," Gilshamed said, very quietly, very seriously. "There is nothing you could ever do that I would not absolve."

Yandumar shrugged. "I could probably think of a few things."

"Such as?"

"Trying to steal Lashriel away from you, for one. And if I weren't so old . . . and so smelly . . . and so *married* . . . I might even have a chance!"

Seemingly against his will, Gilshamed chortled loudly. All sense of decorum he might have held on to instead slipped away upon that mirthful outburst.

Yandumar smiled. "It's good to see you again, old friend, despite the circumstances. You look like a new man."

Gilshamed nodded. "I certainly feel as such."

Leaning in close next to Lashriel, Yandumar whispered, though loudly enough for Gilshamed to hear, "Don't tell him I said this, but I'm pretty sure he has you to thank for the change."

Smiling, she "whispered" back, "My lips are sealed."

Gilshamed turned away, a conflicted look on his face. Utter joy warring with . . . something. Yandumar couldn't tell.

At least the madness is gone. And for good, this time, it seems. A new man indeed. I just need a mark to figure out how much has changed. To find out what's taken the place of the you you've left behind.

"Come along, then," Yandumar said. "I'm sure you'll be wanting to survey the place. It ain't much, but for the foreseeable future, it's home."

He led them down from the raised area, a kind

of platform overlooking the cleared and leveled fields sloping down in terraces to the valley below. Before departing, he looked toward the horizon one last time. His breath caught as he saw the first of the airborne vessels descend fully out of the clouds. It was soon joined by many others, including the countless figures marching into view through the passes on the valley's opposite side.

Exodus approached its end. He prayed exile would prove less deadly.

"What is *that*?" Lashriel asked.

Yandumar turned back to the paired valynkar, finding the prettier one pointing toward the center of the bowl where the mierothi had erected their dwellings.

"That," Yandumar said, nodding at the obelisk in question, "is a voltensus."

"A what?"

"A mierothi construct, my love," Gilshamed said. "In the empire, they used them to detect all uses of sorcery."

"Why would they need one here?"

"You haven't heard?" Yandumar said.

Both of his guests shook their heads.

"Well, according to our mierothi allies, the things have another purpose. One that Ruul hid within their function from the very beginning, even though it was utterly useless until now."

Gilshamed flared his eyes. "You cannot mean—"

"It's designed to keep out the ruvak? Aye, it is. Their skyships, anyway, and anything else of theirs powered by magic. Though gods alone know how."

"Gods . . . and Vashodia."

Yandumar grunted. "As if she sees any difference between 'em."

"I do not know if I would say that. After all, Vashodia is still alive."

"Ha!"

Yandumar continued the tour, circumventing the outskirts of the mierothi town. It was on a hill, relatively the highest point around, and from there they could see a good bit of the land protected under the new voltensus. Though he'd heard it said that the thing's range extended far past the horizon, covering most of Weskara as well as large chunks of Sceptre to the north and Fasheshe to the east, they'd set up their initial defenses well within sight.

Layers and layers of barricades, fortified fighting positions, and staked trenches encompassed a perimeter a dozen leagues long. The outer perimeter—none of it visible from here—was similarly constructed, only many, many times longer. Idrus was even now inspecting the work of the imperial engineers, inserting a soldier's perspective in order to improve them. Though the defenses had been the most crucial, time-consuming project, occupying the land closer to the summit they now walked was everything else that would be needed for what Yandumar had no doubt would be a long, bitter siege.

Cleared areas for tents, hasty dwellings, and land set aside for planting filled the rest of the available space. Even if they'd had another year to prepare, it still would have been cramped. Though the area they hoped to protect was quite large, much of it was occupied by sharp mountains and dense forests. There was simply no way, in such limited terrain, to protect an entire continent's worth of people—what remained of them, anyway—without them all bumping noses now and then.

Even so, their meagre preparations would be better than leaving them to the ruvak. Yandumar almost couldn't wait for the enemy to test them.

I and my swords would like a word with you bastards.

His companions took in the view in silence. Lashriel he didn't know well enough to properly judge her reaction, but she seemed encouraged by all he told them. Yandumar had a hard time imagining what it must have been like on that long road. A place to rest must seem like quite the gift.

But it was Gilshamed he had the hardest time trying to read. So much of his old friend had changed since their last meeting. The madness was gone, much of it replaced, he now saw, with joy, centered around the woman at his side. A woman he clung to with desperation.

It was subtle at first, but the more Yandumar explained of their preparations, the more obvious it became. Gilshamed, he knew, did not see the mighty defenses, nor imagine how effective they would be in keeping those within them safe.

The man saw only a trap.

The frequent glances flickering between his mate and the horizon, which Yandumar had dismissed, took on a different, more sinister meaning then.

Gilshamed was searching for a way to escape.

Despite the fact that it chilled him to see—or maybe even because of it—Yandumar understood. He knew what it was like to lose the only thing you desired; knew it sharper, and deeper than he cared to admit out loud. After struggling for so long, and finally attaining it, the thought of putting it at even the slimmest bit of risk was nearly unfathomable.

But men like us can't always afford the luxury of peace. Not when the peace of so many others rides on our shoulders.

"Bah!" Yandumar said. "Enough with this boring business. I could show you the other half, but it's just more of the same in a different direction." He smiled deviously. "You heard about what happened with my son?"

Gilshamed arched an eyebrow. "If I recall correctly, he and his troops were nearly overrun, until timely reinforced by Jasside."

"*Timely reinforced?* Ha! She pulled his ass right out of the fire!"

Lashriel laughed, and even Gilshamed managed to quirk a smile.

"Weren't you worried about your son, though?" she said.

"Aye. A father always worries. Doesn't matter if they're five or thirty-five, pretending with sticks . . . or *not* pretending, and using swords. At some point, you gotta let 'em go and live their own life. Eventually you learn that the only way to keep the things you love out of danger is to put them in a cage."

"Wise words," Lashriel said. She glanced up at her mate, rubbing a hand along his back. "Isn't that right, Gil?"

Gilshamed frowned, then shrugged, as if caught off guard. "I . . . suppose so."

Yandumar chuckled. "I blame age and my new title for that. Being emperor means I've got too much time to think."

"Gil told me some of what transpired while I was . . . asleep. Was there much trouble ascending to a position so long held by one so foul?"

"Aye. But it was mostly of my own doing."

"Please, you simply *must* elaborate."

"Well, for one, I didn't want to take the abyss-taken throne to begin with. Thank God wiser minds showed me how devastating that would have been. Rekaj's death left a void of power, and if *someone* hadn't filled it in, well, there was no lack of greedy souls who would have snatched up whatever control they could get their hands on. The revolution would have looked like a skirmish next to the bloodbath that would have followed. I was just the unlucky bastard the task happened to fall to."

"It doesn't sound like luck to me."

"What *does* it sound like, then?"

Lashriel smiled. "It sounds like that throne found the right man to fill it. A good man. A man willing to do the right thing even though it's difficult. Even though he just wants to be left in peace."

Yandumar returned the smile, gratefully inclining his head towards her. He realized, of course, that the words were meant as much for Gilshamed as they were for him. He didn't mind, though. *I've no doubt she can do a better job of reaching the man than me.*

"All right, you two, off with ya now. We've plenty to do to get all these people settled. I won't let it be said that Emperor Yandumar the Stubborn wasted time with talk when there was work to be done!"

The pair turned, unfurling their wings, and waved goodbye—if only for now—as they flew off to begin directing the incoming refugees. Gilshamed remained quiet, contemplative, but the look on his face told Yandumar the man had at last shed his shroud of doubt.

". . . **a**nd for the sake of all sanity, put the Tristelkians and Kaunese on *opposite* sides of the camp,"

Arivana said. "If that strutting peacock Prince Galhud so much as *looks* at the premier's daughters again, someone—and I think you can guess who—is going to get their face torn off."

Claris did little to hide her amusement as she wrote another note in her ledger. "I'll see to it immediately. Is there anything else?"

Arivana sighed, running through the day's tasks in her mind. Finding a place for everyone should have been a straightforward affair, if not exactly simple due to the sheer number of people involved. But the egos of the affluent never failed to complicate matters, and the promise of respite from the endless, desperate flight meant that most now had the chance to rekindle old concerns and old rivalries.

Old assery, is more like it.

She was astounded at how quickly pettiness took hold once the threat of death no longer loomed quite so large in everyone's mind. Only the Fasheshish had proven easy to accommodate. Most of their soldiers and civilians had jumped at the chance to roost near the southeastern fortifications, which were still technically within the borders of their country. If they were going to shed blood in defense of a land, it might as well be their own.

Everyone else was a headache.

"No," Arivana said at last. "That will be all. Please send Richlen in on your way out."

Claris bowed. "As you wish, Your Majesty."

As she turned to go, Arivana stood up from the rickety wooden chair that acted as her throne. "Aunt Claris?"

The woman froze, sniffing loudly in surprise. It had been a long time since Arivana had used such a familiar term of address.

"Yes, Your Majesty?"

"I just wanted to thank you, for your loyalty and your service. Countless lives are made better by your efforts every day. My own included."

Claris's face became stoic, unreadable. "You are welcome," she said in a tightly controlled voice.

"And whenever we're in private, I wouldn't mind at all if you started calling me Arivana again. If you'd like, that is."

For a long moment, Claris did not respond, her face becoming even more stone-like with every passing breath. Arivana almost wondered if she had erred.

A tear broke free of one eyelid, and the woman said in a small, quavering voice, "I would like that very much."

Though she now realized it had been building for some time within her mind, the decision had been made on a whim. Which meant Arivana was not prepared for the emotions that welled within her.

"I'm glad," Arivana said, choking over the words. "But please, go. Before we both become useless for the rest of the day."

Claris nodded, drying her eyes, and pushed out of

the tent without another word. The soft padding of her feet had barely faded before heavy footsteps approached. Richlen flipped aside the innermost flap and stopped after a pace, raising an eyebrow.

"You called for me, Your Majesty?"

"Have you acquired the things I asked you for?"

"Yes, but—"

"Are they with you?"

Sighing, he nodded.

"Let's see them, then."

He reached beneath his polished breastplate and retrieved two cloth bundles, tossing one to her. Arivana caught it and immediately pulled loose the knot of cord binding it together. A tattered, dun-colored cloak, much like one any peasant would wear, unfolded before her. A larger cousin of the garment she held dangled a moment later from Richlen's arm.

"You will take me now," Arivana said. She flipped the cloak around her shoulders and pulled the hood low over her head.

"For the record," Richlen said, "I'm against this."

"Duly noted. Now get ready before I change my mind."

If the choice to rekindle familiarity with Claris had been a surprise, this decision was anything but. It had been clawing away at her mind relentlessly, ever since she heard the . . . announcement.

He donned his own disguise, then stepped past

her to the back of the tent. He pushed aside a chest and began unraveling the ropes that tied closed a section of the canvas wall. Once undone, he lifted the now-loose square, admitting a burst of cold wind and daylight.

"Wait here a moment," he said.

He ducked through and disappeared. Arivana edged closer, just able to make out an exchange of whispered words. Footsteps drifted away. Twelve beats later, Richlen's hand appeared, beckoning her with urgency.

She lowered herself and stepped through the makeshift escape portal. Richlen stood alone.

"I sent off the guardsman stationed to this post," he said. "A good lad. Trusts me and knows how to keep his mouth shut. Though, to be honest, I'm not sure why we need to keep this a secret in the first place."

Arivana strode away purposefully, giving him no chance to but to follow. She waited until they'd cleared the tangled maze that was the official Panisian encampment—a task taking nearly a quarter toll—before answering.

"The situation," she said at last, "is volatile."

"I understand that," he said.

"Do you? Tell me, then: what was your first feeling upon hearing Vashodia's announcement?"

He trekked at her side quietly for a time. "Anger," he said.

"And did your fellow guardsmen react the same way?"

"Some did."

"But not all?"

"No."

"A varied response, even among those coming from a similar place. Have you wondered what others might feel who hail from different walks of life? Different countries? Different *species*?"

"I . . . can't imagine."

"Few can. Which is why I need to avoid rumors at any cost. I've no way to predict what shape they might take. No idea how much damage they might cause."

Richlen nodded. "I think I get it now, Your Maj—"

Arivana cleared her throat loudly before he could finish, giving him a pointed look.

He cringed. "Sorry."

She subdued a flash of anger at his lapse, instead gifting him a smile. "It's all right. Just try to remember we're being inconspicuous, hmm?"

Red dappling his cheeks, Richlen nodded. "I'll do better. I promise." After a beat he said, "If you don't mind me asking, what did *you* feel when we all heard the news?"

Arivana lowered her head out of reflex, fighting the pressure that began building behind her eyes.

"Sorrow."

He said nothing after that, leading her on to their

destination as her eyes made a study of the ground before her feet and her mind wandered paths best left unexplored. After time indeterminate, a gentle hand on her shoulder brought her to a stop.

"We're here," he said.

Arivana lifted her gaze at last. A tent sat in the shadow of a nearby cleft of rock. It was perhaps ten paces wide, crude if sturdy, and encircled by half a dozen men dressed in rough-spun wool, each going about seemingly innocuous tasks. She narrowed her eyes and was able, after a moment of scrutiny, to gain the impression of weapons hidden beneath their loose, deceptively shabby attire.

Her heart stammered in protest to what she was about to do.

One of the men set down the axe he was using to chop wood and walked over to them. "Can I help you folks?" he said.

"You can indeed," Arivana said, adding softly, "Warden."

The man flinched, then leaned forward to look inside her hood. His eyes flared a moment later, and he began bending one knee.

Richlen grabbed his shoulder, preventing the man from completing his bow. "Now, old friend, no need for that." He began leading the man off. "Is that stew I smell? Abyss take me, I could use a bowl about now."

Arivana looked past them. The other five had tensed as they studied the scene unfolding. The warden, whose shoulders were now in Richlen's firm—if friendly—grip, waved towards his fellows in a gesture she hoped meant for them to remain calm. Firming up her spine with confidence she didn't feel, Arivana marched up to the tent's entrance, more than half expecting to be challenged. When none came, she stepped through the flap.

Filling all the space inside was a cage.

In one corner lay a cot covered in cotton blankets, while another held a pair of washbasins and a chest of clothes. A stool rested in the cage's center, mounted by a figure who held a book in one hand and a small lightglobe in the other, inhuman eyes peering curiously over the leather-bound cover.

Arivana flipped back her hood, swallowing the lump in her throat. "Hello, Flumere."

The ruvak woman dropped both book and lightglobe, her surprise punctuated by twin thumps. She drew her arms inward, as if hugging herself, and lowered her eyes to the floor. "I . . . don't deserve that name," she said. "Not anymore."

"Sem Aira, then. Believe me, I didn't come here to argue semantics."

"You don't understand my people at all if you think there isn't more to a name than that."

"You're right, of course. I don't know much of *anything* about your kind. I did, however, learn one rather important piece of information recently. I was hoping to talk to you about it."

"Talk about what?"

"This world," Arivana said. "Specifically, that it once belonged to you."

Sem Aira's deep-set eyes widened in all-too-human an expression. "How did you . . . ?"

"It doesn't matter. I need to know if it is true."

"Of course it's true. Do you think we'd invade an occupied planet for no reason? We're not monsters!"

"You're not *human*, you mean."

The ruvak hung her head again. "Those . . . are not my words."

"But you meant it all the same."

Sem Aira said nothing.

"Look, I cannot claim to understand what transpired between our peoples in a past so distant as to be unfathomable. But is not that very gap of time reason enough to render the conflict between us meaningless?"

"Meaningless? My people wandered the void for fifteen *thousand* years! We rode the brink of extinction more times than our own histories could count. Don't you dare—" She stopped herself, breath warbling in her throat. "My apologies, Your Majesty. I have no right to speak to you so harshly."

"Why not?"

"I . . . do not know how to answer that."

"Because to do so would reveal too much about your people?"

Sem Aira shook her head. "Because I don't understand how you can stand there without wanting to rip out my throat. Not after what I did to you."

Arivana felt a tremble coming on, a wave of old hurts she'd just barely managed to keep at bay. She shook herself forcefully, sucking down a breath, and locked her eyes on her former handmaiden once more. "You were just accomplishing your mission."

"I did far more than was necessary. I only needed to place myself next to someone in power, close enough to affect events towards disorder. I didn't need to earn your trust. I didn't need to become your friend."

"But you did," Arivana said in a small, broken voice. "And I have no idea why."

Sem Aira closed both mouth and eyes, spinning on her stool until showing only her back. She didn't look like she would be moved anytime soon.

Arivana clenched her hands at her sides in frustration; not at Sem Aira, but at her own ineptitude in bridging the gap between them, her own failure to understand what once had been, and why she longed so desperately to get it back.

At least we're talking again. That's something . . . right?

She turned to leave, then looked back over her shoulder. "Until next time, Flumere."

The figure on the stool flinched.

Clapping both hands along her thighs to banish the dust that had gathered on her dark leather leggings,

Jasside settled her platform down near Mevon. The lumbering train of refugees stretched out before him into the distance while he marched behind alone, as if he were their sole guardian. The massive warrior turned up his gaze at her descent, his normally chiseled features overcome with an unfettered expression of joy . . . a look marred only by the faintest hint of disbelief.

A feeling that mirrored her own.

It's hard for me to believe it, too. That we're both alive. That we found each other. That after all this time, all this change, we're still enough of who we were to be enough for each other.

But we're here now, and I wouldn't trade that for anything.

"Back so soon?" Mevon said. "I expected you'd be gone all morning."

Jasside shrugged. "I saw an opportunity and took it. And a good thing I did. We won't have to worry about that ruvaki skyship tailing us anymore."

"You took care of it by yourself? I thought their vessels couldn't be defeated by only a single source of power. Weren't you waiting for reinforcements from the valynkar?"

"I got impatient." Jasside pointed behind her. "You see that hill over there?"

He gazed in the direction she was indicating. Faded mountains made a jagged edge of the horizon, but the grasslands between were as flat as a pan. Mevon furrowed his brow.

"All I see," he said, "is a cloud of dust."

"Exactly. It doesn't much matter which way they're attuned when a thousand tons of stone and soil comes crashing down on their head."

Mevon laughed. "That will do it, all right. It looks like the tales don't do you justice."

"What tales?"

"If the rumors are to be believed, you've become at least twice as ferocious since last we were together. From what I've seen so far, they don't tell the half of it."

"That's not a hint of disappointment I hear in your voice, is it?"

"Absolutely not." Mevon smiled. "I wouldn't have it any other way."

She smiled back, hopping down to land gently at his side. He reached towards her, but she held up one hand, palm forward to halt him, and proceeded to guide her platform up and forward with the other. A dozen beats later, it rested upon the deck of the nearest allied skyship.

Turning back to face him, she saw his outstretched arm still spanning most of the space between them, leaving that last slim gap to be crossed in her own way, her own time. Palm upturned, his hand waited, patient and gentle, as if content to remain in place until the all the stars in the void burnt out; yet held firmly all the same, ready to vanquish any who dared try to keep them apart.

In that simplest of gestures, Jasside read a promise of things to come.

She reached with both hands and grasped it.

Their skin touched and she gasped, her power gone in an instant. She could still sense that ocean of eternal darkness, but it was as if she were straining over the side of a boat to dip her fingers in a surface just out of reach, longing to swim in it, shape it once more.

It also brought back memories.

Her mind swarmed with images from their days fighting for the revolution. Their practice sessions where she used her special weave of energy on him, cutting through his nullifying defenses and rendering him helpless. The day that he'd finally gathered enough strength to push off the ground, straining with monumental effort. Touching her to end all games between them for good.

The day she'd finally started to forgive him for the death of her half brother.

"I'll have to get used to this again," Jasside said.

Mevon raised an eyebrow. "Perhaps there's a way to make the transition less unpleasant?"

"What did you have in mind?"

He slid the hand she held up her arm, across her shoulder, then behind her neck. The other wrapped around her back. Both pulled, bringing her upwards to press against his unyielding chest as he bent his face down. She closed her eyes, lifting her chin.

Their lips met, pressing and shifting urgently. Hot breath mixed with her own, smelling of dried meat that seemed to her, in that moment, the sweetest scent in the world. A different kind of energy coursed through her, awakening every nerve.

I'll have to get used to this, as well.

Jasside pulled away suddenly, breathless and smiling. Though she wanted nothing more than to fold up into his arms and kiss the day away, they weren't out of danger yet.

"We should get moving," she said. "But keep that little trick handy. It will do wonders for those awful times we're *forced* to come in contact."

Mevon chuckled. "As my lady commands."

She laughed along with him, punching his shoulder as they turned, arm-in-arm, and began marching forward once more. "It's good to see that you've developed a sense of humor in the time we've been apart," she said.

He shook his head. "I've always had one, I think. It's just that now, with you, I don't always feel the need to hide it."

"Don't overdo it," she said behind a wry grin. "You wouldn't want me calling your sincerity into question, now, would you?"

He stiffened beside her. "I never want to give you

reason to doubt me, Jasside." He sighed, head drooping. "I'm just not sure if I know how."

She looked up at him, pouring compassion into her gaze. "Oh, Mevon, you must know I wasn't being serious. Please, forgive me."

"There's nothing to forgive. And besides, the point still stands. When it comes to relationships, I don't have the first clue what I'm doing. I'm afraid I'll disappoint you."

"Really? Because to me, it looks like you're doing just fine so far."

"How so?"

"For one, you're being honest."

He bent a quizzical gaze at her. "Is . . . there any other way?"

She leaned her head on his arm, chuckling under her breath. "You'd be surprised."

Mevon grunted.

"And," Jasside said, continuing her earlier statement, "there's another thing I think you're doing right."

"Which is?"

"Choice, Mevon. Whatever it was that made you leave everyone behind—"

"I didn't—"

"You can tell me the story later, when you're good and ready. As much or as little as you see fit to share. I wasn't trying to berate you for what you did. I was merely trying to point out that, through all of it, you still chose me."

He nodded. "And you chose me."

"I did. I *do*. So long as we both continue to choose each other every day, nothing in this or any other world can pull us apart."

"You make it sound so easy."

"It may very well be the most difficult thing in the world." She smiled up at him. "Feeling up to the challenge?"

Mevon smiled back. "Always."

"**J**ump!"

Tassariel didn't need to be told twice.

Following Draevenus's advice, she turned from her pursuers, who were scissoring towards her from three separate passages, and leapt through the quickly closing portal into open sky. She unfurled her wings, their glow nearly invisible under a three-way assault of sunlight: the harsh midday sun overhead, the shimmering glare from the sea a thousand paces below, and the reflection from the multifaceted surface of the ruvaki skyship, its hull studded with countless sparkling minerals. Emerging from the dark corridors into such an environment, she was all but blinded.

"Gah!"

She spied Draevenus less than ten paces away, just below her but getting farther away by the beat. His palms were pressed against his eye sockets as he tumbled through the air. If the sudden infusion of light affected *her* this much, she couldn't imagine what it was doing to *him*.

"Wings!" she called, hoping her voice could cut through the whistling wind. *You'd think that after more than half a year, he'd develop an instinct for the things.* "Don't forget about your wings!"

The words must have gotten through, for a moment later he arched his back, dark shapes emerging like a splash of black water. Wings spreading, he righted himself and halted his descent, coming abreast of her.

"Thanks," he said. "What now?"

"What now? This was *your* plan!"

"I know. But I can barely see. I think we may have to improvise from here on out."

"And by 'we' you mean 'me,' right?"

Draevenus at least possessed grace enough to grimace.

Tassariel groaned. "All right. Just find a place to hide. I'll keep them occupied until you've recovered enough of your sight to be useful."

"We're a thousand paces above the sea. Where the abyss am I going to hide?"

"Here." She reached out and grabbed his hand. "I'll show you."

Flying in connection with another was never an easy proposition, and it wasn't helped by the fact that he couldn't anticipate her motions. After a few beats, however, he relaxed, allowing her to guide him.

If she hadn't exactly been the star pupil she knew he'd hoped for, there was no shortage of familiarity between them now, the ease and comfort found in tandem actions, a trust that grew deeper by the day.

I'd almost call it . . . intimacy.

Her breath caught, palms growing slick with sweat at the thought.

She heard Draevenus sigh in relief as they fell under the massive vessel's shadow, cutting out at least two of the three sources of light. Guiding him up under its belly, she found a crevice just large enough to hold him and shoved him inside.

"Wait here," she ordered.

"Are you sure you'll be all right?" he said.

Tassariel grunted laughter. "This will be just like playing Serpent back home."

"Playing *what?*"

"A game favored by valynkar youths." She smiled. "A game I *never* lost."

Sighing, he nodded. "Be careful." His eyes darted to one side, then quickly to the other. "They're coming."

Tassariel pushed away, banking back into the light as eleven ruvaki skyships swarmed into view. Though barely larger than a covered wagon, the escort vessels for the flagship above more than made up for their diminutive stature with their speed and maneuverability.

Let's see if you can keep up with me.

She dove straight down, leading them away from her companion's hiding place, then swooped upwards in a broad, predictable arc. She didn't look behind her. Doing so would only distract her, and was pointless besides. Her first glance at them confirmed they'd already encompassed themselves in their signature muted glow. She knew they wouldn't be where they appeared.

A strange rasping sensation pulled at her mind. She jerked to one side. A moment later, a greenish beam, warping the very air, passed through the space she'd just vacated.

She felt two more gathering their chaotic energy. Energizing, she expelled a burst of power in front of her, propelling herself backwards ten paces instantaneously and dodging the new attacks with ease.

The others readied their assaults, noses pointed every direction to diminish her chances of evading. Before they could get their barrage off, however, Tassariel curled around the top of the flagship's hull with speed they could not match, obstructing their angle. Moments later, she sensed only half still behind her in pursuit. The rest had dipped under the hulking sky-ship, approaching now from the front.

Perfect.

Aided by three already glaring sources, Tassariel filled the surrounding sky with light.

The panic of those piloting the enemy vessels was almost palpable, the air tensing as they fought through their sudden blindness in an attempt to escape. An impact concussed nearby, pulverized stone careening in all directions as two of them collided. The rest veered away, showing her their exposed, illuminated backs.

Tassariel pounced on the nearest one. Her left hand gripped the hull. The right pulled her mace, slamming it down, once, twice, thrice, finally breaking through the thin, rocky skin. Pushing into the hole she'd made, she opened up her palm, filling the interior of the skyship with fire.

She jumped free as the vessel died beneath her, falling a moment before crashing into the flagship just below.

There was little time to admire her handiwork; the rest of her opponents had flown out of her sphere of light and were now firing back into it. Blindly, but the volume and frequency of their assaults ensured they'd get lucky eventually. She was already cringing as chaos cut through her light, encroaching in around her.

Once more, she dove, close enough to the flagship's glittering hull to reach out and touch it if she chose. This time, all the remaining ruvaki escort ships followed. This time, it was exactly what she wanted.

I hope you're ready, Draevenus.

Tassariel eased off her speed, keeping herself just in her pursuers' sight. Angling upwards now, her dive became a swoop, passing back into the shadows beneath the massive vessel. Once directly beneath it, she dipped briefly, then bounced up, losing all velocity as she energized fully and turned to face her attackers.

"Now!" she shouted.

Brilliant rays licked outward from her hands, locking on to each of the eight skyships. Power held them, attuning them to light.

Darkness scythed through from above, unhindered.

One by one, the enemy vessels cracked apart before Draevenus's black, spinning razors. Incredibly, a lone skyship managed to escape the trap, veering away shakily from both sorcerous sources.

The mierothi swept out of the crevice, extending a hand. Dark lightning arced from his fingertips, encasing the skyship trying to get away. He turned his face to her. "Will you do the honors?"

Tassariel nodded, remolding her energy. "Gladly."

She thrust her palm forward. A scintillating orb shot forth. It hit the vulnerable vessel, which in turn exploded in a shower of scorched stone and metal.

Draevenus retrieved his hand, black wings flapping silently. "Well done," he said. "Ready for the big one?"

Tassariel tore her eyes away from the falling wreckage. "Absolutely."

They dove away from the flagship, distancing themselves by several hundred paces before spinning around and hovering. Draevenus began counting backwards from three.

Two days ago, they'd identified this skyship, the largest one for a thousand leagues around. They'd spent most of that time preparing a pair of devices, storing energy in them bit by agonizing bit in order to avoid detection.

As her companion uttered "one" they both raised their arms and directed a tiny amount of energy toward those devices, which they'd placed aboard the flagship during their insertion. Their power reached the devices, each pent up with hoards of energy, and instructed them to release it.

Twin concussions blasted the sky. The ruvaki skyship ripped apart between compounding exhalations of darkness and light. Debris fell, cracking apart like brittle stone as it tumbled down and splashed into the distant waves.

Draevenus turned to her, smiling. "Satisfied?"

Tassariel nodded.

"Good. Then would you mind telling me what this was all about?"

She jerked her head back, surprised by the bite in the question. "I don't know what you mean."

"Yes, you do. You seemed very keen to make this our next target, even though others might have made more sense."

She sighed. "Very well. I wanted it out of the way because it guarded the strait between Mataroa and

Yusan. I didn't want it pestering our back when we cross."

"Cross? Are you mad? We're already deep enough as it is. Yusan has been occupied from the very start of their . . . reclamation. It's their abyss-taken stronghold!"

"True. But how do you explain the fact that a resistance group has been operating freely within their borders this entire time?"

It was Draevenus's turn to look surprised. "That's . . . impossible."

She shook her head. "I confirmed it just last week."

"How?"

"Commune, of course. There are scores of casters on their central island, and as far as I can tell, they've yet to be captured. We're looking for ways to defeat the ruvak, right? That *has* to be worth investigating."

Draevenus took in a deep breath, exhaling slowly. "I can't argue with that." He chuckled in obvious disbelief. "I wonder who's mad enough to lead a resistance for this long."

Tassariel trembled, lowering her head. "My father."

CHAPTER 14

From the shadows, of course, Vashodia watched them gather.

All the pretty little figures milled about by the base of the voltensus, exchanging greetings with those they hadn't seen in weeks or months or years. Or ever. Whether it was Yandumar wrapping Jasside in a fatherly embrace, Gilshamed hesitantly shaking Mevon's hand, Chase whispering harshly to his brother Daye, mother dearest showing off her mewling babe to *anyone* nearby, or Arivana and her advisor introducing themselves to the royal couple of Weskara, every face remained plastered in smiles, every word and gesture molded to fit polite company. Each interaction told a tale, and as the figures rotated, bringing them all a new partner for the dance, every thread of the story changed but one.

"Ah, civility," she said, to no one in particular. "How poignantly you smooth out the jagged edges that form between our messy souls. How well you make liars of us all."

"Who are you talking to?"

Vashodia spun, startled by the proximity of the voice.

A child stood before her, not five paces away, face smeared in dirt and framed by mangy sweeps of hair. The worn if warm-looking coat and lanky body gave no clear indication of age or sex, but Vashodia guessed it to be between six and twelve, and probably a boy.

But really, who can tell with the wretched things?

Vashodia turned so that her hood blocked most of the creature. "Go away, child."

"Who are *you* to call me 'child'? You don't look much older than I do."

"One of the few drawbacks to eternal youth. But well outweighed by the benefits, I assure you."

"Huh?"

"Leave. Now. There are few in this world I consider worthy of my patience. I have none for your kind."

"Got something against Amebites, then?"

"No. Children."

"Hmph!" The child placed hands on its hips, making Vashodia reexamine her assessment of its gender. "Well, if you think you're so much more mature than the rest of us, then you can just forget about playing with me and my friends."

Vashodia burst out laughing. "You came to invite me to play?"

The—girl?—nodded. "We were over around the corner, and I saw you standing here all by yourself. You looked so . . . lonely."

Vashodia felt her heart beat just a little bit louder in response to what felt an accusation. She sneered. "There are worse things to be."

"Like what?"

"Like . . . ignorant."

"Oh, please. What's the point of knowing everything if you don't have any friends to share it with?"

"Friends are a weakness that will forever hold you to expectations you cannot but fail to meet. It's much less agonizing to simply do without."

"Yes, but I love my friends. And they love me. And sometimes it feels like they're all I've got in this whole world, and I wouldn't give them up for anything!"

"Ah, but what if one of them hurts you? Or betrays you? Or dies? How would *that* make you feel?"

The girl—Vashodia was sure of it now—hung her head. "I . . . don't know. Not good. Not good at all. But you can't let that stop you from trying. You can't go your whole life being afraid of getting hurt."

Fire roared to life within her. This didn't just *feel* like an accusation anymore; now, there was no doubt.

Vashodia twisted towards the child, throwing back her hood and lunging forward. "Get away from me, you filthy bundle of rags!"

The girl's eyes went wide and her mouth hung open in obvious awe . . . but it wasn't quite the reaction Vashodia had been expecting. "Cool scales. Where'd you get them from? Can I touch them?"

"What? No, you can't touch them!"

"Why not?"

Vashodia energized, glaring. Shadows began coalescing around her. "Because there are many monsters in this world, my child. And all of them are afraid of *me*."

Finally, the girl spun, nearly tripping over herself as she ran away.

For some reason—the why of which disturbed her greatly—Vashodia did not feel like laughing.

She turned back towards the voltensus, sweeping her eyes across the figures there, many of whom now bore confused expressions. Vashodia knew why, of course: they were waiting for the one who had invited them to begin the meeting. But of course, that person had not yet arrived.

Vashodia knew as well as anyone when conditions were ripe for making an entrance.

Emerging from the shadows between two of the houses along the innermost circle, she glided down the gentle, grassy slope. All eyes turned as she approached: some knowing, others curious, all expectant.

Pushing aside the encounter with the child, she shivered in joy.

It's nice to be back among minds that acknowledge my genius. I can't even image what the world would be like without an audience this appreciative. I do believe I'll keep it.

"Greetings, one and all," she said, not intending to give anyone the chance to speak before her. Or at all. "How splendid of you to make it. You're probably all thinking I invited you here so I could get your opinion on important matters, but really it's only because this was the quickest way to get the word out."

Vashodia paused for breath, growing giddy from all the sharp stares shot her way. "By now you've surely heard the rumor that the obelisk behind you will provide some measure of protection against anything powered by ruvaki sorcery, including their skyships. Let me assure you that this is true. I have it from, what you might call, the *lowest* authority. Former authority, anyway. You can all put your fears of the sky to rest.

"As for our stay here, everything has already been taken care of. The glaciers nearby will provide all the clean drinking water we could possibly need, and more than enough land is undergoing accelerated harvest to fill every belly until bursting. The defenses erected so far are adequate to withstand ground assault, though I'm sure those militarily minded among you can find ways to improve them.

"So calm any dissent stemming from the news about our enemy's origin. Train your young to get them ready for when the enemy decides to test our stronghold—and believe me, they shall. But until then, we have a chance to breathe. Sit back and relax. Lick your wounds. Pack on a layer of fat for the winter to come. Put any last affairs, personal or otherwise, in order.

"Right now, this is the safest place on the planet. To be clear, though, that doesn't mean we should feel content here. I, for one, am not too keen on the idea of the ruvak possessing the rest of our world. So even as we rest, we must also ready ourselves for taking it back."

Spinning on her heel, Vashodia began striding back up the hill immediately, seeking the comforting shadows once more. Behind her, she heard the murmurs begin. Though distant, and growing farther by the step, one voice, deepest and loudest of them all, managed to reach her ears with something approaching clarity. Like the location of the meeting, she knew it to be no accident.

"Nice to meet you too, Vashodia," Mevon Daere said, then grunted. "So much that I didn't understand before suddenly makes sense."

Still marching away, Vashodia smiled.

Draevenus dipped the oar in the rippling water for what seemed the millionth time, the need for speed warring with the need for silence and forcing extra tension into each beat of rhythmic motion. Muscles slick with sweat had long since passed the point of exhaustion, only able to continue rowing through sheer force of will. But even that was starting to run out.

"I think . . . we're almost . . . there," Tassariel said between labored breaths.

Draevenus hazarded a glance over his shoulder, just able to glean the shadowy outline of the woman rowing behind him. "Quiet," he whispered. "Voices carry . . . over water."

"In this wind . . . it doesn't . . . really matter."

He couldn't argue with her there. He'd estimated the trip across the channel on the inland side of Yusan would take two tolls, three at the most, but he hadn't accounted for the headwind, which seemed to push them backwards a pace for every two they rowed forward. The eastern sky was growing brighter with frightening quickness, destroying their cover of darkness.

"Row faster," he said quietly. Belatedly, he added, "If you can."

He switched the oar to the other side of the small boat, giving one arm the illusion of rest. The wooden vessel wasn't much, but he had no reason to complain; they'd stumbled upon it by luck, and it had save them from having to try fashioning a makeshift boat.

Squinting, he peered forward, searching for a hint of the island's coastline, but even his dark-honed vision couldn't make anything out. He didn't know how she could possibly make an assertion as to their proximity to shore.

Unless, of course, she senses other casters of her kind waiting for us. Ruul's light, I'm not ready for that. I've no idea what kind of reception awaits us, and I hate surprises.

He could not detect their kind unless they were actively using their sorcery, something neither of *them* had been able to do in weeks.

Entering Yusan had been simple enough. Nearby ruvaki patrols had rushed to the scene of the destroyed flagship, allowing him and Tassariel to slip unnoticed across the strait and into the woods along the horseshoe-shaped nation's southwestern shore. The countryside had been breathtaking. Autumn had turned the trees brilliant shades of red and pink and yellow, the spine of a mountain range running along the island's length was high and narrow and powdered with snow, and around every bend it seemed a new brook could be found babbling happily and kissed by mist.

Nothing after their arrival, however, could be described as easy.

Every step they'd taken had been drenched in signs of ruvak occupation. Soldiers had been stationed along every trail, and skyships had swarmed overhead by the thousands. Any advance they'd made had been an exercise in patience, as they'd waited for the sluggish occupiers to get out of their way and reveal a path. Too often none did, forcing them to worm their way through or along the edges of enemy encampments. They'd spent most of their journey across the outer island with their faces buried in the dirt.

He wasn't sure if he'd prefer to be back there, or here on the water.

Draevenus shifted his oar back to the other side again. Several drops plunked across the back of his cloak, indicating that Tassariel had done the same. He was just about to ask her how much farther she thought they had to go, when something other than the wind reached his ears.

The thrumming whine, now all too familiar, that preceded the approach of ruvaki skyships.

"Get down," he rasped.

He pulled the oar into his lap and hunched down over it, spreading his cloak over both sides of the boat. He could only hope his companion was doing likewise behind him. The goal was to obscure their profile, making them look like just another lump of driftwood. Though he didn't know the extent of the enemy's detection capabilities, this simple concealment technique had kept them from being discovered so far.

Though, if they actually knew what they were looking for, and made an effort to track us down in a logical, coordinated manner, we might be in trouble. There's one drawback, at least, to their chaotic ways.

Too winded to hold his breath, he settled for calming it to a measured cadence. His muscles rejoiced at the much-needed break. Even knowing they could be discovered at any moment, and pressed into a fight where they'd be heavily disadvantaged, the sudden stoppage of his labors made him relax, far more so than was probably wise.

The sound grew louder, closer, but still he couldn't bring himself to worry. Numb from exhaustion and practically blind, his hearing seemed elevated to almost magically enhanced levels of acuity. He could tell the skyships weren't coming straight at them.

Ten beats later, the whine lowered in pitch and began fading, clearly moving away. Within a mark, it had given way altogether to the wind.

"We're safe, now," he said, straightening back to an upright position with a groan.

"I think we were anyway," Tassariel said.

Draevenus half turned on the bench to look at her. "What do you mean?"

"Didn't you notice the skyship's trajectory? They *avoided* the central island. *Intentionally.*"

"Interesting. I guess that explains why this resistance group has managed to survive this long. Though I'm still baffled as to *how.*"

"Which, hopefully, we'll be able to figure out when we meet them."

"Well, no time like the present." He let go of the oar, letting it slide into the bottom of the boat, and stood.

"What are you doing?" she asked.

"Taking a shortcut." He unfurled his wings, sprouts of darkness no different than what surrounded them. Still, he knew she couldn't fail to sense it. "Care to join me?"

Laughing, she stood as well, setting the deck beneath him to wobbling. "You might want to cover your eyes."

"Why?"

"Do you *really* need to ask that?"

Thinking about it for half a moment, Draevenus realized just how idiotic his question was. "It's not just my body that could use a rest, apparently."

He shuffled around, trying to rock the boat as little as possible, and placed his hands over both closed eyes. Even so, after so long in darkness, the light that flared to life a beat later still nearly blinded him.

The valynkar made a sound somewhere between a squeak and a groan.

"Something wrong?" he asked.

"Let's just say, we might want to get to the island sooner rather than later."

Draevenus didn't need to ask why; he heard the whines returning, piercing the predawn sky. Several of them.

He flapped once, lifting himself into the air, and carefully peeled his hands away from his face. It was no use. "Ruul's light, which way?" he said. "I can't see more than twenty paces, and even then all I can make out is the glare off the waves!"

"Take my hand," Tassariel said. "I'll guide you."

He reached out and felt her palm slip into his, grasping firmly. "Thank you."

"Don't mention it. Do, however, try to keep up."

He felt a tug on his arm and flapped to match pace. The surface glistened below, passing by in a sparkling, lavender-hued blur. Flying into the wind made it shriek around his ears. The whines behind them intensified.

"How much farther?" he asked.

"Almost there. Just hold on!"

"I couldn't let go if I wanted to!"

"What's that supposed to mean?"

"You've got a good grip is all."

"I'm *literally* in the process of saving your backside. Is this really the best time to insult my mannish hands?"

"How is that an insult?"

"Watch out!"

Her hand released his and pushed on his shoulder, driving them apart from each other. A bolt of chaos screamed between them, hissing as it impacted with the surface of the water and turned it into a churning whirlpool.

Another bolt struck the water to his left and two more to the right. A fifth whistled by, slightly higher than the others.

This last one detonated in a maelstrom of sand.

"The beach!" he shouted, eyeing Tassariel's signature glow ten paces away. "The island!"

"I see it!"

He dove forward, spinning as he dodged another round of chaotic projectiles. Trees splintered ahead of him, ravaged by the blasts. Then, he was among them, twisting around trunks that were thin individually, but spaced densely enough to provide a measure of protection. He landed, dismissed his wings, and spun in a crouch. Tassariel came to his side, mimicking his posture.

No more of the deadly volleys came their way. The ruvaki skyships—five of them, he could now see—banked sharply well clear of the island and began drifting away. As if they were children told their friend wouldn't be coming out to play today and sulking back home.

"You'd think this place was cursed," he said, rising out of his crouch.

Tassariel rose beside him, sighing. "Not cursed," she said, slowly turning to face inland. "Just . . . well-defended."

Draevenus followed her gaze. Standing in a broad half-circle behind them were dozens of figures. Both genders were represented, from pock-faced teen to wrinkled elder. Dressed in animal hides or tattered scraps of wool, they all glared at him and Tassariel with almost feral tenacity.

And every last one of them pulsed with sorcerous energy.

A figure approached from the rear, and the others parted to admit him passage. He was a tall man, if slightly hunched in the shoulders, bearing weary eyes far older than his features suggested. Disheveled hair hung just past his neck, the color of the midday sky.

He stopped ten paces away.

And stared.

"Hello, Father," Tassariel said.

The man said nothing. His whole body started shaking, until the spasms seemed ready to overwhelm him. Several of the elder women started towards him, but he dismissed their attention with raised hands and a sharp hiss of breath. Eyes wide, he examined Tassariel for another thirty beats.

Then turned and walked away.

Draevenus looked to his companion's face, unsurprised to see the tears brimming in her eyes. Yet her cheeks remained dry, her jaw clenched, her hands balled up into fists.

He put an arm around her shoulder. It seemed the right thing to do.

She did not resist.

CHAPTER 15

"Thank you for meeting me," Arivana said. "I know you're a very busy man."

Chase waved a hand dismissively. "These days, I'm actually not busy *enough*."

"The enemy still has not attacked?"

"Nothing but probes, I'm afraid. And half-hearted ones at that. I've a feeling they're gathering themselves for something big." He shook his head. "At least we have some time to drill the young ones. I only hope it makes a difference."

"Surely it can't be worse than sending them into battle untrained."

"Perhaps. But until you've survived that first brush with the enemy, the first time a blade swings for your head, you can't know if you're truly a soldier or not.

All the training in the world won't mean a thing if you don't have it in your heart to kill."

"It's been a long, trying journey to get here, and few among us haven't lost someone along the way. Unfortunate though it may be, I think you'll find plenty of hearts that are up for the task."

"We'll see."

Arivana smiled tightly, then beckoned to him. "Please, join me."

She turned, peering down at the open floor as she leaned both forearms on the loft's odd railing. It had a look and feel halfway between metal and stone, and managed to stay warm despite the chill outside, which grew deeper by the day. Jasside had constructed this entire building—and many more besides—out of the strange material, all of it from thin air. It wasn't pretty, but it got the job done.

And they all had more important things to worry about than aesthetics.

Chase joined her at the waist-high ledge and pressed down his palms on the smooth surface. He looked in the same direction as she did, examining the figures below. A few were old, but the rest were quite young. Most were male. They sat, or paced, or wandered, or stared off into the abyss. None spoke. Not to each other, anyway.

"Who are they?" Chase asked.

"You don't recognize them?"

"Should I?"

Arivana sighed. "I suppose not. But we'll get to that. First, tell me, how is your brother?"

"Daye? He's . . . well. As well as can be expected, anyway. I don't think either of us will ever get to used to it when I—his younger brother—have to reprimand him for things like this."

"For disobeying orders? It has happened before?"

"Many times. You should have seen him when he was younger."

"Would that be before or after you two wormed your way into being princes in a foreign land?"

"Both. And what do you mean 'wormed'? We *earned* our place among the Sceptrines."

"A truth you've both proven many times over. Still, I find it odd that you never went back to Weskara."

Chase gazed upward, eyes glazing over. "We both left it young—though, in Daye's case, it would be more appropriate to say he was taken. Even so, by the time we were in a position to leave Sceptre, we were old enough to have built more ties to our adopted homeland than to the one that had given us birth. Besides, it's hard to love a nation whose chief defining trait is purposefully turning a blind eye to the world."

"Oh, Weskara doesn't seem all *that* bad."

He appeared to contemplate that. "Times do seem to be changing. I mean, have you *met* the new queen?"

Arivana laughed again. This time, he joined her.

After their shared mirth had faded, she patted his

arm. She kept the motion easy, natural, but withdrew her hand before he might conceive the gesture as awkward. "I'm glad we can laugh together, Chase. It wasn't that long ago that all our people shared was hatred and bloodshed. If it weren't for the ruvak and their invasion—or, rather, their *reclamation*—we would likely be killing each other still."

His knuckles turned white, shaking as they gripped the ledge. "If it weren't for the ruvak framing us for those assassinations, we'd have never gone to war with each other in the first place!"

A sudden vision of her family flashed before her eyes, their faces still painfully indistinct. All she remembered with any clarity was something that she had never actually witnessed herself.

The flames that had claimed their lives.

The screams.

Even the horrors she'd seen since could never match the nightmare she'd created in her mind. Yet for all the pain it caused, it acted as an excellent motivator.

"You're right, of course," she said at last. "The ruvak deceived us all. And my advisors, at the time, deceived me a second time, propelling the conflict onward for their own gain. But as despicable as their actions were, it only served to accentuate an even bigger problem."

"Panisian presumption of superiority," Chase said sourly.

Her eyes widened. She was surprised he'd been able to arrive so quickly at such a conclusion, especially considering it had taken *her* this long to realize it. "Is it that obvious?"

He nodded. "To an outsider."

"Yes. I see how it would be." She sighed, tucking a strand of hair behind her ear. "People always seem blind to their own flaws, often willfully. I suppose it's no different with nations."

"True. But in both cases, those who can look inward, examining everything without prejudice or mercy, seeing both good and bad as they are, not as they fear or wish them to be . . . well, such a talent is rare indeed."

"Too rare. And as difficult as it is to see your deficiencies, doing something about them may very well be impossible. Just look at *them*."

She punctuated her last word by flicking a wrist toward the figures below.

Chase narrowed his eyes at them again, leaning towards one in particular. "Wait a mark, I *do* recognize one of them. That's the Sultan of Fasheshe. And that boy over in the corner, I'd bet my kingdom that's the Crown Prince of Mataroa."

"He's king, now."

"King? What happened to his father?"

"Dead. Decided to send his house into safety and stand his ground when the ruvak first came. An idiotic move in hindsight, but none of us exactly knew what to expect back then. By the time we mustered a defense, half the rulers of the southern nations had already died, and three others perished due to the strain of the exodus. Only two of the people down there have held their throne longer than a year."

"And so you've invited them all here. But why?"

"I didn't invite them, as such. They're simply . . . waiting."

"For what?"

Arivana pointed to the far end of the lower level as a door opened. "For that."

Claris stepped into the room, instantly garnering the attention of every person present. The silver platter she carried was filled not with food but with folded sheafs of paper, which she handed out to each ruler in turn as she made her way swiftly, smoothly around the room.

"What is she giving them?" Chase asked.

"News, and instructions," Arivana replied. "Though mostly the former."

"I don't understand."

"With the rest of you busy yourselves preparing the defenses, the task of governing the civilians has fallen to me. My council, who have actually become helpful of late, help me make decisions for how best to run things here, for everyone. I try to keep the rest of humanity's rulers informed."

"You don't give them a say?"

Arivana shrugged. "I would . . . if they had any desire to."

"You're telling me they're perfectly happy leaving all major decisions regarding the lives of them and their people . . . to *you*?"

"Not to me. To Panisahldron."

Chase furrowed his brow, as if trying to draw conclusions from her mess of clues. After a moment, he nodded. "I think I'm starting to see what you're getting at," he said. "They've grown dependent."

"Addicted would probably be a better word to describe them. For far too long my nation has been the exclusive supplier of their luxuries, all things fine and beautiful, the manufacture and export of which we've turned into an art. We convinced them that such things were a need and not a want, molding that desire into a drug, and thus shaping their cultures more thoroughly than they ever could themselves. We've been doing this for *centuries*. Is it any surprise it's taking so long to wean them?"

"I . . . see your point."

"I thought you might. But acknowledging the problem is only the first step. In order to begin healing the rifts between us, to give everyone a reason to look to the future with something other than futility . . . it's my hope that you might help me take the next."

"What did you have in mind?"

"I have a proposal for you that I wouldn't dare ask of anyone else. I'm hoping you'll keep an open mind.

Sceptre, in my experience, isn't afraid to do things differently than the rest."

"No," Chase said, smiling, "we are not."

Jasside had just finished pouring the tea when the door opened and a blur of darkness swept in from open sky.

"Honey?" she asked.

Vashodia's eyes burned like embers from deep within her cowl. "I was wondering who had pierced my wards."

"Were you? Really? Who *else* could have done it without dying in any number of painful ways. That trap to turn someone into a block of ice was particularly inventive."

"So glad to see you still recognize greatness when you see it."

"I learned from the best."

Vashodia sighed, then slipped out of her cloak and hung it from a hook jutting out of the wall. Jasside was surprised to see spatters of mud marring the dark fabric. She hadn't known her old mistress to do the dirty things herself.

As the mierothi sauntered over and sat in the seat opposite her—stirring globs of honey into the cup nearest her on the table between them—Jasside gave the chamber an obvious visual appraisal.

"Nice place you've made for yourself," she said.

"But not, I take it, what you were expecting?"

Jasside smiled. "Making your own private dwelling float above the voltensus—*that* I expected. Just as I expected these fine furnishings—the silk sheets on your bed, the bath fitted with constructs to control flow and temperature of the water, the floor-to-ceiling windows that allow you to look down upon the rest of us without allowing anyone else to see in, and the kitchen filled with all manner of devices whose use I can only guess at. What I *didn't* expect was for this place to feel so cozy. So . . . cheerful."

"Would you prefer I craft my lair in a swamp or a cave or some decrepit tower? Perhaps I should fill it with the skulls of my victims? Paint the walls with blood? Make guests enter by way of torture chambers, wander through mazes inhabited by shadow beasts, and crawl past pits that seem to fall through the heart of the world?"

Jasside brought the cup up to her lips, grinning through the steam. "You've been reading too many children's stories."

Vashodia mimicked her movements, taking a dainty sip of her tea, though her smile held no real humor. "What do you want, Jasside?"

"What I *want* is to see how you are doing."

"Checking up on me, are you? Did you forget about the last time we met in private?"

"Just because I'm no longer your apprentice doesn't mean I've stopped caring about you."

"How touching."

"I'm serious. It can't be easy being in your position. Taking on the world's problems as your own personal burden is difficult enough. I can't imagine trying to do it without any friends."

"I have friends enough."

"Who? Feralt and his accomplices?"

Vashodia's eyes flashed dangerously.

Jasside took another sip of tea to hide the joy on her face, even though a part of her was slightly ashamed of it. Not enough to banish it, however.

After all, how often do I get the chance to surprise you?

"I'm not sure," Jasside continued, "if you can count cronies as friends."

"Perhaps not. But what makes you think I need friends in the first place?"

"Everyone needs *someone* in their life who cares about them. With Draevenus away, and Angla understandably occupied, I'm all you've got left. And, if you recall, we *are* still technically family."

Vashodia shrugged. "A few dozen daeloth can make a similar claim. Should I waste my time developing personal relationships with each of *them*?"

Jasside winced. She'd forgotten about the daeloth. Over a year ago, at Jasside's own behest, they'd all ceased using their last names—names derived from their unwilling mierothi mothers. She hadn't thought about how many other Anglascos there might be.

"I . . . don't know," Jasside said. "Perhaps after time has been given a chance to heal those wounds."

Vashodia scoffed. "The only thing time ever brings for certain is death."

"Except to *you*, you mean."

Vashodia giggled.

Jasside shook her head, leaning forward to set her cup on the table. "Look, none of that pertains to why I'm here. If you need anything—anything at all—please don't hesitate to ask. And please don't turn me away when I'm only trying to help."

The mierothi drained her cup, then, gathering a swirl of power between her clawed fingers, erased it from existence. "Thank you for the tea. You may go now."

Sighing, Jasside rose from her chair. She knew quite well when Vashodia had run out of civility for the day. She marched past, pausing in the doorway.

"One question before I go."

Vashodia, hidden now by the high back of her chair, said nothing.

Jasside continued anyway. "What *have* you been doing lately? I've heard reports that say you've been seen standing still for tolls every day, at various points around the colony. I've felt the energy you've been wielding. Care to share whatever it is you're trying to achieve?"

Silence.

I don't know why I even thought she'd answer.

Hands on the door frame, she peered at the city taking shape beneath her. The voltensus was directly below, encircled by the houses and barracks that were part of the original colony. But beyond them, in ever expanding rings, more and more dwellings were springing up due to her labors. Though none were particularly elegant, she'd become practiced enough to create three a day.

She lifted her eyes past them, however, to a vast field milling with figures that, at this distance, appeared merely a smear. Energizing, she focus in on the spot, then made the dash. Her vision blurred as swirling darkness bent reality around her. She landed on the field's near edge with a rush of wind.

Mevon turned from his study of the drilling soldiers. The smile he gave her almost made her forget about Vashodia altogether.

"How did it go?" he asked.

So much for forgetting about her.

"Not as good as I hoped," she answered. "But about how I expected."

He nodded consolingly, then stepped close and raised his arms out wide. As always, he hesitated just out of reach, letting her initiate contact.

As if I could love you any more.

Bracing herself, she curled up her arms and leaned into him. Energy siphoned away, but she didn't mind. She didn't even gasp anymore. The loss of her power took with it the loss of responsibility. It was a comforting illusion, anyway.

Mevon wrapped his huge arms around her, applying just the right amount of pressure. He'd been too gentle at first, but after a little instructing, and assurances that she was *not*, in fact, as fragile as a flower, he'd managed to find the sweet spot.

The combined effects—both magical and mundane—made her feel as if all would be right with the world.

She only wished she felt that way about Vashodia.

"I'm sure it wasn't as bad as you think," Mevon said, his chin brushing the top of her head as he spoke.

"You're right. It was probably worse."

Mevon chuckled, his chiseled chest rumbling with the sound.

"I mean it," Jasside continued. "You don't know her like I do."

"No. But I do know what it is be isolated. To feel alone. She may never admit it to you, and certainly not to herself, but I'm sure she appreciated your efforts to connect with her."

"An effort most likely wasted." Jasside sighed, craning her neck to meet his eyes. "I made a promise to myself that I would touch her soul, that I would reach the frail light within it, surrounded by so much darkness, and help it shine. It feels, every day, like I've failed."

Mevon shook his head, brushing one hand down her cheek. "You don't give yourself nearly enough credit. After all, you managed to touch *my* soul. And I've known few who could have matched the darkness it once held."

Jasside smiled. "You always know the right thing to say to me."

"Do I? I'm just trying to tell the truth as I see it. Isn't honesty our agreed upon policy?"

"It is." Jasside leaned her head against him once more. "It is indeed."

As she nestled in almost complete contentment, she saw out of the corner of her eyes four figures walking together: Queen Arivana and her advisor Claris, along with the Harkun brothers. Unfortunately, the sight of them also reminded her of her responsibilities, which even Mevon's touch couldn't hold at bay forever.

Pushing away gently, she sighed. "I'd better get back to work. More than three-quarters of the refugees are still living in tents, after all."

"Aye," he said, letting her go with obvious reluctance. "And I'd better get back to my trainees before they start killing each other for real!"

Tassariel stared into the crackling flames, which did little to warm her. The ground was too damp, the breeze too insistent, and her padded stump of a seat was too far away from the fire. Dawn was rolling in like a whisper, turning the canopy of tree branches above, most naked but for a few stubborn leaves, into a skein of shadows standing stark against the sky. The sun had yet to add any of its heat to the day.

But none of that had anything to do with why she felt so cold.

Two old women, grey hair held in twin buns by painted sticks, tended the fire, a scene played out at nearly thirty other stone-lined pits. One ladled rice porridge into bowls, a thin gruel filled with mushy vegetables Tassariel couldn't identify, while the other fried fish filets on a large sheet of metal suspended over the flames, scooping the—in Tassariel's opinion—over-salted and undercooked meat onto plates.

Those waiting in line took one of each, bowing and murmuring their thanks to the old women, then moved off to sit and eat and chat amongst themselves. As she'd seen when first landing on this island, they came in every shape and size: young to old, female and male, all bearing the pale, narrow faces characteristic of the Yusanese. But only the young women with babes in shoulder-bound slings had the dark, straight hair of pure natives. The rest all sported various shades of blue atop their heads.

Family, she thought. *My half brothers and half sisters. Yet, in the five days I've been here, none of them have spoken a single word to me. What did you tell them of me, Father? What lies have you spread?*

Her vision slowly fell from the flames, coming

to rest on the moist ground between her boots. She hadn't known what to expect when she'd finally met the man who'd abandoned her before memory had even taken hold. She should have, though. He'd been avoiding her for the last ninety years. What reason did she have to think the bastard would stop now?

Thoughts turning sour, she berated herself for dwelling on it. A pointless use of time that did more harm to her than good. But she knew she couldn't put aside her feelings towards her father much longer. Valynkar were renowned for their delays in dealing with anything the least bit unpleasant. Pushing off resolution for centuries was the norm; for millennia, not unheard-of. When patience is preached like the greatest mark of nobility, few feel the need to hasten confrontation. It was, perhaps, the greatest fault of her kind.

Leave it to my kin to turn a virtue into a vice.

Even now, with her father at last in arm's reach, and the ruvak threatening to end everything, she felt that pull, that small voice that said to deal with it later, to get only what information she needed and be on her way. Another voice, which seemed smaller still, told her that this would undoubtedly be her last chance. She did not yet know which one she was going to heed.

A murmur began some ways off, yet grew nearer and louder rapidly: hissing whispers she'd come to know well. If the inhabitants of this island looked on her with scorn and self-righteous pity, they looked on Draevenus with unbridled hostility. Her father had fought in the War of Rising Night. The mierothi might look different these days, but she was sure no one here would consider them a friend. Tassariel was surprised they had let her companion stay at all. More surprised that no blood had yet been shed.

Draevenus at last came into view, chased by glares as he threaded around the crowds at each fire. He didn't seem the least bit affected by his treatment. In fact, he was . . . smiling.

Please tell me you've brought good news at last.

"Good morning," he said through a yawn, sitting next to her. "I hope I didn't sleep so late I missed breakfast."

Tassariel glanced towards the fire pit. Just outside the circle of stones sat two plates and two bowls, which were being pointedly ignored by the two old women. The first day they'd only set out one, and had refused to give anything to Draevenus. Tassariel had taken her portion and given it to him, making him eat every bite despite his objections, and despite the old women's contentious stares. After that, they'd started leaving two.

She rose and retrieved their meals, then handed one to him and sat back down. "So," she said between her first and second bites, "how did you sleep?"

"Better," he said. "Best rest I've had since we got here."

"Good," she replied, struggling to keep her face impassive.

She knew very well he hadn't slept much at all.

Her father had not made his whereabouts known, and all civil efforts to find out had been blunted. Draevenus had sneaked out of his tent in the dead of night in order to track the man down. The statement about his sleep was prearranged code between them: he had a location.

Now came the tricky part.

They made small talk for the next ten marks, using wide gestures to punctuate their words. Between them, when they were fairly certain no one was looking too closely, the real conversation took place in the form of hand language. She'd learned enough of it in their time together to glean directions, one word at a time.

She finished her meal, then excused herself to freshen up, marching east towards the nearby stream, which the women used for bathing. When she got there, it was occupied, so she turned her back and waited for it to clear. They knew about her shyness. No one would disturb her while she was there.

As the other women gathered their things and began returning to the camp, Tassariel removed her cloak and hung it from a nearby tree. She even bent down and began pretending to unlace her boots—at least until they were out of sight. Once she was sure they were gone, she bolted off into the woods.

Following Draevenus's directions, she crossed one gully, then followed the edge of a draw filled with bracken for half a league. At the two trees fallen against each other, she turned to her left and marched directly into the sun, which was now cresting the treetops. She came to a shallow ridge, slid down, then took three hundred steps towards the mountain peak at the island's heart.

As her companion had promised, the land dipped into a bowl, and there at the bottom rested a small, rocky pool enclosed by looming evergreens.

Through the leaves, she could just make out several figures in and near the water.

Her heart stammered.

She took several measured breaths in an attempt to calm herself. It did no good.

Neither will delaying, but we don't have any other choice. Just go down there and do what needs to be done.

Still feeling wholly unprepared, Tassariel shuffled down the hill and stepped through the last line of trees. Six of the seven figures present turned towards her in alarm.

Four women stood on the edge of the pool, respectively holding a towel, a robe, clean clothes, and a tray with fruit and wine. Two more were neck deep in the water, each gripping washing cloths, whose scented oils she could smell from here.

Between these last two, back turned and only visible from his shoulders up, stood her father.

He raised one hand, flicking it as if swatting away a pest; a gesture clearly indicating that he wanted her gone.

In an eerie, simultaneous motion, the four nearest women set down their bundles.

Then jumped into a fighting posture.

Tassariel tensed, instinct taking hold. Her pulse quickened as she scanned her targets, their balance and speed, how well they moved in relation to each other, predicting both the martial school to which their stances belonged and her chances of victory for the fight to come.

Four against one. They look skilled enough, but they're no masters, and they have no obvious physical advantage, nor weapons or sorcery to bolster themselves. I could win this fight blindfolded.

On the cusp of energizing and entering her own fighting pose, she instead stopped herself, shaking her head.

"My companion and I crossed almost two thousand leagues of enemy-held territory, Father," she said. "And we made our presence *felt*. Though it would weigh little on my conscience, I've no desire to cause harm to your . . . women."

She had another word in mind to describe them—one far less kind—but thought it best to at least *try* to keep things civil.

The four Yusanese women halted their advance, their eyes suddenly filled with doubt. Her father, however, did not respond in any way she could tell. Tassariel took a deep breath, trying to chill the caldron of emotion that threatened to boil over inside her.

"I won't leave until I have what I came for, so you will have to deal with me eventually," she said, forcing calm into her voice when she felt anything but. "The sooner we talk, the sooner I'll be out of your hair. A few words with me seem a small price to pay. I know how little you can stand—" she paused, swallowing "—a nuisance."

Reacting at last, her father's shoulders began shaking, sending ripples through water that had grown deathly still since she'd arrived. The two women in the pool with him leaned in and whispered soothing words as they gently took his arms in their grip.

He wrenched himself free. The women squeaked.

"Very well," he said, his voice deeper than she had imagined, yet thin, almost hoarse, as if he were a man under great strain. She couldn't help but feel he deserved it. "Leave us."

The half dozen women looked six shades of askance, but they did his bidding quickly and without a word of protest. He had them well-trained, apparently. Not that it helped; if all it took to survive the end of everything was to be a colossal ass, she knew plenty of people with enough charisma to save the entire world.

In moments, in far too short a time, the last dripping footsteps faded from her hearing, and she found herself alone with her father, who remained in the pool with his back turned. It was exactly what she'd been hoping for.

Exactly what she'd been dreading.

"Go on, then," he said. "I'm sure you have many questions."

Too many to count.

And I'm not sure if I'm ready to hear the answers.

She supposed it would be best to simply ask about the ruvak, and why they seemed hesitant to approach the island, and how her father and his . . . brood . . . had survived so long. The rest, the personal things, could wait. The petty grievances of an abandoned child were pitiful, pointless, and could be put aside until more important matters were settled. They'd either find some way to deal with the enemy and would have all the time in the world to sort things out, or they'd all be dead.

Tassariel cleared her throat. "Why, Father," she began, voice cracking. "Why did you leave me!"

The man flinched, droplets spraying from the tips of his blue hair. "I . . . I couldn't . . ."

"Couldn't *what*? Raise your only daughter? Fulfill your responsibilities? Wait around when there were so many willing human women ready to make you forget I even existed?"

"No. I couldn't stand to see you anymore."

Tassariel clenched her hands into trembling fists.

"I'm sorry I was such a burden to you," she spat through her teeth.

"It wasn't that."

"What, then?"

He hung his head. "You were starting to look like your mother."

The words struck her like a knife to the gut, breaking loose the first tears from her eyes. "I don't care if I reminded you of her. I was twelve, still a toddler by our people's standards, and my mother was dead. You were all I had . . . and you abandoned me."

"I was not fit to be a father. I knew our people could raise you better than I ever could."

The tears were flowing freely now. "So you're just a coward, then."

"Yes. I am at that."

"Didn't stop you from coming here and spawning abyss knows how many other children. Let me guess, you had an arrangement with the local lords? They supplied you with women and you supplied them with an endless supply of obedient casters?"

He half turned towards her. "How did you find that out?"

She scoffed, wiping the wetness from her chin. "I had a run-in with the Panisian Consulate."

Her father cringed. "I see."

"You see? That's all you can say? They tried to rape and murder me once I found out their little secret. I don't know what's worse—the fact that you copied their operation, or that you send your other children off to be slaves."

He turned to face her now; in her mind, the bravest thing he'd ever done. "You are right, of course. I am guilty of all you have accused me. And guilty of so much more."

"I don't care what else you've done. I doubt it could compare."

"You might be surprised, my child."

"Don't call me that. Don't even think it. You lost the right a lifetime ago, and nothing you do will ever earn it back."

"I know. But—"

"But nothing! I didn't come here so you could confess your sins to me."

"Yet you seem determined to wring them out of me all the same."

Tassariel crossed her arms, feeling fury start to overtake her grief. "Fine, then. If you're so set on unloading your burdens, tell me what other atrocities we can lay at your feet."

"I fought in the War of Rising Night," he said, eyes glazing over as he accessed his ancient memories. "And a case can be made, quite convincingly, that I was the reason we lost."

"What are you talking about?"

"I was young, at the time, only five hundred years old. For most of the war, I was assigned to a position under the man who would one day become your uncle."

"Gilshamed?"

"Indeed. I was there the day he fought with the mierothi emperor. He and Rekaj were evenly matched, neither able to gain an advantage over the other throughout the daylong clash. I was the only valynkar within a dozen leagues.

"And I simply . . . watched.

"If I'd possessed even a drop of courage, I would have come to Gilshamed's aid. Had we defeated Rekaj together, it was said that the mierothi beneath him were more moderate in their stance towards conquest. More reasonable. How much suffering might have been prevented had I not been such a coward? How much death?"

Despite the steam rising out of the pool, Tassariel found herself shivering, her folded arms wrapping around herself sometime during her father's speech.

"Your mother was born just after the war and had no memory of it. She thought she could heal the scars I bore. But even with her ceaseless optimism, she eventually realized she was not up to the task. Not alone, anyway. She thought if we had a child it might mend what even a lifemate's unflinching love could not.

"I tried to convince her it was not worth the risk. So many valynkar women die in childbirth, or soon after, despite the finest in natural and magical care.

Some say that we are too powerful, that to create another like us siphons the life from our very souls. But I was too weak to dissuade her. And you know well enough what came of it. Do you understand what I'm saying?"

Shaking uncontrollably now, Tassariel did not have the strength to answer.

I understand, Father. You wish I had never been born.

Without another word or even a glance toward the man, she fled.

The journey back to the camp passed by in a blur, filled only with the startled faces of those she came upon. No one challenged her.

She found Draevenus and sat down beside him. He didn't question when she buried her face in his chest and let the sobs overtake her. He just wrapped his arms around her tightly and let her cry.

CHAPTER 16

"Do you happen to know what this is all about?" Gilshamed asked, waving the sheet of paper under Yandumar's nose.

The man set his bread on his plate, wiped the crumbs from his beard, and took an unhurried swallow from his amber-colored ale before leaning forward with a squint. "Aye."

Gilshamed raised an eyebrow. "That's . . . all you have to say?"

Yandumar winked. "Aye."

"Care to let us in on . . . whatever it is?" Mevon said.

"Yes, you've piqued our interest, Gilshamed," Jasside added, holding out a hand. "May we?"

"You have not seen the notices?" Gilshamed said, handing the paper to her. "They are posted on every wall and tent pole within the encampment. I even saw some on my domicile."

Mevon grunted. "Must have been put up recently, then." He waved a hand towards the drilling fields, where most of the trainees were also taking a break for lunch. "We've been at it all morning."

Jasside's eyes went wide as she held the paper held before her face. "This is an open invitation to a wedding. A *royal* wedding!"

"Indeed," Gilshamed said. "Yet, curiously, it is lacking in several key pieces of information."

"Such as *who* is getting married."

Gilshamed nodded. "As well as what national matrimony customs will be adhered to, and who is presiding over the ceremony."

"Is that important?" Mevon asked.

Every eye at the table drew to the man.

Mevon shrugged. "I've never been to a wedding."

Yandumar slapped his son on the shoulder. "Well, there's a first time for everything." He turned his eyes toward Jasside. "I'd be ashamed of you if you didn't drag him along. You know . . . for the experience."

She smiled. "I intend to. Still, I can't help but wonder who is—"

"You're missing the point, lass. The notice gives a time and place, don't it? And what does it say there at the bottom?"

Jasside scanned the paper once more. "It gives an open invitation, as I said."

"An invitation for . . . ?"

"For any who wish to attend as audience—" a small gasp escaped her throat "—and as . . . participants."

"Right you are! And with the end of the world just around the corner, who knows how many are gonna want to get themselves hitched? Can't very well put 'em *all* on the invite, now can we?"

Gilshamed narrowed his eyes on Yandumar. "You barely even glanced at the announcement. How can you possibly know so much about it?"

Yandumar picked up his ale again and downed the last half of it in a series of loud gulps. He slammed the tankard down, bouncing the plates on the table. He belched. "You asked who was presiding over the thing, didn't you?"

"I did."

"Well, over an affair this big, only the highest authority can do that."

"The highest . . . authority?"

"Ha! How many other emperors do you know? It's *me*, you golden-haired idiot!"

Gilshamed laughed, joined in his mirth by the others. *Do not ever change, old friend.* "Well, if that is the case, I suppose you and I had better get to work."

Yandumar raised an eyebrow. "What are you talking about?"

"This ceremony is more than just a wedding," Gilshamed said. "An occasion as important as this begs need of a grand speech from whomever has the ear of those in attendance. If I had to guess, I would say you have not even begun to write it."

Yandumar grabbed his hunk of bread and tore a chunk from it with his teeth. He chewed in sullen silence for several beats. "Lucky guess."

"If I'm reading this right," Mevon said, "the wedding is to take place this afternoon. You two had better get ready."

"Yes," Jasside said, leaning on Mevon's arm with a contented look on her face. "And so should we."

Mevon peered at her quizzically. "What for?"

Joined by raucous accompaniment from Yandumar, Gilshamed found himself laughing once more.

"**A**re you sure about this?" Claris asked.

Examining herself in the mirror, Arivana nodded. "We've been over it many times now."

"I know. Just giving you one last chance to change your mind."

"About the dress? Or . . . the other thing?"

Claris laughed. "Either, I suppose. But you've got to admit, that dress *is* rather plain. Especially for a Panisian queen."

"Which is precisely why I *must* wear it."

"Yes, but no powders? No paints? No *jewelry*? Countless eyes will be on you today. I understand wanting to make a statement, but you only get to do this once!"

Arivana tittered. "Only if I do it right."

"Oh, Arivana. How could you not?" Claris leaned in from behind, grasping both arms and resting her chin on Arivana's shoulder. "Everything you touch becomes the purest thing in the world."

Arivana peered at her aunt's reflection, vision blurring wetly. "Stop that," she said, sniffing as she wiped her eyelids. "You'll make me look hideous if you keep it up."

"Impossible. You couldn't pass yourself off as ugly if the whole world depended on it. And you're one of those rare gems whose insides match the out."

"You're making it worse!"

"Am I? Well, I see now why you wanted to skip the powders, little miss river eyes." Claris sighed. "Not that you even *need* them."

"Are you sure? There's still a few marks until it begins, we can—"

"Absolutely not. You're perfect just the way you are, wet cheeks and all." Claris winked. "That boy is going to become one lucky man."

"Abyss take me," Arivana said, pressing both hands to her stomach as it was overcome by flutters. "I don't need reminders about what comes after. About . . . tonight."

"Nothing to worry about there, so long as you remember what I taught you."

Arivana felt warmth flood her cheeks. "I . . . I don't know if I'll be—"

"Trust me, you'll do fine." Claris leaned away, then guided Arivana's shoulders around until she faced the tent's entrance. "It's time."

She took a deep breath. "Right. Here we go."

Half pushed, Arivana walked through the tent's hanging flap. Glacial wind struck her like a hammer, making her shiver and hiss as she fought the urge to dash back inside the tent and grab a shawl.

"I regret," she said through chattering teeth, "that we chose *not* to do this inside."

A cloud of visible breath preceded Claris as she stepped next to her. "Me too. But how in the world would we have found room for all of *them*?"

Arivana followed her aunt's hand as it swept over the masses gathered two-by-two on the field to their left. Some of them old enough to have grand-children, and some even younger than she, they had come from every conceivable nation and walk of life to share in this special day. There were thousands of participants, and the crowd of observers gathered in a ring around them, filling the hillsides and the shadow of the glacier, were beyond her ability to number.

"Countless eyes indeed," Arivana said. "Let's not keep them waiting."

She turned her attention ahead again, and began marching towards a raised platform that had been crafted hastily, yet with care and artistry, for just this occasion. The four figures atop it turned towards her as she approached.

Gilshamed and Yandumar stood on the side opposite from the participants, pausing from their whispered argument over a sheet of parchment to give her a nod of welcome. At the center of the platform, stolid in their dark military uniforms and regarding her with guarded smiles, stood the brothers Harkun. One to stand in the place of honor. The other . . .

. . . to be my husband.

It was strange to hear the word in relation to herself, even inside her mind. Tior's sordid push to get her one so as to plant a royal heir inside her belly had soured the concept. Yet so much had taken place since then it seemed an age ago, and as if it had happened to someone else. Someone weak and naïve and impossibly young.

Someone she could barely recognize.

Encouraged by Claris's too-eager escort, Arivana lifted the long hem of her dress and climbed up the stairs to join the men. Chase intercepted her before she'd gone more than a single step, leaning in close.

"Are you sure about this?" he said.

Arivana raised her chin to meet his gaze. "You're the second person to ask me that in the last few marks. Do I really seem so indecisive?"

He straightened, unable to hide his grin, and shook his head.

"This was my idea, if you recall. This union is important, and will affect the lives of—" she glanced at the waiting crowd "—many. I won't feign modesty just to claim otherwise."

"I know. But my brother still isn't exactly thrilled with the prospect, and to think you might not be as well . . . ?" Chase shrugged. "I just wanted to be sure."

"Well," Claris said, planting fists on her hips. "You can *be sure* that if Sceptre gets cold feet I'll—"

"It won't come to that," Chase said, raising his hands defensively. "On my honor."

"Good," Arivana said. "And as for Daye? Give me a mark and I'll set his mind at ease."

He retreated a step, half-turning to gesture towards his brother. "He's all yours."

Arivana nodded Chase her thanks as she strode past towards Daye, who eyed her approach with obvious reluctance. He hadn't stood so far away as to be *completely* unaware of the conversation's subject.

She paused a pace away, looking up to study him. The gaunt features he'd developed during the exodus had begun to reverse, exuding an aura of gentle strength. Despite eyes that burned with memories of war and loss, his face reminded her that he was not that much older than herself.

Arivana smiled at him. "I hear you might still have some . . . misgivings?"

Daye grimaced. "Please, take no offense. You're a fine woman, but my brother—"

"We're not talking about your brother."

"I know, but—"

"Nor are we talking about you, or even me." She pointed behind her. "We're talking about *them*."

His eyes swept over her head, scanning back and forth across the crowds.

"The people need this," she continued. "Binding together two nations who were very recently at each other's throats helps them to see that our kind can rise above our petty squabbles. That we have the strength to face the ruvak no matter how many they send to kill us. That they have a reason to think that hope is not just for fools.

"I know this may be rather short notice, and we're all still getting to know each other on a personal level, but we cannot afford to wait for a relationship to develop naturally. For people in our position, politics *must* come first. But with patience, and commitment, the hearts will surely follow."

For a long moment he said nothing, lowering his face to make a study of his feet. At last he sighed, lifting his eyes to meet hers. "Has anyone ever told you how convincing you are?"

Arivana gave him a wry grin. "Perhaps. But that doesn't mean I don't like hearing it." She looked over her shoulder and jerked her head at Claris and Chase.

As they moved into place on either side, she held out her arms to Daye. "Now, take my hands so we can get this started before another catastrophe threatens to ruin our wedding!"

Jasside leaned against Mevon, enfolded in his arms: a posture she'd come to favor. They stood close enough to the podium to see Arivana, looking radiant as ever despite the simplicity of her attire, but remained far enough away as to blend in, commanding no position of respect or attention, though no one would question should she demand it. Just two more faces in the crowd, two more lovers come to cement their souls together, for whatever time they had left.

Mevon's voice rumbled above her. "Green?" he asked.

Jasside looked down at herself. A dress the color of spring grass flowed down from her neck to her ankles. It didn't fit quite right, but every seamstress and tailor had been busy with requests and didn't have time to make adjustments. Growing up, needlework hadn't been her most practiced skill.

"What of it?" she replied.

She felt his shoulders bob upwards. "Most of the women here are in white, though a few are in red or gold. You're the only one I see in green."

"There aren't many women here from home. I'm guessing your father didn't allow civilian followers on the ships when you set sail."

"No. But there are women in the Imperial army."

"A few of them. And like you, they're doing this in their formal military attire." She ran her fingers lightly against the red-and-black sleeve of his uniform. "It's strange seeing you in anything but your Hardohl leathers. Where did you even find this?"

"My father had spares." Mevon grunted. "I don't think it was coincidence that he thought to bring my size."

Jasside laughed, pushing herself away to get a better look at him. "I think you look handsome in it."

He smiled down at her. "And you look . . . well, you could wear mud-stained rags and still attract a blind man. In that?" He shook his head.

Failing to suppress a chortle, she punched his chest. "Oh, cut out that nonsense. It doesn't even fit right."

"Mine does, but it's . . . itchy. I can't wait until I can take it off."

She locked eyes with him, throwing up a devious smile. "Neither can I."

Jasside took the greatest pleasure in watching him blush and try to stutter out a response. She spun back towards the platform. "Oh look! They're about to start."

"**A**ll right, I think we're ready," Yandumar said.

"We most certainly are not," Gilshamed said.

"You changed the entire speech at least three times now, and we haven't even finished the ending!"

"Bah. Doesn't matter. I'll think of something. Just do the thing."

"What thing?"

"You know, the 'making me loud' thing."

"I think we'd better—"

"Look, I'm freezing my balls off here, and the young queen over there is wearing half as much fabric. We drag this out any more, and we'll end the day with more bride-sicles than happy newlyweds."

Sighing, Gilshamed nodded. "Very well."

Yandumar turned towards the others, bouncing his glance between Arivana and Daye. "You two ready?"

They both nodded. The boy didn't even seem hesitant . . . anymore.

Unnatural warmth swirled behind him. Yandumar couldn't see it, but knew Gilshamed's spell was now in effect. He cleared his throat.

"All right, listen up!" he began, his voice rumbling across the field and bringing all eyes instantly towards him. "I'm the only living emperor, so that means whatever I say goes. You got a problem with that, you can go ahead and leave now."

A murmur rose from the participants at this, but no one moved.

"That was not in the script!" Gilshamed hissed from behind him.

Yandumar glanced once at the parchment in his hand.

Then dropped it.

Gilshamed groaned. "Shade of Elos . . ."

"Well," Yandumar continued, "since you all stayed, I gotta assume that means you still wanna get married. That's fine. That's good, even. But you all better make sure you're doing it for the right reasons.

"Marriage is for life. Not until it gets hard or inconvenient, or until someone better comes along. *For. Life.* It doesn't matter if you're royalty or you haven't got half a coin to your name, if you get hitched you become partners until the end. *Partners.* Someone to share your journey through life with, no matter what stands in your way. Someone who looks out for the other's best interests because they know it will benefit them both.

"So love and respect your new spouses. Protect them. Cherish them. Give everything you've got to them, and them alone. And abyss take me, listen to them! You can't put two people in a room for half a toll before they find something to disagree on. You wanna be miserable? By all means, let your pride rule, and disregard everything the other has to say, and forget about compromise. But if you ask me, life's too short to live it like that. Even if you're unlucky enough to live for thousands of years."

Yandumar paused, giving his voice a rest and his words a moment to sink in. He knew he was probably rambling, but it couldn't have been worse than that abyss-taken script Gilshamed had scribbled up. Oh, it was moving all right, but the words would've sounded strange coming from him. Besides, people didn't need reminders about the frailty of life, and seizing the opportunity for love before death inevitably came for them.

The ruvak had already hammered that message into every skull.

"I know we all come from different places," he continued, "with as many marriage customs as there are excuses for getting divorced, but I don't got the patience to try working 'em all in. You wanna sacrifice a goat or douse yourself in ice water or have your lady friends beat the groom with sticks, you do it on your own time.

"So as I said, we're doing things *my* way. Short and simple. Just exchange vows of faithfulness and love and commitment, and whatever else you feel like including—so long as you *mean* it—then seal the deal with a kiss. And make it quick before we all freeze to death!"

Mevon turned from his father's speech, grasping Jasside's hands as he peered into her riveting brown eyes.

"I . . . don't know what to say," he said.

"Would you like me to go first?" she asked.

He shook his head. "I'll just end up repeating what

you said, most likely. I want to get this right, but I don't know if what I feel can be adequately conveyed in mere words."

She squeezed his hands. "I understand. How can you express something that can't be seen or heard or tasted or touched?"

"Indeed."

"Hmm." Her eyes wandered for a few moments. "What's that phrase your kind is always using? Something about nailing the last plank on a bridge?"

Mevon smiled. "Even when it's burning."

"Yes, that one. Why don't you try telling me what that means to you?"

He didn't have to think long about it. "It means that once you've started something, you do the right thing and see it through until the end, no matter how difficult it becomes."

She raised an eyebrow at him.

"What?" he said. "Should I consider you a task I need to accomplish?"

"No," she said, laughing. "But you have most definitely *started* something with me."

He smiled again, wider this time. "In that case, I vow to *finish* with you as well, regardless of who or what might try to stop me."

"And I promise that I won't ever be perfect."

"What?"

"Do you *want* me to give you false expectations?"

"Of course not."

"Good. Because I guarantee there will be times I'll be sad or angry or irrational, or that I'll disagree with every word you say just because you say it and hate you just because I know you're right but will never admit it. Some days I'll wake up looking less appealing than a shadow beast and do nothing to rectify it, and eventually I'll grow old and wrinkled and misshapen.

"As I said, I will not be perfect, but neither will I expect *you* to be. And with all my heart, I vow that I will never, ever, give up on us."

Mevon shook his head. "I guess I was wrong."

"About what?"

"What I feel *can* be expressed in words. Now I know what they are."

She smiled up at him, and he saw all he felt shining out from her gaze, with more intensity that he thought possible.

After a moment, she cleared her throat. "Well, it appears we've fulfilled the *first* of your father's requirements."

He nodded, understanding her intent clearly, and bent his lips to hers in order to . . . satisfy . . . the second.

Arivana had given Daye her vows and received his in return. They'd each been prepared in advance, a strict script to ensure all matters of state were covered in detail, with Claris and Chase standing as mutual witnesses to ensure compliance. It was nothing like the fairy tales her mother had told her as a child.

She did her best not to show her disappointment with that fact.

I told him that our hearts would follow. If only I could believe it myself.

Now, as she stood looking up into his eyes with her hands held in his, all that remained for him to become her husband and the new king of Panisahldron . . . was a kiss. But a few moments of awkward stillness made it apparent that neither of them quite knew how to proceed.

She was just about to turn a helpless expression towards Claris, hoping her aunt would somehow find a way to save her, when Daye let out a loud sigh. Surprising her, he stepped forward, sliding down to one knee, so that his eyes were just level with her neck.

"Look," he said. "This isn't what I ever dreamed my life would be like, and I get the sense that you feel the same way. And you're absolutely right about what this means to the people. It's important. Essential, even. But abyss take me if I'm not going to make the best of the situation.

"I've said my vows to the queen. Now, let me say my vows to *you*."

Breath catching, all she could do was nod.

"First, I promise to admit my mistakes and forgive you for yours. Abyss knows I've made plenty already, a trend that would take a miracle to reverse.

"Second, I promise to be gentle with you. You've dealt with more hardship than anyone should have to bear in a lifetime, and shown great personal strength throughout it all. Still, I know that everyone needs someone in their life with whom they can let go of pretense and simply . . . be. I'll do my best to be that someone for you.

"And last, I promise to be patient. I know our hearts won't start beating in harmony immediately, but I'll work towards learning your wants and needs, and sharing your joy and pain, and whatever else it takes until they finally do."

Sniffing, Arivana wiped a tear from her eye. "Something tells me it won't take that long at all."

It seemed to be the right thing to say, for he grinned ear to ear.

She cupped his face and leaned forward. True to his word, he was gentle with her, but she still felt the passion exuding through his lips.

By the time she pulled away, clamoring for breath, snow had begun to fall, brushing her arms and shoulders like cold kisses from a butterfly. Daye looked up at the sky and smiled.

"A white wedding," he said. "It's considered good luck in Sceptre."

Thunder crackled in the distance.

"What about a white *lightning* wedding?" she asked, smirking.

"That," Gilshamed said, stepping near them, "was not lightning."

Arivana followed the valynkar's gaze, lifting her eyes up past the glacier to the high, snow-swept peaks of the mountain. Like a great wintery wave, an avalanche rushed down the slopes, and the crowd gathered to observe the mass wedding was directly in its path.

A heart recently swelled from the unexpected now shattered by the same.

Jasside pushed away from Mevon, despite aching for more. She'd felt something that shouldn't have been: a crack of dark energy released from the mountain's height. Just a sliver, but where it was placed meant the possibility of serious consequences.

A moment later, she felt the ground tremble and saw the wall of snow rolling towards the field like a thick, angry cloud.

She didn't have time to contemplate the how or why of it, or respond to Mevon's questioning stare, or even shout out a warning. All she could do was energize.

Spying a stretch of grass between the participants and the crowd beneath the glacier, she shadow-dashed to it. The noise and vibrations intensified immediately. People began running, screaming, needing no warning to realize that death was coming for them.

Not if I have anything to say about it.

Jasside patted herself in search of the spheres that housed her darkwisps. A wasted moment. Her wedding dress hadn't come with any pockets, so she'd left them behind. Lives would hinge on that decision, made within a false sense of security. It was only a matter of magnitude.

Filling herself with all the dark energy she dared, then more, she erected a barricade across the breadth of the glacier, just behind the last rows of the now fleeing crowd. A thousand paces wide, and a hundred high, she poured everything she had into it, hoping to buy people the time they needed to get clear.

Her heart thumped twice in her chest.

The avalanche struck.

Like a wave breaking over rocks, the snow swept over her barrier, barely slowing.

Cold death swirled down on all sides.

Can't save them all. Just try to save as many as you can!

A strict barrier was useless. There was simply too much force behind the avalanche to try to halt its advance. She had to direct it somehow, away from people to where it would do the least amount of harm.

Down the mountain, to the southeast. The valley there was home to no permanent residences.

It will have to do.

Jasside cast a new barrier. Not a straight line this

time, but a wide curve, channeling the icy, torrential river away from the crowds. Gasping with the effort of keeping it in place, she looked towards the foaming, raging head and realized there were hundreds now in its path that had been out of it before.

And she hadn't a drop of energy left to help them.

A tear rolled down her cheek as they were swept under the snow.

Gilshamed had rushed forward through the air as soon as he'd realized what was happening, but knew within moments of leaving the ground that he would be too late.

By the time he was in position to do any good, it was over.

Heart heavy with loss, he settled down and dismissed his wings. Mevon cradled his new wife, who breathed harshly into his arms, while everywhere else was filled with weeping and wailing as people mourned the lost. The sounds were strangely intense in the hush following the avalanche's expense.

Not even those newly wed had been spared from the mountain's fury.

He had just begun to survey the damage, searching in vain for some way to be useful, when he heard a voice behind him.

"Saboteurs," the voice said. "I'm surprised none of you saw this coming."

He turned to see Vashodia stroll towards him through ankle-deep snow.

Gilshamed sneered at her. "And you did?"

She appraised him with her incessant, knowing glance. "I've been expecting something like this for quite some time. Sem Aira wasn't the only spy the ruvak planted among us, after all."

"You knew," Mevon said, rising as he helped Jasside gently to her feet. "But you did nothing about it? You didn't even think to warn the rest of us?"

Vashodia shrugged. "I didn't think you'd be so stupid as to hold a mass wedding without consulting me first. And beneath a glacier no less!"

"Invitations were posted everywhere," Gilshamed said.

"Not everywhere, and I've been busy since this morning. I didn't even know about it until a few marks ago."

Mevon grunted. "I see now why Jasside had so much trouble with you."

Jasside pulled on her new husband's arm. "Don't engage with her. That's one battle that no one will ever win."

Vashodia giggled. "So glad you still remember that."

"Why did you even come here, then?" Gilshamed asked. "To gloat over your superior foresight? Lives have been lost, Vashodia. Hope . . ." He hung his head and continued quietly, "Hope has been shattered."

"I dare say that was their plan." The mierothi pointed towards the horizon, where dark specks filled the air like a locust swarm, just beyond the influence of the voltensus. "And, alas, our days of respite are finally at an end. Quite a few ruvak fleets have joined the vanguard, tumbling out of the void like . . . well, like an avalanche, I suppose. They now number more than thrice as many as before.

"I do hope you're all ready."

Gilshamed could only shake his head in disbelief before the colony-wide alarms began sounding.

CHAPTER 17

Draevenus honed his daggers for what seemed the hundredth time, casting glances up the trail for what seemed the thousandth. Both activities had become routine as of late, reflexive. The first was merely to pass the time. Only once he realized what the second meant—who he was watching for, and more importantly, why—did he stop. And wonder.

He had admired Tassariel right from the start. Her body, lithe yet powerful, quick yet controlled, along with the skill derived from her calling, carried with it the promise that she would have all the physicality necessary to accompany him, to be both partner and apprentice on the most dangerous journey he had ever made. Seeing her in action had only deepened that appreciation. Yet now, whenever she was within his line of sight, he found his gaze lingering, admiring all the same things about her, but for far different reasons.

And he was running out of excuses to ignore it.

It had begun so simply. Twice he'd been all but blind by circumstance, and on both occasions she'd grasped his hand and led him to safety. Such a small thing. But he was nearing two thousand years of age, and though he'd traveled far more than most, experiencing the vast differences between cultures even from one district of the empire to the next, he had ever only been an observer. An outsider, looking in, desperately wishing to be a part of something, though knowing he never could. Other than when he was killing someone, he hadn't truly been touched in centuries.

The very thought was almost enough to drown him in despair.

Mierothi hadn't mingled with the very populace they'd dominated, and most could hardly stand the sight of each other. The stagnation running rampant under Rekaj's rule had been less about civilization's advance than it had been about his kind's immortal souls. To live forever, to rule in absolution; these things meant nothing. Journey before destination, as the scholars liked to say. But without the latter, the former had no purpose. And without someone to walk at your side, gently holding your hand, even the most adventurous journey to the most promising destination was a lonely trek to make.

Memory being what it was, he hadn't realized how much he wanted it until he started pondering the possibility. That it was Tassariel who had awakened this longing almost seemed a cruel joke. One last jab from the gods in their graves, or the kind of long-planned joke that only Vashodia could pull off, and whose punch line only she could understand. It was impossible on too many levels. Tassariel was a valynkar, for one, and far too young. And any notions of intimacy between them were only due to her need for comfort after her father's cold reception. With the end of the world becoming more inevitable with every day that passed without them finding something that their allies could use, there was simply no time for . . . diversions.

Excuses, all of it. Why can't you just admit that you're afraid?

The thought seemed to come out of nowhere, stabbing him with its virulence, and cutting through all pretense to expose the cold, trembling heart that guided his logic. Thus laid bare, his reasons crashed to the ground, one by one, like timbers felled by an axe-wielding giant.

She is valynkar, but so what? We both came from human stock at one point, and I doubt either of us care what anyone else might think. She's young, yes, but she has actually sought out experience and learned from it, managing to avoid the listless fate of so many who live through millennia. Though a heightened emotional state may have driven her into my arms, she is still thoroughly in control of herself. Most importantly: If the end of the world is truly coming, I'd rather not go through it alone.

Motion drew his gaze down the trail once more, revealing a tall figure in segments between the thin, white-barked trees that dominated the island.

Besides, my gaze isn't the only one that lingers.

Tassariel marched fully into view, her lavender hair shimmering in the sun and hanging loose just low enough to brush her shoulders and neck. She'd taken to wearing it that way of late, instead of braided, making her seem—by human standards anyway—a decade older.

Her eyes found him. True to his estimation, they remained locked in place far longer than normal acknowledgment of his presence could account for. If he could only use one word to describe them, that word would be . . . *intense.*

As much as he wanted to fall into that gaze, to succumb to the desire he knew they both shared, some part of him still resisted. He may have rationalized away all the reasons to abstain, yet couldn't help but think that all of this was somehow wrong, that their shared isolation and hardship had tricked them into feeling things that weren't real.

And he'd lived long enough in his sister's shadow to resent being deceived.

"Back so soon?" Draevenus said, gesturing to the basket overflowing with freshly washed clothes balanced on her right hip. "I thought you'd be gone all afternoon."

She glanced down at the basket, finally breaking her awkward gaze.

Even though it was a discomfort he ached to explore, he was glad for the moment's end.

"Some of the ladies helped me," Tassariel said, smiling feebly.

"Has your father lifted their ban on speaking, then?" he asked, trying to keep it light. Her smiles had become rare, and he wanted to do all he could to preserve them.

She shrugged. Her smile vanished.

He sighed, cringing inwardly. *So much for keeping it light, Draevenus. Might as well bring up her dead mother while you're at it.*

Tassariel trudged to their packs. Setting down the basket, she pulled each article one at a time, hands glowing with heat and light to banish the last of the moisture still clinging to them, before carefully folding and putting them away.

Though he tried to think of something to say as she worked, nothing came to mind that, were he to voice it aloud, wouldn't be many times more awkward than the stare they'd shared a moment earlier. He'd never been the best with words—or women; the combination of the two froze him as surely as winter's heart.

He was saved from any further potential embarrassment when she finished with the clothes and came to sit at his side, saying not a word as she leaned her head on his shoulder. Her presence warmed him in more ways than one.

"I don't think he means to let us leave," Tassariel said.

Draevenus nearly started at the sound of her voice, her mouth so close he could feel her breath on his cheek, smelling of the tart, sweet berries that grew nearby. "What do you mean, 'let' us? And who said anything about leaving?"

"We're wasting our time. You know that as well as I. If there's a weakness to be found about our enemy, we won't stumble upon it here. My father has made it clear he does not wish to speak further, but neither does he want us to go."

"Has he said why?"

"Despite my insistence that we can take care of ourselves, he views leaving this island as a death sentence, and will set his followers to standing in our way should we try. Pointless, but in a way, that's almost . . . nice of him."

"Nice?" Draevenus bit back a less than kind comment about the man. "I'd like to agree with you, but after coming all this way, I don't want to leave until we're sure there's nothing valuable to learn." He sighed, kicking a pebble. "And I don't know where else we might go."

Silence enveloped them as his last words seemed to hang in the air, the weight of them smothering all else. Tassariel fidgeted beside him. She, too, must have contemplated what their next move might be, and had likely come up just as empty as he had.

When he made plans, he always left room for error, for setbacks and improvisation, but rarely did he fathom outright failure. And unlike Vashodia, he didn't have the foresight to layer countless contingencies upon each other, creating a weave so dense it ensured success through the sheer force of probability. Not knowing what they were going to do next made his stomach twist.

Even so, he was starting to enjoy the feel of her pressed against his side despite his reservation, when a sound reached his ears. She lifted her head, and they both turned to face behind them as the noise grew, a shriek tearing across the sky that they had come to know far, far too well.

"Ruvak," he said.

They both jumped to their feet, but before they could so much as take a step, over a dozen figures raced into their camp. As surprising as that was, Draevenus was even more astonished when an elderly woman spoke, barking out an order like a commander.

"To the hill! Go!"

The rest surrounded him and Tassariel, herding them like sheep. And like sheep, they obeyed without protest. As they raced along towards the hill at the center of the encampment, he shared a look with his companion, seeing in her eyes a reflection of his own excitement, and knew that his heart wasn't the only one whose hastened rhythm had nothing to do with the exertion of their flight.

We might finally—finally!—see how they do it. How they repel the ruvak using only light.

He spared only the briefest thought towards offering to lend them their aid. They'd help if things went sour, but this was simply too good an opportunity to pass up, and could very well validate their entire journey.

As they approached the hill, mobs of figures streamed in from all sides, and he was at last able to obtain a clear estimate of just how many people resided here: well over a thousand, mostly women and children. Despite their rush, and the nature of approaching threat, he could see little panic among them. Some of the young ones were even smiling, singing rhymes as they skipped along, or jostling each other as they laughed and raced to see who would be first to the hill.

Passages, carefully concealed in the brush, were opening everywhere he could see. The island's denizens flowed through them to some kind of shelter, but a growing collection of figures remained outside, eyes fixed on the hilltop.

And every last one of them was energizing.

Tassariel gasped.

Draevenus examined her face for a moment, then followed her stare. There, stepping to the very summit of the hill, a space ringed by trees and flattened like some kind of stage, came her father.

The man's eyes surveyed his riveted followers, stopping cold when they swept through Draevenus and Tassariel. Even from this distance, Draevenus could see guilt overcome the man's visage, an expression that seemed horrifically natural. He had heard only little of the man's story, but it was enough to drive away any pity he might have felt.

Now approaching one of the shelter entrances, their herders urged them onwards, gesturing towards the damp, shadowed space. Both he and his companion stopped abruptly.

"I've no time to argue," the old woman said. "Get in."

"No," Tassariel said. "We need to see. To witness."

"Your father gave strict orders, girl. He'd be wroth if anything were to happen to you."

"We crossed half a continent to get here," Draevenus said. "Nothing the ruvak do can surprise us."

The woman glanced towards the man on the hilltop, as if for guidance, but he had begun to energize, gaze lifted to the sky in a sad sort of ecstasy, and it was apparent that he was in no state of mind for issuing commands.

Lips twisting, the woman flicked a hand at them dismissively. "Do nothing stupid," she said before ducking through the portal and vanishing into the shadow of the shelter.

Draevenus flashed a victorious smile at Tassariel, who returned the expression in kind. Together, they turned to face the approaching skyships.

Just as a trio of large, airborne masses came skittering into sight through the treetops, the casters around them pulsed as one. There was no doubt about who led them, however, through whom all that power flowed.

He glanced over his shoulder to see Tassariel's father raise a glowing arm. A moment later, raw light energy shot forth from him in three blinding beams.

Blinking, Draevenus wrenched his gaze forward to track their progress. Inerrantly, the beams struck the three ruvaki vessels, each, he now saw, the size of a flagship. Their hulls glowed white, attuning in an instant.

He held his breath, waiting for revelation.

For almost a full mark, the skyships made no move, neither to advance nor retreat nor attack. They simply . . . hovered. Shapeless statues in the sky. The light emanating from the hilltop remained equally stagnant, a formless flow of light lacking any clear definition or purpose. It wasn't even particularly hot.

"What the abyss is going on?" he asked.

Tassariel said nothing, merely shaking her head as she pointed towards the skyships. The three vessels turned with all the haste of slugs, dipped their noses like chastised children, and flew away.

Frustration and disbelief warred within him as he watched them vanish over the horizon.

Revelation, it seemed, would not come today.

Mevon trudged through the dark streets of the colony, careful not to disturb the burden cradled in his arms. Each step squished from the blood soaking his boots, too much of it his own. He couldn't even smell it anymore. In the past five days, he'd received more new scars than he had in the previous five hundred, and slept fewer tolls than he usually did in one. Not that he was unique in that regard; no one had gotten much rest since the ruvak had renewed their attacks.

Since the day of his wedding.

Mevon risked a glance at the figure he held. Sharp snores stuttered from beneath a face smeared with dirt, while a blond braid dangled over his forearm, ash-coated strands of hair sticking out to all sides like innumerable, wriggling snakes. At least that's what his mind perceived. With fatigue pressing down as heavy as a mountain, he was surprised his hallucinations weren't more frequent or bizarre . . . and that the woman held close against his chest wasn't one of them.

My wife. No, not a burden at all.

As hard as he'd been fighting, Jasside had put him—and everyone else—to shame. Every time the ruvak had attacked, she'd been there. The defensive line was over a thousand leagues long, and they simply didn't have enough troops to mount an effective defense around it all; the bulk of the casters and elite troops spent their time flying between one engagement and the next. She had always been the first to arrive, at times the sole difference between victory and defeat, throwing back their assaults almost single-handedly.

Only tonight had the enemy relented, giving humanity their first true respite along the whole of the perimeter. Upon hearing this, Jasside had collapsed instantly.

As glad as he was that she'd finally get a chance to rest, Mevon couldn't help but worry. The ruvak had proven too smart for his liking, and he knew they were now refining their tactics from the lessons they'd learned during the initial phase of their siege. That they could only field ground troops against prepared fortifications, casters, armed skyships, and sorcerous war engines didn't seem to matter when they had a seemingly endless supply of fresh soldiers, ones who displayed more ferocity and discipline than had those he'd faced before.

And no one could discount the possibility of additional saboteurs in the colony.

All in all, the strategic situation was a mess. Mevon was more than glad to take little part in it, leaving the planning and execution to those skilled in such things, like his father and King Chase. Losing himself in battle had given him more than enough satisfaction.

He glanced down at Jasside once more.

Well, almost *enough.*

At last Mevon spotted their tent among a cluster of others tucked in among the permanent mierothi homes. Technically it was now their shared quarters, since she had given up her house on the domicile to a needy family, but they had yet to sleep in it at the same time. As much as he wished their first night together as husband and wife to involve more than merely sleeping, he knew it was what they both needed most.

Nearing the entrance, he turned sideways, shielding Jasside with his shoulder as they pushed through the flaps, which were three layers thick and tied down stiffly to keep out the cold. Inside, darkness greeted him. As he wasn't yet familiar enough with the tent to navigate it blind, he measured his steps even more carefully than before. It seemed half a toll before he felt his shins bump against the bed.

Sighing in relief that he'd found it without tripping, Mevon began kneeling to set Jasside gently upon the mattress.

Halfway down, his knee buckled.

With his hands full, he had no way to catch himself and tumbled forward into the bed. The frame groaned at the influx of sudden weight, and his head pressed against Jasside's chest, pinning her.

Mevon managed to right himself just as her eyes shot open.

Abyss take me . . .

He could just make out the whites of her eyes, darting about frantically in what could only be panic. He didn't blame her. To awaken in a strange place, in the dark, as a massive figure loomed above you, and without access to your power? He couldn't say exactly what he'd feel in that situation, but in her case, he doubted it would be pleasant.

"Mevon?" she asked in a rasp, her breath rapid and laboured.

"Yes, Jasside. It's me."

"Where are we?"

"In our tent. You fell unconscious after . . . well, from exhaustion."

"The ruvak?"

"Quiet. For now."

A long sigh escaped her lips, which calmed her breathing. "That's . . . a relief. But there's still so much to do. We'd better—"

"*You* are not going anywhere. You'll kill yourself if you don't get some rest." Mevon began pulling away, slipping his arms out from underneath her. "I'm sorry for waking you."

"Five days since our wedding, and I've only just now got you to myself." She grabbed at his collar, yanking his face down towards hers with surprising force. "I have more important things on my mind than sleeping."

This close to her, Mevon couldn't help but smell all the sweat and grime and ash that caked her body, but underneath that was another scent, one wholly her. Wholly . . . feminine.

She wrapped both hands around his neck, pulling him in the rest of the way, and pressed her lips against his with unbridled insistence.

Mevon did not resist, forgetting as well all thoughts of sleep.

Jasside laid against Mevon's chest as it rose and fell with rhythmic regularity, gently tracing the scars across his abdomen with the tip of one finger. His snoring rumbled on without interruption.

Heat lingered within her, only now starting to ebb. She'd felt as if she'd been set on fire, sweet flames licking every muscle and pore, burning her in the most delicious way possible. The ache deep within her was satisfied for now, but she could already feel her desire growing anew.

My first sip of passion. Though it may have quenched me, it also revealed the true measure of my thirst.

She smiled, looking forward to drinking with Mevon, again and again. Something told her neither of them would ever again become so parched.

So long as the ruvak continue giving us reprieve.

Her smile wavered.

There had been a kind of desperation to their love-making, a feeling she'd felt emanating from Mevon even as it overtook her, subduing all thoughts of control. It was as if they were trying to—not make up for lost time, but to fit as much love into their lives before . . .

Before the ruvak take them from us.

Jasside buried her head further into Mevon, nestling between his chin and chest, and felt across the bridge of her nose the slow trickle of moisture.

Touching him had the added effect of rendering her powerless, and with him alone she didn't mind. In a way she'd come to crave it, for it acted to balance her, to remind her that no power in the world was absolute, and make her forget—if just for the duration of their contact—about the crushing weight of responsibility she'd taken upon her shoulders.

But it also left her exposed.

With her passion now sated, her mind fell to pondering the situation that humanity found itself in, coming again and again to a single word.

Futility.

A tear dropped to Mevon's chest, and she quickly wiped it away. She knew it was no use lamenting cruel facts, but if there was a way to shut off her mind once it latched on to something, she had yet to find out how. Humanity was doomed if they couldn't find a way to end the conflict soon, but barring the discovery of a hidden weakness, the only ways to stop the ruvak were to either kill them all, or to negotiate for peace. Both options seemed impossible.

Each engagement saw her allies outnumbered, and in every direction she'd seen the enemy fleets waiting just beyond reach of the voltensus, so many skyships they warped the very horizon. And though she knew the ruvak capable of learning human speech, they'd shown no desire to communicate.

Their only interest seemed to be in . . . extermination.

Rolling onto her back, Jasside pulled the sheets up to her neck, at last feeling the chill that crept in from the night. Though she couldn't banish her thoughts, her fatigue finally started winning out, pulling her down into welcome, blissful darkness.

No sooner had her eyes closed than the colony-wide alarms began sounding, a message in pitches and tones that had become as familiar to her as her own name.

All available hands: to battle.

Thin, pale fingers shook in the morning's chill, holding out a small wooden bowl. Arivana ladled porridge into it. The child moved off, perhaps giving her a smile or a nod of thanks, but if so, Arivana did not see it, nor did she care to. Far too few showed anything like gratitude. If she looked away, they never had the chance to disappoint her.

She'd come here to the part of the camp within Sceptre's borders to get to know the people she'd once thought of as less than human, but had since half adopted by her marriage to one of their princes. To present herself and show them that the ties she hoped to bind between their nations was more than just a game of titles and thrones and treaties. That their lives mattered and that all past animosity was put to rest.

It hadn't seemed to do much good. Like the feel of frost and wind, the smell of human grime and refuse, the whistle of skyships overhead and the muted clamor of battle, too many unpleasant things had become routine. To acknowledge kindness or generosity was a luxury few had enough coin in their souls to afford.

She tried not to judge them for it but did so anyway, time and time again, berating them inside her mind for not showing the level of humanity she expected of them. That it was a standard she herself often failed to achieve was not lost on her. Hypocrisy stung like a snakebite and seemed just as poisonous. And fighting it drained what little hope she'd thought to preserve within her.

It was not the cold, after all, that made her feel so numb.

Eventually the line of people waiting to be served

their morning meal dwindled until none were left. Arivana spun from the table, rubbing her sore arms as she watched for riders from the north. The strike force had flown by half a toll ago to reinforce the harried defense lines. She'd heard the latest reports on enemy tactics, and knew the ruvak would have begun their retreat long before the allied skyships could bear down on them. They'd become too wary, never engaging so much that they couldn't extricate themselves in a hurry. Still, every time they came, they never left without taking a bite out of the human defenders.

We're bleeding slowly. All of us. One giant beast slashed by a million talons a day. It's only a matter of time before one cuts us too deep. When that finally happens, oh how our blood will gush . . .

A shadow fell upon her from the side. Richlen, her faithful guardian, who had barely left her side in months.

He cleared his throat as he followed her gaze. "Worried, Your Majesty?"

She waited for only one person to return from the battle, and she knew he could take care of himself. "No."

He sighed.

"Was there something else, Richlen?"

He glanced northward. "I suppose I should ask if my oath to protect you now includes *him*."

Arivana swung her gaze to see Daye approaching

atop a bedraggled horse. His eyes lit up when he saw her, and she felt herself smiling, her heart beating just a little bit faster as if to remind her that hope wasn't dead after all. Theirs might have been the furthest thing from a fairy-tale marriage, but she could not have hoped for a better husband and king.

His vows had been put to the test even before they'd finished fishing bodies out of the avalanche, yet he'd passed with a nearly perfect score. Even during those first few nights, where she'd cried herself to sleep or thrashed in the throes of nightmares, he hadn't asked for anything, giving her the space she needed to grieve, or holding her softly without expectation. And when they'd finally consummated their marriage, he'd been so tender, so patient, neither pushing nor pulling, but simply taking her hand and walking alongside her to a place she'd never been.

You were right, Claris. There was nothing to worry about. Nothing at all.

The thought made her blush, but on the heels of it came another, which drove away all notions of embarrassment.

These adult pleasures, though welcome, mark the final resting place of my youth. At last the child I once was . . . is dead.

"Yes, Rich," she said at last. "He must definitely be protected."

CHAPTER 18

While Draevenus sat on the damp ground with legs folded before him, limp hands resting on his thighs, and eyes staring sightlessly into the fire, Tassariel began packing.

Her companion didn't notice.

She'd listened as he'd ranted on for days, trying to make sense of what they'd seen, reasoning through every possibility, as if chaos followed traditional forms of logic. Yet nothing he'd come up with had held his attention for long. In the end, he'd discarded everything resembling a conclusion.

He had even taken to questioning the others, the old and the young, casters or mundane souls, singling them out for interrogation in the gentlest sort of way. But few would listen, fewer still would respond, and none possessed the answers he sought. Truth remained to him as elusive as a dove in the clouds.

And when they'd tried to speak with their allies at the mierothi colony, to see if better minds would prevail where theirs had fallen short, they'd found themselves beset on all sides by swirling maelstroms of alien power.

Chaos had invaded commune itself.

They were on their own.

So now, he sat in a trance, leafing through his memories like pages in a book, perhaps thinking he would find some clue hidden there that might shed light on the situation. It was strange watching him. Though Tassariel had learned the skill, as all valynkar did at a young age, she had never used it. A part of her dreaded the day she would need it, for that day would truly signal the end of her mortal life span. Such a fear, however, was faint.

She didn't think she would live that long.

For her part, Tassariel had said almost nothing. She'd spent the last few days in close proximity to Draevenus, enjoying the comfort of his presence, and how perfectly at ease they were with each other. Two people who simply enjoyed each other's company, yet lacked all notions of expectation. She couldn't have wished for a better way to spend her last moments upon this world.

But as day had turned to night, then back and back again, something had begun gnawing on her mind. A sense of duty, and—ironically enough—guilt. For the whole time she'd sat there, content and uncaring, the world had been suffering. And there was something she'd been holding back.

She knew the answer to her companion's most desperate question.

After watching her father turn away the ruvak skyships, it had come to her instantly and instinctively. Yet even knowing that, she didn't see how such knowledge would help them defeat their enemy, and with no way to communicate with their allies, it was pointless to keep struggling on.

That was the lie she'd told herself, anyway.

A lie she could listen to no longer.

She finished packing what few things they still possessed, then strode over to Draevenus. Sighing, she reached down and squeezed his shoulder.

After a moment, his eyes unglazed. Rubbing them, he asked, "What is it?"

"Time to go," she said.

Draevenus stood, yawning, vertebrae popping audibly as he stretched his back. "Is it time for breakfast already?"

She shook her head. "We'll have to eat on the move. We've a long way to travel today, and we can't afford to waste daylight."

He furrowed his brow, then looked about, eyes

widening as he took in the empty camp and the two stuffed packs behind her. "You're serious."

"I am. We need to reach our allies before it's too late."

"Reach them? What's the point if we don't have anything *useful* to report?"

Tassariel grimaced, looking away. "We . . . do."

She was expecting anger from him, but when his hands reached up and enfolded her arms, eyes searching her face imploringly, she nearly cried from the tenderness he showed her.

"Tassariel? What's wrong?"

She met his gaze. His irises sparkled like chocolate diamonds, set in a face that was intense yet, somehow, soft at the same time. "I figured it out, you see. How it is my father keeps the ruvak at bay. I didn't want to say anything because I wasn't sure if it would do any good. I just wanted to enjoy my last moments—" she swallowed "—with you."

His head jolted back, as if struck by her honesty, confused impassivity setting in as he turned inward to examine his thoughts. Yet he could not hide the upwards twitch of the corner of his lips.

"We've a refuge here," he said finally. "A safe place to wait out the end of the world. A companion with whom to spend it. It's a . . . nice thought. I'll admit it had crossed my mind a time or two." He shook his head regretfully. "What made you change your mind?"

"That question is not as simple as it seems. The answer might be messy."

"Take your time."

She contemplated her response for several beats, realizing it was far more complex than she'd first imagined, even if it were the easiest thing in the world to say. "My father's guilt," she said slowly. "It is, I think, an answer to many different questions."

He tilted his head curiously. "I guess I'll have to trust you on that."

"Do you? Trust me, that is."

Draevenus smiled. "With my life."

She felt something stir deep within her at that, a feeling that almost made her forget about their desperation. After a moment, she even remembered to return a grin. "Come on," she said. "I'll answer you in more detail on the way, but we must hurry. We'll have to sneak past my father's watchers. I'd rather not have to—"

"You're not going anywhere."

Tassariel flinched. She and her companion both turned towards the voice, which had called out from the shadows around their camp. A figure stepped into view, then four more, and then dozens, a ring of dour faces flickering in firelight.

They were surrounded.

Defiance came naturally to her, as she locked eyes with her father, a spark of rage that felt both fitting and comfortable. No one she knew would blame her for it. No one sane, anyway.

Suppressing it was the hardest thing she could ever remember doing.

"Before you interrupted me, Father," she began, forcing softness into every syllable, "I was going to say, I'd rather not have to fight our way out of here. I don't think you want that either."

"No," her father said. "Which is why you'll unpack and forget this notion of leaving. The world will find a way to survive the ruvak. Or, it won't. Either way, nothing you do will change that."

"Perhaps not. But I have to try anyway."

"You'll die out there," he said, voice cracking. "I can't let you take that risk."

Tassariel breathed heavily before responding. "As much as I appreciate your concern, I am not yours to protect—you gave up that right a long time ago. We *are* leaving."

Her father's eyes flicked to her companion. "Not with that monster, you're not."

"Draevenus is not a monster."

Her father raised both eyebrows. "You must not know him that well, then. Has he told you how many valynkar he's killed? How many he murdered in their sleep, or with a dagger from behind?"

"Seventeen," Draevenus said. He hung his head. "No. Eighteen. The last was . . . recently."

Her father held up a hand, as if that proved his point.

Tassariel shook her head. "I know very well what Draevenus is, and what he was. Though he hasn't said it out loud, his actions have proven that he is remorseful for his past misdeeds, actions that almost single-handedly forged the bonds that now exist between our peoples."

And, she added to herself, *between him and me*.

Her father's lip quivered. "Do you think the dead care?"

"Of course not. The dead are dead. It's the the living we should concern ourselves with, and I think they'd be grateful."

"Grateful? Pah! He should have that pretty new skin of his peeled off one strip at a time. The only reason I haven't done so is because he came here with you. But if either of you try to leave, you'll be breaking the rules of my domain, and I'll have to revoke my hospitality."

She swallowed, stuffing down a remark about his supposed skills as a host. "I understand that you want to protect your own. So do we. Our friends are out there. Our families. Fighting and possibly dying. They need the information we now have. If you've been in commune recently, you know we can't just send them a quick word. We *must* get to them right away."

"What could you have possibly learned that would make even the slightest bit of difference?"

Tassariel took a moment to glance around at the others, then stepped close to her father, leaning in so only he could hear her.

"That you, Father, may be the most important man in the world right now." Then, even softer, she said, "And that I forgive you. For everything."

She turned away from him then, unable to meet his eyes, unwilling to see what effect her words were having on her father. They weren't really for *him* anyway.

She strode back to their packs, threw one over her shoulder and lifted the other up to Draevenus. Taking her companion's hand, she led him away from the fire and her father and the ring of onlookers, marching through the trees until each was lost from sight behind them, and then unfurled her wings.

No one one tried to stop them.

Mevon strolled into the command center, lifting a hand to greet an old friend.

Idrus did not wave back. "You're late," the ex-ranger said.

Shrugging, Mevon strode over. "My apologies. I was . . . occupied."

"I bet." Idrus shook his head. "I never thought I'd see the day."

"What? That I'd be happily married?"

"That you'd love something more than killing.

Someone. Especially *her*." Idrus grinned wryly. "Do you remember the day we first met her?"

Mevon grunted. "All too clearly."

"She made you piss yourself, if I recall correctly."

"Worse. Though I can't say I didn't deserve it. I had, after all, just killed her half brother."

"Aye. But she forgave you. Takes a special kind of person to do that."

"She's a special kind of woman."

"That she is. And if we had seven more of her, we could put one in each sector, and our defense would get a whole lot simpler. There would be no need for assignments such as the one I have for you today."

So much for pleasantries. "Give me the details."

"In a mark," Idrus said. "We're still waiting on your partner to arrive."

Mevon lifted an eyebrow. "And you called *me* late?"

Idrus shrugged. "Late is punctual for him." He paused, cocked his head, and sniffed deeply. "He's here."

A moment later, two figures staggered through the entrance, the cloying stench of wine and sweat instantly filling the small space. Mevon cast a sympathetic glance at his father, then a disapproving one at Orbrahn, who was only upright due to Yandumar's supporting arm.

His father nodded his greeting towards Mevon, then glanced at Idrus sheepishly. "You said you needed him. You didn't say he had to be sober."

"Bein' sober's overrated," Orbrahn said, punctuating his words with a dainty belch.

"If *you're* to be my partner," Mevon said, "I'd rather do this mission alone."

"But I'm jus' fine!"

"You can't even stand upright on your own, much less be of any use to me. Magic and wine don't mix."

"Nonsense! I'm perfectly capable of performing my duties."

Those were the words Mevon eventually was able to decipher, anyway, after taking several beats to unscramble the man's drunken rambling. He scoffed. "I doubt you could even defend yourself."

Orbrahn hiccuped. "Try me."

Without warning, Mevon lunged towards the man, fist raised.

Orbrahn's hand jolted up. Darkness gathered at his fingertips.

Mevon felt himself go cold.

He staggered, falling to his hands and knees less than two paces from the caster. Nausea born of extreme weakness rose from his gut, but did not spill over. Not this time, anyway. After a moment, he lifted his head and glared at Orbrahn. "You can release me now," he said through gritted teeth.

The young man stepped back, dissolving his strands of dark energy. He ran a hand through his greasy hair, standing erect unaided as his eyes suddenly gained focus. "How the abyss aren't you writhing on the ground in agony?"

Mevon rose, brushing himself off. He was almost surprised at how quickly Orbrahn had shed his drunkenness, but then he remembered that sorcery was a more potent addiction than mere drink could ever hope to be.

"Vashodia's around, is she not?" Mevon said. "Regardless that she calls herself our ally, I'd be a fool not to prepare myself against her. Jasside knows the spell well. I've had her do it to me several times until the effects were minimized."

Orbrahn grinned feverishly. "I bet that's not *all* you've asked her to do to you, eh?"

Involuntarily, Mevon clenched his fists.

"Oh, don't let him work you up, son," said Yandumar. "He's just jealous that no woman will come near him. At least not unless she's had twice as much to drink as him!"

"Fortunately," Idrus added, "there's not enough wine in the whole colony to allow that to happen."

Orbrahn swept a glowering gaze across the room. "Abyss take you all."

"It might," Mevon said, "if we aren't prepared for this mission."

Idrus stepped close, patting Mevon on the shoulder. "Don't worry," he whispered. "I've seen Orbrahn worse and still come through his assignments *mostly* unscathed."

Mevon grunted. "It's not *him* I'm worried about."

"I'm sure you'll be able to take care of yourself. It's why I chose you for this task."

"Which is?"

Idrus stepped away, raising his voice so the others could hear. "Today's assignment is a simple one. One of the defensive positions up north hasn't been attacked in almost a day and a half now. Your mission is to find out why."

Orbrahn gestured rudely. "Recon? Why not send a scout?"

"I have. When the third one failed to report in, I sent for you two."

Mevon frowned. "I don't like it. The enemy going quiet means they're planning something big. And I don't think Orbrahn and I have enough subtlety between us to fill a thimble, much less sniff out what they're up to."

"If I'd wanted subtlety, I'd have gone myself." Idrus sighed, shaking his head. "What I need is someone who can go kick down the hornet's nest and is sturdy enough to withstand a few stings."

Mevon smiled. "Looks like you've found the right men for the job, then."

"Indeed you have," Orbrahn added. "My faith in your ability to command, General Torn, has been restored."

"Ha!" Yandumar barked, nudging the caster with an elbow. "My faith in your ability to respect authority stands on slightly more shaky ground. You'd best get moving so you can start proving my doubt misplaced."

"Elegant words, old man," Orbrahn said, tossing back his hair. "For you, anyway."

Yandumar cranked back his leg, then swung his boot forward.

It met only empty air.

Orbrahn smiled at Yandumar, then gestured for Mevon to follow.

With a sigh, he obliged.

Arivana held a hand to her stomach as the messenger made her report to Jasside. More fighting along the Sceptrine front.

My husband is in danger.

Her belly roiled, as if she'd drunk milk too long left in the sun. The feeling had grown more intense with each mention of battle and, she now realized, in direct correlation with her rising affection for Daye.

"Send wings thirty-six through forty," Jasside ordered.

"Only five?" the messenger asked. "I don't think a hundred casters and a score of skyships will be enough."

Jasside sighed. "It will have to do. The Weskaran front has been unusually quiet all last night and this morning, which makes me believe the ruvak have something big planned. I don't want us to overcommit."

The messenger nodded, then strode to the other side of grassy hill, closing her eyes to enter commune and relay the orders.

Jasside sighed, then looked down on Arivana, her features instantly transforming into an expression of pity. "Worried about your husband?"

Arivana nodded. *I guess I still haven't mastered the art of hiding what's inside. Or maybe, I've grown comfortable enough around you that I don't feel the need to.* "Does this sickness ever go away?"

"To be honest, I don't know," Jasside said. "Once you see Mevon in action, it's hard to think any harm—any *lasting* harm, anyway—could ever come to him. Besides, I usually put myself in just as much danger."

Arivana looked down at the snow-speckled grass. "You must think me so weak. So . . . worthless."

Jasside flipped her wrist. "Don't be ridiculous. Even in war, there are more ways than fighting to prove your value. Without people like you holding things together, people like me wouldn't be *half* as effective."

"You're right. I suppose. But what about the people who don't, as you said, *prove their value*? People who just take and take and give nothing back. Do their lives even matter?"

Jasside snorted. "You *must* be feeling ill. Usually you're the one lecturing the rest of us on the worth of the weak and powerless."

"I know. It's just . . . I spend most days among the

people left behind, left idle, while the rest of you risk your lives to safeguards theirs. While it's true that doing so has allowed me to see uncountable acts of selflessness, compassion, and everyday heroism—in other words, the *best* humanity has to offer—I've also been witness to the *worst*."

"It can't be as bad as what's out there," Jasside said, pointing past the horizon.

"Can't it?" Arivana shivered, wrapping her arms about herself. "Even with the danger we face every day, the most vile scum still stalk this colony. Thieves and swindlers, rapists and murderers. Packs of boys, some as young as ten, have taken to standing guard around their tents and tenements, just so their sisters and mothers can sleep in peace. We've enough to be afraid of as it is—no one should have to fear violation from those who would abuse our lack of a proper watch to satisfy their own sordid pleasures.

"And yet, a part of me doesn't even consider those the worst of them. That kind of evil is at least expected. But those who complain about what they're given without lifting a finger to help, despite obvious and vital needs going unfulfilled on every side . . . *those* people almost make me want to let the ruvak in for a visit!"

Jasside shook her head, frowning. "I'd slap you if I didn't know you were joking."

"If I weren't joking, I'd deserve it."

"Still . . ."

"Poor taste. I know." Arivana sighed. "I'm sorry for taking my frustrations out on you, Jasside. With Claris and Daye busy fighting, and some necessary space between me and my guardsmen, I'm afraid I have no one else to turn to."

The woman's features softened. "I understand, Arivana. Positions of power are often lonely ones, regardless of whether you took your place or were given it. I know you feel the burden of responsibility. I feel it too. It's a good thing."

"How is crushing despair a good thing?"

Jasside laughed. "It means you're doing it right. It you don't feel that weight, people are probably better off without you."

Arivana shrugged. "It doesn't always feel that way. In fact, most times, it feels completely pointless."

"Why do you say that?"

"Just look at us!" Arivana swept a hand over the colony. "Even under a mutual danger to our very existence, we divide ourselves according to such arbitrary means. *Us* from the always malicious *them*. Take away the threat of the ruvak, and we'd be right back at each other's throats."

"Take away the threat . . . ?" Jasside said, as if lost in a dream.

Arivana studied the woman and could almost read the words going through her mind: *If only we knew how.*

After a moment, Jasside shook herself. "Putting

aside differences is harder than you make it out to be, as history has so often proved."

"Perhaps," Arivana replied. "But that doesn't mean it always has to be that way."

"And you'll be the one to change it?"

"Why not?"

"It won't be an easy task."

"Don't think I can handle it?"

"Well, you *are* chafing under the responsibility you already have."

"Only because I have so little actual power. And because people are too afraid to even think about embracing change."

"Are they? Seems to me fear is sometimes the only thing that will get people to reexamine their priorities. My advice? If you're going to start something so ambitious, don't hesitate. By the time things settle down—if they ever do, that is—you'll no longer have a captive audience."

The last two words drove chills down Arivana's spine. Yet, immediately following that cold flush through her bones, another sensation took hold: a curious feeling, like pieces of a puzzle clicking into place. There were bridges that needed to be crossed, but she'd hesitated to traverse them, either because they were brittle or burnt, or simply because no one ever had. She'd been too afraid to do more than creep along the edge.

Not anymore. Even if I have to rebuild each one, stone

by stone, plank by plank, making them sturdy enough for others to follow behind, the path will *be forged. I will no longer allow fear to keep me from forging it.*

She glanced at Jasside, smiling. The gesture was returned for a moment, before Jasside turned to face the messenger who was coming towards them once more at a sprint. Conversations with her always seemed to make things simple. It shouldn't really be a surprise, though. When you do the impossible every day, every problem must seem a matter of mere persistence.

The old woman skidded to a halt, panting. She tried relaying her message, but it was said through too many wheezes to make any sense.

Jasside held up a hand. "Catch your breath first," she said.

The messenger nodded, but there was no gratefulness on her face. All that showed was panic.

"The Fasheshish," she said at last. "They are requesting immediate aid."

Jasside raised an eyebrow. "Are you sure you heard right?" the sorceress said. "Fasheshe *never* asks for help."

It was true. The territory they defended was flat and featureless to every horizon. The ruvak had no way to sneak up on them, and the vaunted Fasheshish cavalry could run down any attempt they made to retreat. Arivana couldn't remember a single time they had called for reinforcements.

"I heard right," the messenger said, still too breathless to affect affront. "The force that arrived at dawn did not withdraw after a brief skirmish as usual. And when they cut off their retreat with a cavalry encirclement . . . ?"

"Well, what?"

The old woman shrugged. "They don't know. The fight continues. And though they didn't say it outright, the Fasheshish are losing."

The look on Jasside's face made Arivana shiver. "Send in Fanilmyr."

"How many wings?"

Jasside shook her head. "All of them. Send the entire domicile."

"But—"

"And get word to Gilshamed. Tell him to be ready."

"For what?"

"For anything."

With the barest flick of her finger, Jasside summoned her floating platform from its resting place behind the hill, and shadow-dashed onto its surface without saying a word. Arivana was not upset by the manner of the woman's departure. She had her own war to fight.

And I have mine.

Mevon finished filling his waterskins from the well, then strapped them back into place along his waist. He lifted an eyebrow at Orbrahn. "Sure you don't want to fill up? We don't know how long we'll be out there."

The caster shook his head, patting the lone, half-empty skin on his belt. "Oh, I'll be fine with what I've got."

"It's wine in there, isn't it?"

Orbrahn shrugged. "Your point?"

"You weren't a drunkard the last time I knew you. What changed?"

"Your old man put me in charge of things back home."

"That's it?"

Obrahn shrugged.

Sighing, Mevon turned away.

With his temporary partner following—or wobbling, to put it more accurately—on his heels, Mevon marched through the outer perimeter. The tents and cook fires were already behind them. The only things allowed here were for purposes of war. Each level was defined by a wide pit filled with spikes, and long planks across them that could be pulled back by defenders during each retreat. In this sector alone, every layer had been captured by the enemy and retaken by his allies dozens of times, averaging more than once a day. Silence had become, to these soldiers, the most suspicious thing in the world.

And today, there is far too much of it.

Only after they'd surpassed the last bulwark and were marching through a forest of bare-branched trees did Mevon look back on their recent trip through the defenses and realize that something was out of place.

"Did something seem . . . wrong?" he asked, continuing to tread through the woods.

"Whaddya mean?" Orbrahn said.

"Back there, in the camp. There was something off about it. About the soldiers."

The caster grunted in clear disinterest. "They were a little quiet. Maybe. Probably don't know what to do with themselves without their daily dose of combat."

"Quiet? They were downright lethargic."

"Not our mission. Not our problem."

Mevon sighed. Perhaps Orbrahn was right. But even so, it did nothing to settle the queasy feeling in his stomach.

They continued on for several marks, traveling deeper into the territory outside the perimeter, yet still within the area affected by the voltensus. It was strange being out here. Mevon had chased down a few enemy groups that had bitten off more than they could chew, but had otherwise stayed within the borders of the encampment. His existence had narrowed to that place. Anything outside it no longer seemed natural.

Despite the lack of animal noises—or perhaps because of it—there was a kind of tension in the air. A sense of something hidden, waiting. The queasiness burgeoned suddenly, and Mevon realized it was not simply instinct. It was too sharp a feeling for that.

The clip of voices returned to his mind, things he'd overheard only half-aware while traversing the perimeter. Men had been complaining about all the vomit. A sickness going through the camp like wildfire in dry grass. The look in every soldier's eyes had been more than mere fatigue.

"How are you feeling?" Mevon asked, stopping and turning to his partner.

"Why do you ask?" Orbrahn said.

"Just answer me!"

Orbrahn lifted his hands in surrender. "I'm fine. Really. The walk is even starting to clear my head."

"How's your gut? Any nausea?"

"No." Orbrahn narrowed his eyes. "What's this all about?"

Mevon closed his eyes, focusing on the sensations within him. His belly continued to roil, but now something new joined the fray. A burning sensation that he knew well.

Blessings scouring him clean.

"You've had nothing but your wine to drink today? Honest, now. It's important."

Orbrahn slowly nodded.

There was only one thing it could be, then.

Poison.

Before Mevon could so much as whisper his suspicions, the forest around them erupted.

Jasside felt her breath catch as she surveyed the scene below her. There, at the edge of a vast desert shimmering in morning light, sat the southeastern defensive perimeter. Manned almost exclusively by the people of Fasheshe, it had stood stoutest of them all, repelling all ruvaki assaults with almost pathetic ease.

It was already half-overrun.

The force sent against it was no mere band of fast-legged skirmishers, the kind meant to disengage before aerial reinforcements could arrive and bound back out of range of the voltensus. This was an army. Fully armored blocks of heavy infantry pounded against the Fasheshish positions, few of which were not already in retreat. Of the cavalry, she could see nothing. Allied and enemy troops swirled together almost everywhere she looked, giving her no clear target upon which to unleash her destruction.

Abyss take me, this is going to be messy.

Directing her platform forward and down, Jasside peeked over her shoulder. Fanilmyr Domicile was approaching, a ragged rock on the opposite horizon. It would be a several marks at best before it was in range, but by then it might already be too late. If she wanted to prevent a rout, she'd have to stall the ruvak on her own.

She popped open her spheres and let loose her darkwisps, harmonizing with them in beats. The activity took as much thought as breathing.

With so massive an enemy force—outnumbering the beleaguered defenders at least five to one—she would need to be efficient, a task she'd become exceedingly adept at. Crafting something from nothing was possible, but draining. Using the resources at hand required far less of her energy.

And what she had plenty of was cold.

Close enough now to hear the screams of dying men, Jasside gathered the ambient chill, scooping up what she needed and forming it into rough balls. Amplifying it. She picked out the places where the ruvak had penetrated deepest, where her allies were in most desperate need of aid, and set to work.

Compressed cold blasted into clusters of her enemy, crushing or hurtling entire companies at a time. Even those nearby that survived the initial attack were slowed to a snail's pace as sudden, biting frost sapped their energy, and made each breath a labor.

Jasside sent her castings down, again and again, killing thousands every mark. Yet against such a tide of flesh, it felt like she were a child on a beach, trying to protect her ill-placed sand castle from what anyone could see was inevitable. In the end, all she could achieve on her own was to buy her allies some time to retreat in orderly fashion, and even at her best, not much of it.

Sweating now, she hazarded a glance back over her shoulder. Relief filled her as she saw that the domicile was nearly in range.

Far past it, however, she saw something that should not have been.

War engine projectiles filling the air.

What idiot called for fire? The enemy is too close for that!

But as the beats thrummed by, and she tracked the volley's arc through the air, she realized what was happening. Too late and too far away to do anything to stop it, Jasside could only watch as the projectiles slammed into Fanilmyr, cracking the unprotected, unaware domicile like an egg.

Rushing wind and the domicile surface growing distant made Gilshamed feel as if he were flying.

Yet his wings were still tucked away.

The two disparate facts throbbed against his skull like the pounding of a thousand hammers. No—that noise was real, stone and marble grinding against each other, rumbling with deafening noise as it all fell away beneath him.

The only thing louder were the screams.

Lashriel!

Ignoring everything else, Gilshamed at last unfurled, bathed in golden glow as he dove through the falling, crumbling wreckage of yet another domicile, eyes searching for a face etched more firmly in his mind than any words in stone. All the valynkar and mierothi combatants had been gathering on the rim in preparation for the battle to come, but she had yet to arrive. If she'd been trapped indoors . . .

No! That's not possible. Not after all we've been through.

He weaved through battered chunks of street and buildings, and innumerable everyday objects that had not been secured, catching flashes of fresh sunlight through the storm cloud of debris.

Dawn. The attack had come at dawn.

The enemy had no respect for light, it seemed. Further proof in his mind that whether or not they survived this war, the age of his people was over. Once the valynkar were gone, darkness and chaos would pick over the bones of the world, twin vultures fighting for every last scrap of flesh. Vashodia alone would ensure the ruvak would never rest easy in their victory, even if she were last living soul with strength left to oppose them.

Cease dwelling on such thoughts, Gilshamed. This war is not yet over, and defeat is anything but certain.

But without Lashriel, any victory would be a hollow one. Meaningless. Without her, the whole world might as well go up in flames.

A flash of violet caught his eye. He angled towards it reflexively. Though haze and rubble made him momentarily lose sight of her, his path of flight remained fixed on the last place he'd seen her. Less than a score beats later, he found himself hovering next to his beloved, who cradled something in each arm.

"Help me," Lashriel cried over the cacophony all

around them, peering up at him with red-rimmed eyes. "There are so many . . ."

Gilshamed blinked. Her words tore his mind loose from its narrow focus. No longer concerned with finding her, he at last was able to take in his surroundings. What he'd dismissed as scattered blocks of lifeless stone were, in truth, falling people.

Falling . . . children.

For the briefest of moments, he wondered what the point would be in trying to save them. Those with the capacity for flight on the domicile were outnumbered hundreds to one. There was no way to prevent them all from descending to their deaths. And even if they could, the ruvak would still lay claim to them in the end. A quick death by falling might even be a mercy.

"Gilshamed!"

He shook himself, energizing, and put such thoughts aside. As always, he would do as much good as he was able.

Thrusting his hands to each side, he sent forth tendrils of light. Dozens strong, he wrapped them gently around as many falling figures as he could, slowing their desperate descent. Locking the magical ropes into place, he summoned more.

Lashriel followed his lead. And soon, others. Within half a mark, the sky was full of sorcerous nets, a mesh of dark and light, catching thousands of the falling. Yet this was only a fraction of the domicile's current population, those unfortunate refugees who had been crammed into every available nook and cranny.

The casters pulled up, slowing their descent, separating farther each beat from the falling wreckage. With soul-crushing finality, what had once been Fanilmyr, a thriving, floating city, crashed tumultuously into the ground.

Mevon slashed and slashed again, dancing backwards in frantic retreat, and still the only thing that kept the ruvak from surrounding him were Orbrahn's waves of crackling darkness, sweeping past him on either side.

More of the enemy soldiers converged. Mevon chopped one head off, but the others nearby pulled back. Capes tied to every back were woven through with fallen leaves. Lying prone, they'd been indistinguishable from the ground itself. He and Orbahn had been practically standing on top of a company when the enemy chose to reveal themselves.

Now, everywhere he could see, the ruvak were giving the pair of them wide berth. The forest was alive with nearly hidden infantry, only visible due to their motion, swarming like a sea of insects through the early-morning mist in every direction. Most of them were already farther south, closer to the defensive perimeter than he and Orbrahn.

Soon, he realized, they would be cut off.

"We've got to hurry," Mevon called, slowing as he came alongside Orbrahn.

"Oh, really?" the caster replied. "Here I thought we might just take a little stroll."

"Enough. Can't you go any faster?"

"I could be a league away in half a dozen dashes if I wanted."

"Jump ahead then and warn the perimeter."

"But what about you? I'm only still here to watch your back. Your wife would *kill* me if anything happened to you."

Mevon raised an eyebrow.

"Right," Orbrahn said. A beat later, he dashed away, leaving transient, inky stains in his wake.

Alone now, Mevon hurried onward. He rushed between trees, up and down hills, and across creek beds, and still the enemy did not close. Sound and motion itched at the peripheral of his senses, but the space directly around him remained calm. Like all things that seemed too easy, he remained wary of a trap.

As he broke through to the edge of the killing field, Mevon saw that it was already in place.

The ruvak had shattered the first two fortifications and were gaining ground on the third. Few stood against them. Most of the humans he could see were falling back desperately, yet sluggishly. If the burning in his belly was any indication, he couldn't exactly blame them. Combat was taxing enough in the best of conditions; attempting to fight while sick or poisoned was an exercise in futility.

All this he took in at a glance, then dismissed in lieu of more pressing concerns. A half-circle of human steel awaited him, all of it held in ruvaki hands. Every unblinking eye tracked Mevon's cautious approach. Without turning, he sensed the other half of the circle closing in behind him. Thousands now surrounded him, an impenetrable wall of spears and shields five layers thick.

At the center of it all, three ruvak soldiers stood ready, faces crazed by unbridled bloodlust. The smallest of them was almost half a pace taller than himself. Where such giants among them had come from, he didn't know, but it was yet another thing about the ruvak of which humanity was ignorant. The list had grown long.

Looks like they want a show. I guess I'll have to give them one they'll never forget.

Mevon stepped onto the killing field, twirling Justice absently as he gauged his three opponents.

Jasside could feel herself growing tired.

Spell after spell flew down from her fingertips, sending hundreds to icy graves with every breath, but her casting was not the source of her fatigue. Indeed, she'd fought longer and harder on many occasions. Yet no matter how grim things had seemed at the time, there had always been hope of both relief and victory, thin as it was.

This time, she had neither.

The noise from Fanilmyr's fall still rumbled behind her, and soldiers—human and otherwise—screamed as they lay dying beneath her, yet these were not the most disturbing sounds she heard. Distant thumps announced the firing of more war engines, the projectiles all falling within the colony. Sorcery snapped, barely felt over the cold ocean of power she commanded, which signified a battle at the very heart of the colony, the place everyone had thought to be safe. The place she now ached to go.

This sector is lost. No amount of effort on my part will change that. Not as long as I'm on my own. There are families back there. Innocents. Children. If I can save even one, isn't that better than what I'm doing here?

Hands trembling, she looked down at the Fasheshish army, whose annihilation now seemed inevitable. All she was doing was stalling it for a little while.

A wave of horror washed over her, all the more revolting for how swiftly it passed, as she turned her back on tens of thousands of lives and began guiding her platforms towards the center of the colony.

What she saw a moment later made her freeze in place.

Flying free of the dust cloud risen from the fall of Fanilmyr came valynkar and mierothi by their hundreds, headed straight for her position.

Relief had come at last.

Jasside turned back around, settled on her course, and resumed her destruction of the ruvaki army.

"The explosions seemed to have stopped for now, Your Majesty," Richlen said.

Arivana lifted her head. The four guardsmen standing in a protective shell around her—as if mere armor could stop a war engine attack—straightened at the words. Another resounding boom made them flinch back into their defensive posture.

Richlen grimaced. "Well, *more* distant anyway. I haven't heard one fall nearby in a few marks. It should be safe to move now."

It had all happened so fast. One moment they were strolling down a street not far from the voltensus. The next, fire was raining down on all sides.

They were inside now. Somewhere. Though how they'd gotten there she couldn't recall. She only had vague recollections of gauntleted hands gripping her arms, lifting her, muffled shouting, and a sense of surreality that even now had not fully dissipated. Richlen's words made sense in only the simplest of ways.

"If . . . if you think so," Arivana said. "I suppose it wouldn't be nice to keep her waiting."

Richlen's eyes widened. "You can't seriously still want to go there?"

"Why not? You said it was safe to move."

"Only to get you to shelter. Real shelter, that is."

"But . . . but I have to build bridges. I need . . . need to . . . cut enough logs before the whole forest burns down."

"I'll help you build a whole *palace* if you want, Your Majesty. Just not today." He paused, looking out the window, then nodded to the other guardsmen. "Time to move."

Before she could protest further about the important things she had to do, she found herself being herded once more. They slipped out the door and into the street, only to plunge straight into a maelstrom of madness. Half the houses she saw were either crumbled heaps or raging infernos. Smoke and screams filled the air. People ran in every direction, most caught in the messy grip of hysteria and lacking any sense of purpose. Some actually seemed organized as they fought the flames and lent a hand to the wounded, but they were outnumbered by the frantic mob, their efforts undone by panic.

All of it seemed muffled, somehow. Distant. Unreal. Like it was happening in another place, another time, and to someone other than herself. Arivana watched the chaos unfolding all around her and felt . . . nothing.

What she saw next, however, shattered her preternatural calm.

A child sat against the wall of a ruined building,

bare feet splayed out before her. A charred doll rested in the girl's lap. From deep within a face stained by soot and sweat and a splash of blood, hollow yet living eyes stared at nothing.

Everything sharpened at once, and Arivana found her eyes watering, ears ringing, and her nose choked by ash. Breath and pulse began racing. Arivana spotted the girl again, reaching out between her guardsmen, but they marched on without yielding, sweeping her away from the child. They turned a corner, and the girl was lost to sight within moments.

"Stop!" Arivana said. "Rich, please, we need to stop!"

Richlen didn't pause or even slow. "Too dangerous," he said, eyes scanning before him as he marched onwards. "Our only priority right now is to get you somewhere safe."

"We're in the middle of the settlement. This was *supposed* to be the safest place around."

Her guardian turned his head slightly, but said nothing.

"There's a little girl back there," she continued, "who looked like she'd just lost everything and everyone she ever knew. She needs our help. It probably won't mean much on the grand scale of things, but it might mean *everything* to her."

And I have too many dead children on my conscience already.

After a long moment, where Richlen contemplated and she held her breath, he simply shook his head. "No."

Fury filled her instantly. What right did a lowly guard have to defy his queen? How dare he refuse her wishes! Even though a part of her knew the futility of her desires, and the danger still present at every step, she let her rage boil, silently glowering at Richlen's armored back as he bobbed along before her.

They continued on for several marks. As the signs of destruction slowly waned, and the permanent buildings became more spread out, she realized at last where they were heading.

The voltensus. The heart of the colony.

She wondered at both the relative peace around them and at Richlen's choice of refuge. But only for a moment. Before she could even hazard a guess as to her guardian's intentions, a cluster of buildings two hundred paces away erupted in fresh flames.

Arivana was thrown to the ground, and the four guards covered her with their bodies in an instant. She peeked through a gap between them, spying Richlen, who crouched with sword drawn, staring in the direction of the inferno.

"There was no volley," he said quietly, narrowing his eyes. "That blast wasn't from a war engine."

She followed his gaze. From between two nearby tenements, six figures emerged, dressed in cloaks and holding bows. Though they looked the part of normal scouts, they were running away from the raging flames and looked more like children caught snatching pastries than soldiers on the lookout for whoever had lit the fire.

And there's something about the way they move . . .

It was subtle, gestures and mannerisms most wouldn't even register as odd. But Arivana had spent over a year in close proximity to Flumere; when it came to impostors, she was something of an expert.

"They're ruvak!" she called.

Without further prompting, Richlen lunged towards them.

One of them raised his bow. And it was only then that she realized it was not a normal arrow fitted to the string.

Wrath-bows? Abyss no . . .

Richlen pounded ever nearer, rushing to close the distance. But he could not span that final gap before the infiltrator loosed his arrow. That heavy, metal shaft, infused with virulent magic, arced through the air.

It didn't travel very far.

Red and yellow flashed, scorching her eyes, but she could not look away. Horror filled her as all seven figures were consumed by flames.

She had no time to grieve, for a second group of disguised ruvak appeared from around the corner of the next building over. Her heart froze in her chest, until she realized they hadn't spotted her yet. Their attention was on something in the other direction.

The only thing of interest beyond them was the voltensus itself.

The infiltrators lined up, fitted arrows to strings, raised their bows . . .

The air darkened.

When light returned, Arivana searched for the ruvak, but could not see them. In the place they'd been was merely a greasy stain upon the grass and a quivering mass that reminded her of the leavings after an animal had been thoroughly butchered.

A dark figure floated down from the sky, drawing Arivana's gaze, and almost lazily touched down near where they'd been.

Planting hands on her hips, Vashodia shook her head. "They just had to burn the grain storage, didn't they? Well, I suppose I'll have to activate yet *another* backup plan."

A wave of power erupted from the mierothi that Arivana felt in her bones. A moment later, the ground started to rumble.

Mevon stopped, one breath away from flourishing his weapon in challenge. Only a dozen paces now separated him from his three huge opponents, each looking as eager as he felt for the contest ahead, but he realized he was now in a position he'd never been in before: close to the ruvak, but not in combat. Not yet, anyway. Each time he'd encountered them before, there had been no deliberation. No chance to speak.

He knew from an earlier report by Draevenus that some among them were capable of learning human speech. Whether any *here* had seemed unlikely. Still, thinking of his friend made Mevon wonder what the assassin would do in this situation. Though the man insisted he was no role model, Mevon had always admired his ability to examine situations and those involved in them carefully, and to pick out the best of what he found.

No harm in testing the waters, I suppose. The worst they could do is laugh at my attempt, which doesn't worry me in the least. I know ways of erasing their smiles.

Clearing his throat, Mevon spoke. "Tell me, if you can understand, what is it that you want?"

A chittering went up from the ringed crowd, and though he didn't know their words, he felt a general sense of amusement rising up from them. The rightmost of his three opponents punctuated the feeling with a snort that would make a bull envious, hefting his massive hammer-like weapon towards Mevon in a gesture lacking all ambiguity. The leftmost one twirled his daggers—each longer than a bastard sword and as wide as Mevon's head—but otherwise remained impassive.

The one in the middle, however, glared at Mevon with naked, seething hatred. He stepped forward, stabbing the air with a meaty finger, froth forming on ragged lips. "You," the ruvak giant said. "Dead."

Mevon grunted. "That much we know. But that can't possibly be all that you desire. What is the point of all this? Do you even know?"

The ruvak's face darkened, as if insulted. But whether that stemmed from his outrage at the question, or from his inability to understand, Mevon did not think he would ever find out. The giant made a sound somewhere between a bark and a chirp—Mevon could *almost* hear the syllables—and gestured to his two companions. They began circling as the one in the middle lifted his blade—an edged, metallic wedge longer than a horse—that looked more like a pointed, oversized cleaver than a proper sword.

Though he was not ashamed of the eagerness within him, Mevon was still a little disappointed that talk had not brought out more than two words from his foe.

It will take a greater speaker than I to reach them. Much greater. Even then, we'll still have to figure out a way to make them listen. I don't envy whoever takes it upon themselves to try to bridge this gap, but I'll do everything in my power to help them.

For now, though, I'll let Justice do the talking.

As the three finished encompassing him, Mevon readied his *Andun*, took a deep breath, and summoned the storm.

Jasside examined the tips of her fingers, which had turned blue from channeling too much cold for far too long. She stared at them, holding her hands up to the sun, less to discern the damage she'd caused to herself—yet again—as to keep her eyes from even brushing across the horror below.

"It is done," Gilshamed said.

She nodded without turning, sensing his golden glow hovering at her side. She did not look down. She couldn't. After staring so long at uncountable tiny figures on the ground and bending every shred of effort towards obliterating them, she no longer had the stomach for it. Even so, she knew a rough estimate of the number of souls that had been rent from their bodies: a quarter million, between the ruvak and the Fasheshish. All in the span of the morning. Much of it by her hand.

Curling her fingers painfully, she clutched her hands to her breast, rubbing them together for warmth, though to little effect. The cold in her limbs, however, seemed paltry before the ice in her heart. Like a cavern frozen deep amongst snowy spires, she felt hollowed out. Knowing how many millions of people waited beyond the next ridge, innocent families that would have been slaughtered without mercy had the ruvak not been stopped, did nothing to temper the pain she felt at the multitude of lives she'd so recently taken.

Though she kept her face stoic so that no one

who saw her would know it, she mourned. For her fallen allies. For the wives and mothers and children who would weep for those they lost. For her inability to see any path, clear or otherwise, that might lead to victory.

She even mourned for the enemy and for how casually she had deemed their deaths necessary.

"We must regroup," Gilshamed said. "They may have wounded us here, but this is just a single sector. We need to ascertain the status of the others."

"That seems . . . wise," Jasside replied.

"Not a single enemy soldier retreated, even when their defeat had become certain, which suggests to me that their actions here do not represent the full extent of their strategy. This attack might even have been a diversion."

Jasside almost scoffed but stopped well short of expressing it. *If I've learned anything about the ruvak, it's that they place no value on individual lives. I shouldn't be surprised to find out that they'd throw away a few hundred thousand of them just to make us look the wrong way.*

At last she turned to face him. Seeing in his eyes as much despondency as she felt drove a spike of alarm through her. He used to be so good at concealing what was inside him. She didn't want to think about why he no longer tried.

"Get your best healers down to the Fasheshish," she ordered, as gently as she could. "Keep the rest ready. I'll find out where we're needed just as soon as I contact—"

Someone in commune brushed against her mind, letting her know they needed to talk. If it were an emergency, she knew they would not be so gentle, forcing their message through. Yet, the brush seemed *too* gentle. Almost casual, in fact. As if it didn't matter how quickly she heard the news, for there was little she could do about it anyway.

Shaking her head to banish her dour imagination, she summoned the barest sliver of energy and sidled her mind into commune.

Orbrahn stood waiting against that persistent backdrop of white. He'd conjured his typical garish costume, complete with lace trim, gold filigree, and gems studded throughout his garments, but none of it could mask the defeated look on his face.

"Where do we stand?" she asked before he could even offer his usual, lengthy greeting.

"Poorly," he replied.

"Give me details."

"The northeastern sector was overrun with the dawn. Ruvak had moved close in the night unseen. We pulled reserves from the north and east sectors, only for them both to be hit by enemy forces several million strong. An entire quadrant of our defense is, essentially, gone."

Jasside closed her metaphysical eyes. She didn't bother asking how this was possible. With the war engines taken over by the enemy and turned against their own skyships, along with the diversionary force sent against the armies of Fasheshe, all their usual forms of reinforcement had been distracted and rendered useless.

"What is Yandumar calling for?" she said, glancing once more at Orbrahn.

"Retreat."

"To where?"

"The center. For now anyway."

Jasside shook her head. "That won't buy us much time. I'll send every available ship and caster to slow down the ruvak. We'll have to—"

"That not why I contacted you," Orbrahn interrupted.

Jasside frowned. "What do you mean?"

"Yandumar has the movements coordinated. I came to you personally because . . . well . . ."

"What is it?"

"It's Mevon, Jasside. He was out there with me when the ruvak sprung their trap. He told me to dash ahead. I figured he'd be fine, but he hasn't reported back in y—"

Jasside didn't hear the rest of what he had to say, dropping back into her physical body. Nor did she hear any of what Gilshamed mumbled to her a moment later. She was too busy pouring energy she could barely control into her platform, urging it into greater and greater speed.

Mevon jerked to his left as the hammer came down. Wind rushed and stone rumbled with such force as to put the elements themselves to shame. Twisting, he spun Justice to ward off a flurry of dagger strikes from the opposite side. He kicked their wielder, buying just enough space to plant himself and level his rod overhead as the great cleaver chopped down. The impact sent jolts from his fingers down through his toes, driving him to a knee.

His three assailants collected themselves, then stepped back to prepare for their next attack.

Within the storm, he had speed enough to see and react to each incoming blow, but despite his blessings, the giants had him bested in raw strength. Mevon had faced similar situations before—namely, against fellow Hardohl—but had always found a way to divide his opponents, snatching small moments within the skirmish that became, in effect, a duel, taking them out one by one.

These three ruvak, however, struck with such precision, such coordination, never leaving themselves exposed, that he had been unable to touch a single edge against them. That they had also failed to draw *his* blood was of little consolation; repeated impacts from parries had shaken him to his core, and he had yet to find an obvious weakness to exploit.

They were *so* careful, in fact, that a casual observer might even think they were toying with him.

He knew that was not the case. He and his peers had fought against them enough times by now that they must have finally learned what worked and what didn't. Wearing him down with small cuts was pointless, for such wounds would heal long before blood loss could become a concern. Instead, every strike against him had been intended to either kill or set him up for a subsequent attack.

So far, Mevon had no answer.

They came at him again. Twin daggers slashed high and low. Mevon made to deflect but saw almost too late that it was a feint. He corrected his answering swing just as a slash from the giant cleaver whistled right over the top of the dagger wielder, who ducked under it. Though Mevon caught the blow, it pushed him backwards a step, driving him to totter on the edge of balance.

Where he felt a presence loom behind him.

If he'd had more than a quarter heartbeat to think, he would have realized there was no room for the ruvak to swing a hammer without risking his companions. He lunged towards the presence, hoping to get close enough to negate the hammer's effect. But as his vision came around, he saw that it was not a weapon that drew near to him.

It was empty hands.

Thick fingers reached for his *Andun*. Mevon regained just enough balance to jerk it out of reach, then danced around his foe, who clutched at empty air, though barely. Outside the ring of the three ruvak for the first time since the fight began, Mevon smiled and swung at the hammer wielder's now exposed back.

Sunlight glinted off twin blades, striking like vipers. Mevon saw that they would be too late to stop his own attack, but that in landing his blow, he'd be hard-pressed to deflect even one, much less both of the daggers.

Guard myself? Or take the wound, but eliminate one opponent? I take a risk either way.

Though he had, from his perspective, all the time in the world to consider, he knew right away which choice he would make. Some fights were decided by the width of a finger; some by the width of a hair.

This one, most certainly, had the feeling of the latter.

Completing his initial motion, Mevon drove one blade through fabric and skin of the hammer wielder's back, all the way through his spine. Steel sliced and grinded simultaneously against flesh and bone.

Mevon snapped his eyes to the metal tips, now closing to within lethal range. Having no time to pull Justice out, he wrenched the free side upward, a task made more difficult by the deadweight still clinging to the other end. Still, he managed to entangle one dagger, turning the thrust aimed for his chest into a glancing slash that bounced off his leather armor without so much as a kissing flesh.

The other blade, however, bit deep into Mevon's left shoulder. Skin and muscle parted in a burst of searing pain, curling away as the dagger cut deeper still. Blood gushed down Mevon's arm. His grip on his own weapon faltered, then slipped away.

Inhuman eyes flared. The ruvak's face was now close enough that Mevon could smell his hot, putrid breath. His foe, it seemed, had obviously not expected Mevon to expose himself.

Relinquishing his *Andun* with his one good hand, Mevon reached up, grasped the ruvak's collar, then slammed him to the ground. He followed by smashing his knee into his assailant's face. Bones crunched like crushed twigs.

Motion caught Mevon's eye from the periphery: the third ruvak, swinging his massive cleaver. Yet, the blow was too safe, on a path that had no chance of intersecting either of his companions.

Mevon had been counting on that.

He leaned dramatically, arching his back until it was nearly touching the ground behind him. The blade whipped past his nose, licking it with wind, then skidded across the ground.

Rebounding, Mevon surged upward. He lashed out a foot, aiming to knock the weapon from the warrior's hand. But his other opponent was not as out of the fight as he'd hoped, and clutched at Mevon from below. His kick connected, but only just, and had too little force behind it to do any damage. The fact was, the third ruvak seemed okay with losing the weapon anyway.

Letting go of the cleaver's hilt, the ruvak grasped Mevon's ankle.

Then, with a shrill roar, the giant flung him through the air.

After a flight and a desperate search that together seemed to take an eternity, Jasside finally spotted them. Everywhere along the northern front, ruvak hordes were swarming over battlements and chasing down the fleeing human defenders, opposed only by a thin line of skyships and sorcerers. A thousand paces below her, however, over a hundred score ruvak stood in a ring, motionless except for the small cluster of figures dancing at their center.

He's there. He has to be there.

Leaning forward on her platform until she was almost completely horizontal, Jasside began her dive.

Wind rushed past her face as she gathered within her as much dark energy as she could hold. It didn't seem like much. Having pushed herself as far just this morning as she usually did in an entire day, her reserves of power had fallen dangerously low, to the point where she doubted her ability to destroy even this meagre force.

But as the ants grew in her sight into mice, and then men, she saw a familiar shock of black hair swirling as the figure it belonged to spun in a deathly dance. With only a dagger in one hand, Mevon fended off a pair of howling ruvak warriors who were astonishing in their size and savagery.

Inexplicably, he seemed to be losing.

Slowing, she could now see his arm, drenched in blood and hanging limply at his side, and a third ruvak giant lying facedown in a pool of orange blood, with Mevon's *Andun* sticking up from his spine like a banner pole.

A plan formed in her mind, and she began its enactment without waiting for a better one to present itself.

Closing her eyes, she quested outward, finding the two strongest heartbeats and homing in on them. The pair of warriors were moving too quickly for any kind of projectile attack, especially in her weakened condition.

But if I form the spell in place instead of sending it . . .

Darkness burst in twin explosions below. When she opened her eyes, she saw only Mevon standing in a cloud of orange mist. The surrounding crowd erupted in a squawking rage. Steel bared, the ring began to constrict.

Sweeping low, she leaned over the side over platform, grasping Justice and yanking it free of the corpse. Then, she guided herself over Mevon.

"Grab ahold!" she called without slowing.

A moment later, Jasside felt the platform lurch

with sudden weight. She rose, one husband now dangling beneath her, as the angry mob closed in on the spot he'd just been standing.

"She's got him."

Yandumar grunted his acknowledgment without looking down at Orbrahn, who sat propped against the railing of the skyship.

A part of him wondered if he'd done the right thing. Naturally, no one would fault him for sending someone to rescue Mevon, but he'd seen too often those in power only using it for their own gain, placing the lives of those they cared about, or those they deemed worthy, over countless others. It's why he hadn't sent a more traditional force, even though they'd been closer than Jasside. As overall commander of the defense, *everyone* was his responsibility. He didn't want to be seen playing favorites.

All I really did was inform a woman about her spouse's . . . predicament. The rest took care of itself. I had no right to deny her that knowledge, and the opportunity to do something about it, not even to assuage my own uncertain conscience.

Though he'd long released his tight hold on his only living son, telling himself it was only a matter of time before battle claimed him, Yandumar still allowed himself a quiet exhale at Orbrahn's news.

The relief did not last long.

Elbow propped on one knee, his wide eyes were fixed ahead on the object his skyship was fast approaching. Had he not suspected who was behind it, he would have called it impossible.

"Get back in commune, then, and keep a close eye on things," Yandumar ordered.

"What's the point, old man? Any fool can see that we're beaten."

"Aye. But we're not dead yet. That'll change if we don't maintain an orderly retreat."

"Retreat? Where the abyss are we going to flee to this time?"

Yandumar narrowed his eyes at what lay ahead. "I think we're about to find out."

As Orbrahn begrudgingly complied with his instructions, Yandumar continued staring, reevaluating the thing's scale every few beats as they raced ahead without the object appearing to change size.

Abyss take you, Vashodia. Even during our own impending genocide, you just couldn't let yourself be outdone.

From the very heart of the colony rose an edifice similar to a domicile, only so colossal it made the valynkar cities seem like toys. The underside was all of dark soil and stone, flaring wide and angled like a cut gem, while the top was sprinkled with familiar houses and tenements, granaries and tents, grasses and roads. And at the center of it all, somehow even more ominous-looking than ever, the voltensus poked toward the sky like a needle.

"Looks like the scorching mountain decided it wanted to fly," Orbrahn said.

Yandumar grunted again. Then, he turned, glaring down at the boy. "I thought I told you to—"

"There's nothing to watch," Orbrahn said, flicking a hand. "The ruvak seem content, now that three-quarters of our defenses are reeling back and aren't pressing the advance. Our wings are holding them off for now. I've instructed the messengers to brush me if anything changes."

Though he saw the sense it in, Yandumar still felt like smacking the boy. The impulse lacked any real strength, however, and dwindled completely from his mind as he turned his attention forward once more.

Eventually, they crested the lip of the hovering mountain and began banking along a familiar landscape. Looking around now, it almost seemed like nothing was amiss. Only the horizon, which showed nothing but the sky, let him know that it wasn't all an illusion. Settling down near the voltensus, he dismounted the skyship and was not surprised at all by who was there to greet his arrival.

"Yandumar, how good of you to join us," Vashodia said, holding up a hand towards the woman beside her. "The queen here was just saying . . . well, actually, she wasn't saying much of anything at all."

Yandumar glanced at Arivana, who indeed looked like she was in no mood for talking. If anything, she looked touched by sadness. But if so, it seemed a lazy sort of sorrow, as if she were too worn out to fully acknowledge the depth of her grief. After today's events, he couldn't blame her in the least.

"So," Yandumar said, turning his gaze back towards Vashodia, "this is what you've been up to all this time."

"Do you like it? I worked so very hard on it. Although, I haven't settled on a name."

"Why not call it 'Vashodia Domicile'?"

"Please. As if I'd take inspiration from the valynkar. In fact, it was my study of the ruvak vessel that gave me the best ideas. You see, while light and dark can form constructs simply by proper application of will, chaos requires a more . . . intentional approach. They rely much more on their thorough understanding of the underlying systems rather than the energy itself. If you know me at all, you can see why I appreciate their efforts."

Yandumar shook his head. "I may know you better than most, yet even I can't explain the tone of admiration in your voice."

Vashodia shrugged. "I admire useful things. It's why I put that same ship I studied at the very heart of my . . . hmm . . . what *are* we going to call it?"

"You're harnessing chaos?" Yandumar said, alarm raising the timbre of his words.

"Of course!"

"How is that even possible? You've no ruvak blood in your veins."

"Oh, I'm not using it *directly*. But in my studies I did find a tenuous connection that allowed me to reshape the latent chaotic energy, augmenting—and even amplifying—my own ample supply of darkness. Whereas light and dark stand in opposition to each other, chaos resides . . . off to one side."

"What? Like three points of a triangle?"

"Don't be silly, Yandumar. It's more like three points of a square."

Yandumar scratched his chin. "Doesn't a square have *four* points?"

Vashodia giggled. "It does indeed! Tell me, smart man that you are, what do you think comprises that fourth point?"

Sighing, Yandumar threw up his hands. "I am not the right person to be having this conversation with."

The mierothi *tsked* at him, wagging a clawed finger. "Once again, I find myself disappointed in you. More importantly, so would your son."

"Mevon? What does *he* have to do with this?"

"Why, he's the answer to your question."

He stared at her blankly for an embarrassingly long moment. "Oh . . . you mean voids."

"Bravo! I knew you could do it."

"Is that why the ruvak react more violently to them than most?"

"Indeed. And why they're so keen to hunt our voids down."

Yandumar nodded. He'd seen just this morning

how far they were willing to go. "I take it you have a plan, then?"

"Of course not."

"But—"

"I have *many* plans. Some are dead, some are in motion, and some . . . well, let's just say I still have a few snakes up my sleeve."

Is that a good thing? "That doesn't tell me much."

"Oh, you wanted specifics? Why didn't you say so?"

Yandumar rolled his eyes. "You know, for all that you claim you aren't the child you appear, you sure do make it hard for the rest of us to believe you."

"Children," Arivana said suddenly, startling him. "We must protect the children."

"And we shall," Vashodia said without hesitation, as if the queen had been part of their conversation all along. "Along with all the rest of the miserable, useless masses. It is, after all, why I built this." She punctuated her last words by stamping a foot on the ground.

"You can't mean to say this vessel will carry everyone to safety?" Yandumar said, not bothering to hide the contempt from his voice.

"Don't be absurd. Large as it is, it only has room on the surface for a million at most. Their salvation will be found below."

"How so?"

"I've carved out space in this vessel's belly to grow food and store water. There will be plenty enough of both for us all to make the journey. I would apologize for it having taken so long to finish, but really, I couldn't have completed it any faster. Besides, you all did such a marvelous job holding back the ruvak—a full three days longer than I'd calculated—that I even had time to add a few special amenities."

Yandumar grunted. "You mentioned a journey but said nothing about a destination."

"Why Yandumar, isn't it obvious? We've seen that the voltensus is adept at keeping out anything powered by chaos—notwithstanding that which I have specifically exempted—yet we are still vulnerable to a concerted, overwhelming ground assault. If only there were a land that contained both coverage by voltensi and a terrain virtually immune to a surface invasion. Do you, most exalted emperor, happen to know of such a place?"

At last Yandumar smiled. "I think I might."

PART IV

PART IV

CHAPTER 19

Leaning into his *Andun*, one end of which was driven into the sand, Mevon kept watch over the Weskaran Waste. It looked different this time. Before, when he'd arrived at this beach alongside his father at the head of an Imperial armada, the desert, for all its desolation, had seemed a thing alive. The dunes had shimmered, bright with heat, and the sands had swirled into ochre mists with every gust of wind. For all humankind's conceit about their supposed dominance, this place had stood as a reminder of nature's harsh indifference to such claims.

But the corpses, bloated and rotting in the sun, spread out beyond the horizon, revealed not a hint of the natural surface below it. Before such wrath, as only thinking beings could inflict upon each other, nature itself had been humbled.

Though the voltensus had accompanied them aboard Vashodia's ark, guarding the long, desperate train of humanity from ruvaki skyships, the second leg of the exodus had been just as deadly as the first. There was no hiding the direction of their flight. Their enemy had used this knowledge to great effect, setting down troops ahead of them. Instead of fighting on open ground, Mevon's vanguard had faced entrenched enemy positions that had had days or even weeks to prepare their defenses. Every step had been drenched in blood, far too much of which was red.

And when they'd reached the swamplands, it had gotten even worse.

Mevon shuddered. If he ever had the chance to fall into a deep enough sleep, he was sure he'd be greeted by nightmares of that place. The ruvak had sprung ambushes with every muck-filled league they'd trodden, springing up from moldy bogs, swinging down from rotting trees, and striking without mercy through every veil of fog. Their squawking howls had filled every waking moment, sounding without surcease from everywhere and nowhere at once. He'd seen more than a few allied soldiers succumb to madness because of it.

Through it all, however, they'd retained hope by repeating a phrase that had become almost religious by the fervor in which it was uttered: *Just hold on until the shore.*

Getting here, however, had proven the easy part; holding it long enough for everyone to board had tested the limits of humanity's collective will to survive.

His father's armada had been waiting for them when they arrived. Those seaborne vessels, along with every skyship capable of holding passengers, had been filled to bursting before setting out across the sea. The round-trip had taken six days and had ferried only a fifth of the population to safety. Standing guard over a stretch of shore several leagues long, with little shelter from the sun, and even less in the way of defensible positions, the remaining defenders of humankind had been decimated.

By the time the fourth wave was halfway finished boarding, it had become clear there would be no need for a fifth.

"It's time to go," Jasside said.

Mevon turned his head to look up at his wife as she floated on her platform just off his shoulder. The stiffness in his neck made the motion laborious. "I've waited so long to hear those words, I'd almost lost faith that they would ever be said."

"It sounds just as strange to say. But you and I are the only remaining defenders still on watch. The rest are already in their berths, and the horizon, as far as I can tell, is still. This continent has seen the end of war."

Mevon glanced even farther behind him. Both sea and sky were spackled by ships, the nearest of them still pushing out from the shore. And distantly, just a dark disc where the two blue realms met, he spied Vashodia's ark locked in place between the land-masses to protect the crossing.

"Good," he said at last.

"If even *you* grow weary of battle, my love, imag-ine how the rest of us feel."

He swept one hand across the lifeless expanse before them. Dead flesh had filled every low place between the dunes, making the landscape flat and featureless but for the occasional skeletal limb poking up from the blanket of bodies.

"I will never tire so long as the cause is just. But this?" Mevon shook his head. "This is nothing but madness."

"You no longer consider defending the innocent as just?"

"You know I don't mean our part in this. I mean *them*. For every human that has fallen, both during the initial invasion and since, we've killed at least ten ruvak. Their use of tactics suggests intelligence equal to our own, yet they come at us with all the slavering of rabid wolves."

"More like rabid raptors."

Mevon almost smiled at that, but the pain from cracked lips halted the expression prematurely. "I think you see my point. This kind of single-minded determination to see us wiped out with no regard for their own lives isn't natural. Whatever drives them goes far beyond mere revenge. Even if Ruul and Elos came here with our ancestors all those millennia ago bearing nothing but ill intent, no ruvak here today could possibly have any memory of it. Hatred this consuming can only be based on a lie."

"And a twisted one at that," Jasside said. "But now is not the time to try unraveling it."

"When *will* it be time?"

"Not long now, I think. Once we reach safety."

Mevon scoffed. "If such a place even exists."

"We'll find out soon enough." She lowered her platform until it was scraping sand right next to him. "Come, husband. Let's go home."

"**A**byss take these clouds," Arivana said. "We'd be able to see it by now, if it weren't for them. Jasside told me that the sight has no equal upon this world. A bold claim, but she's as well traveled as anyone I know. More so than myself, anyway. Before . . . recent events . . . I could count the number of times I'd left Panisahldron on one hand. The nation, I mean. Not the city. Even then, I had never gone far. To my young mind, Corbrithe had seemed the most exotic place imaginable, but now I think I'd find it difficult to even explain the differences between their country and ours. Funny how a change of scenery can alter your perspective so thoroughly. Enjoying your tea?"

Chains rattled as Sem Aira jolted, obviously

startled by the question. Arivana couldn't fault the woman for that. She'd been rambling, and the sudden query had come as a surprise to them both.

Sem Aira stared down at the cup in her shackled hands, a curiously confused expression painted on her inhuman visage. Arivana hadn't seen the need for restraints, but her guardsmen—several of whom were standing nearby, hands on the hilts of their swords—had insisted. Since Richlen's death, she had been unable to deny them anything.

As if in a dream, Sem Aira lifted the cup to her lips, tilting it ever-so-slightly, then lowered her hands once more to the railing upon which they'd been resting. "It's . . . fine."

"Yes, I suppose 'fine' describes it well enough. A bit plain for my tastes, but one cannot be picky in such stringent times. It's not even as if I labored over it myself. An old woman makes it for me every morning. She lost all of her . . . well, let's just say she has plenty of time on her hands and an instinct to nurture, the fulfilling of which seems a balm to her soul."

Arivana sighed, brushing hair out of her face as she turned outward, squinting in a vain attempt to pierce the cool, grey clouds through which they flew. "I see a lot of that, these days. People are doing whatever they can to make the lives of those around them better. Such occurrences are even starting to make incidents of unchecked cruelty and deprivation look like the exception instead of the rule."

"Even the smallest things can make the biggest difference, when people actually take time to make note of the needs in others' lives. Why, just the other day, two brothers gave up their room for Daye and me. It was little more than a broom closet, but it gave us privacy, something few are afforded these days, and something those brothers well knew was the greatest gift a newly wedded couple could receive.

"Humankind is strange, in that way. We're capable of deeds that make the worst nightmare seem a pleasant dream, and yet, at the same time, we can commit acts of such . . . such *goodness* as to drive even the hardest among us to tears. The fact that both extremes can be found within the same soul, well, that is one mystery that may never be solved."

"Why?" Sem Aira said, the words barely audible above the breeze. "Why are you telling me all this?"

It was Arivana who now found herself jolted by an unexpected question. Most notably, because she did not have an answer.

She had intended to bring Sem Aira out of confinement because she thought the woman must be lonely. She couldn't say as such, however. To begin with, it spoke of hypocrisy. How authentic could her concerns appear when it was Arivana herself who had cast the woman into chains? Even in her own mind, the reason sounded false, more of an excuse than anything. But an excuse for what?

Opening her mouth once more, Arivana chased

after her purpose. "I used to think everything was beautiful, once. Not even that long ago. But that was only because I was kept ignorant of all the ugliness in the world, oftentimes willfully so. I've grown up since then. Opened my eyes. Yet, despite all the horrors I've seen, far too many wrought by those closest to me, there's still a part of me that can't help but see the beauty in all things. Or, at least, the *potential* for beauty. I thought I would have to kill that part of me in order to become the woman and the queen that such times needed me to be. But for some reason, it lives on."

Arivana turned suddenly, stepping close so that her face was but a few hand widths away from that of her former handmaiden. "Make me a promise?"

Sem Aira's eyes and the vertical slits of her nostrils flared. "I would, Your Majesty. But I'm not sure a promise from me is worth much."

"It's worth far more than you might imagine. When my kind are gone, yours will be the only promise that means *anything*."

"No, Arivana! That isn't—"

"Don't tell me it's not possible, or even probable at this point. I see no value in trying to ignore the inevitable. Before your people kill us all, I would ask but one simple thing."

Sem Aira lowered her face. Twin tears trickled down her ashen, waxy cheeks, and her protruding upper lip began trembling. Arivana counted the woman's trill breaths, losing track after a score, until at last she inhaled deeply and lifted her gaze.

"If it is within my power," Sem Aira said, "I will not rest until the task is done."

"All I ask," Arivana began, "is that you remember us. Remember that we were capable of so much good. So much . . . beauty. Whether or not we deserve our fate for the sins of our ancestors and our gods, please, tell your people about us. Tell them the story of humankind."

Light blossomed all around them, blinding Arivana with its intensity. Holding up a hand to shield her eyes, she looked out in the direction they were traveling and could see that they had at last broken free of the clouds . . .

. . . and before her stood a monument for which no amount of telling could have properly prepared her. Standing nearly a league in height from sea to clifftop, and bending out of sight only at the farthest reaches of the horizon, the Shelf blazed like a furnace as it reflected dawn's first light.

"Beautiful," Sem Aira said.

Struck nearly breathless by the sight, Arivana could only nod in agreement.

Returning to the Veiled Empire, for the second time, felt to Gilshamed like coming home.

During his previous venture, too many things

about both himself and the land had been askew. He had been a man possessed of singular will, obdurate and obsessive in his desire to see justice wrought for ancient crimes; the continent had seemed a place infested. Now, with neither such obstacle present, he was able to look upon his arrival with fresh eyes, no longer seeing what was different, only how much was still the same.

"It's strange," said Lashriel, who was standing at his side.

They, like all the rest of the valynkar on the domicile, had gathered along the rim to watch as sea gave way to land beneath them. "In what way?" Gilshamed asked.

"After all that took place here, I was expecting to be filled with dread upon returning." She laughed in her gentle way. "Elos must have been thorough in his cleansing of my mind, for I feel nothing of the sort. I would almost say it's—"

"Wonderful," he said.

Smiling, she nodded, then leaned her head against his shoulder.

The expression she and many others wore mirrored exactly how Gilshamed felt. Looking down upon the shadowed crags and snowcapped peaks of the Godsreach Mountains tugged at threads of nostalgia that were woven through his most ancient and cherished memories. His people's banishment from this land had weighed heavily upon every soul old enough to remember it. To not only return, but be welcomed with open arms was a blessing as pure as children's laughter, and just as soothing. The fundamental failure of the valynkar, which had defined them for the last two thousand years, had at last come to an end.

And not even the circumstances that brought us here are able to detract from this moment. Yandumar, you may not have thought much of opening your borders to us, but by that simple act you have helped heal an entire people.

"Even that," Lashriel said, pointing into the distance, "does not make me the least bit uneasy, though I still remember our war with the mierothi as if it were yesterday."

Gilshamed peered where she had indicated, a little east and a few dozen leagues farther inland. Though illuminated by the evening sun, Vashodia's ark, as it had come to be called, still seemed darker than the shadowed land beneath it. A land, he realized as he studied it more closely, with which he was familiar.

A piece of the ark was in the process of detaching itself: a slim spire descending from the massive vessel's very center. It seemed appropriate, then, that a new voltensus would come to rest where once had stood another.

The voltensus that he had destroyed.

He did not think he would change what he had done—even knowing Vashodia was twitching at his strings back then—but he still was not sure if it had been the right thing to do. No matter how pure each side could claim their cause to be, war always signaled a failure of some kind. Whether of decency or diplomacy, it mattered little; diluting conflict to the swing of a sword always seemed to lessen those involved.

This war with the ruvak, he knew, was in no way unique.

Everything circles, around and around again.

When are we ever going to learn?

"Gil?"

Gilshamed looked down at Lashriel, beset by the concern carved into her features. As always, he'd let his guard down around her, letting everything inside show on his face without restraint. "I am well, Lash. There is no need for alarm."

"You are upset by something, though. Do not hide from me what troubles you. You may think me gentle, but I need not be spared from your burdens. In sharing them, our love only grows stronger."

He smiled down at her. "You always manage to remind me, somehow, that we are all capable of being so much better than we are."

"And you're wondering why we so often fail to reach that higher standard?"

Gilshamed shook his head. "I'm only wondering why it has taken this long for everything to shatter so completely."

"Who is to say it has not already?"

He raised an eyebrow. "What do you mean?"

"Well, if the latest tales are to be believed, Ruul and Elos brought us here from another world. That, to me, seems an act of desperation. Could they not have been fleeing some catastrophe?"

"I . . . suppose." He sighed. "But that does not give me any comfort. Everywhere I look throughout history, I see patterns of destruction repeating without end. Must they always culminate in such utter ruin? Are we *ever* going to get it right?"

She leaned closer then, circling her arms around him, and said nothing as she studied the quickly darkening terrain. In doing so, she reminded him with her presence that so long as he kept her close, and held himself open to her, the weight pressing down on his soul seemed just a little bit easier to bear.

Tassariel brushed snow from the branches, then reached down into the trap she'd set the evening before, smiling as her fingers came in contact with fur. Grabbing hold of the limp body, she wrenched it free and held it up before her.

"Looks like we're having hare for breakfast. Again."

She hadn't doubted it would be there. In a land empty of all human occupation, game was always plentiful.

As she drew her knife and began dressing the carcass, however, the upturned curl of her lips persisted.

True, they'd been eating the same stringy meat for weeks now, but the difference this time was that she'd caught the thing herself, the snare crafted and set by her hand alone. Draevenus trusted her enough by now that he hadn't even bothered to check her work. Though she'd failed to learn the first thing he'd tried to teach her, there were other skills besides murder to pass on. And she'd proven herself a most able student.

They had to find *some* way keep themselves occupied, after all. When they weren't running for their lives, things were—for the most part—actually quite boring.

She wiped blood from her hands then gathered up the skin and cuts of meat, leaving the rest for the scavengers as she retraced her steps. In two marks she ducked through the screen of branches covering the entrance to their shelter, a shallow nook under an outcropping. Draevenus waited inside, nursing a fire kept small enough and pure enough that only someone wandering within fifty paces would notice it.

"Hare again, is it?" he said, echoing her earlier words. "It's a good thing they breed so quickly, or I'd worry about our impact on their population."

Stepping over to him, she dropped the bundle of meat in his lap. "It's not *their* population we should be concerned with."

Draevenus clenched his jaw, silent for three long breaths before responding. "We're doing everything we can."

"Not *everything*."

"Abyss beyond, Tass! For the last time, I will *not* leave you behind."

"But you could move so much faster on your own," she insisted. "These wings of mine stand out, drawing ruvak like a beacon, whereas yours are quite literally made to keep you hidden. If you weren't stuck walking with me, you'd probably be there by now."

Sighing, he began picking out slabs of flesh and fitting them to skewers, which he then propped up over the dancing flames. "I've heard all the arguments before, and I won't change my mind. It's too dangerous to go alone."

"Too dangerous for you? Or for me?"

"For both of us. What can either of us do on our own against even the smallest ruvak skyship?"

"We could run. Just like we've been doing for weeks."

"Fine. But who's going to guard our backs at night?"

"Neither of us sleep well anyway. No one is going to sneak up unknowing."

Grumbling under his breath, Draevenus flipped the meat over. Grease dripped and sizzled on the coal, filling the shelter with a savory, if now too-familiar aroma. "There are still too many perils in the wilderness, especially for someone—"

"I am *not* incapable of surviving on my own. Not anymore. When was the last time you had to find clean water on your own? Or forage for edible plants? Or scout out shelter? Or even—" she gestured sharply at the fire "—set a trap for our breakfast. I can do everything you've taught me without thinking, Draevenus. Nothing about being alone scares me anymore."

Nothing pertaining to my safety, anyway.

Tassariel turned from him and knelt by her pack, tying the fresh skin to four others they'd acquired and treated in recent days. She couldn't look at him right now. Her attempt to approach the problem with logic would run afoul if she even so much as looked into his eyes. He might have been a stone-faced killer once, but now, it seemed, he couldn't keep the smallest thing he felt from showing up in his features.

The problem, she knew, was that he cared too much about her. So much so that he was placing her, quite literally, above everyone else in the world. As much as she wanted to cling to that feeling of being wanted, and to bask in the warmth that came with such attentions, there was too much at stake.

And I'm not yet jaded enough with this world to welcome its end.

"Perhaps," she ventured softly, "we could try commune again?"

Draevenus grunted. "Itching for another skirmish, are we? You *do* remember what happened last time."

"Yes, but that was weeks and leagues ago. And before the ruvak swarmed us, I swear I felt something a little bit different than our previous attempts. As if their grip on commune was starting to slip."

"I felt nothing like that."

Tassariel shrugged. "Perhaps they're more concerned with strangling the dark than the light. Vashodia and Jasside, after all, are the two most powerful beings alive. It makes sense that the ruvak would spend more effort opposing them."

"Maybe." Draevenus plucked the finished skewers from the flames, handing half to her, then bit into a sliver of meat.

Sitting opposite the fire from him, she did the same. They both chewed in silence for a time. As much as she enjoyed having a full stomach, the meat itself went down almost without registering to her senses. Only after the final scrap was in their bellies, and every last drop of grease had been licked from their fingers, did Draevenus lift his gaze to her once more.

"All right," he said. "We'll give it another try."

Tassariel nodded, breathing deep to settle her nerves. To be honest, she wasn't sure if she was more excited for possible good news, or more worried about another failure. But after so long walking empty, quiet lands, either was a change she would welcome.

After they'd both finished securing everything loose back in their packs, in the likely event that they had to run on short notice, they settled down on the ground, legs crossed and backs resting against each other.

"You should go first," Draevenus said. "If you're right about their hold slipping, then you're right about their focus on dark. If we're going to find a way through, it will be light that leads the way."

"Thank you for showing such confidence in me."

"Thank you for earning it."

Tassariel energized. Closing her eyes and holding her breath, she plunged into commune.

A familiar dark sky surrounded her untethered conscience. More familiar, in fact, than it had been in some time. The swirling, every-color clouds that had beset every recent visit were, if not gone, then faded, diminished to the point that they were no longer the dominating feature of this realm.

It wasn't victory outright, but it *was* progress.

She cast her gaze in the direction of the colony, eager to see if any stars were visible. What she saw, however, only confused her.

While there was light of a sort, it was wrong in too many ways. It was dim and indistinct, less like individual points than it was like a reflection in murky waters. And whatever it was did not reside at the colony. The direction was right, but the distance was much too vast. It was almost as if . . .

Popping out of commune, Tassariel jumped to her feet.

"What is it? What's wrong?" Draevenus asked,

THE LIGHT THAT BINDS 493

rising himself and putting his hands on two dagger hilts.

"I have good news and bad news," she replied. "Which do you want to hear first?"

Draevenus groaned. "The bad, I guess."

"We won't be joining our allies at the colony."

"But why? What happened to them? *What did you see?*"

"The good," she said, ignoring his queries, and failing to hide her smile, "is that you get to take me to see your home."

CHAPTER 20

It was strange and bittersweet to see Mecrithos from above. For Yandumar, it was a city filled with too many memories, few of which were good. Victory over Rekaj, his marriage and ascension to the throne, and all the reforms he'd enacted to try to make the empire a better place, were all shadowed by losses that had stolen his joy. Yet for all that, he had always viewed it as a magnificent city, a feat of architectural and civic brilliance that, if not as polished or sparkling as some other places in the world, still impressed through sheer scope and audacity.

From this high in the air, however, all notions of greatness vanished. It seemed but a child's maze hastily formed in the dirt by an unsteady finger. When viewed in relation to the mountain upon which it sat, not to mention the vast countryside around it,

Mecrithos appeared insignificant. But even though it seemed new and unknown, the truth was, he still felt he was intimately acquainted with the city. Distance didn't change what he knew.

The same, unfortunately, could not be said about the ruvak.

What had been bothering him, he realized—indeed, what had been clawing at his mind ever since the city he called home first came into view—was how little they actually knew about the ruvak. When he'd declared war against Rekaj's regime, he'd had thorough knowledge of the empire's inner workings, knowing not only the evils they committed, but the motivations behind every act of cruelty. The blood he'd shed in that revolution, while undeniably tragic, he still considered just.

He had no such comprehension of their current enemy. While protecting the innocent from violent aggression could never be considered wrong, the fact that he could make no sense of ruvak purpose filled him with a futile kind of madness. It was hard to feel justified when he could see no point to the bloodshed, to the countless lives lost on both sides of the conflict.

War always signaled a breakdown in reason. War without meaning was the very essence of insanity.

"We're almost there, Emperor."

Yandumar broke from his study of the land below, glancing over at Orbrahn. "No 'old man' this time?"

Orbrahn shrugged. "Takes a special kind of

caring to be as insubordinate as I am. That and the wine. This is the me you get when I've run out of both."

"I can solve *one* of your problems just as soon as we reach the palace. As for the other? Well, I can't fault you for the lack, but you'll have to find it again in your own way and time." Yandumar sighed. "As will the rest of us."

He stepped to the opposite edge of his command ship and watched as it swept low near the lip of Gorat-ismyr Domicile. A crowd had gathered there, though a small one. As much as he would like to address every refugee at once, there was simply no feasible way to do so. He'd have to rely on the rulers gathered below to pass on the word to their people.

What was left of them, anyway.

As soon as he felt Orbrahn's spell take effect, amplifying his voice, Yandumar cleared his throat and began.

"Welcome to my empire," he said. "Strange as it may be to say, this is the safest place in the world, at the moment. I'd like to say I had hoped to greet you under better circumstances, but then I'd be lying. I'm not much of a diplomat, and the idea of sitting down to dinner with foreign dignitaries to discuss trade agreements and treaties and whatnot . . . well, if the abyss came in personalized flavors, that's what mine would taste like.

"But nevermind all that. For the time being, we're

under no threat of attack from the ruvak. The Shelf guards us from the sea, and the voltensi guard us from the sky. I have ships patrolling both in any case, which should give us fair warning should our good friends from the void make any attempt to invade. Breathe, all of you. As deeply as you can, for as long as you can. Unfortunately, I don't know how long that will actually be.

"But for now, we *do* have peace, and we must make the most of it. Your people are all being settled in temporary towns my citizens have been working hard on building for the last few months. It will be crowded, I'm sure, and anything even resembling luxury will be in dreadfully short supply. But at least they'll all be safe, and sheltered, and fed.

"As for you, rulers and generals and crucial figures in our campaign against annihilation, I open this entire continent for your use, and issue this one command. Go! Disperse and enjoy yourselves. Explore whatever suits your fancy and take time to find yourself again, however that may be achieved. This war has tested us, stretching us beyond what we thought was possible. I'm sure we all need an opportunity to just . . . relax."

Sensing nothing but relieved eagerness from the crowd, Yandumar turned away from them, nodding to Orbrahn. The boy lowered his hand, releasing his spell.

"Well, that's over with," Yandumar said. "Let's get

on to the palace. You'll be needing your wine, and I'll be needing—"

"A proper bed?" Orbrahn said, lifting one eyebrow.

Yandumar grunted, then smiled as he looked down and watched a single, small skyship lifting up from the city. "That . . . and a certain someone to share it with."

In another mark, the tiny vessel had reached his own and disgorged its small flock of passengers. Two Imperial Guard stepped off first, followed by Derthon, who looked surprisingly calm for someone taking their first trip on a flying contraption. Then again, not much could rattle him. Even if Yandumar could see the face lying beneath the wrapped bandages, he was sure its expression wouldn't change much whether the man was standing still at guard for half a day, or cutting foes in two with the curved blade strapped at his waist.

Following Derthon came a pair of women who, while similar in their ability with sharp objects, were just as different in most other ways.

"She didn't want to wait," Ilyem said to him, in what might have been apologetic fashion. He'd sent her ahead to deliver news in person and let the palace know to prepare for his arrival.

The other woman, as always, had her own plans.

"Where is she?" Slick Ren demanded, planting fists on her hips.

She might not have been as slender as when they'd

first met—palace living was a far softer business than running a criminal enterprise, after all—and the grey in her hair had almost overtaken the red, but Yandumar couldn't recall a more welcome sight.

"Nice to see you too, my dear," he said.

Slick Ren's lips pressed into a tight line. "I'll give you a proper homecoming soon enough. But if I so much as glimpse a single black scale—"

"Vashodia is far away, I assure you. Do think I'm crazy enough to bring her *here*?"

"Well, you *have* been known for the occasional lapse in sanity."

"What? Like marrying you?"

"Among other things, yes."

"Well, I've had enough bloodshed to last anyone a hundred lifetimes. The last thing I need is you two going at each other's throats."

"Oh darling, it will be *me* going for *her* throat . . . and she'll never see it coming."

The breeze dried the sweat from Jasside's skin as she lay against Mevon's chest, only to moisten it again as intermittent gusts caught mist from the waterfall. Bright sunlight shone down from a clear, open sky, reflecting from her husband's eyes, which matched the hue of the wild grasses upon which they lay. Its warmth was just enough to counteract the wind's cooling effect.

Not that she lacked when it came to heat.

"I'm . . . sorry about that," Mevon said.

Still struggling to control her own heaving chest, Jasside noted with amusement the hint of breathlessness to his words. She'd made him work for it, this time. "What could you possibly have to be sorry about?"

"After that apple fell from the basket, I saw you bend over to pick it up. And . . . well . . . I'm not sure I gave you much of a choice after that."

Jasside laughed softly, remembering his hands reaching for her from behind, forceful and insistent with need. Yet, even then, he'd paused, waiting for her to give assent before letting his desire take hold, infecting them both with its insatiable passion.

"Did my response give you even the slightest indication that your touch was unwanted?"

"Well, no, but—"

"Then you have nothing to be sorry for."

"Still. Twice before breakfast? We've never done *that* before. I don't want you to think I'm being greedy."

"Impossible," she said. "The only reason we haven't done so before is that we were too busy. Not to mention that after a day of fighting we had barely enough energy for, what some would call, 'the basics.' I'm glad we finally have time to . . . explore."

A smile split Mevon's face open wide. "Me too."

There was a kind of surrender to love, she realized. To truly commit was to make of one's self a gift, and to give it freely. Finding someone who would not only take that gift and unwrap it with care, but also give of themselves in return was a thing she'd seen all too rarely. That she could perform this exchange with Mevon, a man she'd once hated with every fiber of her soul, well, she needed no more proof of miracles than that. Without forgiveness, unconditional love simply could not exist.

She reached past him and snatched an apple, one of many that had tumbled into the grass after the basket had—along with her robe—found itself strewn on the ground. She bit into the glossy skin, chewing slowly, and let the cool, sweet juices salve her parched throat. With that last bit of uncomfortableness finally relieved, her body relaxed into a state of complete satisfaction.

Rolling onto her back, she stared up at the sky, content in every way imaginable. After Yandumar ordered everyone to go enjoy themselves, she'd brought Mevon to this place, a spot near enough where she grew up to be familiar, yet far enough away from anything resembling civilization to be considered secluded. She'd formed a small building for their shelter, though they hadn't done much inside it but sleep. Instead, they'd spent their time exploring the nearby terrain, searching for plants to eat, and just simply . . . being. No battles to fight, no people to save, no desperate orders to give or follow.

It was exactly what they'd needed to rediscover both themselves and each other.

And yet, she knew it wouldn't last.

"I like it here," she said, after nibbling the apple down to the seeds, then tossing the core away. "Wouldn't it be nice if we could just stay here forever?"

"Yes," Mevon said. "It would."

"We could plant a garden and hunt occasionally for food. We'd only go into town when we felt like it, and not because it was expected of us, or because we were needed. We could live out our lives in peace. We could even, if you wanted, raise a family. I would add a new room to our house every time . . ."

"That sounds lovely," Mevon said, wrapping an arm around her and hugging her close. "That sounds lovely indeed."

Sighing, she nestled back into him. It was nice to fantasize about the future, even if the odds of it ever coming about were anything but in their favor. "How long, do you think, until they call us back?"

Mevon grunted. In that short exhalation, Jasside read volumes. They both knew how clever and persistent the ruvak could be.

"Not long," he said.

Jasside did not disagree.

"**C**ome on," Lashriel said, tugging at his hand. "We are almost there."

Gilshamed stumbled along behind her. He did not know where they were going, or why they had to walk the last half a league instead of flying, but neither point of ignorance concerned him. He was with his love, alone and untethered to all responsibility. Nothing else seemed like it could possibly matter.

"Just over this hill and it will be in sight. Oh, I cannot wait for you to see it!"

Gilshamed smiled. Though he was only a few centuries older than her, it appeared as though the last two thousand years had simply not affected her. She still retained the relatively youthful vigor that he remembered in his ancient memories, and it was a good thing that she did; that energy, that exuberance for life and all that came with it, was the only thing that had been keeping him going.

After another few dozen steps, they neared the crest of the hill. Lashriel swept a hand out before her, smiling widely as she announced, "And here we . . ." She trailed off, her arm slowly dropping to her side.

Before them was nothing but an ashen wasteland.

"I don't understand," she said. "It's supposed to be right here."

Gilshamed surveyed the valley, which was covered in old lava flows that had long since crusted over, only allowing a few scattered patches of foliage to poke through the grey. "There is little about this place that tugs at my memory."

"It is the same for me. But that should not be so!

That is Mount Elurath right there," she said, pointing to the solitary, snowcapped peak rising high out of the plains. "And where we stand now is a league and a half from the summit, on the leeward side. We should be able to see—"

Words succeeded where the vista had failed, and Gilshamed felt memories older than the empire spring back to life within his mind. "Taranis Valley," he said. "The place where we first met."

"I was but a student at the youth retreat here, and you one of the mentors. It was quite scandalous when we started courting, especially since you were five times my age and already being groomed to take your place on the High Council."

"It was your eyes that first ensnared me, but your compassion that held me in the trap. I always was drawn to the very things that I lacked."

"As was I." Lashriel gestured forlornly to the view before them. "But that place is gone now."

The mountain must have erupted during or soon after the Cataclysm, wiping away one of the more cherished places from their youth. She did not have to speak it out loud for him to understand why she had brought him here. Despite her best efforts, he had felt himself slipping away, caring less and less every day about the fate of the world.

It was difficult to believe in hope when it seemed less real than dreams.

"I had intended . . ." Lashriel shook her head. "I suppose it does not matter anymore. Let us depart. It was a mistake to come here."

"No," Gilshamed said, wrapping an arm around her shoulders before she could unfurl. "You were trying to give me a reason to fight on. A reminder of better times to sustain my will through the dark days ahead. That you would even try means much to me, my love. It is no fault of yours that the very land beneath our feet has been irrevocably altered from the days of our youth."

"So much has changed," she admitted. "But the land is the least of it. There's not a culture around today that I recognize. They've become so alien to me that the ruvak themselves do not surprise me. Even you and I are different from the way we would like to remember ourselves."

"My love for you will *never* change."

"Yes, it will—and that's a good thing," she said, catching the look of protestation on his face. "Change may always be frightening, but it is not always bad. Our love today looks nothing like what it did when our hearts first latched on to each other. In another thousand years it will be different still. Should we sorrow over those lost flutterings that so dominated our young selves? Should we rage against the incessant machine of time that will eventually destroy what defines our love today?"

"Of course not, but we—" He stopped himself, shutting his lips just before they let loose the words that would do her the most harm.

Unfortunately, as always, she knew him too well.

"You do not think we will live that long."

She did not speak it like a question. *Around you, my love, my soul remains ever unguarded.*

"No," he said, after a long moment.

"Perhaps you're right. But I do not think that matters."

"How could it not matter? If I cannot save you, then *what is the point?*"

She stared once more toward the place their old retreat had once stood. "For the youth, of course. For the children alive today, and all those yet to come."

"I do not care about them. Only you."

"I know. I, however, *do* care. I care about them a great deal, and I will fight until my last breath to ensure that their day has a chance to dawn, even if I do not live long enough to see that sunrise. But I do not have your strength, your courage, your implacable will to see a task through to the end.

"You lived for two thousand years sustained only by a dream, and in the end, you turned that dream into a reality. All I ask is that you help me do the same."

Gilshamed lowered his eyes. Her words had stung him. Not in any malicious way, but it hurt to hear them all the same.

"I have been selfish," he said. "And my vision seems as though trapped in a tunnel. You are, as ever, entirely right about me. I cannot continue fighting for you alone. But for your dream? For all those for whom your heart pours out?" He smiled. "Now that is a cause worthy enough to claim my *full* attention."

Arivana watched as the sun shed its last light over the vineyards. Neat rows of plants rolled out over gentle hills as far as she could see, which was even more impressive considering her skyship floated fifty paces above the ground. Thousands of field hands stirred below, laughing and joking with their sun-burnished brethren as they finished up their daily labors, the fruit of which quite literally now rested in her glass.

She saw several of them staring up in her direction, a response she'd grown accustomed to; flying vessels were still a rare sight in the empire. She held up her glass in salute, smiling as the sunlight danced within the swirling liquid like wildfire. The figures all waved back and released jubilant ululations.

"I'm normally more of an ale person," Daye said as he stood beside her. "But this isn't bad."

Arivana glanced over at his wine, as red as blood whereas hers was only faintly pink. "Though I'll not argue the quality," she said, "that particular vintage is too strong and sour for my tastes."

"And yours is much too sweet."

"Well then," she said, pausing to take a sip. "It appears we've both found a drink to suit our temperaments."

Daye frowned. "I'm not *that* sour. Am I?"

Laughing, Arivana patted him on the arm. "Leave it to you, my king, to hear only the perceived slight while missing the compliment entirely."

He grunted as he lifted his own glass and tapped it against hers with a sharp yet short-lived ring. "Well spoken, my queen. As always. I suppose I'll have to learn that particular skill eventually."

"You mean speaking well? Don't be silly. The less you speak the more people are reminded that you hail from the *barbaric* north. Silence, on your part, will only intimidate them into doing whatever we ask of them."

"Are we tyrants now, to bully others into doing our bidding?"

She shrugged. "We could be, if we wanted. The throne hasn't had this much true power in thousands of years."

"Sounds like fun. What sort of foul rules should we force upon them first?"

"Oh, I don't know. Maybe we could make everyone be nice to each other?"

"Outlaw meanness? They would absolutely hate us for that."

"We could outlaw hate, too."

"If we did, they'd just find a loophole through pettiness and sulking."

"Yes, but once we sentence them to acts of altruism and charity, I'm sure their attitudes will change."

"Now *that* is wishful thinking if ever I heard it."

"True," Arivana said with a sigh. "Being a tyrant is more difficult than I thought."

"Plenty of people still manage it," said a voice from behind them. "It's not that hard when people willfully blind themselves to any cruelty not immediately directed at them."

She and Daye both turned as the figure approached them. "Claris," Arivana said. "I take it our course is set?"

"Just waiting on your word to depart," Claris replied.

"Depart?" Daye said. "We just arrived here this morning and you already want to leave?"

"Why not? I've had a lovely time learning about the wine-making process and sampling the best this land has to offer, but there's so much more of it out there to explore!"

"We've already seen half of this entire continent, it seems. Will you not be satisfied until your eyes have claimed the rest?"

Arivana spun outward, scanning a horizon quickly succumbing to long shadows. "But it's . . . all so beautiful. True, many parts of it are different from what I've seen elsewhere, but it's no less stunning a sight. Some places we've come across already have been unique enough to steal my breath away.

Beauty takes so many forms and is measured differently by each observer. I would never forgive myself if I didn't take the opportunity to find it everywhere it lies. Especially here, in a land that's been so long a mystery."

"I couldn't agree more," Daye said, reaching out grasp her hand. "I just find it a shame that true beauty can usually only shine amidst the ugly things in this world."

He squeezed gently, and she felt something pulse through her. Though his touch had never been unwelcome, not even from the awkward start of their relationship, it had never been something she necessarily craved. Something had changed that, somehow. As their eyes met and did not waver in their mutual regard, she realized that this was the first true moment of intimacy between them.

Claris cleared her throat. "Well, if you won't be needing me . . ."

With reluctance—or perhaps to leave them both wanting—Arivana broke her gaze, glancing over at her aunt. "Do me a favor before you go?"

"Anything."

"She may have declined my invitation to join us in today's affairs, but I wouldn't want her to miss out. Would you please bring Sem Aira a glass of wine?"

"It would be my pleasure. Which kind?"

"Any kind she likes," Arivana said, turning back to her husband. "She's no longer a prisoner, after all."

Vashodia skipped along the bottom of the Chasm, sending waves of power down every canyon, cave, and crevice. Darkwisps spilled into the main floor of the massive wound in the planet, flushed out by their thousands. Her spheres feasted. Every pocket in her robe was already stuffed with newly formed homes for her little friends, and she'd even begun filling the sack strapped over her shoulder. It wouldn't be long before that, too, was full.

It was strange that so many of the disembodied souls would choose to linger here. She understood the aesthetic appeal, of course, but not the instinctive one. When she'd shattered the Shroud, most of the darkwisps trapped within it spilled out into the world at large, seeking out lightwisps, and thus, a long-overdue end to their presence upon this world. That had been just as she'd expected.

"Then why are all of you still here? Were you waiting for me? Did you know that I'd come back someday and have need of you? Well, *need* is perhaps too strong a word. You are, after all, not much more than a *means*, a convenient way to more simply reach an end.

"Which end, you ask? Oh, please. As if that mattered. Plan A is forgotten, plan B a distant memory, and plan C . . . we don't talk about plan C. Honestly, why even bring it up?"

The sack was getting heavy, now. Vashodia slowed.

"All I know is that the game is coming to a close. And, as always, I play to *win*."

She formed in the air beside her a basket of sorts, imbibing its bottom with repulsive force, then dropped the sack inside the floating contraption. Her burden removed, she straighten her back and brushed her hands together.

"That's better. And thank you all so much for your participation. I'm afraid I'll have to solve this little mystery another day. But trust me, no matter how things turn out, I will still have plenty of *those* to look forward to. Now——"

All other thoughts subsided in an instant as she felt someone brush against her mind. She had not expected that. Indeed, she'd even taken steps to actively block all attempts to commune with her.

From every source but one.

She plunged into commune, barely giving herself time to form before saying, "It's about time, brother."

"Vashodia!" Draevenus said. "Thank Ruul I got through. You've no idea how good it is to see a friendly—well, to see *your* face, anyway."

"How lovely to see you too. Did you have a nice trip?"

"Heh. Very funny. Now why in the abyss is everyone back in the Veiled Empire?"

She shrugged. "We might have had a setback or two. No matter. I'm preparing a contingency that, while on a somewhat longer timetable than I had initially hoped, should prove effective in seeing our ultimate end met."

"*Our?* Don't try fooling *me*, sister. There is no 'our' about anything you do."

"Brother, you wound me! Everything I've done has been for the benefit of others. Believe me when I say, future generations will thank me."

"If they do, it will only be because you alone survive to write the history books. All the praise in the world means nothing if it comes without choice."

"Oh, bother your negativity. I suppose you contacted me for a reason? Please get to it."

"A reason? Abyss *below* do we have a reason!"

"And that is?"

Draevenus smiled at last. "Rally the troops, Vash. Tassariel may have found a way to end this war."

CHAPTER 21

Jasside listened raptly as Tassariel told her tale, afraid to even breathe lest she miss some crucial detail. Vashodia wouldn't, she knew. And of all those who had gathered to hear the news, her former mistress gave her the greatest worry. She could count on Mevon, Arivana, and even Gilshamed to maintain level heads, and combine their intellect with whatever new information arose to construct the best possible course of action. With Vashodia in the room, however, even the most stolid will could become subverted. Usually, no one even knew it was happening.

". . . and so," Tassariel concluded, "when my father turned those ships away with nothing but purest light, I knew exactly what it meant. What relationship exists between our magic and theirs."

"Oh, yes. Tell us, please," Vashodia said. "Enlighten the feeble minds of those of us too stupid to figure it out ourselves."

Tassariel frowned. "Are you saying you don't want to hear it?"

"Do go on," Jasside said, throwing a quick glare at her former mistress before facing the valynkar woman once more. "She's just mad you know something she doesn't. It's an . . . unfamiliar feeling to her."

Vashodia waved a hand dismissively. "All knowledge will be mine eventually. And I am *such* a patient little girl."

"Then why berate her?"

"I merely find the notion that she and my brother *actually* stumbled upon information that could be considered useful—crucial, even—a bit preposterous."

"But . . . isn't that why you sent us?" Draevenus said.

"What?" Vashodia said, sounding surprised by the question. "Yes, of course. I mean, I had hoped you would. Naturally."

Jasside sniffed out the lie immediately, and judging by the expression on his face, so had Draevenus. For one thing, Vashodia never *hoped* for anything. She made calculated decisions based on well analyzed information and several lifetimes of experience. The future, to her, was one of likelihood, not hope.

But if you didn't expect their mission to succeed, why send them at all?

Another look at Draevenus, whose face softened with glistening eyes, provided her answer.

You sent him away to keep him safe, didn't you?

Granted, penetrating deep into enemy-held territory wasn't typically considered risk-free behavior, but in this case it made a kind of sense. His particular set of skills would have allowed him to pick his engagements, fighting only when relatively sure of victory, while keeping hidden the rest of the time. If he'd stayed with the main group, he'd have been exposed to far more danger. His sister had even sent along a companion in case things became . . . messy.

Vashodia always *did* have a soft spot for her brother. Perhaps, there was hope for her soul yet.

"I believe we are deviating from our purpose in gathering here," Gilshamed said. "I, for one, would like to hear what my niece has to say."

"I agree," Arivana added. "Please, Tass, tell us what you've learned."

Tassariel stepped forward, risking only the briefest glance at the glowering Vashodia. "As I was saying," she said, "our sorceries interact in a most peculiar way. You casters have seen it firsthand, I'm sure."

"They attune to us," Vashodia snapped. "We know this already."

"Yes, but it is more than just becoming similar to either light or dark. It's deeper than that. More . . . personal."

"What do you mean?" Jasside asked.

Tassariel paused for breath, and when she spoke again her voice took on a wondrous, breathless quality. "When you use magic, you're exerting your will on things outside yourself. Each time you do, I think, a piece of you goes with it. Now, light and dark are too opposed for us to feel any effect when used one against the other, but with chaos it's different. If not exactly a middle ground, it seems almost like a bridge of sorts. And when our energy touches theirs, so do our souls."

Vashodia rolled her eyes. "There aren't enough days left in my life to explain how wrong you are."

"I am *not* wrong," Tassariel said, straightening her back.

Jasside was torn between defending Tassariel and agreeing with what her former mistress had taught her. She knew the deeper mysteries of the energy coruscating throughout the universe. She'd seen the way it worked on the most fundamental level with her own eyes. She even had theories as to how humankind had come to harness it, and nowhere did they allow for something so intangible as the soul.

But what if I'm wrong about that?

She peered down at the diminutive mierothi, dressed as ever in dark robes, and asked herself an even more disturbing question.

What if she is?

"When you fight the ruvak," Tassariel said, meeting Vashodia's unwavering stare without flinching, "tell me, what is it that you feel?"

"What I *feel*?" Vashodia giggled. "Why should I feel anything at all? Clever as they are, it's still just sweeping away maggots."

Tassariel nodded. "Arrogance, then. And disdain." She turned to Gilshamed. "What about you, Uncle?"

He sighed, eyes lowering. "Futility."

Tassariel began turning towards Draevenus, but stopped halfway as they both made sharp, whispering inhales. It seemed to Jasside that neither of them wanted to hear what the other felt. At least not in front of a crowd. The valynkar woman instead cast her gaze upon Jasside, lifting an inquiring eyebrow.

"Hate," Jasside said, furious with how easily the word had come to her. "Hate . . . and fear."

Mevon, at her side, gently squeezed her hand.

"As it is with most other casters, I'm sure," Tassariel said.

"So you're saying what, exactly?" Mevon asked. "That the *ruvak* feel what we feel when we fight them?"

Tassariel nodded.

Mevon grunted. "That explains why the fighting grew ever more bitter as the war dragged on. When it comes time to kill, no matter the justness of your cause, there's little room in your heart for anything considered *good*."

"No. My father, on the other hand, felt none of those things. All he felt was guilt. And I think we can all agree that those who are consumed by guilt don't often face their problems."

"No," Gilshamed said quietly. "They run."

The room fell silent as everyone contemplated the words already spoken. Jasside's mind ran wild with implications.

If we could make them feel something good, something other than fear and hate, futility and guilt, what might happen then? All efforts at communication have been met with silence so far. Maybe we've just been speaking the wrong language.

But Vashodia didn't seem to see the connection. "This is all pointless," she said. "What are you going to do? Spit rainbows of happiness at our sworn enemy and expect them to lay down their arms?"

Jasside's elation slipped away at the words. Not because of any vehemence on the speaker's part, but because of how nonchalantly they were spoken. They were enough to make her feel foolish for her recent thoughts, which, she knew, was exactly Vashodia's reason for saying them. Even so, unfortunately, Jasside now found it hard to disagree with her former mistress.

For all her faults, the woman knows a lost cause when she sees it.

Not Gilshamed, though. "What would *you* suggest, then?" he asked, staring down at Vashodia.

"Nothing we have done thus far has done more than delay our eventual fall. Even this reprieve is only temporary. I am certain that no one present is under the illusion that the voltensi will hold the ruvak back indefinitely."

"Which is why we must go on the offensive," Vashodia said.

"Are you mad?" Draevenus said. "Never mind, don't answer that. But trust me when I say, leaving this continent in anything other than clandestine elements is suicide. You don't know what's out there."

"On the contrary, dear brother. I know *exactly* what is out there. Including the fact that no more reinforcements will be arriving for our friends from the void."

Jasside was about to ask how she knew as much, had even opened her mouth to speak the question, but shut it without a sound, shaking her head. Vashodia was ever miserly with her sources of information. "What's your plan, then?" she asked instead.

Vashodia smiled. "Well, they're spread out at the moment. Many are consolidating their hold on the lands beyond, while the rest are probing the empire for a breach point. You know all about that, don't you, Gilshamed. Tell me, if you'd had a few million friends helping you out, would it have taken more or less time, you think, to find your way in?"

Gilshamed only frowned.

"Precisely," Vashodia continued, as if he'd answered. "We're lucky they haven't found one already.

In the meantime, a few well-timed strikes against vulnerable strongholds and logistical points, and the ruvak will start thinking twice about an assault. Now are there any other arguments, or can we start smoothing out the details?"

Jasside looked up at Mevon, searching his face for guidance. Though he appeared troubled, mirroring her own feelings on the matter, after a moment he merely shrugged. Glancing around the room, it didn't look like anyone was about to raise an objection. She sighed, settling into the idea of a long, slow war of attrition that would likely see them all die of old age—including the valynkar and mierothi—before the conflict was over.

That is, until one small voice spoke up from the quiet.

"No," Arivana said.

She held her breath, waiting for someone to shame her into silence. Vashodia, however, only crossed her arms, holding a smug look on her face that said *I can't wait to hear* this, louder than if she had shouted it.

As for the rest . . . well, it was hard for her to describe what she saw. There was a kind of yearning there, in each rapt visage, a longing for something they all needed yet were too afraid to grasp. Not that she could blame them. She knew that maintaining even a thin grip on hope, especially when faced with such impossible odds, required an extraordinary expenditure of energy.

One benefit of youth, at least, is that I have plenty of that to spare. Maybe even enough for the rest of you.

"I may not be a caster," she said, "but if I'm hearing correctly, it seems possible that we might influence the ruvak with sorcery in a positive way. Although it's easy to make it sound absurd by using words like 'rainbows of happiness,' the idea should not be so easily discounted. At the very least, I think we should give it a try."

"Give *what* a try?" Jasside asked.

Arivana shrugged. "I have no idea. Obviously, those of you who *can* use magic will have to work out some sort of process. All I'm saying is that we should travel this path first before going on the offensive. Because once we do, nothing but scorn will come from our efforts to begin talks of peace."

"Peace?" Jasside shook her head. "As much as I'd like to believe it's possible, nothing we've seen from the ruvak suggests that they're interested."

"Which is exactly what Tassariel was pointing out. If what she says is true, then we can't know peace is impossible until we give it a chance. That's all I'm asking for."

"And in the time it takes to try, our opportunity to turn the tables will have passed."

"Is that *you* talking?" Arivana tilted her head towards Vashodia. "Or *her*?"

Jasside's eyes narrowed in anger, but it was replaced just as quickly by shame. A moment later, the anger returned, only this time it was directed inward. Arivana understood the reaction perfectly. The woman had probably told herself not to let her former mentor influence her thoughts, yet had still failed.

We can set all the wards in the world, but there's no guarding against those we care about the most.

"The ruvak aren't all that different from us," Arivana said quietly. "And if anyone can claim to know that, it's me."

Encouraged by the lack of challenge, Arivana swallowed and trudged onwards.

"This war doesn't need to end with the total annihilation of one species or another. I *have* to believe that. I hope you all do, too. Now, I can't guarantee any attempt using this newfound knowledge will succeed. Far from it. In fact, I expect any gamble we take will have odds so long as to make a betting man weep with joy just for the chance to pick against us. Still, I think it's a risk worth taking. If we could just get them to pause—just for a moment—and see us as something other than a hated enemy . . . or see themselves as something other than righteous avengers . . ." She shrugged, lifting her eyebrows.

With her point as defined as she could make it, Arivana ran out of words to say. She looked around the room, searching every set of eyes to see who—if anyone—would support her.

The first person to do so was the last person she had expected.

"She's right," Mevon said.

All eyes turned to him as he spoke. Most people seemed surprised, though none more so than the queen. He gave her a nod, and the look of gratitude that came over her features—and Jasside's gentle pat on his arm—let him know he was doing the right thing.

"Anyone can see that the ruvak are fanatics," he continued. "And knowing what we do about their origins, it isn't hard to see why. They've been banished from their home for thousands of years, every moment a reminder of what they lost, and blaming all their suffering on a nightmare from the ancient past. Blaming us. For whatever they knew about us from that first encounter, so long ago, surely grew more sour with each telling, painting humanity in ever more grotesque light until our extermination must seem not only righteous, but the only thing that matters.

"They've convinced themselves of this, I'm sure, and are too blinded by it to accept the truth. If we could open their eyes for even a single moment, they might see the lie for what it is. Will they change their minds? Who can say. But like Arivana suggests, I think we should give them that chance. Because sometimes," he added, angling his gaze to look down upon his wife's glowing, upturned face, "that's all people need to turn away from the darkness in their hearts and turn instead to something better.

"Something . . . good."

Tassariel smiled. This was exactly the kind of response she had both hoped for and feared, but now that the moment was here all apprehension vanished. And though the momentum was building, she could tell it hadn't begun rolling just yet.

Time, perhaps, for one more little push.

"I agree," she began. "And I think it's important to remember, that though the ruvak have committed atrocities against us, we've done far worse to ourselves. We all came from different lands and walks of life, and at one point our peoples warred, killing each other with bitter savagery that not even the ruvak could match. Yet . . . here we are. No matter what lies behind, I think it's time to start looking forward. And I, for one, don't want to live in a future where we wiped out another intelligent race without at least *trying* for peace."

"Neither would I," Draevenus said, stepping up next to Tassariel as the vision faded from his mind. Another gift of insight from Ruul that felt as if it would be the last.

Vashodia is the key, Ruul had told him. *Through her, all possible outcomes flow. Yet, she is an imperfect creature. Though she will resist, you must guide her, Draevenus. You, and the others gathered to your cause, must remind her that no matter how superior she may be in matters of the mind—yes, even unto both Elos and myself—that she cannot discount matters of the heart . . .*

"Not you too," Vashodia said, appearing legitimately wounded as she stared up at him. "I thought you, of all people, would have more sense than to fall for this sentimental nonsense."

He shook his head. "You know me better than that, Vash. You just don't want to admit that the days are long past when I would stand blindly at your side."

"I never thought of you as blind."

"Blindly loyal, then. But that was back when you and I agreed—if not always on methods, then at least on our goals. Nowadays, even that can no longer be said."

"I'm to stand alone, then? With not even my brother to have my back?"

"I'd like to—I really would—but in this you are, quite simply—" he swallowed before finishing "—wrong."

She crossed her arms. "Survival is wrong now, is it?"

"At the cost you suggest? I don't know. Maybe. But despite the fact that you think you've accounted for every possible factor, there's one I know you've left out."

"And that is?"

"Love, sister. You said it yourself, not too long ago—it can be a useful tool. And for this, it might be just the one we need."

She flicked a hand angrily. "Love is for the weak."

"So you name every person here. *Every* person. That includes yourself."

Finally, she laughed, a bitter sound he'd come to expect from her every time she coiled about herself, turning away any chance of connection with the outside world. "There's no room in my heart for anything so pointless. All that is within me . . . is darkness . . ."

"**Y**ou're wrong about that, too," Jasside said.

Vashodia sneered at her. "Don't tell me you still claim to know me. That assertion has been proven false, time and time again."

"I don't need to know you, or anyone else for that matter, to know that no one is capable of darkness alone. Because I see, now, the light in every soul. The light that binds. That strips away differences. That has the capacity for things like compassion and forgiveness and love."

Shaking her head, Vashodia turned her back on everyone. "You're all fools. I will take no part in what will surely be a suicidal venture."

"Suicide, eh? Sounds more appealing than what's in store for the rest of us."

Jasside turned to see Yandumar standing in the doorway. "Is there news?" she asked.

"Unfortunately," Yandumar said. "I just got word that a ruvaki fleet is dropping troops on the Frozen Fangs, just outside the influence zone of the southern territory's voltensus."

"Have they reached the mainland?" Mevon asked.

"Not yet. But they will by the time we get there. The few troops we have stationed there won't hold them for long."

"Well then," Jasside said. "If we're going to try something, it will have to be now. The only question left to answer is, who should go?"

"I will, of course," said Mevon, smiling. "Don't think you can spit in the abyss's eye without me."

She smiled back at him. "I hadn't planned on leaving you behind."

"I'll go too," Tassariel said.

"And me," Draevenus added.

Jasside nodded to them. She had expected no less but was still grateful for their lack of hesitation. The four of them should be able to protect each other while staying unnoticed until . . . well . . . until they did what needed to be done. However that might end up looking.

"I think I should go, as well," Arivana said.

Jasside felt her eyes go wide at the words, but it was Tassariel who spoke up first.

"I don't think that's a good idea," the valynkar

woman said, putting an arm on the queen's shoulder. "You're no fighter, and wherever we end up will be dangerous."

"Maybe. But if we're to make a gesture of peace, surely we'll try to avoid fighting if at all possible?"

"What about the refugees?" Jasside added. "You've taken to overseeing their care. Who will do that if you're gone?"

"Claris can fill in in my stead. She's been doing most of the work anyway. Besides, there's someone I need to bring. Someone whose presence may mean the difference between being killed outright . . . or being heard."

Nodding, Jasside swallowed the lump in her throat, understanding the queen's point, even if she didn't like putting someone so young in harm's way.

But Arivana is a child no longer, and if we fail, no place in the world will be safe.

Jasside looked to see if Vashodia had any parting words but couldn't find the short figure anywhere. She'd likely already departed to save the world on her *own* terms. "Very well," Jasside said. "Try to get some sleep tonight, everyone. We leave at dawn."

CHAPTER 22

Though it was officially summer, this close to the empire's southern tip meant that on a warm day you only needed one heavy coat instead of two. But as he was high enough to see both of the Frozen Fangs, despite the hundred leagues between them, up where the wind slashed the skyship's front edge like icy knives, even the two he had on weren't enough to keep Yandumar from shivering ceaselessly.

And I'll be too far from any fighting for the heat of battle to warm me up. Probably a good thing, though. These old bones creak just from strapping on my weapons. They'd probably break if I actually tried to swing one.

He glanced down at the troop formations marching across the tundra far below. Hundreds of rough squares, each ten thousand strong, stretched from horizon to horizon, hazy stains crawling like snails towards the two barren, frosty peninsulas. Already, it was the greatest force he'd ever seen assembled in one place, while millions more waited in reserve, only held back by the distance and time it took for the limited transports to make the round trip. Two days until the next wave arrived, then three more for the one after that. If things took a bad turn, he'd have to choose between holding out for reinforcements or sending those skyships into battle, knowing the latter would mean no more help was coming.

A choice he was almost certain he'd have to make.

This far from the action, he could only really affect things on the strategic scale, and so had appointed the two best tactical minds he knew of to command each front. General Idrus Torn had the western Fang, and King Chase Harkun of Sceptre had the east. Casters were placed with every unit whose sole task was to report in constantly, allowing those commanders to maintain a clear picture of the battlefield and maximize effectiveness of their troop placement. No one was under any delusions in that regard. There would be no heroic stands or brave charges, just a steady, slow retreat while conserving the lives of as many troops as possible.

They didn't need to defeat their foe, after all, only delay them long enough for his son and those with him to complete their task.

If success was even possible.

No, don't think about that. You've been through too

much to give in to despair now. Besides, if they fail, the only thing we'd have to figure out at that point is the best way to die. And death hasn't scared me in a long, long time.

"There are few reasons for smiling these days," Gilshamed said, striding up next to him. "If you are willing to share, I would like to hear yours."

Yandumar grunted, just now aware of the state of his own face. "Abyss if I know," he said. "Maybe I'm just relieved that—one way or another—this will all be over soon."

"Yes," Gilshamed said, smiling himself, if with little joy. "An end to conflict does sound appealing, I must admit. As long as I have lived, I have far too few memories of peace."

"You're not alone in that, old friend. But we've no one to blame but ourselves, really. No one forced us to live as we have, thinking if we fought long and hard enough we'd eventually run out of enemies. If anything, we only created more."

"Has a bit of wisdom finally come to you in your old age?"

"Bah! I just no longer see the point in lying to myself. If that's all it takes to qualify as wise, then—" he shrugged "—it's not hard to see how we got into this mess in the first place."

"Indeed."

As it so often had in the past, that single word birthed a long moment of companionable silence.

Memories rushed forth of the first time it had happened between them, back before they'd even returned to the Veiled Empire from their separate exiles. Even then he'd realized the value of such instances, and had begun to realize just how good a friend Gilshamed would become.

Yandumar clapped a hand on the valynkar's shoulder. "We've been through some dark days together, old friend. I pray we'll only have to do it this one last time."

"As do I." Gilshamed paused, his eyes glazing over momentarily. "It is strange to think about the path that led me here. I once defended this land against those who would take it by force, and when that failed, it was *I* who became the invader. Now, I defend it once again, completing the circle begun these two millennia past against an enemy far older still, all while fighting alongside those who were once the bitterest of foes."

"About as strange as some nobody soldier becoming emperor of this abyss-taken land."

Gilshamed smiled. This time, it even showed hints of real amusement. "In that, old friend, you are most certainly correct."

Yandumar dropped his hand from Gilshamed's shoulder, only to wave it across the vista before them. "I suppose it doesn't matter how we got here. I'm just glad that two used-up old men are still around when it matters. That maybe we can even make a difference and leave something behind for the generations to come. Something other than regret."

"A better wish I have yet to hear." Gilshamed's gaze darted past him, and the valynkar cringed. "Let us hope we have strength enough to make it come to pass."

Yandumar turned, then sighed immediately when he saw Orbrahn marching towards them. "What is it now?" he demanded. "The transports delayed by another abyss-taken storm?"

"What?" Orbrahn said. "No, nothing like that. I just received word from our forward scouts attached to the local garrisons."

"Have they begun contesting the crossings yet?"

Orbrahn shook his head. "They never got the chance. They're retreating as we speak . . . what's left of them, anyway."

Too soon. The ruvak had to cross a gorge fifty paces wide from the last ice pillar to reach the mainland, and would have been vulnerable to even a handful of defenders. They should have held for longer than this. "What happened?"

"They were in position, ready to throw back the first bridges, when the attack came. From the sky."

"Impossible," Yandumar snapped. "We're well within range of the southernmost voltensus. No ruvaki skyskips can fly here."

"I didn't say they were *ruvaki* ships, did I?"

Yandumar felt his blood go cold. "How many?"

"A few dozen that we know of. But that was more than enough to smash our outposts along the Shelf. They could be hiding more."

"They shot down hundreds of our skyships in battles past. We'll have to assume every one of them. But how they abyss did they get them working again? Not to mention figuring out how to fly them?"

"That, at least, is explainable," Gilshamed said. "When the need for casters became too great, we began modifying the controls so that anyone skilled enough could become a pilot. It was expedient at the time. None of us foresaw this . . . drawback."

Yandumar sighed. "The next wave is still two days out. Looks like we'll need our winged assets involved in matters sooner than we had planned."

Gilshamed nodded. "I will move them forward and instruct them to keep their eyes on the sky. You do realize that once we commit our own skyships—"

"I know!" Yandumar paused and took a deep breath, unable to believe that the dreaded decision had come so soon. He turned his gaze toward Orbrahn. "Tell Chase and Idrus that we can forget about trying to slow the ruvak. From this moment forward, we're in a fight for our lives."

"No, no, no," Tassariel said, leaning over Draevenus and pointing. "*That* one is for pitch, *that* one is for roll, and *this* one is for yaw."

Draevenus scratched his forehead. "Then what does the lever do?"

"Thrust. You'd know that if you were listening the first time."

"Hey, I'm trying. And how did you become such an expert at piloting anyway?"

"Jasside taught me."

"Ah. Well since she designed the ship, I suppose I'll have to trust you, then."

"You didn't before?"

"Umm . . . yes? I mean, of course I did. Absolutely."

"You're a horrible liar."

"Not true at all. Why, I once persuaded an entire village into thinking I was the mayor's long-lost son. *Without* wearing a disguise."

"Really?"

"No. But I had *you* convinced, didn't I?"

"Well . . ."

"Admit it!"

Tassariel straightened, crossing her arms. "Fine. Now, are you ready to start piloting or not?"

Draevenus shrugged. "The ship is flying perfectly on its own. Why ruin a good thing?"

"Because it's your shift. And if we *do* have to change course, that moment is *not* the best time to learn how."

"Point taken." Draevenus exhaled heavily, reaching for the controls. "I suppose you just—"

The skyship lurched. Tassariel heard glass breaking in one of the cabins below, and from the deck came a nauseated cry.

Ebony hands shot upward as if they'd touched something hot. A moment later, the vessel's flight smoothed out, the balancing mechanisms within returning it to equilibrium automatically.

"Easy," she said, leaning in again—much closer this time. She slipped her fingers through his and guided his hand back to the controls. "You just need to be a little more gentle."

He turned towards her, opening his mouth as if to speak, but the motion only brought his face in line with her chest. And with her blouse hanging just loose enough, he couldn't help but get an eyeful. His gaze lingered a beat longer than an unexpected glance could account for—not that there was much to see—but somehow, she found herself smiling.

And why should that surprise you, exactly? It's not as if he were some lewd, gawking stranger. He's been far more than that to you for far longer than you want to admit. Just be glad he's finally seeing you as a woman.

With his eyes now fixed firmly forward, peering out the glass windows of the pilot's cabin into the setting sun, Draevenus cleared his throat. "I'm not sure if I'm cut out for this."

Tassariel lifted an eyebrow. "Oh? I've seen you put a dagger through an eye at twenty paces. Hands that nimble—" she paused to give one a squeeze "—can handle this."

"Yes, but I had hundreds and hundreds of years to perfect that one skill. Learning new things—quickly, anyway—hasn't always worked out for me before."

"Well, there's your problem. Stop living in the past so much, and instead start living for the now."

Because, she didn't need to add out loud, *that might be all we have left.*

His gaze shot to her, penetrating in its intensity. Tassariel matched it. Neither looked away.

After a long moment, he smiled. "You've convinced me. I think I'll give it another try."

"Good," she said, returning the smile. "Just remember, no one expects you to be perfect. Just keep trying to improve and learn from your mistakes. That's all anyone can ask."

"Right."

He placed his hands on the controls once more, but this time his motions were slow and steady, and the ship responded in kind.

"Tassariel?"

"Yes?"

"I've been meaning to tell you. I . . . really like the color of your hair."

"Thank you, Draevenus. That's a very kind thing to say."

"Feeling any better?" Mevon asked, holding Jasside's hair as she dabbed at her lips with a cloth.

"A little," she replied. "Sorry about that. I'm not used to being on skyships where I'm not the one controlling it. I didn't realize how much it would affect my stomach."

"No need to apologize. Besides, most of it went into the waves."

"Small consolation, that. Do me a favor?"

"Anything."

"Next chance you get, give your friend a hard time about his flying skills."

Mevon grunted, looking over his shoulder at the pilot's cabin. "I think he has other things on his mind."

He helped her to her feet, then watched as—one hand to her stomach—she followed his gaze. A beat later, her eyes widened.

The gestures and smiles, the lingering gazes, the tense yet comfortable way they moved around each other; even to someone as new to it as Mevon, it was impossible to miss.

"They're . . . in love," Jasside said, eyes glistening in wonder.

"Aye," Mevon said, feeling as much in awe as she looked. "I wonder if he even knows."

"Come, now. He can't be *that* oblivious."

"If you'd asked me a week ago, I probably would have told you it would take a miracle to open that man's eyes to the possibility, buried as he is under that much regret."

"Sometimes, all it takes is the right person to come along."

"The right *woman*, you mean."

Jasside shrugged, grinning wryly. "It's not *my* fault men are mostly idiots when it comes to matters of the heart."

"True," Mevon said, laughing. "Still, it never ceases to amaze just how much it can change you, how little a man who knows love resembles who he is without it."

Jasside sighed, spinning away then leaning against his chest. "That," she said, "is the only thing that gives me hope that this might work."

Mevon wrapped his arms around her, bending his nose to the top of her head and breathing deeply of her familiar, comforting scent. "Have you worked it out, then?"

"Tass and I developed a method that should at least get their attention. But how effective it will be? How long that effect will last?" She shook her head. "There's no way to tell until we try it. We've run out of guarantees, I'm afraid. All we have left is faith."

Mevon grunted. "No wonder Vashodia wanted nothing to do with this."

His wife's laughter seemed the sweetest thing in his ears. Not only because his attempt at humor succeeded—a rare enough occurrence—but because he'd been able to impart upon her some small measure of joy. He didn't always feel like he knew what he was doing, being a husband, but moments like this let him know he was at least walking in the right direction.

And the fact that joy is even possible, when all seems so bleak, well . . . that gives me all the faith I need.

Arivana collected fresh goblets—pewter, this time—as Daye finished cleaning up shards of shattered glass and spilt wine. Strange as it was to see a king on his hands and knees wiping the floor with an ever-reddening cloth, Sem Aira's reaction seemed stranger still. She'd begun moving from her seat as soon as the skyship had finished its unexpected motions, as if to be first to the mess, only to stop herself willfully, shaking her head as she sat back, eyes going cold and watchful again. Yet as Daye discarded his spent rag and retrieved another, the waxy, grey fingers carefully folded in the woman's lap still twitched from time to time, obviously uncomfortable to be idle while royal hands labored.

All in all, Arivana didn't know what to make of her former handmaiden's behavior. Despite her efforts to reach through to her, it seemed that after all this time, still nothing had changed. Not for the first time, she wondered if it was a mistake to have come.

"All taken care of," Daye said, straightening his tunic as he returned to his chair. "Let's hope Draevenus is done testing this vessel's limits."

Arivana forced a smile to her lips, determined to escape the dismal thoughts swirling around her head. For the plan to work everyone needed to do their part to perfection, and much of her task—as simple as it seemed in the grand scheme of things—required her to walk a knife's edge with every word and gesture, a balancing act that had already been going on for some time. Though she felt confident in her ability to pull it off, the strain of maintaining her act had begun to wear on her. Her only consolation was that the end was finally in sight.

And abyss take me if I'll be the reason we fail.

Lifting the pitcher, Arivana filled the three new cups with equal measures of wine, then handed two to her companions. She brought the last to her lips and drank deeply enough to feign an air of relaxation without seeming too eager. The smile she swept towards Sem Aira came more easily this time.

"Drink up, Sem," Arivana said, flicking her hand casually toward the untouched cup. "I'd hate for any more of this fine vintage to go to waste."

"Fine vintage?" Daye said. "Is that what you call it? Give me a warm mug of Sceptrine ale any day over this swill."

"Oh really? I seem to recall you finishing off each of the last three—no, *four* bottles I opened. That doesn't seem to me the actions of a man barely tolerating his drink."

"You can't blame me for taking what enjoyment

I can under less than ideal circumstances. It's not as if we could swing by the great breweries of Taosin or San Khet and fill the hold with the best ale on the planet."

"Why not?"

Daye shrugged. "Too far out of the way."

Arivana laughed, reaching out to give her husband a playful shove. It wasn't the best joke in the world, but humor was in such short supply these days any attempt at it seemed worthy of celebrating. Besides, it had accomplished its intended effect. Out of the corner of her eye, Arivana caught a twitch at the corner of Sem Aira's mouth as the ruvak finally took hold of her wine.

"I suppose it is," Arivana said. "I do hope I'll get the chance to try it someday."

"I thought you hated ale?" Daye said.

"Maybe that's because I haven't yet had yours."

"Ah. Well, if anything can change your mind, that first taste will certainly do the trick. If not, the second will."

"I think you're underestimating the impact of first impressions."

"Oh, I won't dispute their importance. But sometimes, the best things in life are the things that take some getting used to. In my experience, you'll never find a greater champion for a cause than one who initially stood against it, only to come around after realizing what they were missing."

"Now I think you're *over*estimating the seriousness of alcohol." Arivana paused to take another deep pull on her drink, then turned to Sem Aira. "What about you? Do you prefer wine or ale? Or perhaps something else? I'm sure you've had all kinds of drink we've never heard of, and which most humans would find unpalatable."

The way the woman's expression changed sent a swell of hope throughout Arivana. It became the face of someone who had waited a long time for their chance to speak while knowing they had something meaningful to say.

"Well," Sem Aira began, "there is this one liquor I used to favor. It's fermented from the fungus that grows on the . . ."

She trailed off, dropping her head as she shrank into herself once more.

The hope, newly arisen within Arivana, crumbled into dust.

"I know what you're trying to do," Sem Aira said. "I just don't understand."

"Understand what?"

"How the two of you can act so comfortable around one another, let alone around me. Not that long ago your nations were slaughtering each other without mercy or remorse, yet you sit here talking as if it never happened, as if all that pain and hate has already been forgotten. And *my* people? They view your entire species as little better than the insects we feast upon, yet you speak to me as though I were some old, long absent friend. None of this makes any sense!"

Arivana leaned back in her chair, exhaling as she reached out a hand towards Daye, who grasped it with all the firm tenderness she'd grown to both want and need. "I don't expect it to. Not all of it. Not *yet*. All I can really explain is that Daye and the people of Sceptre have forgiven me and my countrymen. Though we did nothing to deserve it, they understand what too few do—that hatred and revenge may feel natural, but they only cause more damage in the long run, and most of it to those who hold it in their hearts.

"They form the easy path to take when one has been wronged, the path of destruction so often masked as one of justice or righteous recompense. To achieve true healing, however, requires you to walk a most unnatural road, one far more difficult to tread. But, in my admittedly short experience, I've found that the things truly worth doing are the ones that test you along the way. It's those very trials that let you know you're heading in the right direction."

Sem Aira peered at Arivana with narrowed eyes, sucking air in through her vertical nostril slits like someone on the verge of erupting. After a long, silent moment, the ruvak set down her cup and pushed it away. Arivana could tell that the woman knew the truth: that time was running out for them all.

"Where are you taking me, anyway?" Sem Aira asked.

Arivana glanced to Daye, who met her regard with a nod. She turned back to her former handmaiden. "Home."

CHAPTER 23

Yandumar jerked awake as a hand fell on his shoulder.

"Wasn't sleeping," he said, rubbing his fists into his eye sockets as he leaned forward in his chair.

"Your slurred words suggest otherwise."

Twisting his neck, which set off a brief struggle with coughing, Yandumar cast a baleful eye on Gilshamed. "Just the cold, old friend, I swear. My lips are half-frozen."

"I could do something about that, you know."

Yandumar shrugged. "The soldiers fighting below don't have that luxury. Until this is over, neither will I."

"It looks unlikely to end anytime soon." Gilshamed smiled. "But if it does—"

"Then I'll be cold until I die."

"As will we all."

Yandumar stood, stretching as far as he was able

before joints started popping with pain, then pulled his coats closer about him. He glanced briefly out past the rim of his skyship. It was night, which meant the sites of active battle, with their steady if slim exchanges of sorcery and power-infused weapons, were visible to the naked eye. A quick count revealed roughly two score such places. No big surprise either way.

"Have you heard any news?" Yandumar asked.

Gilshamed shook his head. "I was about to ask the same of you."

Sighing, Yandumar nodded, then raised an eyebrow. "To the table?"

The valynkar lifted a hand behind them, gesturing towards the center of the vessel's main deck, which was covered in a loose patchwork of canvas faintly resembling a tent. "After you."

"How kind," Yandumar replied, coughing again as he lurched into motion. "I look an abyss-taken fool trying to keep up with *your* pace. I ain't as young as I used to be."

"Trust me, old friend," Gilshamed said, falling into step beside and slightly behind him, "with all that has happened, even *I* am starting to feel my years."

"Bah! What are you now? Three thousand? Four? Why, you're barely middle-aged for a valynkar. You don't get to start grumbling until those absurdly golden strands on your head start looking like a slightly less precious metal."

"If we make it through this alive, something tells me I'll get the opportunity to complain."

That, old friend, is one very big "if."

They pushed through what constituted an entrance together, and Yandumar was immediately blinded by the light blazing from every possible angle. It took a good mark of blinking until he could see clearly again. Half a dozen figures stood around a low, broad table, which glowed with pulsing, sorcerous light.

It had taken all of two days until his messenger corps—all casters too young to take part in the fighting directly—had tired of his constant questions. Clever things that they were, they had devised a system that would constantly feed him and his subordinate commanders with all the information they could ever require, all without need for a word to pass between them. Thus, the table danced with conjured images of light and shadow, depicting up-to-the-beat details about troop placement and combat status, casualties, supplies, enemy activity, and a dozen other things. He'd even set a young boy to keeping a scrolling list of all the dead, but that lasted less than half a week; the list quickly became too unfathomably long for a single soul to manage, and he couldn't spare any more to help.

So many fallen, and we can't even be bothered to remember their names.

Yandumar wasn't sure why that bothered him so

deeply. After all, there would soon be no one left to do the remembering.

No one *human*, anyway.

He and Gilshamed stepped up to the table and set to examining the situation. The thin, jagged line of human defenders—represented by spectral blue lights—had been pushed several hundred leagues northward, onto the border between the tundra plains and the mountains that spanned the breadth of the empire's southern territory. The two fronts had become one as individual units dug in, fought, retreated, or simply licked their wounds.

The angry, red blob that stood for the enemy occupied all the rest of the displayed space.

As if numbers alone and the salvaged human skyships weren't enough of an advantage, the ruvak had even more surprises in store. Wrath-bows and shock-lances by the thousands, and nearly a hundred war engines, had shown up on the front lines on the third day of fighting, turning the tide in several key engagements. They'd been running for their lives ever since.

"So," Yandumar said after his all-too-brief study of the strategic situation, "it's going about as well as can be expected."

"Yes," Gilshamed said, shaking his head. "How soon until they begin threatening your population?"

"All the towns and villages along the mountains have been evacuated, and it's another two-day march beyond the passes to the nearest city. I'd empty them too, but . . ." Yandumar shrugged.

"If the ruvak break through," Gilshamed said, unnecessarily completing the thought, "there will be no place left to find refuge."

Yandumar closed his eyes. "Aye."

Every breath in the room stopped as one. After a moment, he heard the first sorrowful whimper.

He leaned close to his companion, lowering his voice. "Hope is a funny thing. It can lift souls to greatness not otherwise possible, but it's so damned fragile. No need to be swinging hammers at it."

Gilshamed dropped his head. "My apologies, old friend."

"Forget it. No, seriously, put it out of your mind completely. We've enough things to worry about to get hung up on little mistakes."

"I know. Still I—"

"Still *nothing*. We do the best we can, but perfection is impossible even in ideal circumstances. With the pressure we're under? Ha! I'm surprised I haven't mistaken you for Slick Ren yet!"

"Is my touch so gentle to be perceived as a woman's?"

Yandumar grunted. "Not in the least. Of course, that's exactly where the confusion comes from!"

Gilshamed smirked. "Well, the next time I see your wife, I will be sure to tell her how little you think of her femininity."

"Much obliged, old friend. Much obliged." He

clapped Gilshamed on the shoulder, almost forgetting for the moment all that was at stake.

Almost.

"Speaking of family," he said after a moment, "have you heard anything from our secondary front?"

"I was in contact with Tassariel this morning. All she told me was that she thought they were getting close."

"Nothing else?"

"I'm afraid not," Gilshamed said, shaking his head. "They could be arriving as we speak, or still days away. By necessity, I allow her to initiate contact. I wish I could tell you more."

"It's all right. They ain't dead yet. Until they are—" he swept an arm over the table "—it looks like we still have work to do."

Draevenus saw it first. He'd been expecting it.

There'd been something wrong about his time in Yusan. Something so subtle only a thorough examination of his memories had revealed it. It was a good thing so many moments had been worth storing.

The attacks upon Tassariel's father had always come from the east, but where they were located, the only thing east of them was open ocean. And it wasn't called Endless for nothing. Arivana had confirmed it, a fact every Panisian child knew as a matter of course: eastward of the continent were waves and little else. But the attacks had to come from somewhere, and the ruvaki skyships he'd seen, even the command vessels, were all too small to launch the squads that had come against them.

Something was out there, he'd insisted. And whatever it was, it was *big.*

None of them had been prepared for just how right he was.

He'd first spotted it about a toll past noon. Just a dark blot on the horizon at first, but it soon resolved into a sharp-peaked dome. Jasside had immediately cloaked their own skyship in darkness, sure their destination was imminent. But as the tolls dragged on, and night fell, and still the monolith's lowest part had yet to be revealed, the scale of it dawned on them all. Even Sem Aira had been left speechless, for though she knew what it was, she'd never in all her years been so close.

She'd whispered a word none of them understood. A blessing or a curse, he couldn't tell. When Arivana had asked, the ruvak woman had told them all what lay before them.

The Cloister, where the heads of every avenging clan gathered to conduct their war.

He didn't bother telling her that "war" was the wrong word. That "genocide" was far more fitting. Though he still wasn't quite sure why she was with them, he left all such matters to the queen. He'd done his part leading them here. He was sure Arivana was somehow doing hers.

As the sun began rising, and the mountain-dwarfing vessel came fully into view, he took hold of Tassariel's hand. She didn't resist.

"Are you ready for this?" he asked her.

Her fingers curled tightly around his. "As long as I'm with you, I'm ready for anything."

Mevon announced soon after that he'd spotted an entrance. Draevenus released Tassariel, and the two of them began checking their weapons.

Vashodia strolled through the streets of Mecrithos, sickened by how happy everyone seemed. Though words of war were whispered with every other breath, replete with concern for loved ones sent to battle, the people of the city went about their daily affairs with an obvious sense of pride, an attitude far removed from the dull pallor of drudgery that infected every downcast or snarling visage the last time she'd been here.

Yandumar was a good ruler, apparently.

How wonderful.

She did her best to ignore everyone as she picked up her pace, drawing her hood even farther over her face to prevent another mother from approaching with worry over a small child wandering the streets alone. The gambit failed. Two women tried to stop her between the gateposts of the city's highest district and the palace, bringing the total to nine since she'd first entered Mecrithos. On principle, she didn't kill anyone she didn't think deserved it, but such annoyances always tested the bounds of her self-imposed rules.

As her steps finally came to a halt outside the palace gates, two guards crossed their halberds in front of her.

"You would dare try to stop me?" she said, more amused than anything.

"Course not," one of them said. "Just thought we'd give ya fair warning."

"Against what?"

"The empress," the other guard said, "she don't want you here. Told us to kill you on sight."

Vashodia raised her head. "Is that so?"

"Aye," the first guard said. "But us and the boys got to talking and figured that'd be a bad plan for everyone involved."

"Don't get us wrong," the second guard added. "We love and respect ole Slick Ren, but there ain't no use dying in a fight that could only have one outcome."

"Still," the first guard said, "if you wanna avoid trouble, best do your business quietly. Keep hidden and our boys won't bother you, but if'n you start making a scene . . . ?" He shrugged. "Won't have much choice at that point."

Vashodia smiled. "I think we understand each other perfectly, then. Now, will you kindly open the gates for me? Or will I have to . . ."

The guards both gestured behind them. A beat later, the ornate metal bars began creaking apart.

For the first time in years—and perhaps the last time in her life—Vashodia entered the Imperial palace grounds of Mecrithos.

Taking the guards' excellent advice, she glided behind the library, avoiding the main thoroughfare to the palace proper. Though she didn't fear confrontation, the inconvenience of sneaking to her destination was only a fraction of that were she to force her way there. Simple math kept to her to the narrow, vine-strewn paths that eventually led her to a servants' entrance halfway around the back side of the ghastly structure. She slipped in behind a maid bearing a bucketful of freshly extracted milk.

Gliding through the once-familiar hallways, ducking into alcoves and side passages to avoid what few servants she came upon as they bustled between errands, Vashodia couldn't help but notice the changes. Though the palace had been rebuilt with an essentially identical layout, the atmosphere felt wholly different. Gone were the grotesque statues, paintings, and sculptures that depicted images of mierothi dominance, and the lightglobes—dark blue or purple at their brightest—placed far apart to accentuate the shadows. Though the current decor fell short of cheerful, Slick Ren had at least livened the place up.

Vashodia hated it.

Her path eventually led her near the royal chambers, where she exited from the servants' passage to another, even more hidden one, risking a brief use of energy to rearrange the molecules in the wall to allow her transversal of a seemingly solid mass. In complete darkness now, she smiled. This was the escape tunnel. To her left was the entrance to the royal bedchamber, while the path right would lead her out of the palace entirely to a narrow trail that led down the back side of the mountain upon which the city lay.

Vashodia turned left, marched half a dozen paces down the stone passageway, and without hesitation pressed the button hidden in the mortar between two bricks.

No one had bothered to change its location during the rebuild. Vashodia giggled as a section of the wall swung open in a blaze of firelight.

She marched into the private quarters shared by her once-servant Yandumar and no-one's-servant Slick Ren, feeling confident that it would be empty. It was the middle of the day, after all. With the emperor away, the empress surely had too many things on her plate to be caught sleeping in.

Her assertion was confirmed after a cursory inspection of the bedchamber. Though she had a sudden urge to pry, she ignored the closets and dressers, reluctantly making her way to a spot on the wall near cupboards full of wineglasses. She found another hidden button near the floor, and marched through the swinging wall before it had even finished opening.

A square platform awaited her. A pedestal held a single lever, pointed up, while dark, drafty emptiness surrounded her. She flipped the lever down and held on while the sorcerous construct began its long, quiet descent.

Vashodia checked her pockets twice in the mark and a half it took to complete her downward journey. She was far below the palace now, below the city even, at an equal elevation to the base of the mountain. She stepped off the platform and began down the only path available, her footsteps echoing off the distant borders of the cavern. Two hundred paces.

Then she stopped and looked up towards the pinnacle of the voltensus.

"Hello, old friend. It has been a while."

A memory gripped her then, exposing her to a vulnerability she hadn't thought to guard against. She remembered the face of the soul trapped within the obelisk. A face not that dissimilar from her own: young, girlish . . .

Mierothi.

This was the master voltensus, after all, capable of controlling the others. It needed to be stronger, more loyal. Who better to inhabit it than a childhood friend of the one who oversaw their construction?

The conquest of this empire had seen all of her people change. But that moment had been the one where she realized they'd gone too far. That she could no longer support a regime bent on cannibalizing its weakest members to strengthen those already in power. She'd hidden away what little was left of her soul, and began laying plans to undo the very evil she'd helped to ascend into dominance. Though her exact goals had changed along the way, somehow that purpose had always remained steadfast.

Confronted by more than she had been prepared for, Vashodia fell to her knees. She'd come here to harness the voltensi. With the proper instructions, the boundaries of their effect could be temporarily altered.

In a single stroke, she could disable every ruvaki skyship on the planet.

None of her supposed allies had known of this capability, and she hadn't felt like telling them. Their gamble for peace had preoccupied them to the point of blindness. Even as frustrating as their stance was, Vashodia couldn't help but wish them well. She'd done her best to keep Draevenus alive through the centuries, and Jasside had managed to remind her that she still had a soul. And that, broken as it was, it could still be mended.

Sighing, Vashodia reached into her pockets. She

withdrew the two soulstones she'd crafted and set them before her. One each for the only two people in this world who meant anything to her. They both still glowed, indicating that her brother and former apprentice yet lived.

"I'll give you a chance. I can do that, at least."

She waited, kneeling, watching the two rocks for tolls, unblinking eyes expecting any moment for the stones to lose their glow and crumble into dust as the connected lives met their end.

But they never did.

What she witnessed instead defied all expectation.

In an instant, the glow from both soulstones faded to the barest whisper of a spark, but the matter itself remain whole.

Jasside and Draevenus weren't dead. They had simply gone beyond her reach. Out of bounds. Invisible.

For the first time in her life, Vashodia didn't have the slightest idea what to do.

Tassariel, considering herself the lone representative of light, was first to step off their skyship after it docked inside a relatively isolated opening near the midpoint of the monolithic Cloister. A single, unarmed ruvak was witness to their arrival. Tassariel sprang towards him, wrapping the inhuman male in a chokehold before he'd even begun to flee. The body in her arms soon fell limp and unconscious.

The rest of her companions disembarked right after her. Together, they began treading the interior passages of the impossibly massive vessel.

Draevenus joined her beside the first portal as the others crowded in close behind. "You remember the plan, right?" he asked.

She tried not to roll her eyes. "Avoid detection but don't draw our blades. Spilling blood will undermine our whole purpose in coming."

The mierothi sighed, nodding. "Right. Sorry. Didn't mean to patronize. It's just—"

"No more apologizing," she said, flexing her fingers. "All that's left for us . . . is action."

The only response Draevenus gave her was a smile.

She glanced back over her shoulder as the others moved up to join them. Daye was first among them, with Arivana close behind, one guiding hand on the elbow of Sem Aira, who was bound at her wrists by ropes. Jasside kept several paces behind those three, and though she hadn't energized yet, Tassariel knew the woman could activate a spell in the span of half a breath. Mevon brought up the rear, head and eyes on a constant swivel.

"Ready?" Draevenus asked her.

Tassariel nodded.

They dashed through to the next hallway, splitting to either side. Draevenus leapt forward from shadow to shadow until almost out of sight, then gestured towards her. She repeated his motions, surging past him with care to keep herself exposed for as little time as possible. Once far enough, she turned to wave him on. The others followed, keeping close enough for hand signs to pass from her or Draevenus, but far enough to retreat without detection should the need arise.

It was a game of patience played as hastily as they dared. There was a lot of ship to search, and none of them knew exactly what they were looking for.

The skyship seemed strange in so many ways. She'd been aboard other ruvaki vessels, and while each had different flavors, they all seemed similar in purpose: tight interiors, built for economy of space and function. The Cloister felt nothing like that. Soaring archways lined every hall, full of color and light, if each a little faded, and footsteps echoed down endless, tiled corridors. Whereas on other skyships she'd never been able to escape the feeling of being on a moving construct, here it felt like being on a mountain.

And undeniably, the Cloister felt *old*. Ancient. A piece of living history stronger than the pillars of the Valynkar High Council. The dust that filled her lungs with every breath held a stale quality reminiscent of a tomb, if not half so cheerful. Something—perhaps a lingering memory from the time of her possession— told her that Elos himself had seen this very vessel long ago, before humankind had ever stepped foot upon this world.

Every beat spent inside the infernal thing scraped away at the hope that they would ever make it out again alive.

From ahead, Draevenus flashed her a hand sign. It was different than she'd expected. Tassariel turned around and motioned for the others to gather close, then trotted towards the mierothi.

"What is it?" Jasside asked after everyone had arrived.

Draevenus motioned over his shoulder. "There's a staircase, just around the corner. I was thinking we should take it."

"Maybe," Mevon said. "But which way? Up . . . or down?"

Arivana patted Sem Air on the arm. "Any thoughts?"

The ruvak shook her head. "I do not know this place. It is as alien to me as I must seem to you."

Tassariel caught herself staring at the woman, and nearly flinched when those inhuman eyes grazed past her own. She'd been trying to tell if Sem Aira were lying, she realized. But even watching as closely as she could, nothing about the woman seemed the least bit deceitful.

"Let's go up," Tassariel said.

"Why up?" Draevenus asked.

"I don't know. It seems logical for the ruvaki rulers to take the highest vantage point, doesn't it? Besides, it's better than going nowhere."

Nods greeted her last words—even from Sem Aira—and they began marching up the wide, spiraling staircase.

They took on a similar posture as before, but due to the constrained space the gap between them all shortened to a single revolution of the steps. Every footfall resonated with far too much noise in her ears, but after a while she took a small measure of comfort from that. No ruvak had reason to be as quiet as she was being. They wouldn't even try. If anyone else was actually on this accursed skyship, she was confident her friends would have ample warning of their approach.

For almost a toll, they trudged onwards and upwards. Though they passed countless landings leading into each level of the Cloister, no one suggested that they exit the staircase—the air from the landings was sour. Stale. Even more lifeless than the one they'd entered on. What they sought would not be found on any such floor.

Not that we've any clue where it will be found. I only hope that we'll know it when we see it. If not, the ruvak won't even have to kill us. We'll wander these endless halls until we die of old age.

After pausing to catch her breath and rub loose a cramp in her leg, Tassariel looked up to find Draevenus at her side.

"Are we giving up tactical movements?" she asked.

"I'm not sure it matters," Draevenus replied.

"What do you mean?"

He planted one foot on the next stair and tilted his head. She followed, keeping pace. Their elbows brushed together every other step, but she didn't move away from him. Neither did he move away from her.

"Tell me what you sense," he said. "What do your instincts say is waiting for us?"

"I don't know," she replied, without thinking. "I'm too tired to try feeling anything beyond this stairwell."

"As they intend, no doubt. I can't exactly blame you for not seeing it yourself."

"Seeing what?"

Draevenus sighed. "We're being watched."

Cold flowed to the base of her spine, making her shiver despite the sweat drenching her skin. "Are you sure?"

"Instincts," he said, patting his chest but in no boastful manner. "I've had more time to hone them. Especially for situations like this."

Tassariel didn't feel inclined to argue that point. "What do you think it means, though? If they know we're here, yet haven't tried to stop us . . . ?"

"They either don't consider us enough of a threat to warrant to bother rousing a defense, or—"

"They're leading us into a trap."

"Aye." He leaned close. "We must continue to be wary, but I don't see any more need for stealth."

"Agreed. What about the others?"

"I'll drop back and talk to Mevon. I'll be surprised if he hasn't already come to the same conclusion."

"Instincts?"

He nodded. "Instincts."

Draevenus slowed his steps, leaving her once more in the lead. As he fell from sight behind her, she couldn't help but think they were missing something. That there was perhaps a third option to explain the enemy's reticence.

That no matter what we do, it won't make the slightest difference in the end.

She tried to shake the thought away, but it refused to dislodge from her mind. And before she could announce victory, or concede defeat, something more pressing stole the rest of her attention.

The stairwell had at last come to an end.

Mevon stepped out alone into what proved to be a wide-open concourse, sniffing deeply. It smelled different from the other levels. Whereas the emptiness of them seemed the kind born of long neglect, the kind here seemed only temporary. The maze of suspended walkways, terraces, and sheltered alcoves before him was as still as a ruin, but held only a fraction of the dust. Whatever for, it had seen recent use.

If something is going to happen, it will happen here.

He advanced another dozen steps, fully isolated and exposed to every corner of the concourse.

Nothing moved.

Mevon knew why.

With a sigh, he gestured behind him, urging his companions to emerge from the stairwell. No use delaying the inevitable. When there was no way to avoid a trap, the best thing to do was force it to spring when you were at your most ready. And if he was being honest with himself, Mevon was itching for some action.

Justice was in his hands, yet turned perpendicular to his normal grip. Striking with the flat of his blades went against all his training, all his instinct, but that was what they'd all agreed upon. He would need to maintain absolute control.

Seeing his beloved approach, and knowing what was in store should he fail, he had no trouble summoning the storm. No trouble at all.

A beat after his companions all joined him, the ruvak did the first predictable thing he'd ever seen them do.

"Here they come," he said.

From every shadowed corner, they emerged. Hundreds in the first breath. Thousands by the time he'd made a full sweep around with his eyes, with more pouring in every beat. He twirled his *Andun* once, conscious to retain his altered grip, but remained otherwise motionless.

He felt the three casters behind him energize at last.

Though they were too slow to raise barriers against the first attacks, Mevon wasn't. Projectiles of some kind pierced the air in front of him. He flicked out Justice to meet them, sending the metal shards spinning towards the cavernous roof far overhead. Sparks of dark and light snapped on either side as Tassariel and Draevenus began batting more of them from the air with pinpoint applications of sorcerous power.

Ruvaki troops closed in from all sides, silent but for the stamping of untold feet on the floor. They displayed none of the squawking savagery of those he'd faced before. They were disciplined, focused; two things he considered far more deadly than rage.

The missiles stopped two beats before they drew within striking range. With less than twenty paces now separating them, Mevon tensed, preparing to lunge forward to meet them.

But they drew no closer.

The front ranks slammed to a halt on all sides with unnatural swiftness. Those behind continued forward, crashing into the backs of their compatriots with bone-crunching effect. Their silence was broken in a wave of cries laced with surprise and pain.

Mevon looked over his shoulder at Jasside. Torrents of power reached out from her raised hands to the shield she'd erected, which let nothing through.

Though the ruvak continued crowding around, testing the barrier at every point, they were, at the moment, in a stalemate.

"They've played their hand," Mevon said. "What now?"

"Now?" Jasside said. "Well, I suppose we could always ask for directions. Anyone know how to say 'take me to your leader' in ruvakish?"

"It's not called that," Sem Aira said, surprising Mevon with the very sound of her voice. "But they're speaking an odd dialect. Very old-fashioned. I'm having a difficult time understanding them."

Mevon grunted. *He* had a difficult time taking anything the woman said at her word. "If you can't translate, then why did we even bring you?"

"She said difficult, not impossible," Arivana snapped at him. The queen turned up an eyebrow toward her charge. "Isn't that right?"

Sem Aira hesitated, then nodded.

Mevon wasn't the least bit reassured.

He swung back to survey the enemy and was just in time to observe a ripple pass through them, stifling all movement and sound within those thousands in a mere heartbeat. He couldn't even hear them breathe.

From a wide, dark doorway directly opposite the one his party had entered from, Mevon witnessed the emergence of six . . . things.

He couldn't properly call them figures, for the very air around them was warped, spilling chaotic energy like blood from crossed wounds. Mevon's whole body ached in a way he'd not felt in years, not since Voren had begun laying waste to the Imperial palace with twisted power not his own. He took a step towards them without even making the decision to do so.

"Jasside," he called out in warning.

"I see them," she replied.

"Is it a problem?"

Jasside paused before answering, and Mevon felt the first twinge of what might be real fear. "I . . . don't know. These aren't mere conduits. If they were, I'd put the odds in our favor, but I don't have the slightest idea what they're capable of. But I can tell that those we've faced before were only borrowers of ruvaki sorcery. These are its *true* masters.

"If we weren't currently averse to shedding blood, it would make for an interesting day."

"What do we do?" Tassariel asked.

"Prep a shield, just beneath mine, then we'll both add another layer just to be safe. Daye, join Mevon in the front. If the opportunity arises, I may lower a section of the shield to see if I can bait them into striking one of you. Draevenus—"

"I'll stay on guard for any deceptions," the assassin said. "And keep an eye on all our backs."

"What about us?" Arivana whispered, huddled close beside Sem Aira.

"Stay low, but be ready to move if we call for it," Mevon advised.

The queen twisted her lips, obviously frustrated by her relative weakness, but she merely nodded and tugged her charge down into a crouch behind him. The king squeezed her shoulder, then bent down and kissed her forehead before joining at Mevon's side.

"Ever been used as bait before?" Mevon asked him.

"Plenty of times," Daye replied. "In Sceptre, princes are chosen by their merit, and I was the youngest one so named in a century. I didn't earn that honor by sending other men into danger in my place."

"Though nothing quite like this, I imagine."

Daye barked out a single burst of laughter. "No. Nothing like this at all. I may be a void, but there are few enough casters in Sceptre that I didn't often have to face them."

As he and his companions arranged themselves to meet the coming adversary, Mevon felt a newfound appreciation for their courage. Though Draevenus he knew and welcomed, the others were mysteries to him, and he hadn't trusted that they would be worth bringing along. Step after step, they'd proven his doubts misplaced.

Though he had kept them within his peripheral, Mevon now turned his full attention to the six beings as they drew nearer. The crowd of mundane ruvaki warriors had backed away twenty paces, and those directly before him had parted, clearing the way for the eye-twisting entities, whose exact movements even *he* had trouble tracking. Every time he looked toward one, it seemed to have already moved somewhere else. No—like it had never even been where he'd first thought them.

They're doing more than just playing with our eyes—they're playing with our minds.

The six spread out, surrounding them, working chaotic energy in ways he could not discern. That they had drawn within spitting distance without testing the shields set off every instinct, but he was constrained by their mission.

Jasside's muttered curse was all the warning he had before the floor fell away beneath his feet.

"I don't care how many times you've done it already," Yandumar said. "Check. Them. *Again!*" He slammed a fist on the table once each to punctuate the last three words.

He remembered a time when such an action would instill a dose of healthy fear into his subordinates, but the six young casters about the table only rolled their eyes in exasperation before closing them and slipping into commune. He even heard one of them mutter something about a crazy old man, but couldn't pin down which it had been. Not that he could blame them, exactly; most people didn't fly into a rage when given supposedly good news.

"What seems to be the problem?" Gilshamed asked. He'd been in commune himself until a moment ago and had missed what had prompted Yandumar's fury.

"Idiots," Yandumar spat. "It's always the idiots who make a mess of everything."

The valynkar waved towards the currently unpresent messengers. "Are you speaking of them?"

"Them, or the people giving them their reports. There's no abyss-taken way they could all be this wrong."

"How so?"

Yandumar pointed at the glowing figures along the table. "Look for yourself. I'll burn my empire's coffers to the ground if you don't see it in the next three beats."

He watched as his friend's eyes narrowed in study of the presented information . . . then widened. *Two* beats later. "Can this be true?"

"No. It can't. Which is why I'm making these idiots check their sources again."

"But if it is—"

"It's not."

"*If* it is," Gilshamed repeated, ignoring him, "then it can only mean one of two things."

"I know, I know. Don't think I haven't thought about it. But there's no use jumping to conclusions before we know anything for sure."

"Not even for the sake of hope?"

"*Especially* not for that. I might accept my fate should the worst happen, but there're plenty down there in the mud and snow that ain't as old and bitter as me. Most are too young to have ever known pain. I'm talking real stuff. Agony and loss that leaves you curled up and making puddles on your pillow. If word gets out before we confirmed anything, and those soldiers get their hopes up only to see them smashed to pieces before their eyes?" Yandumar shrugged. "I don't think I have to tell you why that's a bad thing."

"True. But look at what we were facing just before this happened. You and I have twisted our brains into knots moving our forces around to reinforce weak points, and we've only just managed to prevent this tenuous line from breaking. I think our troops could use a bit of good news for a change."

Before he could refute Gilshamed's words, the half dozen messengers returned to the waking world. Yandumar fixed them all with a hard stare.

"Well?"

"It's as we said," replied their spokeperson, a pimple-faced boy whose name Yandumar kept forgetting. "No units are currently engaged. There hasn't been an active battle for the last half a toll."

Yandumar closed his eyes, sighing. He knew exactly which two options Gilshamed had hinted at, the only two reasons the ruvak would pull back after having nearly broken them already: the strike team had either won through and bargained for peace . . . or the enemy had something even worse in store.

"Relay to every commander," he said, forcing

calm into his voice. "Tell them to give their troops what rest they can, but keep an eye out."

"Keep an eye out for what?" the boy asked.

Yandumar grunted. "Anything."

He flinched as distant peals of thunder rumbled through the air. More joined them, some closer, some farther away, and he moved towards the open doorway without even thinking.

"Just what we need today. A storm, on top of everything else."

Gilshamed joined him, his gaze cast towards the evening's earliest stars. "This is no storm, old friend. How can it be when there isn't a cloud in the sky?"

Yandumar squinted. The bright spots above him grew larger, closer, and he could now make out smoky streaks trailing behind each one in the sky. "Those aren't stars . . . are they?"

Gilshamed had already returned to commune.

But Yandumar knew his message would arrive too late.

The air continued rumbling as thousands of meteorites fell among his scattered troop formations, crashing into the ground with fiery effect. He spun back into the room, but didn't need to wait for the information on the table to update.

"Call the retreat! All units pull back through the passes. We'll hold there, if we can."

It took a while for all his messengers to acknowledge, struck to their core by the bombardment of reports they were each receiving. The order was probably unnecessary. He could see the ranks breaking and falling back even as he watched more meteors dive down from the sky. Still, when chaos struck, that was when it was most important to maintain order.

Or, at least the illusion of it.

I've bought you all the time I can, son. If you're still alive, and you still have a chance, please . . . hurry.

Arivana felt as if she'd plunged into a sea of darkness, floating freely but for the current of stale air from below, which grew faster and louder with each beat until the loose flaps of her dress started whipping about her so hard it stung. When she heard her companions shouting invisibly somewhere around her, her only thought was how absurd that was.

Fear had gripped her so tightly, she didn't even have breath enough to scream.

A body collided with her, an elbow or heel painfully impacting her rib cage and sending her into an uncontrollable spin. Her ability to orient herself, or even tell up from down, fled as she twisted again and again.

They'd been almost to the pinnacle of the Cloister, higher above the sea than most mountain peaks, but their fall couldn't last forever. Mathematics hadn't been her strongest subject, but she was skilled enough with numbers to know that their time was running out.

At least it will be quick. A fall from this height . . . I'm sure we won't even feel it.

It seemed silly, but she felt thankful for even that small relief. She knew of people who had experienced more pain or sorrow in their lives than she had, but as for trouble? She'd had quite enough of *that* in her sixteen years. A death free of complication was almost welcome.

The bright, lavender-hued light that blazed to life a moment later, however, made her forget all thoughts of dying.

Tassariel's wings illuminated what she now saw was a wide, roughly circular shaft, and some of her companions as they fell through it with ever-quickening speed. Arivana tried in vain to keep the valynkar in sight as she spun, and at last filled her lungs with enough air to do more than gasp.

"Tass! Help!"

Every rotation, Arivana craned her neck to keep her winged friend in view as long as possible, but doing so only made it clear that Tassariel was not moving any closer. In fact, she'd grown noticeably farther away.

Arivana shouted again, but it didn't seem to make a difference. Tassariel was reaching for, then grasping, another figure by the shoulders. She spun him around to get a better grip, allowing Arivana to see who it was.

Mevon Daere. Of course she'd rescue him. He's more valuable to our mission than me. More useful.

She searched through the shadows and found Draevenus flying towards her husband, his black wings spread like something out of a nightmare. Where Jasside and Sem Aira were, she couldn't tell. She didn't know how much weight two sets of wings could carry safely to the ground, but she didn't think it would be enough to save them all.

We'd always known success would likely require sacrifice. I only hope the others can finish this without me.

What brief hope she'd felt at the flare of Tassariel's wings faded once more as she fell. She closed her eyes, exhaling deeply. Every source of stress expelled, every worry waned, every muscle loosened into numbness.

She did not brace for impact but instead embraced her end.

It was . . . colder than she expected.

Arivana felt herself jerked suddenly to one side, the ice tightening across her chest.

She opened her eyes.

Something blacker than the shaft wrapped like a tentacle around her torso. She traced it out toward two sets of eyes, dimly reflecting the glow from Tassariel's wings. Feeling herself being pulled again, she saw the eyes grow bright.

Arivana stumbled onto a flat surface as two sets of arms curled tight around her.

"I've got her," Jasside shouted.

"Can we set down yet?" called Draevenus from above.

"Almost. I just need a little more time."

"Well, hurry it up, will you? These louts are getting heavy."

"I don't . . . want to hear you . . . complain," Tassariel said, pausing for breath every few syllables. "You have . . . the easy one."

"Are you calling my husband fat?" Jasside asked.

"No. Just . . . cumbersome."

"Well, you'll just have to deal with him a few moments longer. He can't touch down while I'm still shaping the platform."

Arivana felt her weight begin to settle in and looked down to see a smooth, featureless surface below her feet, spreading outward even as she watched. Though she'd seen Jasside perform near-miracles on countless occasions, she had somehow forgotten the woman's ability to fashion things out of thin air.

Sheer panic had a funny way of destroying all semblance of faith.

"Are you all right, my queen?" Sem Aira asked, alone in embracing her now that Jasside had turned her attention elsewhere. "Your heart is beating faster than a galloping horse."

"I am now," Arivana said. "I just thought—for a moment, anyway—that I was going to die."

"How could you? Didn't you hear them shouting?"

"Shouting was *all* I heard. I couldn't understand a word of it."

Sem Aira shook her head, a smile painting her face. "They were coordinating from the very moment we began falling, making a plan to ensure no one fell for long. Did you truly believe they'd give up so easily?"

"I did, I'm ashamed to admit. Thank you for helping see my faith restored."

The ruvak tensed slightly at this, pulling away. Now that the tension had passed its peak, she once again became distant and quiet, her face plagued by consternation. It was a look Arivana had grown quite used to in the past few weeks.

The platform slowed further, jostled momentarily as the flying figures above them—following Jasside's permissive gesture—let down their burdens, Draevenus groaning in relief while Tassariel collapsed onto her back, gasping for breath. Daye lunged towards Arivana, scooping her up into a tight embrace.

"I'm okay," she assured him between kisses.

"I know," he said. "I just heard you shouting. You sounded so scared."

"Of course I was! But I should have known better. Our friends would have never let something so trivial as a disappearing floor get in the way of completing our mission."

He chuckled, then kissed her again.

Jasside guided the platform towards the shaft's outer wall, slowing them until they were hovering in place. The sorceress swept her hand across the surface in front of them, and it vanished in an instant, emitting a dull, green light from the chamber beyond. The platform slid through the hole, and Arivana followed her companions, sure she wasn't the only one relieved to be back on solid ground.

"Sweep the room and find us an exit," Jasside ordered.

Tassariel and Mevon were already moving away in opposite directions. Draevenus, however, didn't budge.

"What then?" he asked. "I don't know about you, but I'm tired of running around without a plan."

Jasside nodded. "What did you have in mind?"

In answer, he faded into shadow. The voice that spoke next seemed to come out of nothing. "You had the right idea when you suggested we ask for directions. We just need to find someone who's a little more willing to provide them."

Draevenus remained still as the enemy circled in, growing closer with each of his shallow, silent breaths. The use of sorcery had drawn them, as he knew it would. But with their trap already sprung, the ruvak that came against them were disorganized, their nature made manifest in the chaotic pattern of their attacks.

Jasside and Tassariel lured them, with Mevon guarding their backs. They ran along preordained, circular routes, filled with as much dark and light energy they could sustain as bands of Cloister guards pursued. The more that joined in on the chase, the more manic it became.

And all the while, Draevenus waited in the shadows.

Your opportunity will come soon enough. All it takes is a good plan—which we have—and a few drops of patience.

His own, he was glad to see, was about to be rewarded.

A squad of ruvaki soldiers slowed as they came abreast of the hallway in which he was hiding. One pointed down it, and they turned as a flock of birds in his direction. The fastest among them raced by first, obviously eager to close with their enemy, yet in their haste they left some stragglers. One in particular, a smallish ruvak sporting a limp, shuffled behind the rest of them by a full dozen paces.

He'd passed up other opportunities because they hadn't quite been ideal. This one, however, was like a gift from the gods.

Draevenus kicked off the wall behind him, surging towards the straggler. Both arms reached for his target, one covering the mouth while the other curled tightly about the neck. He wrapped his legs around the ruvak's body, clenching his thighs and hooking his feet together to pinch both of the guard's arms to his sides.

The creature struggled, writhing in a vain effort to throw Draevenus off for almost ten beats—longer than he'd anticipated. Eventually, though, the limping leg gave way and they both toppled to the cold, tiled floor. Another score beats with the air cut off, and the figure fell limp in his grasp.

Draevenus released him and jumped to his feet immediately. In nineteen centuries of this kind of work, he'd never known anyone who could fake a loss of consciousness convincingly. Grabbing his prize beneath the shoulders, he began dragging him to the designated meeting point, glancing up and down the hallway to make sure the way was still clear. The guard's squad had already turned the corner, none having so much as glanced back. No new faces had shown themselves.

He paused only once, drawing a dagger to carve a symbol into a post. To most, it was nothing: a random set of scratches or a crack in the paint. To those with keen enough eyesight, and who knew what they were looking for, it would deliver the intended message. On their next pass of the adjoining corridors, he had faith that Mevon would see the sign and advance to the next phase of their plan.

A mark later, he kicked open the door to the chamber where the rest of his companions waited.

He heard the familiar ring of drawn steel, and twin feminine gasps of surprise.

Daye sighed a beat later, returning his sword to its scabbard. "You could have knocked, you know."

"No time," Draevenus said, dumping the guard at the feet of the two women. "Another squad was about to turn this way."

"Is he even alive?" Arivana asked, squatting beside the prisoner. "He looks so . . . stiff."

"He gave me a bit more of a fight than expected. But yes, he's still breathing."

Arivana sighed. "Let's get on with it, then."

Catching his eye, Daye said, "Take the top half? I'll get the bottom."

"What about her?" Draevenus asked, tilting his head toward Sem Aira.

Daye shrugged. "She'll be fine."

Draevenus leaned in close to man, lowering his voice so the two women couldn't hear. "Are you sure?"

"I trust her enough. She won't try anything. And if she does, Arivana can handle it."

"I don't know if I feel comfortable letting—"

"Look, we all had our part to play in this. Sem Aira was my wife's responsibility. If she has faith enough in the woman, then so do I. So should we all."

Draevenus tapped his fingers along his dagger hilts, musing the man's word for several beats. "So be it."

He stepped around the unconscious ruvak until standing over his head, then knelt, pressing his knees into the arms as Daye lowered his weight onto the legs and waist. Draevenus peered up at Arivana. "Ready?"

The queen tugged Sem Aira closer gently, sharing a quick glance with her before nodding.

Draevenus pulled a stone from his pocket. Jasside had conjured it just before she'd taken off with the others. He wasn't sure exactly what it was, but it smelled strongly of salt, and she'd assured him it would do the trick.

He placed it directly beneath their prisoner's nose.

The figure jerked beneath him, alternating between coughing, sneezing, wheezing, and squawking out what could only be curses. Draevenus wasn't worried about the noise; the walls in this place were thick.

Once the tirade had passed, for the most part, Arivana and Sem Aira knelt at the ruvak's side.

"Go on," Arivana said.

Sem Aira took a deep breath, then began speaking to the prisoner in their own language.

The exchange went on for some time. Sem Aira did most of the talking at first, but eventually the guard began adding to the conversation. Based on her facial expressions, however, he wasn't giving the answers she was hoping for.

More than once, Draevenus caught the prisoner's

gaze fall to the bindings on her wrists. The words that came out of his mouth after carried a vitriol that needed no translation.

Knowing the others couldn't keep the ruvak running in circles forever, he waited until a lull in the conversation, then interjected. "Well? Has he said anything useful yet?"

Sem Aira hesitated a moment, eyes filling with fear, then shook her head. "I'm sorry. He's being very reticent. All he keeps saying is that it's too well-guarded and that we'll never find it."

"He said both those things?"

"Well, yes. As a single thought, but that is the best translation I can come up with."

A single thought? Too well-guarded . . . we'll never find it. Something about that seems contradictory. But knowing the ruvak, it might not be.

"Ask him where it is again," he said. "But slowly this time. And do it over and over until he either gives you the right answer, or I tell you to stop."

Sem Aira nodded, turning her gaze towards the guard again.

Draevenus stopped listening. The answer that he spoke didn't matter anymore. The only thing that did were his eyes. And though they flicked around in seemingly random patterns, each time the question was asked, they inevitably paused for the briefest of moments while staring at the same exact spot on the ceiling.

"That's enough," Draevenus said. "Tie him up."

"But he didn't answer," Sem Aira insisted.

"I wouldn't say that," he said, smiling. "He pointed us in just the right direction. That's good enough to start, and I know the person who can lead us to the finish."

Jasside concentrated, furious with herself for not thinking of this earlier. She'd known the power the ruvak commanded was peerless when it came to deceiving the senses. The best way they could guard their most precious assets was to ensure intruders had their instincts tied in knots. Logic then dictated that the place they would be found would be the place they never thought to look. A place surrounded in a powerful layer of chaos magic, yet one so subtle that it rebuked all sense directed towards it without letting anyone realize they'd been turned away.

Now, she hovered once more in the very same shaft they'd fallen down earlier, sending out hair-thin tendrils of darkness throughout the shadows inhabiting the Cloister around her. With the information Draevenus had given her, and a remembered lesson from Vashodia about seeing past the bounds set by chaos to reveal the true nature of that which it tried to hide, it was only a matter of time before she found what they were looking for.

As long as they don't find us first.

Her companions sat on the platform around her, doing their best to keep quiet. She had debated sending them out as a distraction, but decided against it. The ambient darkness in the vessel was weak before the unrelenting torrents of chaos, but she was confident it was enough to mask her actions. Besides, once she found the place, there was a good chance an alarm of some kind would be set off, and she wasn't even sure she would know about it. When the time came, they would have to move quickly.

A hundred tiny tentacles reached out from each fingertip, probing aimlessly. She didn't try to guide, leaving them to wander and turn as they willed. She focused not on where they were going, but rather on where they'd been. Try as they might to obfuscate, the ruvak still occupied physical space. If she was right, those subtle flows of chaos that surrounded their destination would unerringly turn away her little, black tendrils without giving them a second thought.

All she had to do was look for the one place none of them ever went.

After almost half a toll of sweat-filled search and careful analysis, she finally found what she was looking for.

Without a word, the others began getting to their feet. Maybe it was the slight acceleration of the platform; maybe it was the determined smile on her face. Whatever it was, the feeling of readiness overtook the air around her as solid, controlled breaths left seven sets of lungs. It was the moment before they all headed into danger unknown, with no hope of ever walking out again, yet none of them faltered in their resolve, or made the slightest mention of retreat. Despite all the battles she'd faced before, this was the first time in her life when she felt she knew what it meant to be amongst heroes.

It was a shame that the moment was ruined by another bout of nausea.

Again? I thought I was over this.

Jasside reached a hand down to try to soothe her writhing stomach, a feeling that had come on out of nowhere, and fought down the acidic bile rising up her throat. All while keeping the platform moving towards their destination.

She turned her attention towards her tasks—what few she had left in this world—as a means of distracting herself from the discomfort. Whether it worked or not, she was glad to feel the nausea fade by the time she'd flown them all as far as the shaft could take them.

"This is it," she said. "Once I open the way, there's no holding back. We go in fast, keep close, and don't let anything stop us until we're in position. None of us know what to expect, but as long as we continue to trust that we have each other's backs, I know we can survive anything they might throw at us."

As far as rousing speeches went, hers certainly

lacked the polish and fire of great leaders such as Gilshamed, but it seemed to impart the confidence she hoped to share with her companions. Mevon stepped in front of her, every muscle rippling with readiness as he nodded tightly and gave her a small, secret smile. She saw reflected on his face the depth of the conviction she'd been trying to convey.

She lifted a hand to rearrange the molecules of the wall before them with a brushstroke of dark energy, then guided the platform through.

Yandumar watched the command ship disappear behind white-clad mountains fifty leagues to the north, on its way to Fyrdra, the capital city of the nearest district, to begin emptying it of civilians. When it had gone, he turned back to the palisades. Metal spikes lined the wall before him, pointing outward, a set of steel teeth to ward off threats from the frozen plains. This was the largest and most centrally located fortress along the southern frontier of his empire, guarding the only major pass between the empty lands before him and the inhabited regions behind.

It was where he had chosen to make his stand.

"Are you sure about this?" Gilshamed asked from his side.

Yandumar grunted. "Are *you?*"

Gilshamed leaned forward, exhaling deeply as he

wrapped gloved hands around a pair of spikes, displaying a depth of exhaustion Yandumar had never seen before in the man.

"I am weary, Yan," Gilshamed began. "All the ships have been wrenched from the sky, half our troops are slain, and hundreds of my kin will never spread their wings again. The other passes are narrow, and the soldiers you sent to each of them will be able to hold for days, if not longer. The fastest way through is here . . . and the ruvak know it."

Yandumar clapped the valynkar on the shoulder. "I hear ya, Gil. Now tell me your reasons *not* to stay."

Tired as he knew him to be—almost as tired as Yandumar felt himself—it took Gilshamed a moment before he appeared to get the joke. A ghost of a smile painted his friend's lips. "Even here, at the end of all things, you never change."

Yandumar shrugged. "Too late now, for better or worse."

"Worse, I am sure."

"Ha!"

He turned to survey what troops remained with him. A hundred thousand were still in reserve, but could only travel by foot and were weeks away, while half that many were spread out along the mountain range, backed up by flying patrols of mierothi and valynkar to ensure no ruvaki troops sneaked through. Here, he had the rest. He'd known it might come to this, so he'd held Ilyem and her Hardohl, along with the Imperial Guard—what little remained of both—out of the fighting, to stay fresh and prepare this fortress for siege.

Three thousand men and women.

To guard three thousand paces of ground.

Against three million unrelenting enemy soldiers.

That was the closest estimate, anyway. But at least it was only ground assault they had to deal with. All the sorcerous weapons, on both sides, had long since run out of destructive energy, and there were no casters with strength or time enough to recharge them. The battle here would be one of swords and arrows, of steel and blood and grit. The kind of fight in which he used to excel.

And perhaps I can again . . . one last time.

"Do you remember when we fought to capture my son?"

"I do."

"Well, old friend, as far as I see it, there are no emperors or councilors here. Only soldiers. Do me one last favor and help me feel like one again."

Gilshamed nodded.

Yandumar drew his swords, tightening his grip as power flowed into his limbs, just as the foremost ranks of ruvaki troops marched into view below.

Mevon had been ready for opposition of some kind, but not like this. Elite guards, such as those three he'd fought in on the foothills of Sceptre, or sorcerous wards, or even mundane traps and obstacles and mazes to keep them ensnared.

This fog that surrounded them had not been what he'd expected.

Sometimes filled with bright colors, sometimes absent of anything but grey; sometimes slow and wet and cold, sometimes swirling with dryness and heat; sometimes echoing his footsteps for what seemed like leagues, sometimes smothering his very breath.

But always . . . always blinding.

Had he not insisted they travel in a line while holding on to each other, he was sure they would have all drifted apart by now, left to wander the mists alone until their bodies gave way to hunger and thirst. Though he led, he had no idea where they were going. Already, his sense of time had twisted, forestalling any guess as to how long they'd been inside. None of his companions so much as whispered. They must have felt as he did: a certain kind of fear that came when facing the unknown and unknowable, which left you bereft of all but the most basic instincts.

And when even those fail to provide direction, all you have left is stubborn perseverance.

So he marched on, feeling foolish for finding comfort in the grip of his *Andun*. Something told him it would be of no use.

"There's . . . something up ahead."

Mevon jolted to a halt and pivoted until facing

behind him. The words had sounded as if they'd come from the other side of a thick, glass window, and he was having trouble locating their source.

"Who said that?" he demanded.

"*I* did," Sem Aira said, lifting a hand and pointing. "Look there."

He turned again and squinted in the indicated direction. After a moment he saw what she must have meant. Something solid, in a place where nothing seemed to stay the same, not even the ground beneath his feet. Something *real*.

"I see it, too," Jasside said. She caught his gaze, offering an expression that said, without words, *I love you*, and *lead on*, and *be careful*, all at once. That her face also held that same formless fear wasn't worth considering.

Mevon glanced quickly over his companions, to make sure they hadn't lost anybody, then began treading towards what he hoped would be the final stop on their trek.

The fog continued to billow. Judging distance was impossible, and more than once he lost his way entirely. But the place showed up again each time. It was almost as if it *wanted* to be found, but only by those willing to devote themselves to the journey.

Or maybe I'm just going insane, which isn't an impossibility. If my father is any indication, I'm headed there eventually.

Just when it seemed like the trip was never going

to end, Mevon stumbled forward into a roughly circular area completely free of fog. Looking up and around, he saw that they were surrounded by scores of strange, ephemeral shapes, hanging suspended by nothing he could see.

Each of them reverberated with oceans of chaotic energy. Combined, it felt enough to drown him.

Before he could so much as open his mouth, something closed in around them. He thought it was the fog again at first, but it was stronger, more malevolent, singeing the very air around him until he felt as if he were about to choke. All without coming into contact.

If it can do this without even touching . . .

"Collapse!" he called.

His companions, if they hadn't been expecting the command, still knew exactly what to do. Mevon stayed still, while Draevenus and the women came to huddle together at his back, reaching hands to him or Daye, who closed in the tight formation from behind.

The assault—for he was now sure that's exactly what it was—continued, but grew no more potent. After almost a mark of withstanding it, Mevon knew the faceless enemy dared not press their power any closer.

"ENOUGH!"

The chaos withdrew, but only but a hair.

"If you could kill us, you'd have succeeded by now. And if we'd wished you dead, we would not have come aboard this vessel so quietly. We came to talk. So cut the theatrics and show yourselves!"

For a moment, he almost thought they would. But the assault did not diminish. In fact, it couldn't seem to make up its mind, waxing strong one moment, from one direction, only to wane weak again the next. It was either an attempt to throw them off-balance . . .

. . . or these ruvak aren't as unified as we thought.

Before he could follow up that thought with any sort of logical response, he heard them: voices, crackling and chittering like a flock of mad birds, echoing from everywhere in the chaotic soup surrounding them.

The rush of sound struck him like a cleaver, cutting through all reason, all sanity. He fell to his knees and held hands over his ears. To no avail. The voices continued pecking away at his mind, his soul, devouring all sense. Justice crashed to the floor without only a muffled thud to mark its fall.

But then . . . something changed. One voice screeched out a note disparate from the others—*loudly*—bringing many to immediate silence. Within a few beats, another joined this opposing chorus. Then another. And another. And though it didn't seem to defy the ongoing assaults, it did seem to draw some of their focus away.

It wasn't long until both discordant melodies sang in equal strength. A moment later, the assaults on body and mind abated, at least temporarily, followed by the most surprising thing yet.

Someone spoke in his own tongue.

"Speak then, human," the scratchy ruvaki voice said, echoing in strange harmony with itself. "Speak, and tell us why you have come."

Mevon looked over his companions, his friends. He met each gaze, and found in all of them the encouragement he needed to go on. It didn't feel right to go first—talking had never been his strongest skill— but if they knew one thing about the ruvak, it was that they respected strength. There was no doubt in his mind, then, that they respected *him*.

"We are here," he said, "to ask you for peace."

From what seemed a million separate throats, cackling laughter followed his words.

"We are winning this war, in case you could not tell," said another voice, just as odd as the first. "What need have we of peace?"

"You call this a war? It hasn't felt like that. Not from my side. It felt like extermination. Like genocide. And with how many of your own soldiers' lives you threw away for the slightest advantage, it most certainly felt like *madness*."

There was a momentary silence, the kind that always preceded an enraged outburst. He was sure they hadn't expected to be insulted.

He pressed on, not giving them the chance to voice their anger. "I'm sure you consider your cause, and everything done in its name, just. Among my people, there are few who could claim to understand justice as I do. I was born into a life that preached it above all else. All else, that is, but loyalty. But when those two seemingly wholesome things are wrapped in unquestioning and unconscionable violence, then what you end up with isn't wholesome at all. It is vile. A poison unto all it touches. A rancid stain upon everything it claims to stand for.

"It is everything I used to be."

He paused again, for breath, ostensibly, but also to gauge his audience. Silent they remained, but it had changed, no longer one waiting in anger, but one steeped in contemplation. He hadn't been confident when his companions had elected him to engage first, but at least they seemed to be listening.

"I killed a man, once," he continued. "It didn't mean much to me at the time. Just another criminal delivered his sentence. Just another countless victim to my supposed justice. But I didn't really know anything about him. I didn't know . . . didn't know . . ."

Mevon felt an arm slip gently around his, and didn't need to turn his head to know that Jasside now stood at his side, whispering without a word to go on.

"I didn't know that he *stood* for something. Something I couldn't understand at the time. He stood for hope. He stood so that his actions could help create a better life for those he cared about. A better world. And somehow, his sister, who stands here beside me, not only found a way to forgive me for his death, which I caused in my ignorance, but also . . . to love me.

"It's not the kind of love I will ever think I deserve, but it *is* the kind of love that has made me want to be a better man. A man at least partially worthy of the gift she has given me."

As Mevon and Jasside pressed their foreheads together, Draevenus rose to his feet. Though this hadn't been part of the plan, he knew that his normally recalcitrant friend had run far past his quota of words for the day, and that *he* had something valuable to add to the conversation.

"My tribe, the mierothi, once declared war on the valynkar. Darkness and light . . . it seemed appropriate that our peoples should stand in opposition. It seemed . . . inevitable. And for almost two thousand years of separation, our mutual animosity grew, festering like an open wound dragged around in the mud. When we finally crashed together again, it was no surprise that it came accompanied by bloodshed.

"Yet a moment came when we either could have renewed our hate, or put it behind us. I chose the latter, and one among them, thankfully, agreed. Since then, we've learned to look past our differences, all those insignificant things that divide us, and focused instead on the things we had in common. Once we put old, pointless animosities to rest, we found that those things were much more numerous than we could have guessed."

Something gripped him: a feeling he'd grown familiar with, yet hadn't experienced in so long he thought he'd never feel it again.

Ruul.

The vision came clearer than it ever had before. Not just a memory of the time he'd spent in that cave, but something deeper. Older. A shared memory from Ruul himself.

He felt his mouth move, depicting all that he could see.

"He called himself Ruulan, and he wandered the void for thousands upon thousands of years, carrying with him innumerable sleeping hosts. This world was the first he found that might serve as a home for them. A place they could finally find new life, and for himself, at last find some rest.

"But it wasn't as empty as he had first assumed.

"This world's creatures struck out at him, threatening his very existence, and that of all he carried within him.

"Ruulan called out for help.

"Only by a miracle was the entity known as Durelos close by at the time, and came to the aid of Ruulan, striking down those who assailed him and sending the rest fleeing deep into the void. Even so, such actions were not enough to save Ruulan, who fell to the world in ruin and flames, burning the very sky in his descent.

"In their ignorance, they had both caused so much death and had no way to repair the damage. Ruulan released his hosts, damaged as they were, and Durelos, compelled by compassion to remain, did the same. In time, the world came to be theirs, these humans, and all memory of how they had come to be here faded into myth and legend, only to be forgotten entirely.

"But those we came to know as gods did *not* forget. Only they were powerless to stop us from shutting them out from our council, and we came to war among ourselves, time and time again, ignoring all that bound us together in search of blind, greedy advantage. They knew that a time would come when this world's original inhabitants would return, and that the only way to prevent another catastrophe was to . . ."

Draevenus slumped to his knees, panting, drained of all energy by the insistent force of the vision. Even so, the last word of it managed to force its way past his quivering lips.

". . . sacrifice."

For a dozen labored breaths, the space around him remained empty of all sound, and that strange, chaotic energy did not resume its assault.

But what he felt a moment later let him know it wouldn't last.

A wave of dark washed across the face of the entire planet, as if dredged from the very depths of the abyss.

The ruvak erupted into screams.

Yandumar shouted in triumph, lifting twin blades dripping orange blood as the latest assault upon the fortress turned back. Nine attempts, and the wall had yet to be breached. His three thousand stood strong, proving their value far above their meagre number, having suffered fewer than fifty losses so far.

He was honored to fight at their side, a feat only made possible by the energy coursing through him courtesy of his oldest living friend.

"You've gotta do better than that!" he shouted at the backs of his enemy, as they retreated across the two-hundred-pace-wide killing field. "This is *my* Imperial Guard you're dealing with. So long as even one of them remained standing, this fortress will hold forever!"

A shout went up from along the palisades, and thousands of blades rose to join his own. His words were a lie, and every one of them knew it. It didn't matter that the enemy had finally run out of tricks. His men might last a few more days until exhaustion and countless small wounds caught up to them, while the ruvak could field fresh troops with every surge. Still, that wasn't going to stop them from going down swinging.

Yandumar turned from the wall as the Guard began making use of the break in combat: binding cuts, fixing or replacing damaged gear, throwing food down their throats, and hunkering down to snatch what little shut-eye they could afford. Despite fighting for most of a day already, he felt little need for rest.

"Gil, ole friend, I haven't felt like this in ages," he proclaimed as he marched over towards the valynkar. "You put something special in that mystical concoction of yours this time?"

Gilshamed smiled but shook his head. "Not at all, Yan. But you've been too long gone from the fight. This first renewed taste of it must make the effects seem stronger."

"That so? Next you'll be telling me you're only giving me half the usual dose."

"Well, I *have* had to conserve my energy, while dividing it between healing the wounded and pushing back the most vicious of ruvak assaults. I cannot say for certain—"

Yandumar raised an eyebrow, watching as Gilshamed clamped his jaws shut, then spun to look northward, his golden eyes wider than he'd ever seen before.

"What . . . has she . . . *done?*" Gilshamed whispered.

It took Yandumar three whole beats to put together what he was talking about—what *she* Gilshamed meant—which was probably about two beats too long.

"Vashodia," he said, trying not to make the name sound like a curse. "What'd she do this time?"

Gilshamed shook his head once. "I do not know. I suspect, however, that the whole world is about to find out."

The words soon proved prophetic.

It began with a jolt, which sent him crashing to his knees. He lifted his head to see Gilshamed in a similar posture, and looking beyond him, most of the Guard were also struggling to keep their balance.

He had just enough time to right himself and catch his breath before the rumbling began.

Half helping and half helped by Gilshamed, Yandumar stumbled to the palisades. The shaking intensified. Within a mark, he heard a deep snap and watched as the ground along the center of the killing field began cracking open.

From that gap poured no natural kind of darkness.

In a blink, the split lengthened to either side, flowing across the hills as far to each horizon as he could see.

Then, it began to widen.

Jasside knew why the ruvaki masters were in an uproar. No caster on the planet could ignore the raw oceans of power being unleashed half a world away. Although, perhaps *raw* wasn't the right word to describe it. For all its wide-reaching effects, the energy felt controlled, shaped for a specific purpose. And while there was no doubt in her mind about who was responsible, without access to her power, there was no way to determine exactly what was going on.

Standing on the tips of her toes, she leaned as close to Mevon's ear as she could. "I need to let you go."

He turned his mouth towards her ear, whispering in return. "Are you sure?"

"It will only be for a moment. Stay close, will you?"

Mevon smiled. "Always."

Jasside released his arm. The presence of her power returned in an instant, like a sudden plunge into icy waters. She didn't hesitate to grasp it.

After that, it was a simple matter of following the energy from its source out to where it was being expended, and tracing the boundaries of its effect. The task was made difficult by the distance, yet she had it finished in five beats.

What she found was . . . unexpected.

As she released her power and took hold of Mevon's arm once more, Jasside couldn't help but laugh.

"What do you find so funny?" screeched a voice.

The cacophony around her dimmed, as if holding its breath in anticipation of her response. "Vashodia," she said. "My old mentor, and the one responsible for your current outrage. I didn't think she could surprise me anymore. She isn't exactly known for her mercy."

"Mercy?" another unseen ruvak said. "The snake has sundered the very surface of our world!"

"It isn't the first time. Nor the last, I imagine."

"Is that your plan, then? If you can't have this planet, then you'll destroy it beyond hope of repair?"

"Not at all. But the quantity of power she's wielding right now has the capability to do all kinds of things, many of a far more devastating nature. Namely, to destroy every last vessel of yours in an instant."

"Lies!"

Jasside shrugged. "Considering the source she's drawing on—the very source keeping your skyships out of my empire—I'd say it took her quite a bit of effort to make it do anything else."

And though I might never know what caused her change of heart, perhaps my influence played some small part. Either way, I can rest assured knowing I did everything I could to reach her.

Whatever had happened, and why, didn't really matter at the moment, though. Vashodia had handed them the perfect opportunity, and Jasside knew better than to question her good fortune.

She cast her gaze upon the young queen. "It's time."

Arivana nodded at Jasside, then glanced up at Daye. "Keep a hand on me, please. We're going."

A flash of distress crossed his features, the hesitation of both a soldier and a husband to send her into more danger than himself. As much as she loved him for that, she loved him all the more for his ability to push past it, knowing what needed to be done.

"I'll be right here the whole time." He reached to her shoulder and squeezed once, gently.

"You're not going to tell me to be careful?"

"I think we're too far gone for careful. Just be . . . queenly."

She smiled. "*That*, I can do."

Settling her nerves with a deep breath, she took a long step out from the group, positioning herself so as to be visible by those strange pods, half seen through swirling mist, which supposedly held the ruvaki masters. Once set, Arivana reached behind her, lifting the rope that bound Sem Aira's hands, and tugged the woman forward to join her.

"My queen?" Sem Aira said, her face a maze of confusion. "What are you doing?"

She kept her voice a whisper, so that only her companions could hear her.

"Sem Aira . . ." she began, then stopped and shook her head. "Flumere . . ."

Her mind emptied. All their plans had come down to this moment, all their hopes resting on the next few beats in time, and how the ruvak would react . . . and she couldn't think of anything else to say. It seemed appropriate, somehow. Any words that might sway the ruvak had already been said.

All that mattered now . . . was action.

Arivana drew the small, ceremonial knife from her belt and sliced through Flumere's binding.

Before the woman could do much more than blink, Arivana reversed the blade and thrust the hilt into her old handmaiden's newly freed hands.

Arivana closed her eyes, and waited.

For five beats, there was no sound. Not even a breath. But at last the silence was broken by a deep ruvaki voice, the kind used to being obeyed without question. The kind that took pleasure in it.

"Kill her."

Five more beats. Then ten. Arivana kept her eyes closed, knowing there was nothing more she could do to influence events. From the moment they had flown free of the Veiled Empire, they had each considered their lives forfeit. And not only their own, but that of all humankind. What they hoped to achieve was a gamble only the truly desperate would even attempt.

All they had to keep them going was faith.

The second silence shattered with a muted metallic ring, as the knife fell faintly to the floor.

Tender, inhuman arms wrapped around Arivana, embracing her with fierce affection. She gasped in surprise, feeling a ready well burst forth from behind her eyelids, and hugged the woman back as strongly as she dared.

"Oh, Arivana," Flumere said between sobs. "How did you ever think I could hurt you?"

"I didn't," Arivana replied in kind. "Not even for a heartbeat. We just needed *them* to know that."

Arivana punctuated her words by sweeping an arm through the air above her.

As if the gesture was a signal of some kind, the ruvaki masters began screeching in incoherent rantings once more. This time, however, it had the feeling of a pointed debate, with wave after wave of shouts in opposing pitch thrown back and forth across the foggy, bitter air overhead.

Soon, the sound was joined by magic.

Chaos billowed and snapped and rolled, collapsing around Arivana and her companions like an avalanche. Just as it seemed like it would crash upon them, it drew back, yet not far. The argument in unintelligible words had crossed over to become an argument of energies, surging closer and farther away as those opposed fought back against those in favor of their annihilation, turning the air acrid all the while.

Yet within moments it became clear that the virulent strands were growing ever closer.

Tassariel watched Jasside mouth the words that, even shouted, could not be heard over the maelstrom now surrounding them.

You know what to do, they said.

This was the moment they'd planned for, practiced for, but now that it was here, she began shaking and felt her throat go dry. Before this tempest of chaotic power . . . she was *nothing*.

Remotely, she saw Daye pull on Arivana and Sem Aira, bundling them at his feet before spreading both legs and arms wide. Mevon took up a similar stance on the opposite side, and the two men leaned in until their fingertips were nearly touching. Draevenus and Jasside huddled close beside her. The three of them, by design, were in the center of the protective circle, such as the two men could provide, yet not in contact with either of them.

They had a job to do, and it could not be done while voided.

She sensed the two dark casters energize. They put their energy to work instantly, threading through gaps in the circle to deflect metal shards that came shrieking out of the gloom.

Now, Jasside's lips pleaded. *I need you to go first.*

Trembling, Tassariel fumbled for her own power, yet came up short of grasping it, again and again. What had once been an act as routine as breathing had suddenly become like trying to swim up a waterfall.

But when Draevenus grabbed her face and pressed his lips against her own, she remembered that she didn't need to swim at all. Though she'd lost them once, she still had her wings.

Time for me to fly.

Light filled her.

She looked towards Arivana. So young, yet she'd been wise enough to find a way through hatred, to put animosity to rest and put love in its place. She could see it in the way the queen gazed upon Daye's face and clutched at Sem Aira: two who had once been her enemy, but now counted among those she called friend. The love that swirled around them seemed almost palpable, as if Tassariel could reach out and grab it.

And from the man before her, there was no *as if* about it. She could feel it, a warmth and passion flowing from him to her like heat from a hearth in winter. It was the greatest gift she had ever received, greater than she had ever expected or even hoped for. Returning it felt the most natural thing in the world.

Her fear forgotten in the face of such overwhelming beauty, Tassariel lifted her hand, spilling forth purest light from her fingertips. Though she held only a fraction of the power her father had when he'd first planted the idea in her head, it was enough to spread fully throughout the maelstrom beyond. The light didn't *do* anything—it didn't need to—but its very presence forced the smallest measure of order on the chaos.

Order saturated not with guilt, but with love.

Jasside squinted against the sudden brightness above her, and patted Draevenus on the shoulder. He tore his ebony gaze from Tassariel's glowing face, his own features filled with something she'd never seen in him before. Something very much like happiness.

It's up to you now, she mouthed to him, as the torrent of chaos and squabbling ruvaki voices were still drowning them in noise.

Draevenus nodded his understanding. Reluctantly, he pulled back from the valynkar and thrust his hands to either side, sending out tendrils of darkness to replace her own in blocking the incoming projectiles.

The ruvaki masters were at last attuned to light, and nothing else stood in her way.

Time to end this.

Jasside gathered her power. Though she didn't think she would need all of it, she wanted to make sure she had more than enough to accomplish the job. The amount that filled her would have made a younger version of herself drool with envy. Like so many things, this had been Vashodia's doing. That woman trapped in a girl's malformed body was always planning ahead, thinking in terms of centuries when the next best had trouble thinking in years. Yet for all her forethought, Vashodia hadn't steered events towards this moment.

This was all my doing. It's up to me to get it right.

She looked up, able to sense, if not see, the ruvaki masters floating in their pods, which she now knew were meant to prolong their relatively clipped life spans. Yet, despite the importance of her task, which required she place herself firmly in a certain frame of mind, she couldn't help but find herself drifting in the opposite direction.

All the battles and bloodshed, the countless enemy soldiers eradicated by her hand, and even more innocent people trampled beneath the weight of ruvaki hatred. So much pain spawned by these very figures, suspended helpless—though they knew it not—above her. All of it could be made right with the barest thought or flick of her wrist.

Justice could at last be served.

Her upward gaze drifted over to Mevon's down-turned face. She knew that this was *his* influence talking, but also knew that he'd berate her, gently of course, for letting such thoughts linger as long as they had. What was easy wasn't always right—abyss, it almost *never* was—and too often, what people passed off as natural, as *normal*, even, were the worst things anyone could possibly do.

She'd seen what walking of the path of vengeance and hatred did. She'd been walking it her whole life. Now, it was time to try forgiveness.

Mevon's eyes locked with her own. The love evident in that gaze filled her soul, but not, as she had hoped, to brimming. Jasside focused, looking inward, surrendering all thoughts of pain as she searched for the part in her that needed nothing else but love.

It was then that she discovered her second surprise of the day.

Delving within her own body, Jasside found not a single heartbeat . . . but two.

My child . . .

She raised one hand next to Tassariel's while the other landed gently over her abdomen, smiling as she released a deluge of dark energy into the maelstrom above.

Vashodia knew she had made two mistakes.

The first was obvious, as her brain kept endlessly reminding her: She'd listened to her heart.

Abyss take that accursed thing. I thought I'd rid myself of its influence millennia ago.

She had wasted her only opportunity to deal a crippling blow to the ruvak, one from which they'd never recover. And not only that, but using the power of the voltensi to divide the continent and cut off the invading army had suspended their latent function.

Ruvaki skyships had begun pouring into the empire almost instantly.

And try as she might to coax them back to life, she'd drained too much of their power for a swift recovery. It would take them days at least to return to normal. Based on their flight trajectories, the ruvaki fleets would be at each outer voltensus in tolls. That this central one might last a month wouldn't matter much when every human soul on the planet—besides herself, of course—lay beyond abyss's gate.

Vengeance would come in time—of that she had no doubt—but it would pale before the outright victory she had planned.

If, of course, her second mistake didn't lead to a very swift end.

Accessing the voltensi had drained *her*, as well. So much so that she'd been left unconscious on the floor for abyss knew how long. And when she'd awoken, just moments ago, there'd been a dagger held sharp and cold across her throat.

"Hello, Vashodia," Slick Ren whispered into her ear from behind. "I've been waiting a long, long time for you to slip up. It looks like today is my lucky day."

Vashodia groaned. Even if she had strength left to access her power, she could never get over her own weakness. A weakness that, despite her unmatched skill and foresight, had thrown a spike into the wheel of her plans, time and time again. Which had made her wait far too long to eliminate Rekaj from the equation, among other things. Which made her— she shuddered to even think the word—*reliant* upon others to fulfill her bidding.

Vashodia was . . . slow.

"Don't make a move," the empress demanded. "I want to enjoy this."

"How did you find me?"

"I rebuilt this palace using the original plans, even

if I did change most of the decorations. Did you really think a secret hallway leading from the royal bed-chamber would escape my notice?"

"I was careful."

Slick Ren snorted. "My guards are loyal. Though, in fairness, I don't suppose you'd know what that was like. All *you* ever inspired was fear."

"It's the easiest way to control people."

"One tool among many. I never understood why you limited yourself to the tactic, but now I see— you were too arrogant to think you'd need anything else."

"I was—I *am* without equal, in almost every re-spect. Arrogance is justified."

"*Confidence* can be justified, even if it's rarely earned. Arrogance? Never."

Vashodia grunted in contempt. "What do *you* know? You're nothing but a trumped-up thief who weaseled her way into the bed of the man everyone knew would become emperor. Do you really think I wouldn't take steps to protect myself? Steps you wouldn't see before you woke up in the abyss?"

The words, she hated to admit, were a bluff. That accursed heart of hers had filled her thoughts, prevent-ing her from taking any such insulating measures. She really needed to look into ways of eliminating its influence for good.

If I survive this, that is.

Though she couldn't see it, Vashodia practically

felt the woman sneer behind her. "If you had anything in place, you'd have activated it by now."

"Would I? I happen to have a fairly benign association with your husband. Killing you would put a
damper on our relationship."

"Cheeky bitch."

"Whore."

Just as Vashodia felt the steel press down a little
tighter on her throat, she heard the soft shuffle of
footsteps approaching from behind.

Both of them grew still. After a moment, Vashodia
felt Slick Ren draw in a breath as she turned her head.

"Why did you come?" the empress asked. "I told
you I would handle this alone."

When no answer came that she could hear, Vashodia knew who stood behind them.

"No," Slick Ren said, in response to an unseen
query. "We were just having a friendly chat. Weren't
we, little miss cancer-on-two-legs?"

"As friendly as they come," Vashodia mockingly
agreed. "Why don't you join us, Derthon? Though,
I'm afraid I haven't prepared any tea."

The footsteps sounded again, closer this time,
and soon the man himself strode slowly into view.
He looked strange, wrapped head-to-toe as he was in
bandaging cloth. It was no surprise, really. The last
time she'd seen him, Vashodia had been removing
the last strip of skin from his body. It wasn't something people exactly recovered from.

His hands flicked in a pattern Vashodia couldn't recognize. Though she'd learned many of the sign languages that had cropped up over the centuries, this one was foreign to her; a private speech built between brother and sister alone.

"I will *not* release her," Slick Ren said. "Have you gone insane?"

Bandaged hands flowed together again.

Behind her, Vashodia felt the empress shake her head. "She doesn't deserve your forgiveness."

Despite her best efforts to keep it at bay—especially after its recent outburst—Vashodia felt her heart stirring once more.

Derthon knelt in front of her, placing his forehead a few finger-widths away. He raised both hands toward her face. One dipped under her chin, grasping his sister's wrist and pulling it—and the blade held tightly in her grip—away from Vashodia's throat.

The other traced down the side of her face, in what could almost be called a caress.

The man coughed, then bored his gaze into her skull.

"I . . . pity . . . you," he said in a raspy, throaty voice.

Released at last by Slick Ren, Vashodia fell limp to the floor.

Long after the two siblings had left her, she dredged up the will to rouse herself. When she took a look around her, she discovered something unexpected. Something—dare she even think it—*good*.

Both soulstones were glowing like they had from the moment she'd first created them.

Jasside and Draevenus were both still alive.

Vashodia closed her eyes. Over the span of several marks, she recovered enough to energize to the barest degree, then tapped into the energy circuits of the voltensus, reaching out to sense what was going on in the farthest corners of the empire.

The ruvaki skyships that had entered from the western, eastern, and northern territories had all turned around. Those that had entered from the south were settling down near the stranded ruvaki army.

It took her a moment to realize that they were loading up with soldiers, one by one, before flying away once more.

CHAPTER 24

It was a rare cold day in Panisahldron, when a wind carrying chill from the mountains of Kavenmoor never rested, and the sun stayed hidden behind clouds. Such days had always stood out to Arivana, not only for their rarity, but also because each time they came was an excuse to try on all her winter clothes, which were usually packed away in some dusty trunk, only thought about when taking trips up north. They were some of the few occasions when she and her sisters could all get along.

It's funny how finding a common interest, something mutually beneficial, made us forget the petty bickering for a time. I guess it's hard to hate someone when you can no longer ignore your similarities.

The cold wasn't the only thing rare about the day, however. After weeks on end of clearing rubble from the ruins, they were finally ready to begin re-building.

Tens of thousands of carpenters and masons, ar-chitects and engineers, and countless unskilled hands had come together for the undertaking, and now toiled in the streets below. Daye had taken to his new role as her people's king, and was even now down among them, taking part as much as he was directing them like he was supposed to. No one had any plans to reconstruct it exactly as it had been before. Not only would it be nearly impossible, and take far too long to accomplish, most people—herself included—knew that ludicrous displays of wealth were no longer necessary. Beauty would always be a major part of her people's identity. Just not the kind found on the *out-side* anymore.

All the survivors really needed was a place to call home.

Amidst the hammers and nails, stone blocks and wooden planks, Arivana also witnessed the occasional flash of sorcery, either bright or shadowed, as structures reached various stages of completion. Though none here could form solid matter from thin air, as could Jasside or Vashodia, magic still made many aspects of construction both easier and quicker. It wasn't even noon and the first building—a modest tenement—had already sprung up. And just below where her skyship hovered, she watched as a second was guided into its final shape by two familiar flying figures.

Tassariel maneuvered each massive, prebuilt segment onto the framework, then held it in place while Draevenus secured it by driving metal spikes with a quick flick of both wrist and magic. Together, they were able to do in a few marks what would normally take a hundred workers tolls to accomplish. The roof was the last piece. After it settled, Draevenus drew a mallet from his waistband, breathed deep, and gave the whole thing a good smack.

A cheer rose from the workers below as the building failed to crumble into dust.

"Looks sturdy enough from up here!" Arivana shouted.

The two turned towards her, necks craned skyward and smiles on their faces.

"Why don't you come take a break before you start on the next one? I'd say you've earned it."

Reaching out to each other, they rose skyward, hand in hand. After gliding over the railing of Arivana's skyship, they touched down gently beside her. Tassariel smirked as she dusted herself off, while Draevenus scanned the view below, taking an exaggerated breath in a gesture of deep contentment.

"Refreshments?" Arivana ventured, indicating the table beside her, which held mulled wine and a plate piled high with freshly baked pastries. "Or are you both too self-satisfied to indulge in such trivial affairs?"

"Hey!" Tassariel said, planting her fists on her hips.

"Don't blame *us* for taking satisfaction in a job well done. *You* were the one who asked us to come here."

"Only because I was sick of listening to how bored you were patrolling the armistice zone back in that dreary, broken empire."

"I never said I was bored."

"You didn't have to. Oh, don't get all huffy on me, Tass. I could read between the lines of your messages easily enough. You're not the kind to sit still. Why, not even a week after we flew free from the Cloister I could tell you were growing restless." Arivana plucked a slice of melon from the plate and dropped it into her mouth. "I knew you were bound to grow weary of guarding a peace no one had the heart—or stomach—to break."

"All right," Tassariel said, lifting her hands in surrender. "I admit that after it seemed my old one had become temporarily obsolete, I've been on the search for a new Calling ever since. I've already learned so much, just in the short time we've been here. Enough to know that this . . . occupation . . . might have enough in it to keep me busy for a century or two."

"Well, far be it from me to ridicule your newfound purpose in life." Arivana picked up the decanter and poured its contents into two tall, thin glasses, then looked up as she started filling the third. "What about you, Draevenus? As much as Tass here has taken to her work with zest, you've seemed downright enraptured!"

The ebony-skinned man smiled at this, and for several beats his eyes glazed over, a sign of one delving into their memories, as Arivana had come to learn. When at last his trance ended, he resumed his inspection of the labors going on below, only this time his eyes glistened with something like gratitude.

"It feels good to be doing something constructive, I think," he said. "Adding something to the world after a life spent subtracting."

Tassariel swiped the two filled glasses and stepped over to him, pressing one into his hand. "Well, for the time being at least, no one needs the kind of help we used to provide." She raised the one she'd retained. "To a future free of expectation."

Draevenus raised his own. "To a future free of blood."

Arivana quickly filled the third one and joined their toast, adding, "To a future free of . . . unnecessary boundaries."

Three glasses touched together with a reverberating clink. Arivana and her guests all took a short sip. Then, dispatching smiles between them and disregarding all propriety for a midday repast, threw back their heads and gulped until only the most stubborn red drops remained.

Draevenus dipped his head towards her in appreciation. "A local vintage?"

Arivana nodded. "Our most popular brand."

"A bit less sour than I'm accustomed to. And much

more sweet." He reached out towards Tassariel, who seemed to instinctively meet his hand halfway. "I think I can get used to this."

"Me too," the valynkar woman said.

"You'd better." Arivana refilled all three glasses. "We recovered several thousand barrels of this stuff from cellars deep enough to avoid the destruction, but little else. If you choose to stay, you'll be drinking nothing but this and water."

Tassariel sighed loudly. "It will certainly be a burden. But somehow, I think we'll manage."

"Speaking of managing," Draevenus said, flashing his eyes at Arivana before gesturing towards the sky, "it looks like your appointment has arrived."

Arivana followed his gaze, then watched as the small skyship came to a landing on the wide deck of her own.

A skyship of ruvaki design.

Moments after it had settled down, a figure emerged from the lone entryway, dressed in strange finery somewhere between a woman's nightgown and a man's military uniform. But the face atop the attire was one as familiar as could be.

"Ambassador Grusot," Arivana said, bowing. "It is good to see you again."

Sem Aira returned the bow, fidgeting with her collar as she straightened. "Please, Your Majesty. Things need not be so formal between us."

"Is that so? Well then, you'd better stop referring

to me as 'Your Majesty' or 'my queen' from now on. Otherwise, the blame for formality will lie solely at *your* feet."

Both she and the ruvaki woman regarded each other sternly. But after half a dozen beats, smiles overtook their artificially dour demeanors and they rushed towards each other, embracing like the fast friends they both had stopped denying that they were.

"You look so good," Arivana said. "It's amazing what proper fitting clothes and a touch of cosmetics will do. And is that perfume I smell?"

"No. I've just been eating a proper ruvaki diet for a while now. This is what I naturally smell like."

"Really?"

In a decidedly human gesture, Sem Aira rolled her eyes. "Come now, Arivana. I'm not *that* good of a liar."

"I'd hope not. It's not the best trait to have if you've been tasked as the primary liaison between two recently warring peoples."

"Speaking of which," Sem Aira said, a sudden sense of nerves settling in her features, "I need to ask you a favor."

"Name it."

"It's . . . about the armistice."

Dark thoughts threaded through Arivana, stabbing like icicles. "Your masters haven't changed their minds, have they?"

Sem Aira emphatically shook her head. "Nothing like that. I assure you, their stance has remained firmly changed. However, Jasside managed such a feat, it seems to have stuck."

"Is it the resettlement zone? If Yandumar is giving you fits over the land he seceded—"

"That's not it either. We're quite happy with the territory given us for rebuilding our civilization. The cold makes us feel right at home, and there are plenty of perfectly suited caves and caverns for growing our primary crops."

"What's the problem, then?"

"It's our soldiers. The sudden reversal has left them confused. Angry. The more vocal among them are even saying our leaders have been charmed somehow."

Arivana whipped her head towards her other companions. "Is that even possible?"

Draevenus shook his head. "There are a lot of ways to influence a person, but nothing so severe or long lasting. That's not what's at work here. Jasside did something I've never seen before. Something . . . unprecedented."

"After I exposed them," Tassariel began, "she took what I can only describe as a piece of her soul and gave it to each and every one of them, showing them in a way they could not deny that we were equals, and equally worthy of the right to exist."

"*How* she did it, I don't think we'll ever know," Draevenus added. "But even my sister would be impressed."

Arivana nodded, then turned back to Sem Aira. "What is it you need from me, then?"

The ruvak sighed. "I don't know, exactly. Some idea for preventing an insurrection, I suppose. Any idea at all. Both me and my masters are at our wit's end."

Placing her hand on Sem Aira's shoulder, Arivana gave her a warm, comforting squeeze. "We walked into the very maw of the abyss together and came out not only victors, but also allies with the those who once sought our destruction. We can figure this out. Trust me."

Sem Aira smiled.

Arivana knew that their two peoples needed a bit of distance from each other for now, to allow time for the war's fresh wounds to heal. Even so, communication between them needed to stay open, lest they become strangers once more. Managing such a fine balance was a task she once would have balked at. But now?

Transitioning from war to peace has become something of a specialty of mine. It's one burden I won't ever mind bearing.

The Gulf, as it had colloquially come to be called, dominated any vista one might attempt to view from this place. The rent through the land was as wide as any canyon in the Chasm and ran far beyond either horizon, as if some titanic entity had gripped each end of the continent and pulled apart until it tore. While its birth had helped put an end to hostilities, it now acted as the only border between humankind—in all its various forms—and the planet's original inhabitants, returned once more.

"Something funny?" Yandumar asked of him.

Gilshamed only now realized he was smiling. He waved to indicate the Gulf looming before them. "Even in her restraint," he said, "Vashodia still found a way to outdo herself."

"Of course she did. It's in her nature. She's not the kind for half measures."

The shadows dancing across the thousand-pace gap seemed to agree.

"Have you heard from her?" Gilshamed asked.

"Not a squeak. And don't tell me why that should make me nervous. I already know."

Gilshamed smirked. "Are you afraid she might start making new plans?"

"Afraid? No. Only the unknown worries me much, these days."

"You are sure of it, then?"

"If she hasn't gone dark to begin the next phase of her grand plan, the only explanation left is that she's *actually* undergone a change of heart. Do I really need to spell out for you which of the two is more likely?"

"I see your point." Gilshamed sighed, uncertain if he would live to see the culmination of her next scheme . . . but *quite* certain that he did not care. "But to be honest, old friend, I do not want to talk about Vashodia anymore. I think I've had enough of her for a lifetime."

"Me too. Abyss, I'm not sure you'd find a soul on this planet that wouldn't agree with you. Especially the ruvak."

Gilshamed nodded. While Vashodia would always be a problem, the ruvak were a different matter. With patience, he was sure they could be resolved in time.

That is, after all, why I am here.

He looked to the east and to the west, scanning along the near side of the Gulf for two faraway objects as they gently descended. Were he to stretch out his arm and hold a silver coin between thumb and forefinger, the image would be similar in both size and color to the two vessels now moving into what would be their final resting place.

If the Gulf was to be the border between the ruvak and the rest of humanity, the last two surviving domiciles of the valynkar would be there to keep the peace.

Gilshamed watch with rapt attention as they settled along the edge between darkness and light, and the immense vines dangling beneath them were guided to root within the freshly made cliffs.

We can no longer keep thinking ourselves above others.

Instead, it is time to start seeing eye-to-eye with our fellow denizens of this world. To be both bridge and barrier. To ensure peace has its fair chance to reign.

He returned his attention to his immediate surroundings once more, settling on the friend he knew would never live to see true harmony in the world. A fact that nearly drove Gilshamed to tears.

"What will you do?" he asked, unsure if he'd been able to keep back that thread of emotion from his voice.

"As emperor?" Yandumar asked, raising an eyebrow. "Or as a man?"

"The former, for a start."

Yandumar shrugged. "My empire has already started to break apart—literally. Why not give it a good shove out the door?"

"You're going through with the disbanding, then?"

"Might as well. It's a big place, this continent. A lot of different people with a lot of different ways of thinking and doing things. It was never meant to be burdened under solitary rule. By this time next year, the empire will be gone."

"Are you not the least bit worried that this is an inopportune time for such a drastic change? Weakening yourself just as the ruvak take up residence along your empire's southern border does not seem the best way to maintain stability?"

"The empire doesn't care anymore. The Free

States of Ragremos, however, might have a thing or two to say about it."

Gilshamed smiled, clapping Yandumar on the shoulder. "In that case, old friend, let me extend the approval of both myself and the Valynkar High Council. Not that you need it, of course."

"Ha! You got that right."

"What about the latter, then? What are your plans as simply a man?"

"I'm getting too old to have much use for plans, Gil. But to start, I'm gonna follow in my son's footsteps for a change."

"How is that exactly?"

"I'm taking a few well-earned days off!"

With a sack slung over one shoulder, Mevon strolled up a hill that had become quite familiar to him in the past year. He knew every rock and tree, every flower and bush, every twist and turn and scrape along a path that saw few feet but his own. He'd never been in one place so long. Even during the half decade he spent stationed in Thorull, he'd been constantly on the move, resting little in his endless pursuit of justice. Never able to appreciate the things he had around him.

Never taking time for things that *mattered*.

He rounded the last bend and stepped between two tall oaks that stood sentinel over the trail's entrance. A modest meadow lay beyond, filled with scattered wildflowers in reds and purples and yellows from the treeline on either side all the way up to the gently sloping banks of the creek running cool and clear from the waterfall.

Mevon left behind the dirt ruts of the trail and made his way towards the meadow's lone structure, striding through grasses that came to his knees. It looked different than it had the first time he'd been here. Jasside had initially formed it for function, a temporary enclosure to ward out the elements while they took their last rest before what they thought would be the end. Since their return, he'd added a frame of logs to the outside—to make it fit in with the other buildings in the town below—and his wife had decorated, adding color and character, in addition to modifying the house for a more extended stay: smoke rose from a chimney set in one of three new rooms; trees and bushes and other plants lined one side of the house, bearing all manner of fruits and vegetables and herbs; a stack of wood he'd split rested along the other; behind it lay a series of barrels and crates, filled with preserved meat and drying skins that he'd brought back from his hunts, along with a supply of the last and finest wines the now-dead empire had produced—a belated wedding gift from old friends.

The sight of this place, more than anything ever had, made him feel like he was home.

Mevon pushed through the door, careful to keep it

from knocking against anything, and set his sack on their table. As he began removing the contents one piece at a time, setting each down with exaggerated care, Jasside strode in from the bedroom.

"Did you find everything?" she asked in a gentle voice, sliding up next to him and running a hand up his back.

Mevon grunted. "And then some. I practically had to run out of there before people started shoving things into my sack. They still insist we're not charging enough for your vials of remedy."

"Oh, they'll get used to it. This town was robbed of its healer when I left to join the revolution. The least I can do is offer a discount."

"Doubly so." Mevon pulled out the last object within the sack—a spool of thread—and held it up to her with one eyebrow raised. "You could conjure all this stuff yourself, you know."

"I *do* know. But they'd get suspicious if I just gave my remedy away. Besides, it gives us a way to connect with people. *Normal* people. Not the kind that want or need us for anything."

Mevon rolled his eyes. "Speaking of which . . ."

"The mayor didn't ask you to become sheriff again, did she?"

"Not this time."

"Good."

"But the sheriff did."

"Oh no! What did you tell him?"

"The same thing I always do—I'll be there if the need arises, but until then, he doesn't have to start searching for a new job."

Jasside reached out to pat his arm. "I'm . . . sorry."

"I might believe that if you weren't trying so hard to hold back your laughter."

"I wouldn't have to," she said, dropping down to a whisper, "if little ears weren't so sensitive!"

Mevon took his arm in hers and shuffled quietly into the room from which she'd come. His heart beat like a drum as he stepped up next to the crib and peered down at the tiny life sleeping peacefully within.

Of all the many reasons he'd ever had, this was the greatest one of all to smile.

CODA

Serit Kai Ul-Daeris watched the other children play energy tag, frustrated that they wouldn't let her join in. Those designated as "it" would take turns tossing mostly harmless orbs of light or dark or chaos at their fellow participants, who tried to avoid such attacks by running, or ducking behind one of the many trees ringing the hillside, or unfurling their prepubescent wings for a short burst of flight.

Of these things, Serit Kai could do none. So she watched, and waited.

But she did not pray.

She'd long ago given up hope that she'd be allowed to join her classmates during recess. Or what she called *unscripted time*. The teachers ensured everyone played nice while under their supervision, but only kept a close enough eye while the students were out-side to avoid broken bones and bloody noses.

Instead of sulking on the sidelines for her turn at "fun," Serit Kai stomped away through the small patch of forest bordering the school grounds. Within two marks, she'd found and pushed through the loose board on the boundary fence. Another three saw her to the forest's end. It came abruptly, and with a harsh blast of wind, opening up to a vista that more than made up for her peers' inability to include a freak like her.

Heart racing, she took tiny steps until her toes were hanging over the cliff's edge.

And stared straight down at a drop of several thousand paces.

They said a great city had once rested on this mountain. Mecrithan, or something like that. Not that she knew what a city was, exactly. Sure, the teachers showed them in projections during history lessons, but no one actually *lived* in one anymore. They were a relic of the ancient age, when limited means of transportation forced everyone to dwell in cramped proximity to each other. Sitting in a class-room with eleven other students was bad enough. She couldn't imagine sharing a few square leagues with millions.

Though the valley below her didn't contain a city, it did, however, hold one of the largest gatherings of activity this world had seen in a few millenia. Serit

Kai Ul-Daeris came here almost every day to gaze upon it. Forgetting, for the moment, all the morons who surrounded her and dwelling instead upon the place where everyone actually knew what the abyss was going on.

A place where she might not have to be so alone.

"Do you come here often?"

Serit Kai tensed, yet was proud of herself for not squealing or jumping in fright, like one of her pathetic classmates surely would. She scanned the cliffside in search of the voice. It didn't take her long to find a figure dressed in strange, dark robes standing as close to the edge as she, not twenty paces away. Judging by stature and vocal inflection, Serit Kai presumed the speaker to be a girl about her own age.

"Perhaps I do," she said, crossing her arms. "Perhaps I don't. I see no reason to tell you one way or the other."

"Smart girl," the other said, speaking as slowly as her grandmother. "Never give up information freely. Always make sure your audience *earns* it."

"I don't recall asking for your advice. *Or* your approval."

The other girl turned towards her. Though her face was hidden within a shadowed hood, it still gave off the distinct impression of a smile. "Feisty, this one is."

Serit Kai felt the spark of rage light within her. But she'd had so much practice subduing it—and other emotions—that she made sure not to let even a hint of it show on her face. Anger was only useful, after all, if she could direct it, instead of letting *it* direct *her*.

"You're strange," she said, testing a low-level insult to see if it had any effect. "I bet your own mother gave up on you years ago."

"How perceptive! Though you are correct in your hasty surmisal, you'd have to go back farther than mere years to find the point in time when my mother realized I was not the tame creature she wished me to be. Quite a bit farther indeed."

"Why haven't I seen you around school before? Why do you talk so funny? Just who the abyss *are* you?"

"You'll figure it out," the other girl said. "Or you won't. In which case I'll be most disappointed."

"That'll make two of us, then."

"Wishing to watch the launch alone, were you? I don't blame you. So many whoops and hollers. So much unbridled emotion. So many people wishing to capture your every word and gesture in hopes of garnering vicarious attention. Much better to view the event from afar. A distant yet unobscured cliff, for example."

Serit Kai suppressed the growl that nearly burst forth from her throat. She was used to the petty and pedantic social stigma from her supposed peers. This was something different. This other girl knew too much about her. About the *real* her. The one she hid from the others. And she was far too casual in her surety for it to be merely good guessing.

Who are you?

The question remained in her mind, this time, for she remembered the response to when she'd asked it out loud.

She had to figure it out.

But I don't know enough about her, yet. Time to stop acting like such a child and decipher who it is I'm dealing with.

Serit Kai knew the other girl was no student. She was connected with the activity below, somehow—maybe even central to it—yet she did not want the attention it naturally drew. She also, apparently, had a keen insight into the mind, able to glean indisputable truths about people she barely knew.

Taking this evidence, and what she could tell about the girl's physical characteristics, only a single possible candidate sprang forth in her mind.

"No," she said, shaking her head. "It's impossible. You *can't* be her. You can't!"

"Why ever not?"

Serit Kai shivered inside her coat. She had no use for the gods; not the new, not the old, and certainly not the ancient. There was only one person, in her mind, who was worthy of such devotion as the deities inspired.

"Because," she answered at last, her voice like a mouse, "Vashodia Everchild has no reason to visit *me*."

The other girl let down her hood, putting all doubt to rest.

Serit Kai felt her throat go dry. It wasn't every day she got to meet her idol.

"I'm afraid," Vashodia began, "that you are quite mistaken. I have a very *good* reason to visit you, Serit Kai Ul-Daeris. And not just because you are a blood descendent of some dear old friends of mine."

"I am?"

"Never mind that. Tell me why you're an outcast."

The question stunned her with its abruptness and total lack of etiquette. "It's because I'm a freak," she answered instinctively. "My parents decided it would be a good idea for their offspring to sport all three types of energy within their blood. Abyss cares if that means none of them will ever fully manifest."

"Won't they?"

Serit Kai couldn't hold back the emotion any longer. "Of course not! Everyone knows that! I have all the power in the universe at my fingertips, only I've had my hands cut off at the wrist. It doesn't matter that I can feel them all when I'm about as close to harnessing them as an abyss-taken void."

Vashodia smiled warmly. "You certainly are a rarity, child. Even in this supposedly enlightened age. It is a problem I have too long neglected in lieu of more pressing matters."

"Like what?"

"Like . . . utopia."

"Utopia? What's that?"

"It is a word whose origins lie in a past far older than you could possibly imagine. It is the dream towards which people will never cease to strive. It is a world transcended into perfection." The other girl giggled. "It is *impossible*."

"If it's so impossible, then what's the point of even trying?"

"Better to keep society walking the path that leads towards it, rather than let them race down the one leading away. Such an endeavor is a worthy use of one's time, I think."

"What does any of this have to do with me?"

Vashodia gestured to the valley below. Serit Kai looked that way and watched as the latest greatship kicked off its thrusters in a burst of fire and smoke, and began its long ascent towards the void.

"Our efforts to reach the stars have been ongoing for half a thousand years now. I can rest assured in the fact that, no matter what happens to *this* world, all of sentient life will live on. Somewhere. So I've decided to turn my attention back to the kind of studies that used to interest me."

"What kind of studies?"

"The kind dealing with things that everyone considers impossible. Mysteries that few even recognize as such, much less expend any effort towards resolving."

Vashodia raised an eyebrow. Serit Kai felt energy cascading through her, dark in nature, matching the

Everchild's famed source of power. It latched on to something inside her. Something she'd always felt, yet had never been able to grasp. A strange, familiar beast that sported three heads, all of them now fighting to be the first free from her fingertips. Though modern education gave it a different title, it was the old name that sprang into her mind.

Magic.

"You may not ever sprout wings," Vashodia said. "But in no time at all, I can teach you how to fly."

The End

ACKNOWLEDGMENTS

I'd like to start by thanking my past self for having the requisite intestinal fortitude to finish writing this book. Real life circumstances aside (because we ALL have stuff to deal with), writing the last book in a trilogy is tough. Especially when I hadn't ever planned for this story to span three novels. Sure, when I first dreamt up the sundered world, I had a good idea about what *might* come after *Veiled Empire*, but when my publisher informed me they wanted a pair of sequels, I must admit the first thing I felt was dread. *Shadow of the Void* was hard enough, being my first time under an actual deadline; *The Light That Binds* stepped it up to a whole new level. How on earth was I supposed to wrap up all the characters and conflicts and story threads in a satisfying manner, while still . . . you know . . . writing a good book? I'm still not sure if I managed to pull it off, but at least I can say that present me is satisfied with the work that past me produced. And future me? Well . . . he's never satisfied with *anything*, it seems.

On a serious note, I'd like to thank my editor, agent, and family. Again. Most of the time, I have no idea what on earth I'm doing. You all make it possible for my creative side (which spent far too much of my life suppressed) to even see the light of day. I think everyone has at least one story to tell. Thanks for allowing me to share some of the ones inside of *me*.

To all the people who worked behind the scenes to turn this book into a reality, and whose names and faces I'll probably never know (or remember), thank you.

And to everyone along the way who has ever inspired me by sharing their stories and passions, and encouraging the rest of us to find our *own* dream, there doesn't yet exist a word in the English language strong enough to express my gratitude. And there probably never will.

ABOUT THE AUTHOR

Born in 1983, **NATHAN GARRISON** has been writing stories since his dad bought their first family computer. He grew up on tales of the fantastic. From Narnia and Middle-Earth to a galaxy far, far away, he has always harbored a love for things only imagination can conjure up. He counts it among the greatest joys of his life to be able to share the stories within him. He has two great boys, and an awesome wife who is way more supportive of his writing efforts than he thinks he deserves. Besides writing, he loves playing guitar (the louder the better), cooking (the more bacon-y the better), playing board/video/card games with friends and family, and reveling in unadulterated geekery. He can be found on Twitter and Facebook: @NR_Garrison and facebook.com/author.nathan.garrison.

www.nathangarrison.com
www.harpervoyagerbooks.com

Discover great authors, exclusive offers, and more at hc.com.